From Across the
Ancient
Waters

From Across the Ancient Waters

MICHAEL PHILLIPS

BARBOUR
PUBLISHING

© 2012 by Michael Phillips

Print ISBN 978-1-61626-585-4 (Paperback)
Print ISBN 978-1-61626-673-8 (Hardback)

eBook Editions:
Adobe Digital Edition (.epub) 978-1-60742-758-2
Kindle and MobiPocket Edition (.prc) 978-1-60742-759-9

Cover design: Faceout Studio, www.faceoutstudio.com

Published by Barbour Publishing, Inc., P.O. Box 719, Uhrichsville, OH 44683,
www.barbourbooks.com

*Our mission is to publish and distribute inspirational products offering exceptional value
and biblical encouragement to the masses.*

ecpa Member of the
Evangelical Christian
Publishers Association

Printed in the United States of America.

DEDICATION

To Robert James Nigel Halliday,
A man of integrity, truth, and depth of character,
whom it is an honor to call my friend.

—A Note Regarding Locale—

Whenever one is blending fact and fiction, certain disclaimers and clarifications are necessary. Everything that follows is fiction, the characters, the setting, the story. Authors are often asked about the locations in which their stories take place. Some settings are truer to the reality of place than others. I have searched high and low to find the settings of some of George MacDonald's Scottish novels, only to arrive at the conclusion that those settings existed only in the author's mind. In the case of his novel *Malcolm*, however, the details of locale in the story match precisely the reality in and around the northern Scottish village of Cullen. Readers do the same with my books, with similar results. Some are based on factual places, others are not. In the case of *From Across the Ancient Waters,* the location of the story is set along the north coast of Wales. But the specifics of the villages and coastline and roads have been changed and adapted for the sake of the story. If you visit North Wales, you will *not* find a village called Llanfryniog or the promontory of Mochras Head or Westbrooke Manor or the cave on the beach. The setting, as well as the story and characters, is entirely fictionalized.

The Region of Gwynedd, North Wales
at the Northern Expanse of the Cambrian Mountains

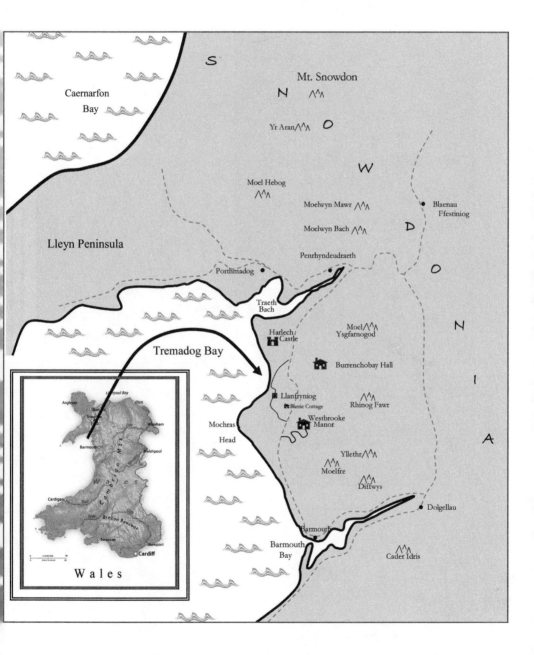

S

N

O

W

D

O

N

I

A

Mt. Snowdon

Caernarfon
Bay

Yr Aran

Moel Hebog

Moelwyn Mawr

Moelwyn Bach

Blaenau
Ffestiniog

Lleyn Peninsula

Penrhyndeudraeth

Porthmadog

Traeth
Bach

Harlech
Castle

Moel
Ysgfarnogod

Burrenchobay Hall

Tremadog Bay

Llanfryniog

Barrie Cottage

Rhinog Fawr

Westbrooke
Manor

Mochras
Head

Yllethr

Moelfre

Diffwys

Dolgellau

Barmouth

Barmouth
Bay

Cader Idris

Wales

Liverpool Bay

Anglesey

Flint

Bangor

Snowdon

Wrexham

Barmouth

Welshpool

Cambrian Mts

Cardigan

Brecon Beacons

Swansea

Newport

Cardiff

PROLOGUE

The Fate of the Rhodri Mawr
1791

*T*he blue-green sea of the Irish Ocean between the treacherous coastlines of eastern Ireland, northern Wales, and southern Scotland could be as placid as any of the thousand inland lochs for which the three Celtic lands were known.

Saint Columba had been borne safely over it to Mull more than a millennium before. He had carried a new spiritual destiny to Scotland's western isles, which would spread throughout all Britannia. But when the seas of the north Atlantic rose in unexpected fury, beware to all who challenged them, whether conquering Roman or Viking, whether Irish saint or Welsh pirate. At such times, the waters of this Celtic triangle, no respecter of persons, sought victims to add to its ancient tomb of the watery deep.

Such a fate had come suddenly upon the vessel of dubious reputation known as the *Rhodri Mawr.*

A fierce blast from the north bent the struggling ship's aftermast dangerously toward the slate gray waters of an angry sea. The imposing craft, stalwart and fearsome when sailing out of Penzance two days before, now bobbed like a plaything as it bottomed into a trough between two giant swells of St. George's Channel. The leading edge of the second wave rose ominously then sent its white-tipped crest

9

smashing into the prow with such violence that it seemed the ship's massive stem must burst into matchsticks from the blow.

The front third of the ship disappeared as if swallowed whole. Two seconds later it reappeared out of the tumult. Somehow it was still in one piece. Water pouring over the sides, the pointed bowsprit shot toward the sky. The swell that had swallowed it now spewed the boat as a mere toy upward in a dangerous arc.

Thus repeated the downward crash and heavenward flight of the two-masted English brigantine as it had for hours. Each disappearance between titanic billows seemed to all appearance its last. Only by a miracle had it managed to remain afloat so long. Helpless against the elements, its crew was too exhausted to think what terror must be their inevitable portion. The gods were in control now. Such men as these, however, had not spent their lives befriending whatever deities made the fate of men their business. Nor was it likely that a heavenward flight would be the final journey of their souls. It was doubtful any would live through the descending night or that the *Rhodri Mawr* would enter safe harbor again.

The secret of Dolau Cothi seemed destined for a deep, black, unknown grave somewhere near the home of the giant serpent *Gwbert-ryd*, whom superstition credited with such violent storms and the shipwrecks that resulted from them.

Water was not just threatening from below but also from above. Rain slammed onto the deck with a ferocity that made visibility impossible. The crow's nest had been abandoned hours before. Nothing could be seen from it. No man could survive atop it.

The *Rhodri Mawr*'s crew had ventured into these waters on a mission now forgotten in the battle for survival. As the storm rose quickly, the captain thought to find some sheltered inlet in Cardigan Bay. But the anger of Gwbert-ryd swept upon them rapidly, turning every inch of this Celtic sea into a frothy boil. No shelter was to be found. Had they only known that the drift of the current had taken them northward into Tremadog Bay and that they were now floundering within three hundred yards of the rocky coastline, it might have been different. But through the falling mist, none knew how close safety lay.

The bow slammed into another wall of water yet more violent than the rest.

"She's taking water!" cried one of the mates, clinging desperately to a ragged end of hemp to keep from being sucked overboard.

With the wind roaring and the tattered remains of sails flapping, his warning was lost to the prince of the power of the air. The nearest of his fellows had been thrown onto the deck thirty feet astern.

A sharp crack sounded.

The tall front mast swayed dangerously. . .rocked the opposite direction. . .then another splintering crack. Suddenly the thick round timber lay across the deck in the sea. Even if she survived the storm, no ship could navigate without its rigging.

It mattered little. The next instant a tremendous wave slanted high over the bow, battering the side with mortal force. Another shattering blow followed to starboard. A deep groan creaked below deck.

Those aboard seemed destined to live out the poet's words of the ancient rime:

> With sloping masts and dipping prow,
> As who pursued with yell and blow
> Still treads the shadow of his foe,
> And forward bends his head,
> The ship drove fast, loud roared the blast,
> And southward aye we fled.

The *Rhodri Mawr* pitched dangerously to port. It took but one more split. Now the aftermast snapped from its base and tumbled overboard. The stem could no longer absorb the blows from the raging sea. Side-timbers began to splinter. Within seconds the forehull of the *Rhodri Mawr* was breaking up. Now indeed did the sea set about in earnest its business of making matchsticks of this once sturdy vessel.

"Over the side!" sounded cries from all parts of the ship. "Save yourselves. . .she's tearing apart. . .we're going down!"

In panic, most of the crew leaped overboard to keep from being knocked unconscious on the lurching deck. Within minutes the brigantine's three lifeboats were in the water. Whether they would fare better than the mother ship was doubtful.

There was one on board, however, who did not so hastily leap to his doom. He would outwit the legendary serpent of the deep with more than a brief prolonging of his own life. He had seen the signs an hour before as the winds whipped up the frothing cauldron. He knew what must be the result. He knew these waters better than his fellows. From the shape and flow of the waves, he had deduced what even the captain had not realized, that land could not be far off.

As his mates struggled above deck, he descended into the depths, to the captain's quarters, empty now except for its most precious cargo. With the floor pitching and yawing under his feet, he lugged a great black chest from the closet. The thing was nearly too heavy to lift. He could not hope to swim a foot bearing it. The contents would sink faster than a great iron anchor. But there might yet be a way to save the treasure within it.

With all his might, he lifted the reliquary and struggled toward the stairs. Inch by inch he made his way up then onto the next flight. A great crash sent the box from him as he toppled onto his back. Luckily its lock held. He scrambled to his feet, retrieved his booty, and continued toward the sea-deck. Hearing both masts crack, followed by shouts everywhere, he knew the ship's fate. If he could just get himself and the box overboard.

He reached the air to see lifeboats being tossed from above. All about, his fellows were scrambling overboard. No one paid him heed. None saw what he lugged behind him.

Another lurch of the deck sent the chest from him again. Picking himself up, he dragged his bounty toward a mass of corked netting. Hastily he wrapped it amid several folds, securing the strands to its precious load.

The *Rhodri Mawr* swayed one final time then lurched sideward. The motion flung him off his feet, over the bulwark, and into the sea, tangled in a mass of cord and chest and hemp and cork. Bobbing up into the dim light of dusk, he gasped for air. A length of cord remained connected to the bulwark. In seconds the sinking ship would pull the chest and netting and himself down with it.

A wave dashed him below the surface. He sent his fingers groping toward the sheath at his side. As his head surfaced again, his hand bore aloft a shiny blade. He plunged through the netting toward the ship.

A minute more and the *Rhodri Mawr* capsized to its side. Half its deck was now underwater, its keel exposed, the lower hold filling rapidly.

As the ambitious pirate felt himself pulled down in the sinking vortex, three quick slashes from his knife released him safely from the doomed ship, adrift with a lifecraft of cork and netting.

Thirty seconds later, the mighty vessel above him tipped further and slowly sank out of sight.

The rocky shoals of this coast were unforgiving. It took not many minutes for the squall to reduce the three lifeboats to floating debris. Futilely gasping for breath between twenty-foot waves, those of the crew who had trusted them found themselves clinging to mere scraps of wood. Most would not be heard from again. As they had given their lives to the sea, the depths now became their final resting place. If the serpent Gwbert-ryd was near, he must certainly be satisfied with this day's work.

The great hull slowly settled to the bottom and came to rest almost in one piece. There the waters, though frigid, were calm. After its gallant struggle, the *Rhodri Mawr* could finally rest in peace.

Under the water it rumbled on,
Still louder and more dread:
It reached the ship, it split the bay;
The ship went down like lead.
Stunned by that loud and dreadful sound,

Which sky and ocean smote,
Like one that hath been seven days drowned
My body lay afloat:
But swift as dreams, myself I found
Within the Pilot's boat.

And now, all in my own countree,
I stood on the firm land!
The Hermit stepped forth from the boat,
And scarcely he could stand.

No one ever saw the tangled mass of ship's netting, held afloat by great balls of cork no storm could sink, bobbing up and down as it bore two parcels—one human, the other filled with that which men would kill for—away from the wreckage toward the coast of Mochras Head, overlooked through the mists of the storm, by the green hills of Snowdonia.

PART ONE

Stranger in North Wales

1867

ONE

Strange Benefactress

A girl of indeterminate age stole with stealthy step into a narrow lane leading perpendicular to the central dirt road of a coastal village in North Wales.

Whether she had just pinched a sweetie from the post or a half-penny roll from the baker, the quick furtive glance behind as she disappeared from view of the three or four humble shops of the place would surely prompt an observer to think, whatever her business, that she was up to no good.

The tiny flaxen scamp was soon swallowed by shadows of high stone rising on both sides of her. Immediately she broke into a run.

Noiseless as they were swift, her steps took her quickly through the buildings of the village. Moments later she was racing across a wide green pasture. Several black-and-white cattle grazing in its midst paid the flight of the girl no heed.

In truth, the small Celtic lass was no thief at all. That her two hands and the single pocket of her threadbare dress were empty gave all the proof necessary that nothing untoward had taken place during the three or four minutes in which she had darted into the village and out again unseen. In actual fact, her exit had been made with one less encumbrance on her person than she had entered with. Her errand on this day had been one of giving not taking. She had been discharging a debt of kindness from her young heart.

The only evidence left behind that she had been in Llanfryniog at all was a small bouquet of wildflowers—dandelions and daisies mostly, with a few yellow buttercups sprinkled among them—plucked on her way into the village from the field next to the one through which she now ran. She would have left something of greater value on the latch to Mistress Chattan's side door if she had had it. But the blooms were free and abundant, available to all for the having, and the only gift she could afford to bequeath. Flowers were thus the normal commodity of the unusual commerce in which she engaged.

At this hour of late afternoon, the front door of the inn swung back and forth on its hinges every few minutes. This was the time of day when the region's miners came to relax with their afternoon pint before trudging home to their suppers. Already the place was bustling with animated talk and laughter as ale and an occasional whiskey flowed from Mistress Chattan's hand. The tiny bouquet on the door of the lane that opened into her private quarters remained unseen for some time.

What manner of woman it was who thus served the men of the mine their daily ration of liquibrious good cheer was an inquiry that would have provoked heated discussion among the respectable wives and mothers of Llanfryniog. Though they were no more genteel than she, they were far from pleased that their husbands made such regular visits to her establishment. That the thirsty miners and fishermen of the region contributed so much to the health of Mistress Chattan's cash box was as much a grief to their wives as it was a boon to the innkeeper. No one knew Mistress Chattan's antecedents. Neither were they inclined to ask about them. But the women were suspicious. They would cross the road if they saw her ahead, like the priest and Levite of old, in order to pass by on the other side, little knowing what curses and imprecations she muttered under her breath against them.

Having left the small floral token of goodwill, not fragrant but nonetheless precious in the eyes of him who made girls and flowers and surly old women together, one would assume the recipient and the girl on intimate terms and that the discovery would bring a smile to the good Mistress Chattan's lips.

In fact, only the day before the proprietress of Llanfryniog's single inn—which boasted only three little used rooms but whose pub contained six frequently used tables—had given the girl a rude whack along the side of the head. This had been followed by a string of harsh words that ought not to be heard from a lady's lips.

But Mistress Chattan was no lady. And when she discovered the small nosegay on her door later that evening, a silent oath passed those same lips, more vile than anything spoken against her customers' wives. She knew whence came the gift and was anything but grateful.

On one thing were the wives of Llanfryniog and Mistress Chattan agreed—the young imp and daughter of Codnor Barrie was a menace.

Half the women of the village, like Mistress Chattan on this day, had at one time or another been the recipient of some such insignificant remembrance, usually wildflowers, from the strange benefactress of Llanfryniog. To chastise her or tell her to mind her own business, in the words of Solomon, only succeeded in heaping burning coals upon their own heads. Where one nosegay had been the previous day, a larger one would be found the next.

Most had learned that the best way to keep little Gwyneth a safe distance from their homes was to bite their tongues. Their policy was either to ignore her or treat her with distant civility. Rebuke or anger acted as too ready an incentive to the girl to repay evil with kindness—a sentiment they would all have endorsed in church every Sunday but which, when they found themselves on the receiving end of it, they found disconcerting in the extreme. Where she had come by such an absurd notion, they could only guess.

"There goes the Barrie girl," said one of the village wives to her neighbor over the low stone wall between the gardens at the back of their two cottages.

Both women paused a moment and watched as the unruly head of white sped through the field of green.

"Aye," sighed the other. She added a significant click of her tongue for emphasis. "But where does she come by her strange ways?"

"From her mother, some say."

"Mere gossip. No one on this side ever saw the mother."

"She must have been an ill one, to have given the world such a girl."

" 'Tis the auld grannie, if ye be asking me."

"She's no grannie to the lass."

"Who's kin is she, then?"

"The father's, I'm thinking. Though what relation I can't rightly say."

"What of the girl's mother, then?"

"They say she was cursed with the evil seed."

"Where did you hear such a thing, Niamh?"

"From them that know."

"Nobody knows who she was, except that she came from over the water, where the man should never have gone looking for a woman. I hear she had the blood of Irish kings in her veins."

"Now 'tis you who's spinning tales, Eilidh. How would an honest man like Barrie have got such a wife? Whether her blood ran blue or no, I can't say, but 'tis more likely that of knaves."

"Aye, ye may be right. There's rascals and kings alike above us."

"Whatever the color of her blood, the mother passed *something* to the girl that was not altogether of this world."

"Unless it came from her daddy."

"Codnor Barrie? No, I'm thinking it must have come from the mother or the grannie's side."

"No matter. 'Tis with us now. And none can escape whatever it be till she's gone back to wherever she came from."

TWO

The Gray Cliffs of Mochras Head

*T*he course taken by the girl as she disappeared from the two observant busybodies led south of the village. Beyond the grazing cattle behind her, she ascended a gradual slope of uncultivated moorland and soon arrived onto the precipitous promontory known as Mochras Head.

Having completed her errand of grace, she skipped merrily over the terrain of gentle green as if possessing no care in the world. That the plateau across which her steps carried her overlooked a peaceful sea from a height of at least two hundred feet above the craggy coastline caused this Celtic nymph no alarm. She had roamed every inch of these regions since she could walk. The mystery of the sea lay in the depths of her being. Her soul felt its majesty, though she knew not why. These high perches above it were her favorite places in all the world.

Her father taught her that the cliff distinguishing this seawardmost point on the eastern curve of Tremadog Bay was not to be feared, and she trusted her father. Only she must keep three paces from it, he said. From there she might feast upon the blues and greens and grays of the sea to her heart's content and dream of what lay beyond.

Though they knew nothing about her, everyone in the village knew that the girl's mother had come from across these waters. Codnor Barrie loved the sea for his mysterious wife's sake. His daughter shared the mother's blood and was likewise a child of the sea. The father saw in young Gwyneth's countenance daily reminders of the only woman he had ever loved. He knew that the sights, sounds, and smells of the water drew the girl and made her happy. Whatever evil the women of Llanfryniog attributed to the radiance shining out of them, the far-off expression in Gwyneth's pale young eyes kept the melancholy memory of his wife quietly alive in the humble man's heart.

The girl paused and stooped to her knees. She then stretched flat onto her stomach and propped her chin between two small fists. There she lay and gazed out to sea.

It was a warm afternoon in early June. The fragrance of the new spring growth of grass on which she lay wafted gently on the warm sea breezes. What rose in her heart as she lay on the grassy carpet were feelings and sensations no words could explain, no images contain. The world's splendor exhilarated her spirit. For Gwyneth Barrie, that was enough.

How long she lay, she could not have said. When the sun shone and school was over and her papa was at the mine, time did not exist. The sea stretching out like an infinite blanket of green, the moor above it, the hilly woodland rising away eastward toward the peaks of Snowdonia— these all comprised the imaginative playground of her childhood. She was at home on every inch of the landward expanse of them.

The sea beyond, however, remained an intoxicating mystery. She could stare at it for hours. Yet still it withheld its secrets.

She knew that her mother had lived somewhere on the other side of it, and that she had been born in her mother's country. That connection with her unknown origins, and with a mother she had never seen, made the sea a living thing in her soul.

Inland from the girl at a distance of some five or six hundred yards, two riders on horseback trotted slowly down the road toward the village. The gray and the red they rode were well groomed and exquisitely outfitted. The two young people were themselves dressed in riding habits that none of the local peasantry or miners could have afforded for their sons or daughters. Their two hats alone might have cost a month's wages for half the working men in the village.

"Hey look, Florilyn," said the older of the two, a youth who had just turned eighteen. He had seen the girl walking along the promontory as they came onto the plateau. "There's the witch-girl! How about some fun!"

"Like what?" answered his sister, younger by two and a half years.

"To see the little scamp try to outrun a horse!"

"Go chase her yourself, Courtenay," said the girl called Florilyn. "She gives me the shivers. Besides, she's afraid of no animal. She would just stand there and let you charge straight at her."

"Then I'll run her down!" Her brother laughed.

"And have Rhawn's father to answer for it!"

"He wouldn't do anything to me. Father wouldn't let him."

"You might be right. But I have no intention of making the girl angry. She'd probably put a curse on us or something. Suit yourself, but I'm going to see Rhawn." She urged her mount forward down the incline.

A few seconds later her brother followed. Bullying is not a sport enjoyed in solitude. He wasn't quite brave enough to upset the strange child by himself.

THREE

Unknown Ancestry

*H*aving no idea she was an object of conversation between Lord Snowdon's son and daughter, the girl they had been watching rose and continued on her way. After some distance, she turned toward the great blue expanse below her and suddenly disappeared over the side of Mochras Head.

At this point along the promontory, she *was* allowed within three paces of the edge. For between the northern and southern extremities of the rocky face, the cliff had worn inland through the eons, creating a slope seaward from the plateau noticeably more gradual in its descent. Down it a well-worn path crisscrossed back and forth until it reached a sandy beach. The inviting narrow strand was approximately forty yards in width at high tide between water's edge and the bluff and stretched away in both directions under the shadow of the lofty headland.

Down this sloping trail the girl now made her way. She bent occasionally to pluck a wildflower from amongst the rocks beside her or kick at a pebble beneath her feet. Three minutes later she ran down the final winding slope and emerged onto the white sandy shore, bright almost to brilliance as it lay between the blue green of the sea and the gray-black of the rocky promontory. Her descent was not unlike that of the wide-winged sea birds—whose antics she glanced up at now and then with hand to forehead. She never tired of watching as they played on the currents and breezes between the cliff and water, occasionally dropping from great heights to the sea, almost paralleling the very trajectory she had herself just taken.

The joys of exploration and discovery of late afternoon were no doubt heightened by the fact that her days were not entirely filled with happiness. School was a painful ordeal for Gwyneth Barrie. She was slow of speech and insecure among the other children who were quick to make her the object of their derision. That she never defended herself and silently accepted the teasing of other children in the village as the natural order of things, invited their jeers all the more.

Her stature, too, tempted cruelty. As it has in all times, the smallest and least aggressive in the animal kingdom are singled out by others of their kind for intensified scorn. Poor Gwyneth had the misfortune to stand a head shorter than any other boy or girl her age in Llanfryniog.

No one but her father knew exactly how old she was. Everyone considered her several years younger than she was. The women who had suckled her, as they grew to fear her, had done their best to forget. The years, however, passed more quickly than they realized. Most assumed her eight or nine. She had actually just turned thirteen.

Pure white hair—lighter than was altogether natural, the old women said with significant expressions—added yet one more visual distinction to make her, in the eyes of young and old alike, more than merely different but *peculiar* from other children.

Codnor Barrie, stocky, muscular, and a harder working man at the slate mine than most, stood but a few inches over five feet. It was therefore no surprise that his daughter should also be a bantam among her peers. He had suffered similar indignities in his own childhood and youth. It had been assumed that by some quirk of nature his two average-sized parents had produced a dwarf for offspring. But Codnor grew into manhood manifesting no dwarflike attributes other than a simple lack of height.

None in Llanfryniog had ever laid eyes on his wife. Assuming from the daughter that she must have been as tiny as he, they would have been shocked to see her on her wedding day in Ireland, neither short nor blond, towering four inches above beaming young Codnor Barrie.

Notwithstanding his diminutive stature, in all other respects the Welshman, widowed less than two years later, had lived a normal life. This did not stop two or three of the low-minded men of the village from thinking that he, like his daughter, came from an inferior class of humanity. After several pints of stout in Mistress Chattan's pub, such boors often made him the object of their base jokes, exactly as their sons did his daughter.

Courage, however, is measured by other standards. Young Gwyneth possessed more valor than any of her schoolmates among the things of *her* home—whose roof was the sky and whose furnishings and friendships were provided by nature itself. It required no fortitude to ridicule the defenseless. But let the heavens open and unleash their torrents, let thunder roar and lightning flash, and young Gwyneth Barrie was out the door of the school into the midst of it, rapture in her eyes. All the while her classmates cowered near the black cast-iron stove waiting for the tumult to pass.

Likewise not a youngster among them would tempt fate by walking toward the hills at dusk for fear of the water-kelpie of the mountain lakes. *Gwberr-niog* was known to come out only at night. They were as terrified of waking his hunger for human flesh as the fishermen who braved the waters of the Celtic triangle were of arousing his cousin-beast Gwbert-ryd. Gwyneth, however, romped and played among the trees and hills near her home as happily with a moon overhead as the sun.

Nor would any of the boys and girls of Llanfryniog on the cheeriest of days have crept among these rocks and caves where Gwyneth now frolicked beneath the promontory. Legends of dead pirates and live beasts abounded. Her own fearlessness only confirmed in the eyes of fellows, schoolmaster, and old wives of the village alike that Gwyneth Barrie exercised a closer acquaintance with the dark forces of the universe than was healthy in normal people.

Fear being a healthy ingredient in the human constitution, Codnor Barrie's daughter possessed her appointed share. But she was well on her way at an early age to recognizing what *should* be feared and what should *not*, a vital distinction to a life of contentment.

Thus was young Gwyneth Barrie suspected of being preternaturally abnormal from other children—a view given credence by the impediment of her speech—freakish, queer, perhaps not quite "all there" according to Llanfryniog's gossips. Even the calm sagacity of her countenance, it was assumed, hid something sinister. Had she been a prankster, mean-spirited, or a giggly simpleton, she would scarcely have been given a second thought. That she spoke little, and was *better* than other children, made her an object of mistrustful and dark speculation.

Her light hair, shooting out from her head in the disarray occasioned by being raised by a man not a woman, surrounded features pale but full of health. Out of their midst gazed wide, knowing, trusting eyes of deepest blue green. Their shades were as changeable as the sea itself. At one glance, they seemed to reflect the blue of heaven, at another the emerald green of several inland lochs at the height of spring's snowmelt.

Young Gwyneth's ageless face was one any thoughtful grown-up would pause over with mingled admiration and question. In truth, who could not admire the graceful loveliness of childhood, a beauty still dormant but waiting to blossom? In the midst of their awe, however, rose the riddle of those empyreal eyes. They surely possessed some secret that might be worth knowing but which would not be easily discovered. The face bore a complexity of expression only a true Celt could recognize. And then only one who knew the old mystery of the ancient race.

That her dead mother was no native to Gwynedd and, said some without a wisp of evidence to back up the claim, was more than a little disreputable herself strengthened the conviction that the odd child, if she was not one already, was well on her way to becoming a witch. The child's tongue was cursed. That alone was a sign that must be heeded.

No good would result when she came of age.

Hopefully before then she would disappear from among them.

Codnor Barrie himself came from a decent Welsh family. He was mostly respected among his fellow workers. He had no complaint against him other than falling in love with an Irish lass who had borne him a witch-child and then promptly died for her trouble. The poor widower was left alone with his baby. The good little man may have named his daughter for the Snowdonian region of Gwynedd. But that could not prevent her being what she was.

Once her peculiarities became evident, Barrie was offered no more help by the women in the village such as they would have given any other poor father with a daughter to look after. Those who had nursed and bathed her in infancy now feared for the day the curse of the growing girl would come upon them. They wanted nothing to do with her. The Christianity so deeply embedded in their Celtic blood was heavily laced with superstitious remnants of the paganism out of which it had grown. They trembled at the sight of her floral bouquets as maledictive charms against the doors of the village from the nether regions.

The mother's untimely death, though rarely spoken of, was never forgotten. What could it be but a verdict from on high? It was only a matter of time before similar judgment was rendered upon the daughter. Doubtless some ill-fated misfortune would eventually fall upon Barrie himself for allowing the evil to invade Snowdonia from across the Irish Sea.

Four

Secrets of the Sea

*G*wyneth ran to the water's edge and skipped merrily along it for some distance, then slowed. She realized that the tide on this afternoon lay uncommonly low. The flat, wet expanse of sand was much wider than usual. She gazed all about then returned in the direction from which she had come. She passed the end of the path from above then continued northward where a rocky shoreline gradually encroached on the expanse of sand until replacing it altogether. A stormy few weeks had prevented her coming here for some time. With the tide so low, she could again explore the crags and boulders and caves at the water's edge.

Two or three minutes later she was scrambling about the base of the rocky headland, scanning the small pools left by the tide for tiny sea creatures and plants. Living things of all kinds and species gladdened Gwyneth's heart. Hers was a continual search to discover new forms of life she had never seen before, whether insect or flower, weed or bird, tree or unusually colored rabbit. On this day what drew her attention where sea met land happened to be the limpets, sea snails, mussels, tiny crabs, whelks, cockles, and water bugs made newly accessible in the swirling eddies of the extraordinarily low tide.

The tide on this day lay lower than it had in years. The waves of previous weeks against the rocks and inlets of the promontory had rearranged the sandy floor of the caves and beach. The largest of the boulders remained unchanged. Yet the surface beneath Gwyneth's feet was different as she scampered over it. Some rocks of great size previously exposed were nearly covered with sand. Others whose mere tops were partially visible before had been to all appearance thrust upward into the light of day. With every rise and fall of the tide, new changes came to the coastline.

She walked into the largest of the caves, which sat at the foot of the sloping bluff where the beach sand mostly gave way to rocks and boulders. Its height was sufficient that she could explore to a distance of thirty or forty feet inside it without bumping her head. It was one of her regular haunts, though only when the sea was calm and never when the tide was in its flow. Smooth slate walls beside her as she entered glistened black from constant salty spray.

The tide was still in retreat, and on this day there was no cause for concern. Gwyneth knew the signs of the sea, knew when danger was present and when it was not. She never allowed curiosity to compromise safety. She was, in truth, more "there" of intellect and savvy than most of the villagers had any idea.

If she was different than other children, the distinction came more likely as the result of genius than fatuity. Like most genius, however, it was invisible to the commonplace mind and would be slow to reveal itself. Whatever rare gift she possessed yet lay at rest, growing, deepening in the invisible recesses of her character, awaiting the kiss of a prince to bring it awake in power.

By now the shadows of afternoon were lengthening. The westerly sun cast its slanting rays against the cliffs of Mochras Head. It had not yet descended far enough on its daily journey to hover at the horizon and throw its light directly into the yawning mouth the girl had just entered. But dim visibility shone inside the cave as the tide approached low water.

Gwyneth walked gingerly into the blackness, hands spread in front of her. As well as she knew the place, subtle changes in the sea floor made her cautious lest some stone or wall of rock loom before her unseen.

All at once her toe caught something half buried at her foot. She stumbled and fell onto her stomach and elbows at once. She cried out softly, more from surprise than pain, as she hit the wet-packed floor. Quickly recovering herself, she rolled to one side on the sand and lifted one knee.

Suddenly a terrified shriek echoed through the darkened chamber.

A foot away, two dark eyes were staring straight at her!

Black and vacant, however, they were eyes that saw nothing. The human skull, whose empty sockets leered silently in the blackness, lay two-thirds buried in the sandy cave floor. Thin light from the cave's mouth played eerily on the polished bony cranium. That its season for seeing was long past only heightened the dread of the hideous spectacle.

Gwyneth sprang to her feet and sprinted for the safety of sunlight. She did not once glance back in the direction of the macabre object uncovered by the storm. Not easily frightened, Gwyneth's young heart now clutched at her chest with the horror of the unknown.

Lightning and rain and legends of lake creatures were one thing.

Dead human heads with black holes for eyes were another!

She dashed across the open sand, turned for the promontory, and scrambled frantically along the narrow trail. All the way up the rocky bluff the way she had come earlier she ran as if her life depended on it.

Reaching the plateau above the sea, she scarcely slowed. With what remaining speed her feet possessed, she set out across several fields and then over the wide moor toward the stone cottage at the edge of the hills where she and her father made their home.

FIVE

Lord and Laborer

*F*rom a high vantage point overlooking plateau, town, harbor, and the coastline of the sea for miles, two watchful eyes beheld the curiously speedy retreat of the girl away from Mochras Head inland across the flat moorland below.

It was not his custom to walk alone on the rolling hills and solitary high meadows of his estate. He was not a great walker. He preferred the back of a horse for transport to his own feet. But afternoon tea had precipitated a disagreeable dispute with his wife. Roderick Westbrooke, the Viscount Snowdon, had therefore sought the out-of-doors, not for whatever solace it offered but merely to get away from the house. His annoyance required movement to quiet itself.

Though his stables were well stocked with suitable mounts for any occasion, he was in no mood for a ride. It was too late in the day for that. He had wandered out with no particular destination in mind. He ambled aimlessly up from the house, kept on longer than planned, and now a mile from the manor still had none.

Lord Snowdon paused at the sight below him. He stood observing the flight, now across the road that connected the village of Llanfryniog to the main north-south thoroughfare. At length the blond-headed figure disappeared from his view.

Gradually he now made his way down the slope he had climbed. Descending a dense thicket of pine and fir toward a stream where it passed through a corner of his estate, he eventually completed a wide arc back toward the front of the house.

If only it *was* his estate, he mused sardonically. . .in *all* ways. That his name appeared on the title was such a mockery when he possessed no means by which to rule and enjoy life as a lord and viscount ought to be capable of.

The ridiculous inheritance laws could be so confounded unjust. They gave a man property and title but no means to use them if those means had been squandered before his time!

He had known all that, of course, when he married the earl's daughter. *Her* wealth and *his* property seemed made for each other.

He had not paused long enough at the time to consider the consequences if she ever proved stubborn. Now he found himself on the horns of that very dilemma.

Technically, of course, it *was* his estate. The ground itself, the land, the house were entirely his possession. But what good did property by itself do a man? He couldn't *spend* dirt or trees or grass or the stone blocks of which the manor was made.

He had to find a way to win her over to his point of view. . .or else find some other means to raise the cash he needed. The opportunity before him was one he mustn't let slip by. True, it was only a yacht. But he had his heart set on the purchase. Yet without his wife's funds, the thing would be dashed difficult, if not downright impossible.

⁊⳾ℯ

Meanwhile, the child Roderick Westbrooke had seen reached the stone cottage of her home and burst inside. Her father had only moments before returned from the slate mine north of the village. He spun around at the sound of the door nearly crashing off its hinge.

"P–P–P–Papa, Papa," stuttered his daughter. "Th–th–th—"

"What is it, Gwyneth, my child?" asked Barrie as he calmly

approached with open arms. He had long ago learned that to soothe his daughter's agitation was the quickest remedy for the difficulty of her tongue.

"It's a. . .a h–h–h–h—"

Her father sat down and took her lovingly into his lap as if she were as young as the villagers thought her. He smiled with reassuring patience.

"Th–th–th–there's a head, P–P–Papa," she finally blurted out. "It's b–b–b–buried in the s–s–s–sand."

"Where, Gwyneth?" asked Barrie calmly.

"In th–th–th— In the c–c–c–cave, P–P–Papa."

"Where, Gwyneth?"

"B–by the w–w–water. I stumbled over it and fell d–d–down."

Her father stroked her wild hair and gently rocked her in his arms. Gradually she calmed.

"Are you hurt, little one?" the miner asked.

"No, Papa," Gwyneth replied, leaning her head against his chest. Already the cave apparition was beginning to fade. Since she was not one ruled by fear, neither did she cling to it on the rare occasions it visited her. She was happy to let it go. She would soon laugh at the memory.

Assuming his daughter had seen some oddly shaped stone, or perhaps come upon a fragment of sheep bone fallen from the plateau above, Barrie thought it best to avoid further mention of it.

The two chatted casually a few minutes.

"Shall we have some tea, Gwyneth?" asked the father at length.

"Yes, Papa," she replied, jumping down from his lap. "I will boil water." She ran across the floor, picked up a small iron kettle, and dashed outside.

Her father rose and followed her toward the small kitchen that occupied half of the larger of the cottage's two rooms. Upon arriving home, he had restoked the stove with coal and already begun water boiling for potatoes. He now bent to check the fire again then tossed in a second small shovel of fuel from the scuttle.

A moment later, Gwyneth lugged in the kettle of fresh water. She placed it on the stove.

He tossed a handful of potatoes into the iron pot, now beginning to steam, beside it. "Did you get bread from Grannie, Gwyneth?" he asked.

Her face fell. "I forgot, Papa," she answered. "I meant to after I went down to the sea. But I forgot and ran straight home instead."

"No harm done. We shall go see Grannie together while the potatoes boil."

Adjusting the flue of the stove, Barrie turned and took his daughter's hand. They left the cottage together and made their way down the sloping hillside toward the sea and to the village of Llanfryniog.

Six

Trouble in Glasgow

A sneaking figure of a lanky youth of sixteen sprinted along a wide Glasgow street. The echo of tinkling glass from a breaking shop window faded behind him. In his hand he clutched the booty he had retrieved through it.

He had no need of the antique sterling silver mug. Neither did he have the slightest interest in whatever money it might fetch. The shiny object struck a momentary fancy as he passed, nothing more. Mere seconds after spotting it, a brick from a nearby alley crashed through the window. The next instant he was sprinting along Gallowgate, mug in hand and a smile of youthfully devilish triumph on his face.

The mere thrill of theft drove him. It had been brought on by neither necessity nor upbringing. The lad's training had in fact instilled an altogether different set of values than those of the lifestyle in which he had been engaged for the past year or two.

Unlike the most common of thieves, this youth came of wealth. His was a home highly respected in the city. He had been given all the privileges of his station yet was now doing his best to mock them. Like many adolescents—ruled by a lust for autonomy, seduced by premature self-reliance, possessed of self-gratification, and eschewing common sense in the choosing of associations—he had reached fourteen and suddenly found the constraint of goodness intolerable. Within another year, he had burst its bonds altogether. The adventure upon which he had now embarked contained just enough danger to act as a stimulant to his rebellion.

His only creed at present was to make mischief and to do that which was certain to be "disapproved of." That such self-indulgent behavior could make anyone truly happy was doubtful. Nevertheless, such was the lad's *motive operandi*. And he had given himself wholeheartedly to it. Whether the training he had received in his early years would in time reemerge to reverse the present decline of character, he alone would be capable of determining.

Clinging to the stone building at his left, he shot into a narrow close leading away from the wide thoroughfare. He could not help smiling to himself at how absurdly easy crime really was.

Suddenly his eyes shot open, and the smile disappeared from his lips. Thirty yards in front of him stood a policeman!

His running feet clattered to an echoing halt on the cobblestones. The evening fell momentarily silent. The boy stood as one paralyzed. His eyes drifted down to the large mug glistening in his hand.

With cocky nonchalance, he turned and began to saunter in the opposite direction. He had only taken a few steps, however, when he heard the policeman's booted feet behind him. They were coming with steadily increasing tempo in his direction.

He wasn't about to wait to see how this turned out!

In one quick motion, he tossed the mug clanking onto the stones of the alley, then turned and sprinted back for Gallowgate. He could outrun any policeman in Glasgow. He had no intention of being caught with the evidence.

"Stop. . . Hey, you!" shouted a voice behind him. "Stop, I say!"

Calling out again and with whistle blaring, the policeman broke into a run. But though he took up the chase with vigor, the lanky legs of youth quickly widened the distance between themselves and the middle-aged bluecoat.

A quick glance by the young rogue over his shoulder confirmed that he was out of danger. He continued at full speed, however, as the whistles and shouts gradually faded behind him. Around a corner he flew, along a long block, across the deserted street, left again, and—

Suddenly a great crash was followed by exclamations of astonishment and cries of pain. The teen went sprawling over the rough stones of the street and landed in a heap against a brick wall. Angry curses burst from his lips as he began to pick himself up.

Before he could completely recover, a great hand seized the scruff of his neck and hauled him back to his feet. "Ay, 'tis you, is it, young Drummond?" said an unmistakable voice attached to the bulky frame he had collided with. "I thought as much. Ye'd be advised tae watch oot a mite better whaur ye'd bound."

"Yeah, yeah," the youth replied testily. "I might say the same for you, coming round the blind corner without letting a bloke know you're there. Just let me go, will you!"

"I want tae ken what ye're aboot runnin' through the streets this time o' the evenin'."

"I'm about nothing that's any of your business!" shot back the boy. He struggled in earnest to free himself, but to little avail. His captor was three times his size. The lad threw a nervous glance over his shoulder.

As he feared, soon another set of feet came running heavily toward them. "Stop him, Forbes!" shouted the exhausted pursuer. He lumbered to the scene, breathing heavily. "Keep a tight grip on him or he'll bolt."

"He's aye gaein' nowhere, officer," replied the policeman called Forbes. "I've a good grip o' him. Noo, young Drummond," he said, turning again to the boy, "why dinna ye tell me what ye've been aboot like I asked ye?"

SEVEN

The Village

*T*he village of Llanfryniog of North Wales spread out in random disorder away from the main street running through its center.

Several shops—the post, a baker, a dry goods store, a butcher, and a green grocer—were supplemented by a dozen or more homes that boasted an assorted miscellany of goods in their windows. Most of their offerings—from sweeties to tobacco to eggs, milk, potatoes, turnips, apples, candles, jams, and an infinite variety of homegrown and homemade products—could be purchased for a penny or two, but rarely more than a handful of shillings. Even this latter, however, would have been a considerable sum for most who passed by and gazed at the simply offered wares. There were also a variety of services available from a blacksmith, a cobbler, and a doctor from their homes on the outskirts of town.

The school and the chapel, the same white-harled steepled stone edifice serving for both, stood at one end of the town. Beyond it the single wide street turned toward the harbor, gradually narrowed to a single lane not quite wide enough even for two farm wagons to pass, and skirted the coast northward for another mile before veering inland to connect again with the main road north where it led a course around the waters of Traeth Bach.

At the opposite end of town, walkers through Llanfryniog passed two other churches, symbolically facing one another from opposing sides. The wide thoroughfare then continued straight south, rising through farmland above the sea toward the plateau of Mochras Head. There, like its northern counterpart, it wound back inland to reconnect to the north-south road connecting Blaenau Ffestiniog in the mountains near Snowdon with Barmouth where the River Afton emptied into Barmouth Bay.

Near the top of the Mochras slope, a private avenue led off the main road east and inland into the foothills. An imposing iron gate across it with gatehouse beside stood some fifty yards off the main road. From this impressive entryway, the approach led along a winding tree-lined course of some half a mile up a continuing incline to Westbrooke Manor. The largest mansion for fifty miles sat at the base of the Cambrian range, which, as the hills surrounding it increased in height, led some miles inland to the southern peaks of Snowdonia.

Though it was a mere village housing a thousand people or less, its proximity to Westbrooke Manor, as well as the small natural harbor in the protected waters of Tremadog Bay, gave Llanfryniog the distinction of being of ancient date and of a certain historic importance. Centuries earlier it had been a sort of sister village to Harlech, the administrative seat for the surrounding coastal area. That Harlech Castle—built in the late thirteenth century by Edward I, dominating the region for centuries, and considered by some the most perfect castle design in all Britain—was now reduced to a stupendous but impotent stone shell took nothing away from the historic tradition of both towns.

Notwithstanding that serious judicial functions had long since passed to the larger cities of northern Wales, Llanfryniog continued as home to a lay magistrate, whose duties were largely at the behest of the viscount and involved minor civil matters. It was his daughter, in fact, whom the viscount's son and daughter had come to town on this day to visit. Neither viscount nor magistrate, however, benefited from the services of a local policeman. For that they must depend on

Porthmadog to the north or Dolgellau south and i.
fifteen miles distant.

It was not a serious deficiency. The need for ei
enforcement or legal proceedings in such a rural oasis,
fishing, and slate mining occupied most of the waking hou. ⌐ı ιτs working
men, was rarely felt. That they enjoyed their stout, and occasionally
partook of more than their wives might have wished, belied the fact that
these were good men, devoted to family, church, and the friendships that
bound their community together. Nearly to a man, in spite of conflicting
religious affiliation, most would have given their lives for any other. They
would indisputably have bound together in common cause against any
foe, no matter what the odds, whether real or imaginary.

If the Celtic blood of their ancestors had inbred a troublesome
flaw into their collective nature beyond an occasional hot temper, it
was an affinity for the bizarre, the paranormal, and the occult. Their
religion, whether Catholic, Anglican, or Protestant, was so laced with
superstition as in some respects to be scarcely distinguishable from the
paganism of its ancient origins. The staid memberships of both Catholic
and Church of England houses of worship, along with those of the
more enthusiastically minded Methodist chapel, could all have quoted
chapter and verse from the lexicons of doctrine that had been drilled
into them from their infancies why the other two were false expressions
of Christianity and theirs the true.

In actual fact, however, all three tended to see God as an almighty
magician and shaman, rather than as the loving Creator-Father of
humankind. Ritual, doctrinal legalism, and the idea of vicarious sacrifice
passed down from humankind's prehistoric ancestors remained the
pivotal elements of their creed, not obedience to the commands of the
Creator-Son nor the sacrifice of self-will He exampled.

This grotesque intermingling of the Christian gospel with medieval
druidism presented a particularly frustrating challenge to the truth-
loving ministers and priests who came among them through the years.
Sadly, it also provided a singular opportunity toward manipulation and

mind control for those pulpiteers of less honorable repute.

As if in visible manifestation of this occult religiosity that existed in the very air of the place, a small house constructed mostly of wood, whitewashed on its exterior, stood near the heart of the village. It had been built at the intersection of two narrow lanes—out of the way of most foot traffic and carefully avoided by those whose routes took them in proximity to it. The very architecture of the dwelling bespoke mischief if not outright devilry behind its weirdly appointed and colored exterior. A steep-slanted roof was accented by curious ornamentation at the four corners and with a spooky weather vane atop it. The purple paint on doors and window frames and an assortment of statues about the garden, including trolls, fairies, goblins, and a miscellany of bizarre figures and gargoyles, all indicated dubious if not outright evil intent.

The scrupulously avoided dwelling might easily have been a dwarf's cottage from some fairy tale transplanted out of the depths of Germany's Black Forest. How it came to be *here*, in this Welsh village where gray stone predominated, no one knew. That it predated by half a century or more its present occupant was certain. Yet almost by seeming preternatural contrivance of the gods, or of powers from more subterranean regions, the place had apparently been perfectly designed for its present mistress, even though she had been in Llanfryniog only a dozen or so years.

A small wood sign above the door, ornate with Celtic symbolism, snakes, contorted animal shapes, and leering faces, read: MADAME FLEMING, PSYCHIC—FORTUNES AND FUTURES FORETOLD.

None in the village knew why the enigmatic "Madame Fleming" had chosen this coastal village to set up her shop of doubtful wares or where she had come from. No one for a moment thought the name on the sign her *real* name. She was rarely seen. When she did chance to be about—with long flowing dresses of bright colors, sashes and scarves and kerchiefs of reds and pinks and oranges and purples about the head, and gaudy jewelry dangling from ears and neck and wrists—there was no mistaking her. Rumors abounded about the woman's age. These ranged from fifty to one hundred and five.

How she supported herself was an equal mystery. About this, even more rumors were part and parcel of the undercurrent of talk that circulated among the women of the place. Ideas were as far reaching as that she possessed independent wealth, to the existence of a dead husband of means, to her being "kept" by the viscount with whom she shared a secret he could not afford to come out.

If Madame Fleming, so called, had not come of gypsy origins in Bohemia or Bulgaria, she certainly looked the part. Except that gypsies, as associated as they were with sorcery and clairvoyancy, did not generally stay so long in one place, pay their bills, and establish themselves in communities it was their intent to fleece. That the woman had been here for so long and that no charge of misconduct or failure to meet her obligations could be laid at her doorstep argued for other antecedents, perhaps halfway reputable, than of gypsy tradition.

Neither man nor woman, neither miner nor fisherman, neither lord nor lady nor commoner was ever seen coming or going from her establishment. Yet she remained a distinct presence in the midst of the town and always paid baker and butcher in cash. The whole thing was an enduring mystery.

A private door opening into a dark and narrow lane leading away from the central district of Llanfryniog afforded ample means for further gossip. That it was never locked, and its hinges kept well-oiled for reasons of silence and secrecy, added credence to the rumors, despite all appearances, that she actually had paying customers. Some of them were said to be regular, including those who sought consultation from as far away as Chester. But there were also said to be some among the local populace who walked to and from her back door unseen from their own homes less than five minutes away.

At this time of night, with summer nightfall descending, though an occasional clandestine caller might extend his or her hand in the light of a flickering candle to have its lines read by the shadowy Madame

Fleming, it was Mistress Chattan's establishment on the main street that was doing the brisker trade.

By this time, the two young riders had returned to the mansion up the hill that was their home and were concluding an uneventful dinner in the dining room of Westbrooke Manor with father and mother, Lord and Lady Snowdon, the viscount Roderick and his wife, Katherine.

EIGHT

Ale and Information

*T*he evening wore on. Dusk deepened.

One by one the miners, having had what drink they could afford, left the inn for their wives, potatoes, tea, and, if they were fortunate, children who loved them and appreciated their hard work to put what meager provision they could on their tables each night.

A scruffy man probably in his fifties, although with features hard and difficult to assess, cast a look about the deserted street of Llanfryniog then walked into Mistress Chattan's inn. He was not a man who even had a place to go. He had left home at fifteen and never returned. He had not seen his father nor mother again. If he regretted his prodigality, he had never admitted that fact.

It takes humility to face the regrets of life honestly, and this was a man who had not yet become acquainted with the eternal imperative of humility. When he had had enough of the seafaring life, he had betaken himself to a career in subterfuge and charlatanry—turning whatever information came his way, or that he could coerce out of others whether willing or unwilling, into profit to himself. His methods had become more ruthless through the years, as befit the atrophy of whatever conscience he once may have possessed. He was a man better avoided.

He walked inside and quietly took in the two or three men seated at one of the tables. He walked slowly across the floor and found a chair at the far end of the room. His business would keep until they were gone.

An aproned woman approached, large though her step was soft. Hair graying slightly, her face showed weariness from the long day. She was, however, always eager to oblige a new customer.

The man glanced toward her.

"It's not a room you'll be wanting, I'm thinking?" said the woman.

"Just your darkest ale," replied her visitor.

She turned away. A minute later she returned with a tankard.

The man began to sip slowly and in silence.

One by one the other men rose. With a few final words to the proprietress, they gradually wandered out.

At last the stranger and Mistress Chattan were left alone.

"Another ale, if you please, my good woman," he said.

She brought it.

He tossed a half-crown coin on the table. It jingled in a circular motion until it fell silent.

Mistress Chattan scooped it into her fleshy palm. "I will bring you back what's due you," she said.

"Keep it," said the man. "There'll be another to add to it if you can provide me with a small piece of information."

Mistress Chattan's eyes narrowed imperceptibly. In her business, where talk was cheap and where the liquid inventory of her stock-in-trade tended to loosen tongues, she had come by more than her share of secrets. Some were harmless; some not so. That it was in the nature of her position to occupy the occasional *rôle* of confidante was in truth one of the perquisites of her profession. Over the years she had, by subtle art, by attentive ear, and by skillfully placed sympathetic comment, gained much information that might be useful to possess.

Indeed, Mistress Chattan knew far more about Llanfryniog's people than they had any idea. She possessed two or three juicy secrets concerning which she was biding her time until some profitable opportunity presented itself. At such time, she would either divulge what she knew or, if the price was right in the opposite direction, vow on a Bible, which meant nothing to her, to keep silent forever.

Giving away information, however, was another matter. She was a woman who knew how to guard her tongue. But as the man had rightly surmised, what she might or might not know could be had. . . for a price.

"Make it a gold sovereign," she replied after a moment. "If it lays in my power, I will tell you what I know."

"You are a shrewd one, if not a shrew."

"If you think to hurl insults at an honest woman, you best keep a civil tongue in your mouth," she spat. "One more such word and you'll get nothing from me."

"Tut, tut, lady, I was paying you a compliment. I shall give you your pound and one, then. It's easy money for you. All I want to know is where to find an old man by the name of Drindod."

"There's Drindods and there's Drindods," she replied cryptically.

"Toy with me and you'll lose your sovereign."

"There's at least six Drindods within a mile of my door. Another ten within five."

"This one's called Sean Drindod."

Mistress Chattan took in the information without divulging her chagrin. She did not like the look in this fellow's eye. Nor did she know where the old man could be found. She had heard the name. But she knew nothing more. And she had no doubt that this man would come back and slit her throat if she played him false.

"You can keep your sovereign," she said reluctantly. "If you want to know where old Sean Drindod is, you'll not hear it from my lips. But for what remains of the half crown, I will tell you of one in town who knows things. For a sovereign she will tell you what she knows."

"How do I find her?"

The stranger to Llanfryniog left Mistress Chattan's inn a few minutes later and sought the dark lane. Through quiet hinges no one heard, he was led into a secluded parlor. There a candle and incense burned in the gathering darkness.

The low conversation that followed between the stranger and the clairvoyant proved satisfactory to both parties of the exchange.

NINE

Drastic Measures

A Glaswegian man and his wife sat silently at a well-appointed supper table. A third place setting had been prepared. The chair before it was empty. They had waited until dark but had finally gone ahead with the meal. Every swallow, however, was made difficult by the concern visible in their eyes and by the ache eating at both their hearts.

It was not the first time the two had eaten late and alone. Yet upon every successive occasion of their son's absence, deeper anxieties arose concerning what might be the cause.

The house in whose dining room they sat was of obvious culture and refinement. The man's study upstairs, though lined with bookshelves, was sufficient to contain but half the volumes in his possession. Books spilled into most of the other rooms of the house, including this. On an ornate sideboard sat a handsome silver tea service. Furnishings everywhere bespoke wealth.

All such comforts, however, this man and woman of God would have traded in a heartbeat in exchange for the opening of the eyes of him for whom both now silently prayed.

Their affluence had been sought by neither. It was the mere result of the circumstances in which they found themselves.

The man's father was an earl. Though the title would not pass down at his death, he had already split most of what remained of his fortune, after what he had given away, between his son and daughter, keeping only enough for him and his wife to continue the missionary endeavors to which they had devoted their latter years.

In truth, the earl's son and his wife possessed a healthy fear of the balance of their account in the Clydesdale Bank. Unlike most couples of means, they took no pride in it nor based a moment's security upon it. The unusual man and woman regarded their wealth as a holy possession, not theirs at all but rather a stewardship that had been placed in their hands. It was not theirs to spend but rather to *administer* by prudence, prayer, and wisdom. They were of that exceptional breed in the spiritual realm, rare but thankfully not extinct any more in their own time than such were in the Lord's, though as infrequently found in society at large as in its churches—a humble and unpretentious man and woman of wealth.

"Where *can* he be, Edward?" said the woman finally. The question came from her mouth in scarcely more than a whisper. Either words or tears *must* at last burst from her mother's heart. For the moment she preferred the former.

Her husband shook his head. The only possible response was a pregnant sigh born of anguish too deep to find expression.

Nothing more was said. They continued to eat sparingly.

Their silence was interrupted fifteen minutes later by a knock on the parsonage door.

At the sound, the woman's hand unconsciously clutched at her heart.

The man rose quickly and strode from the dining room to the front door. He opened it and saw a policeman standing on the porch.

"I'm sorry tae be disturbin' ye, reverend, sir," said the transplanted native of Inverness who had come south years before and now wore the blue of a Glasgow bobby. "I'm afraid I found yer laddie up tae nae good again."

Beside him, with the large highlander's grasp firmly around the boy's bicep like a vise, stood the young thief. The expression of profound vexation on his face could not have been less indicative of repentance.

The vicar glanced at his son. His expression betrayed nothing. But his heart ached within him.

Behind him his wife approached. It was all she could do to avoid tears. She knew they would only make her son despise her the more.

"Thank you, Constable Forbes," said the vicar. "We are greatly indebted to you."

"Beggin' yer pardon, Mr. Drummond," added the policeman in an apologetic tone, "this will be the last time I'll be able tae bring the lad home tae ye this way. The next time, sir, it will be the tollbooth for him, even if he is but a lad."

"I understand."

"And there will be a bill comin' for tonight's damage."

"I understand, constable. Thank you very much. We will take him now." The vicar stepped forward, took his son by the arm, led him inside, and closed the door.

"Percy, *why* do you do these things?" said the vicar's wife once they were inside. Her voice was soft, though urgent. At last she could hold in her emotion no longer. She looked away and began to weep.

The boy struggled to free himself from his father's grip, but the man's quiet wrath was smoldering. He had finally had enough of his son's foolish antics. All fathers, no matter how long-suffering, how loving, how patient, have their limits. Vicar Edward Drummond's had finally been crossed. "Answer your mother!" he said angrily. He shoved the boy down in a chair and stood towering above him.

His son shrugged his shoulders. "I like to," he said insolently. "I enjoy outwitting the stupid policemen. I would have gotten away tonight if I hadn't stumbled, and if there hadn't been two of them."

"It's a game to you, is that it?"

"Of course it's a game. What else would it be?"

"How can you ask that after all we've taught you. . .all we've given you?" said Mrs. Drummond, bursting into sobs as she collapsed in a couch across the room.

"It is pointless to argue," said the vicar. "I don't know what evil spirit has overtaken you, or why. I do know this," he added in a tone of greater finality and resolution than his son had ever heard, "we *will* have no more incidents like this evening's."

The youth glanced up briefly then away. His father's words jolted him out of his testy nonchalance. They sounded eerily like a threat.

"I will *not* rescue you from your own folly again," the vicar went on. "If you persist, you *shall* find yourself in jail like Constable Forbes said. If it comes to that, I will not bail you out. Is that understood?"

The sixteen-year-old son sat sulking. He realized he had pushed his father too far. He had never heard such a voice of command. His father rarely became angry. It was obvious he had aroused something more dangerous than mere anger. That was righteous indignation.

One of his father's favorite sayings from the Bible was, "Let your yea be yea; and your nay, nay." His father was not merely a man of his word. He made no idle promises—or threats. What he said he would do, he would do.

The minister's son realized he had best lie low for a while.

"Go upstairs to your room," said the vicar after a moment. His voice had calmed but rang with no less authority.

Percy rose and went. To say that he *obeyed* would hardly be accurate. Mother and Father wondered if he had ever truly laid down his own will for the chosen purpose of doing what another commanded him. In the present case, however, the boy recognized the expediency to himself of departing his parents' presence at the earliest possible opportunity. This he therefore did.

To be banished to his room at sixteen, like a child, was a profound humiliation. But young Percival Drummond, though he may have been a rebel, was no fool. He was enough of a realist to know that his room at home was better than any of Glasgow's jail cells.

The parlor fell silent. Supper was by now long forgotten. Mrs. Drummond's breathing occasionally caught on a lingering sob.

At length her husband turned from where he had been standing still as a statue. He walked slowly to the couch. He sat down beside his wife and placed an arm gently around her shoulders.

"What did we do wrong, Edward?" she said in a broken voice.

The vicar sighed deeply. How many times had they asked that question of themselves during the past year? "I don't know, Mary," he replied softly. "If it continues, I don't see that I shall have any other option but to resign my vicarage."

"Surely that cannot be God's will."

"Nor can it be His intent that the son of the parish minister is running through the streets of Glasgow as a common burglar. Sadly that seems exactly our situation."

They remained silent a few minutes more.

"What would you think of our sending him to my sister?" said Drummond at length.

"In Wales—you mean. . .to stay?"

"I don't know—perhaps for an extended visit. The country might do him good. School will be out in a few weeks. At the very least, we could try it for the summer. When fall comes, we can see what the situation is then. School is doing him no good anyway."

"Do we really want to send him away from home, Edward? What if he doesn't return? I don't think my heart could take losing him at sixteen."

"We have as good as lost him as it is," rejoined her husband. "The city is trying its best to corrupt him. I fear for his soul if *something* is not done. The country has been known in some cases to exercise a therapeutic influence. Whether it can exorcise his spirit of foolishness and rebellion," he added with another long sigh, "I do not know."

His wife nodded. Her heart was breaking for her son. She was willing to consent to anything that might help. "He would never agree to it," she said.

"I shall give him no alternative," rejoined the father. "He is young enough that he is still dependent upon us for everything. I often wonder if he would have been better off had we been paupers. If his salvation requires it, I will cut him off without a farthing."

"Knowing that he stands to inherit all we possess, he would bitterly resent it."

"He is possessed with a spirit of resentment anyway. I doubt we can make it much worse. Character is the only inheritance worth giving. At present our son is in fearfully short supply. I would sooner give away my entire half of my father's fortune than allow Percy to squander it to his own demise. Hopefully time will not make such extreme measures necessary."

"I am in favor of anything that might help," his wife replied. "What do you think your sister's husband will say?"

The vicar smiled. "My brother-in-law is a man I can never predict," he said. "Roderick might refuse our request. On the other hand, it would not surprise me if he took a liking to Percy. That Roderick makes no claim to being a man of religion and has always looked down on me for my profession, would give him and our son something in common. They might find themselves forming a friendship on the basis of their mutual antipathy toward me!" he added, chuckling at the thought. "In fact," Drummond said, rising from the couch, "I like the idea so much, I think I will go up to my study and write Katherine straightaway."

TEN

Evil Night

*T*he night in Llanfryniog grew late.

Wispy elongated fingers eerily bisected a near full moon only recently risen above the silhouette of the mountains to the east. The ethereal thin horizontal clouds did not substantially reduce the light from its pale glow but did portend this night's omens of sinister intent.

A powerful man, whose appearance might have indicated him one of the region's slate miners but whose hands and mannerisms indicated other means of gaining his daily bread, had let the evening pass until an hour when respectable persons had taken to their beds. Leaving Madame Fleming's, he now slunk through the deserted streets of the coastal Welsh village. The occasional lone bark of a dog was the only sound that divulged life.

He was careful that his steps were not heard. None saw him sneaking among the shadows of their abodes on his nefarious errand. It may have been unwise to talk so freely to the woman he had just left. But unless he was a poorer judge of character than he thought, she would not talk. If that changed, she could easily be bought off—or eliminated.

His own connection to the man he had come to Llanfryniog to find had come about years ago by one of those chance encounters destined to alter the course of life forever after. While most of the others in the

Dolgellau pub that night dismissed the drunken man's stories of pirate treasure with the laughter of their own whiskey-soaked brains, he had been sober enough for his ears to perk up.

For the next hour, he had listened attentively across the dingy tavern. An hour after that, he followed the man out and struck up what conversation was possible in his wobbly state.

It was enough to convince him that there existed more than a grain of truth to the man's story.

He had carefully arranged to meet Drindod again. . .and again, professing friendship and standing him drinks—the surest way to an alcoholic's heart. Gradually he learned more. He had not learned enough, however, to lay his hands on what the man claimed was the key to the location of the booty, a certain gold coin of exceedingly ancient date.

He had patiently waited all these years without success. He had tried every means of persuasion possible to loosen the old fool's tongue. He had craftily spoken with every septuagenarian and what few octogenarians remained within fifty miles, carefully and without betraying his intent.

But years continued to pass.

One by one they went the way of all flesh. Whatever knowledge they possessed passed with them. Fewer and fewer remained from that fateful century when fortunes were made—and hidden.

He had finally discovered where the man was from. After Drindod's retirement from the seafaring life, he had followed the old salt back to the home of his childhood.

Then came a day when he realized the time could be delayed no longer. If he did not act soon, it would be too late. He would be left with nothing. He did not intend to let this night pass without discovering more about the mysterious coin.

Pausing momentarily beside a wall of stone, the figure now hurried across a wide dirt street then along it another hundred yards. Though a conglomeration of cottages were scattered about inland, the buildings thinned northward along the shoreline beyond the harbor. With stealth he approached the seaward side of the street. Light from the moon was shielded by the low building in front of him.

The Fleming woman's description matched the place exactly. He crept toward its corner, paused briefly, then moved around it and temporarily into the thin glow. He did not hesitate. He set hand to the door and quickly entered. No homes in this region possessed locks.

A sound of startled wakefulness from the occupant was brief. "What are... Who are you?" he said in the darkness.

"Shut up, old man," growled a low voice at the bedside. It made no attempt to disguise itself.

"What are *you* doing here, Rup—"

A large hand clamped over the aged lips. "Quiet, I told you!" rasped a whisper which could not hide its menace. "Get up. You're coming with me."

The sleeping old man could hardly argue. Already his unwelcome visitor had rousted him from bed and was dragging him from the cottage in his bedclothes. The old man of eighty struggled feebly as he was pulled from his home. But the hand across his face prevented so much as a peep from escaping his lips.

Twenty minutes later, away from the village on a lonely expanse of shoreline and beyond the hearing of all save the waves, which never slept, at last assailant and hostage stopped.

The younger of the two released his prisoner and threw him rudely to the sand. "I've been patient all these years," he said. "Now I want to know where it is."

"I don't know what you mean," said the old man. He attempted to climb to his knees.

A rude kick sent him toppling over on his back. "You told me there was a coin."

"A small thing, of no value."

"You said it would lead to the rest."

"I was drunk. I didn't know what I was saying."

"Maybe the whiskey loosened your tongue to tell the truth."

Silence was his only answer.

"Where is it, Drindod! I want it. . . I want it all!" He bent to the sand and raised his hand to strike.

"I told you before. The old man was dead by the time I saw him."

"Then how did you get the coin?"

"I never had it."

"You said you saw it."

"Only once. And just for a moment. I could never get my hands on it."

"But you know who has it. Tell me and I may let you live!"

"She has it!" the old man burst out, at last divulging his secret of many decades. "She's had it all along."

"Who? Tell me!" cried the younger man. He grabbed Drindod with a huge fist and viciously yanked him to his feet and within six inches of his own leering face.

"Little. . .little Bryn," whimpered the old man in terror. For the first time in three-quarters of a century he spoke the nickname of his childhood acquaintance of that fateful day.

"I've never heard that name! Who are you talking about?"

"I tell you, the girl has it. She would never give it to me. It was she who found the body. She was just a little girl."

Enraged at what he took for another lie, the hysterical prodigal seaman clutched his prey by the throat. A loud whack sounded across the wrinkled cheeks. The blow sent the weak old man sprawling again to the ground.

A few more wrathful attempts to coerce the information from him gave way at length to the full force of the younger man's fury. The struggle was brief. Soon all that could be heard was the rhythmic inflow of Tremadog's waters.

Five minutes later a shadowy figure, alone now and unseen of human eye, scrambled across a few rocks and up onto the moor. It then hastened northward away from the village.

Behind him, on the very shore whose secret had possessed him in vain for seventy-six years, lay the form of him who now followed the salty old pirate to a place it might be hoped was better than this.

ELEVEN

Condemned to the Country

*T*he first sensation to reach sixteen-year-old Percival Drummond's ears the morning following his arrival in the Gwynedd foothills of North Wales was the sound of a bird chirping somewhere in a tree outside his window.

He and his father had reached his uncle's home by coach after dark the night before. A round of tedious reintroductions to relatives he had not seen for five years had been punctuated by looks from his two cousins, Courtenay and Florilyn, that did not invite optimism about his prospects. Boring conversation followed on stiff chairs with tea altogether too strong for the occasion. Mercifully he had finally been allowed to retire for the night to his new quarters.

A prison cell would be a more apt description! Maybe he had been wrong—a Glasgow jail *might* have been better!

How would he possibly live through the summer in this country wasteland?

Perhaps after his father left, Percy thought, he could steal some money and make an escape. There might be some fun to be had out of this after all!

He turned over sleepily, stuffed his pillow over his head, and did his best to go back to sleep. But it was no use. The blasted bird was too close, too loud, too persistent. If he had a gun, he would shoot the infernal thing. If it insisted on waking him every morning, he would see about getting one! His uncle surely had a well-supplied gun cabinet somewhere about the place.

Reluctantly he climbed out of bed, dressed with the enthusiasm of one preparing for his own execution, and left the room. He descended to the main floor of the house. He heard voices coming from the breakfast room. The last thing he wanted was to see anyone.

The gnawing in his stomach, however, reminded him that such a thing as food existed and that sixteen-year-old boys consumed great quantities of it. He therefore walked along the wide corridor toward the sounds and entered. He found his aunt and uncle and father seated about the table.

"Ah Percival—good morning!" exclaimed his uncle.

"Hello, Uncle Roderick," he replied with an imperceptible nod. He did not offer much of a smile to accompany it.

"Come, Percival," said his aunt Katherine, beckoning him to one of the empty chairs. "The tea is just come."

Percy approached and sat down. Somberly he took the plate offered by his aunt and helped himself to generous portions from the contents of several platters on the table.

"I see nothing to be gained by glossing over the affair," said Edward Drummond as his sister poured tea into Percy's cup. "I have been explaining to your uncle Roderick and your aunt Katherine exactly the nature of, shall we say, our *problem* with the authorities in Glasgow. Should you think to dupe them, Percy, rest assured that I have urged watchfulness. There are no false pretenses about your presence here. They know what you have done and exactly why I have requested that they take you in for the summer."

Percy busied himself with breakfast. He saw no advantage in making a reply. His father's words rankled, but an argument now would not help his cause.

"Don't worry about a thing, Edward," put in Westbrooke with

blustery confidence. "We shall have an amiable time of it. Although I dare say the country life may be more dangerous than you bargained for," he added, laughing.

"How do you mean?" asked the vicar.

"Tilman Heygate, my factor, came to the house early this morning to tell me that the body of an old man was found on the shore a mile south of the harbor just after daylight by one of the village fishermen."

"Who, Roderick?" asked Mrs. Westbrooke in alarm.

"Old Sean Drindod."

"The poor man!" she exclaimed as her hand came to her mouth.

"Drowned?" asked the vicar.

"No, actually. That's the curious part," answered Westbrooke seriously. "Seems his neck was broken."

"What happened?" asked his brother-in-law.

"No one knows. There appears no sign he'd fallen among the rocks. I'll ride into town later this morning and speak with the magistrate. At the moment it appears he was murdered."

His wife gasped as her face went white. Silence fell around the table.

Lord Snowdon quickly resumed his zestful spirits. "I assure you such occurrences are most out of the ordinary." He laughed, though his wife's face remained pale. "As I said, Percival will be most welcome. We shall make a man of the young Scotsman! Once he has a taste of the country life, you may never get him back to Glasgow."

"Thank you, Roderick," replied the vicar. "You cannot know how much this means to Mary and me."

"It is the least we can do for your brother, is it not, Katherine?" replied the viscount. He glanced briefly across the table to his wife. "If the lad proves troublesome," he said, throwing Percy a quick wink and grin, "I shall hire him out to one of my tenants to help with the sheep shearing or send him to sea on one of the fishermen's boats. Eh, Percival, my boy? Hard work and country air—that's what's wanted. We shall provide both in good measure."

Lord Snowdon's words rang a little hollow in his wife's ears, seeing as how he had never taken the slightest interest in making a man, as he put it, of his own son, who would sooner have jumped over the moon than soiled *his* hands in the matted wool of a dirty sheep. But the moment her brother's letter had arrived from Glasgow with its request, the viscount had perceived his opportunity to reestablish himself in his wife's good graces. Well knowing her family's notions of spirituality and Katherine's fondness for her older brother, Westbrooke determined to assist her side of the family in the matter of their wayward son. Secretly he hoped for the result of his wife's loosening up her purse strings. Toward that end he would make himself everything an aristocratic country uncle should be to a Glasgow-bred youth. Thus he would win favor with the brother-in-law *and* his wife.

Whether eighteen-year-old Courtenay would greet the presence of his city cousin with equal jubilation was doubtful. He had behaved himself last night. Yet from the moment Percy's eyes met those of Courtenay Westbrooke, his elder by a year and a half, it was clear that a contest for supremacy was inevitable. Courtenay's fifteen-year-old sister, Florilyn, was every bit the equal of either boy in feisty self-centeredness. But she would gain her ends by wile rather than bluff. She possessed the face and physique of an eighteen-year-old, with cunning and coquetry in equal measure. She was already turning more heads among local old youths than either of her parents had any idea and had bewitched several to attempt foolhardy exploits to gain her notice.

That both young Westbrookes were as spoiled as money could make them was as much a grief to their mother as it was object of humorous jocularity to their father. The viscount was not a man for whom character was life's highest ambition, either for himself or his offspring. Even now, with the evidence before his eyes every day, he yet remained oblivious to the danger he continued to perpetuate by pampering his son and daughter in their self-indulgence. Westbrooke was of the school that taught a man to get what he could and watch out for number one. His foresight, therefore, was not altogether perceptive in the matter of what he might be passing down unto the third and fourth generations of his progeny.

The axiom "Lead by example" works in many directions. The result generally reinforces tendencies already well established within the garden of personhood. A good example is not usually sufficient to counteract a bad one willingly emulated. In this case, as their father was the stronger personality of the marital union, the children had taken his model as their standard. Neither Courtenay nor Florilyn had any desire to become a saint. Both appeared likely to be granted their wish.

Breakfast concluded, Percy wandered back to his quarters. Alone again, he stood for a moment gazing absently out the window, then turned again into the room and threw himself on the bed. It was less than twelve hours since their arrival. Already he was bored silly.

His father found him unmoved forty minutes later.

Their good-byes were stiff and awkward. Hoping for a word or glance or gesture that might indicate a softening in his son's soul, the vicar remained a moment more beside the bed.

But none came.

Drummond turned at length and left the room. Tears gathered in his eyes as he made his way down the hall.

An hour later he sat in the coach on his way to the train that would take him back to Glasgow. *God*, he prayed silently, *his mother and I have done the best we knew. It certainly did not turn out as we had hoped.* He sighed disconsolately then added in an inaudible whisper, "Do what You can for him, Lord. Fulfill the words of the proverb that he will one day return to the training we gave him."

Shortly after lunch—a strained affair with aunt and uncle now that he was alone with them—Percy wandered out behind the great house. He had seen neither of his cousins since the previous night and was glad. As much bluster as he tried to wear, he was, after all, still a boy in many ways. One would think that city life might have made him more worldly wise than his country-bred cousins. Just the opposite was in fact the case. Without any noticeable spiritual component to their existence, in spite of their mother's efforts, and a sense shared by both of their own superiority as wealthy son and daughter of a lord, Courtenay and Florilyn had matured rapidly in that ugliest of character flaws—hauteur. They were in love with themselves.

Percy Drummond, on the other hand, had grown up as the only child of a manse. That fact alone had shielded him from many of the very influences bearing such foul fruit in the personality gardens of his cousins. He at least had *heard* values espoused that, though he now eschewed them, had been part and parcel of the soil in which his being had sent down its first roots.

Percy's rebellion was a phase of youth. The conceit of his cousins was more deeply endemic to their natures. It would thus be more difficult to purge.

Twelve

The Stables

For the rest of the day, which seemed fifty hours long, Percy wandered about, did his best to avoid human contact, returned to his room, stared out the window, lay on his bed, wandered out again, and nearly went mad with boredom.

The family did not gather for dinner as the viscount and Courtenay were gone to the neighboring estate. A buffet had been spread out in the dining room. Percy ate with his aunt, though the conversation was mostly one-sided on her part.

Slowly the evening wore on. Dusk descended on North Wales. A gorgeous sunset rose over the sea to the west but was lost on Percy. Alone in his room, he stared out the window into the dusky gloom. All below him the house was quiet. It had been since the striking of ten. Everyone had long since retired.

It had been a warm day. The evening remained warm as well. Percy's window stood open. Straight out from him, midway up into the sky, a few reminders remained of the brilliant reds, yellows, oranges, and purples of the sunset that had come and now were gone. No noticeable disturbance of the air came to his face. Yet he felt the faintest tingling of the sea somewhere about his nostrils, borne inland on breezes too light to be felt by the skin. He continued to gaze in the general direction of the ancient Green Isle of Ireland, which was supposed to be out there somewhere. Closer at hand he could just barely make out the fading dividing line between the blackening green of sea and the faint dimming goldening blue of sky.

What was on his mind, even sixteen-year-old Percival Drummond himself could not have said. He was young for introspection and unaccustomed to the exercise though its season was approaching. How far away and long ago Glasgow seemed—another world from this.

He reflected on the incident that had sent him here in the first place—the theft of the sterling mug. It was not the first such incident.

What had possessed him to do such things? So remote it now seemed in his memory.

What caused the reckless streak within him? Was his rebellion directed against his father? If so, again came the question—why? Did he resent his father's profession? Had he been trying to discredit him, make him look foolish in the eyes of his parishioners?

For now, such questions remained unanswered.

The only sounds coming from outside were crickets, turning the darkness into their own chirping symphony. From the stables behind the house, whenever the crickets paused to rest their leggy instruments, the occasional stamp of horse's hoof or snort of nose and lips broke the silence.

He knew his father had sent him here to change. But now the question rose, and with it an inexplicable annoyance: Did he *want* to change?

A last vestige of insurrection rose within him.

I am who I am, Percy said to himself with mounting indignation. *I am not my father. I am no one but me. I shall do as I please! Nothing will change me!*

He turned from the window and took several restless paces into the room. Realizing there was no place to go, he turned toward the window again.

He swore under his breath, hardly pausing to reflect that his father, peaceful man though he was, would whip him if he heard such from his lips.

He closed the window with a bang, angry at the crickets, angry at the tomfool of a horse who was keeping the stables awake, angry at the peaceful and fragrant air, angry at the sea, angry at the mountains, angry at his father for sentencing him to this ridiculous place.

He spun around and walked toward his bed and threw himself on his back. Mercifully sleep eventually brought an end to the tedious day.

Percy awoke the following morning, fleetingly thought himself back in his bed in Glasgow, then realized with a sinking feeling that his waking had brought a return of the bad dream.

His second morning in Wales passed much like the first. By noon he was going so mad with cabin fever that he had to get out and find *something* to do.

After lunch he left the house again, determined to find some way to pass the afternoon.

In truth, Percy was more insecure than he let on. He was not quite sure of himself here. He was out of his element and could not help feeling a little ill at ease. He fancied himself more a man of the city than he actually was. Whether he would allow that insecurity to be transformed into humility, or would encourage it to fester into smoldering bitterness against his father—the most natural, though illogical, target of youth's imagined grievance—only he would be able to determine.

Once outside, Percy walked around one wall of the huge stone manor house. He soon found himself among hedges and roses and flowers. As yet they held little fascination for him. He was not alive to the mysteries of growing things. Realizing he had entered an enormous garden, he turned and retraced his steps.

Give him the streets of Glasgow and he would be at home anywhere. But here in the country—with limitless space in every direction, with green all about, with the blue vault overhead, without people and with only solitude and emptiness, and with such blasted quiet everywhere— he didn't know what to do with himself.

He kicked petulantly at the gravel beneath his feet. He had to do *something*.

He made his way aimlessly toward the opposite side of the house. Soon he found himself wandering in the direction of the largest of several outbuildings surrounding the manor. From the sounds and smells and general look of them, he realized that he was approaching the barn and stables. Though he knew how to ride as well as a half dozen city lessons had made him capable, it could not be said that he was a great horseman. But if he was going to spend the holiday here, he thought to himself, he would probably have to acquaint himself with this place. He continued toward the buildings.

The wide wood-planked door of the largest barn stood open. He walked inside.

Dim light and the mingled aromas of hay and horseflesh were the first sensations to reach his eyes and nose, followed almost immediately by a more pungent bouquet, at once enchanting and repulsive depending on one's love or antipathy toward all things equine. It was the strong smell of manure.

A snort or two sounded from deep in the darkness. Percy glanced about, sniffing with some discomfort. Gradually his eyes accustomed themselves to the shafts of dusty sunshine slanting through the doors at each end and several openings high along the walls.

Suddenly a voice he could barely understand broke the silence.

"You'll be Master Percival Drummond, I'm thinking," said a crusty, thick Welsh tongue.

Startled, Percy spun about. Ten feet away stood a lanky man of fifty-five or sixty, clad in blue work trousers, boots, and worn green shirt. His sleeves were rolled up to the elbow, and his hands clutched a pitchfork.

"Uh, yes. . .that's right," said Percy, recovering himself.

"Pleased to make your acquaintance," said the man. "It's Hollin Radnor you're talking to, my lord's groom. Were you wanting a ride, Master Drummond?"

"Well. . .sure, I suppose so—if you don't mind."

The groom turned and ambled deeper into the huge barn.

Percy followed, continuing to look about as his eyes adjusted to the surroundings.

"Your second day at the manor, is it?" asked the man.

"Yes, it is."

"No better way to acquaint yourself with the country than on horseback. Here's just the one for you, Master Drummond." He paused beside a waist-high stall. Inside stood a light grayish-brown mare, with white forehead star and two white stockings on her forelegs.

"What's its name?" asked Percy.

"Grey Tide," replied Radnor. He pulled down a saddle from the rack nearby and lugged it to the stall. "Like the water of the sea after a storm."

"Not wild like a storm, I hope," said Percy. He could not prevent his tone betraying a hint of nervousness.

The groom laughed lightly. "Don't you worry about a thing, Master Drummond. She's the gentlest creature in the place. Though's she's fast enough with Lady Florilyn in the saddle. For today, you just enjoy a quiet ride to get your bearings of the estate and hills."

Satisfied, though still a little fearful, Percy watched as the groom opened the stall, spoke a few words in Gaelic, then proceeded to saddle the mare.

He had never ridden other than on the flat grass of Glasgow's city parks. He had never been more than a mile from the stables where he took his few riding lessons. Nor had he ever ridden alone. He was still trying to decide if this was such a good idea when, a few minutes later, the groom led him through the back door of the barn to stand near the mounting block.

"All right, then, up you go," said Radnor, offering Percy a hand.

Still wondering if this was wise, Percy slowly mounted.

"Follow the road there up the hill," added the groom, pointing ahead of him. "In half a mile you'll come to the high gate. After that you'll have the whole of Snowdonia in front of you!"

THIRTEEN

On the Slopes of Gwynedd

ollowing the groom's instructions, Percy rode tentatively away from the stables.

He had hardly gone a hundred yards, and was still within the precincts of house and garden, when suddenly the form of his cousin appeared from behind the trunk of a great beech tree. If her unexpected movement startled the mare called Grey Tide, the animal showed no sign of it other than a brief upward jerk of the head.

"Where are you going?" asked Florilyn Westbrooke. She stepped into their path, reached for the rein at the mare's nose, and stopped her.

"Just for a ride," answered Percy.

"Where?"

"I don't know. . .nowhere. Just there—up in the hills, I suppose."

"You must be a skilled horseman."

"Not really. Why?" asked Percy.

"To go out alone. . .on our wildest horse."

"The man back there in the barn—I've already forgotten his name—he said she was perfect for me."

Florilyn saw the quick look of anxiety that passed through Percy's eyes as he spoke. She met it with a mischievous smile of her own.

"Oh. . .Hollin?" she said with pretended innocence. "One thing you will learn is that he is the biggest liar around here."

"Why would he—"

He did not have a chance to finish his question.

As quickly as she had appeared, his cousin now leaped aside, ran to the back of the horse, and gave its rump a great swat, followed by a piercing shriek.

The mare lurched forward, nearly throwing Percy backward onto the ground. Desperately trying to keep his seat, he grabbed frantically for any piece of mane or saddle his hand could find. The next moment he found himself hanging on for dear life as Grey Tide galloped out of the grounds. Florilyn's laughter echoed in his ears.

In less than ten seconds, which nevertheless seemed a lifetime, his mount slowed. Gradually she resumed a gentle walk away from the house. Knowing full well that his cousin was still watching behind him, Percy did his best to regain his composure after the brief scare and do so without looking back.

Vowing to get even with the little vixen the first chance he got, he tried to relax. Slowly the manor receded in the distance behind him.

After passing through the eastern gate of the estate ten minutes later, Percy found himself on open hillside. He continued at a slow walk. Now that it was behind him—and now that he had survived it!—the memory of his brief skirmish with death atop a galloping horse filled him with a sense of exhilaration. As a result, he quickly gained confidence as he went. This was nothing like the lessons he had had at twelve on the Clydebank. He had to admit it was an agreeable sort of activity once he was comfortable enough to trust the beast underneath him.

For one accustomed to the rolling hills and dales of Ayrshire, the countryside over which Percy Drummond now made his way might not have appeared scenic or beautiful. To the young Glaswegian, however, though he would persist yet for a while in trying to convince himself he hated the rugged and mountainous aspect of the place, it could not help but strike into him a vague sense of awe.

Beautiful, perhaps, it would not be called by some, but wild certainly...

big, high, even magnificent. If rugged starkness possessed an allure not found either in city street or tidy countryside, that appeal might explain why the ancient race of Brythonic Celts, now known as the Welsh, had made their home here. He supposed the area through which he now rode was like the highlands of his native Scotland. But in his two or three sojourns up Scotland's western coast with his parents, he had never paid much attention to the scenery.

At present grass grew under his mount's four iron shoes. Upward ahead in the distance, however, stone seemed the chief characteristic of the landscape, here black, there containing reddish hues, but mostly gray. He continued to make his way through low-growing shrubbery and a few small woods. The highest ridges ahead, however, were so rocky as to appear mostly bare.

Several peaks loomed rather than towered in the distance. They were not of particularly great height, though remnants of snow could yet be seen on one or two. The topography rose steadily eastward from the sea into the northern reaches of the Cambrian Mountains, of which Percy could now see the summits of Rhinog Fawr, Yllethr, and Diffwys stretched out as in a line some four or five miles inland. The lower slope of Moelfre was nearer at hand and partially obscured the latter. Blue billows of clouds drifted lazily in the blue expanse overhead.

It was altogether a lovely summer's day for a ride. Had Percy Drummond been more a friend of nature, he would have derived immense pleasure from it. If the truth were known, he was actually enjoying himself more than he was likely to admit. He was more than a little proud of himself for holding his seat for so long as well as he had. The spectacular grandeur about him could not help but prick certain hidden regions of soul to which it was designed to speak.

Northward out of sight from here, the range of inland peaks rose amid craggy precipices and high-notched passes through the range to its highest point, Wyddfa, "nesting place of the eagles," known in English as Mount Snowdon. The treeless granite gray peak from which the region took its name overlooked the whole of North Wales. It was the highest summit in Britain south of the Scottish highlands, second only to Ben Nevis, with which it shared an uncanny likeness.

Percy found himself riding for some time along a trail that gradually and circuitously ascended upward and northeastward. Whether it was actually a trail or not, the horse followed it on her own. Cresting a small rise, he heard the tinkling of bells.

A moment later, a rambunctious flock of sheep suddenly appeared nearly upon him, scrambling and bleating their way along the ridge. Seconds later Percy found himself in the middle of a tumultuous sea of white. Neither horse nor sheep paid the other heed, though the mare paused while the little white balls of wool passed, scurrying and baaing around her feet.

A stocky lad followed behind the flock, a black and white sheepdog at his side. "*Prynhawn da,*" he said as he came near. "*Sut mae?*"

"I'm sorry," replied Percy with a confused expression. "I'm afraid I don't understand you."

"Then 'tis I who should be apologizing," said the boy with a smile. "I said good afternoon to you. Fine day for a ride, it is."

"Yes—thank you. I had no idea anyone else was nearby," said Percy. "I must admit you startled me. I'm not too good on a horse."

"Looks to me you are doing right fine. I shall get my sheep out of your path as quickly as I can."

He cried out in the strangest voice Percy had ever heard, uttering some unintelligible mixture of command and singing chant. Whatever its meaning, the animals all understood the ancient Welsh tongue. The sheep burst into a frenzy of motion, scooting along at suddenly doubled speed. The dog leaped eagerly into action and scampered about at their heels with sudden frenetic urgency.

Percy took the young shepherd for several years older than himself, though he was in truth seventeen. His stout frame was not as tall as Percy's, yet broad and muscular. The brown, leathery skin of face and arms, from constant exposure to the harsh coastal elements, gave an appearance of age beyond his years.

"The name's Stevie Muir," the boy said. "I live over the hill there." He pointed behind him.

"I am Percy Drummond," said Percy.

"New to Llanfryniog?"

"Visiting," answered Percy.

"Da. Then let me say '*Croeso i Cymru*' to you!"

Confusion on Percy's face was his only answer.

" 'Welcome to Wales,' in your tongue."

"Thank you," nodded Percy.

"I best be on my way." The boy called Stevie laughed. "My little flock is already leaving me behind!" He broke into a jog to catch them, whistled once, then turned. "You'd be welcome for a visit anytime," he called back. "We're over the rise there, in the little crook of the next valley. . .a little stone cottage."

"Thank you," said Percy.

Stevie waved then turned and hurried after his sheep.

Percy resumed his ride in the same direction. A short distance farther up the gently rising slope, he paused and turned around in the saddle to take stock of where he had come. Whatever might be the horse's condition, his own hindquarters were sore. He would gladly have dismounted and walked awhile. He was not at all confident, however, that he would be able to get back up on the mare by himself.

Spread out below him, at a distance now of perhaps two miles, stretched the coastline. Between the ocean and himself sat his uncle's imposing stone mansion of Westbrooke Manor from which he had come. The eight-foot-tall stone-block wall of the boundary of the estate meandered across moor and through field, into woodland, and a good way up this same slope and out of sight, in a great circumference of four or five miles surrounding the great house. From this distance the estate did not appear so huge. In truth, however, the viscount's property measured in the thousands of acres. Only a portion of it lay enclosed by the high stone wall in the immediate vicinity of the manor.

Lord Snowdon owned most of the village of Llanfryniog as well, and nearly all its cottages and the poor homes Percy saw scattered about the moorland and into the hills. His tenants paid him, through his factor, semiannual rents. Though they could at times prove difficult to bear, they were not so crippling as they might have been. His people considered the viscount a reasonable man, though generally stern and aloof. Most harbored no reason either to love or hate him. That they did not tremble when they saw his factor approach on horseback was a good sign. Though neither did they smile.

The sea today offered the beholder intriguing shades of blue and green. From the high vantage point of his ride, the white stretch of sandy beach below the bluff straight ahead of him was obscured from Percy's view by the cliff edge. Farther to the right, however, the sand surrounding Llanfryniog inlet, at the southern extremity of which the body had been found, and the slate roofs of the village beside it, glistened in the westerly afternoon sun. Sails of a few fishing boats from the harbor dotted the surface of Tremadog Bay, as the waters were known between Point Mochras and the peninsula of Lleyn, faintly visible at a distance of some fourteen to sixteen miles to the west. Northward from Percy's outlook, the spires from another great country house, constructed of more reddish-looking stones and appearing like a castle from this height, rose above the coastal moorland.

As he gazed about him, Percy realized that he had come a good distance. He had better return down the slopes. If he wanted to know more about these hills, he would find out another time. He had already ridden farther than he intended.

He urged his mount on. Perhaps the mare now sensed the direction he wished to go, for she veered to the left and they began a descent, where they would circle around and return to the estate by the front gate. He decided that Grey Tide was the horse of choice for him. She seemed to know that he trusted in her.

FOURTEEN

Nosegay from a Tiny Friend

*A*nother hour passed as the lone rider from Glasgow made his way out of the hills on a course roughly southwest. His route brought him below the estate on the wide moorland plateau overlooking Mochras Point as it sloped down to the inlet and village. Feeling relatively at ease in the saddle by now, though tired, he even urged Grey Tide into an occasional light trot for a few moments.

Mostly occupied with the ground in front of him, he glanced up to see a small girl a hundred yards ahead walking casually toward him. With seemingly aimless step, she was apparently on her way to nowhere. She stooped to the ground every now and then. As he drew close, she glanced up, stopped, beheld him steadily as he came toward her, then shielded her eyes from the sun and smiled.

"H–h–hello," she said sweetly, stuttering as she spoke. She did not seem embarrassed by the fact.

Percy reined in and looked down from his high perch. "Good afternoon to you," he said, returning her smile. He did not realize it, but it was the first intentional smile he had sent in the direction of another human being in a long while. That of the girl, along with the wide trusting gaze of her deep azure eyes, was so infectious there was nothing to do but return it.

"W–w–what are you doing riding G–G–Grey Tide?" the girl asked, patting the horse's wide stomach without hint of fear.

"You know this horse, do you?"

"I know all the horses at the m–manor."

"Do you indeed! Why is that?"

"Because I love horses. I love all animals."

"Do you live at the manor?"

"No," replied the girl. "I live over there." She pointed behind her, but Percy could see nothing. "That is where I have *my* animals," she added, turning back toward him.

"Do you have horses?"

She shook her head. "I wish I did. M–m–most of my friends are smaller. But why are you riding one of Lady Florilyn's favorite horses?" she asked.

"I am her cousin."

"Oh!"

"I am here to visit for the summer."

"From where?"

"From Glasgow."

"That is a b–b–big city, isn't it? I think I have heard of it."

"A *very* big city," laughed Percy.

The girl's eyes widened. "Have you been to London?" she said. "I want to see London someday."

"I am sure you shall," rejoined Percy. "And Glasgow, too. Perhaps you shall visit me there one day."

Her face brightened yet more. "Visit *you?*" she said.

"And why not? I am *here*. Why should you not go *there* when you are older?"

"My father is poor. How would I get there?"

It was a turn in the conversation Percy had not anticipated. He had merely been making conversation. "Those things have a way of working out," he said breezily, glancing about.

The girl's silence brought his gaze once more down to her face. Her wide round blue eyes still stared straight up into his. "Grannie says always greet a stranger with flowers," she said simply.

"So—" Percy smiled, in the absence of suitable reply, a streak of wit seizing him—"you consider me a stranger, do you?"

"I've never seen your face before."

"Then what do you intend to do about it?"

"Give you the flowers I picked for you, of course," replied the girl with an innocent smile. She brought her hand from her side. "Here," she said, reaching up and handing him a small handful of tiny wildflowers.

Percy hesitated as he took them. The heart of the sixteen-year-old rebel was suddenly touched by the kindness of the child-stranger. He hardly knew what to say. He hadn't expected such a response to his attempted humor. The droll smile faded from his mouth as he spoke again.

"Surely you meant these for someone else?"

"I picked them for you," she replied simply, still gazing into his face with wide, innocent eyes. "Now that I have given you flowers, I must know who you are. What is your name, so I shall know whom to ask for when I go to Glasgow?"

Percy could not help laughing with delight. He hardly even noticed that as she had grown more comfortable talking with him her stuttering had lessened. This girl was absolutely too charming! The fact that he was out in the middle of the countryside, so far from the city where he was accustomed to behaving like a surly youth, brought out of him responses very different even than he would have expected.

That the girl herself—at one moment so young, at the next seemingly ageless in her innocence—had evoked his laughter and the unexpected feelings that had gone with it was not a fact he paused to consider. As they spoke, their respective ages of thirteen and sixteen—the girl such a child in the eyes of the boy, the boy such a man in the eyes of the girl— did not enter the matrix of either's consideration. Both could have been fifty; both could have been five.

"My name is Percival. . .Percival Drummond, at your service," replied Percy at length. "My friends call me Percy."

"What would you like *me* to call you, Mr. Drummond?"

"You must call me Percy. What is *your* name?"

"Gwyneth Barrie."

"Then, Gwyneth Barrie, I am happy to make your acquaintance." Clutching the floral gift in his left hand, he bent down from the mare's back and extended his right as far toward her as he could.

She reached up and placed her tiny palm inside his and shook it.

Percy pulled away his hand, sat back upright, and looked for a moment at the humble bouquet. Again the thoughtful mood swept over him. "But. . .why did you pick these for me?" he said.

"I saw you coming," replied the girl.

"You didn't know me when you picked them. Surely you don't give flowers to *every* stranger you pass."

"Only those who are going to become my friends."

"You knew that about me?"

"Of course."

"How did you know?"

"I saw on your face the look of a friend. So I picked them for you as you rode toward me."

Percy gently lifted the tiny nosegay to his nostrils. He breathed in of the earthy fragrance in which was hidden the faint perfume of something sweet. When he looked up, already the girl had left him and was making her way up the hillside.

Percy stared after her then turned around in the saddle with a mysterious smile of question on his lips and slowly continued on his way.

FIFTEEN

Cardiff

I tell you I've seen it with me own two eyes!" said a raspy voice.

The candle in the center of the table between the two men danced on the hard-bitten, deep-chiseled miner's face. The light revealed eyes nervously in motion lest unwanted ears venture too close.

"Maybe you have, and maybe you haven't," said the other. His tone was calm and measured. "But I pay nothing without seeing it with *my* own two eyes."

The corner of the darkened pub fell silent. The man who had just spoken, his accent betraying that he was no native to this region, sat doing his best to swallow his annoyance. The other, whose accent was barely intelligible to his ears, took a long swallow from the tall mug in front of him. The Englishman had come here to make what he understood was a simple arrangement with a longtime Welsh coal miner of greater cunning than most of his fellows gave him credit for. The man was said to possess information his employer had been seeking. He had not been told the fellow was an opportunist and shyster as well.

Most of the business conducted within the buildings, offices, and storefronts of Bute Street in the burgeoning Welsh city across the channel from Bristol at the mouth of the River Severn had to do with one of two things—coal or shipping. This port, which at the beginning

80

of the nineteenth century had been little more than a township, had grown rapidly with the industrial nation's hunger for coal. Cardiff was well on its way to becoming a great metropolis and seaport. It sent around the world that valuable black commodity from the nearby mines which lay in abundance beneath the mountains north of the city. English, Irish, and Scots flooded daily into South Wales, brought here by industry. They were now as numerous in Cardiff as its native Welshmen.

Neither coal nor shipping, however, was on the minds of the crusty miner or Englishman across from him. The two had been engaged in low conversation in a darkened corner of a cellar pub half a block off the busy Cardiff thoroughfare long enough that the Welshman had downed a pint of dark strong beer and was well begun on a second. With the other paying, he would consume as much as quickly as he was able. It was not the sort of establishment in which the Englishman felt altogether comfortable. He had heard stories about Cardiff that did not put him at ease. But he had been told he would find the man here. He hoped the information he possessed would make it worth his employer's while.

"And see it you shall," the miner said, "but it's far to the north, in that part of Wales called Snowdonia. I won't take you there without five crown up front. Then it'll be fifty quid more when your own eyes flash at the sight."

"They told me you were a thief, Bagge," said the Englishman. "Now I believe them. But you'll not get a brass farthing from me without *some* kind of proof."

The miner smiled, if such it could be called. Though he had scarcely enough teeth left to make much use of, his lips parted in devious delight. A low chuckle rumbled in his throat. A Cardi was known for having short arms and deep pockets, and this old-timer took the Englishman's comment as the highest form of praise. To outwit an Englishman in any financial transaction represented the ultimate triumph.

The man called Foulis Bagge brought a dirty hand to his chest and patted the outside of a ragged grimy coat once or twice with significant expression.

"Are you telling me you. . .*have* proof?" asked the other.

"Right here," replied Bagge, patting his coat again.

"Let me see it."

"Let me see the five crown."

The Englishman hesitated a moment then reached into his own vest pocket and retrieved a small handful of coins. He placed ten on the table between them.

In less than a second they were gone, swallowed up in the miner's blackened hand with the marvelous speed of a frog's tongue snatching a fly from midair.

With the coins secure in an unknown receptacle somewhere among his garments, he now slowly drew back the flap of his coat with one hand. The other crept slowly and mysteriously inside it. His fist emerged a moment later, clutching a small leather pouch. Untying its neck with deliberation, occasionally sending his cunning gaze across the table, he held it out to allow the other man a brief peep inside. The Englishman's eyes widened at the sight. Even in this dim light there could be no mistaking the contents.

The five crowns, however, only purchased him two or three seconds. Suddenly the bag withdrew, was yanked shut, and disappeared after the coins.

"This came from the place you told me about?"

"It did."

"You could lead me to it?"

"For fifty quid, Sutcliffe, I'll carry you there on me own back."

After a few minutes more conversation, the Englishman rose and departed the pub, leaving the toothless Welshman to his third pint. He squinted briefly as he climbed the dirty stone stairs back into the sunshine then turned again into Bute Street.

After a block's walk, he stopped and stepped quickly into a large, handsomely appointed black brougham whose owner had been waiting.

The moment the door closed behind him, the driver above called out to his team of two. The windowless carriage jostled into motion.

"Well?" said the man seated inside.

"He is exactly what I expected, crafty as a Cardi and twice as greedy."

"Will he do it?" asked the other, whose voice left no doubt of his aristocratic upbringing.

"I think for the right price our slimy friend Foulis Bagge would do anything, including sell his own grandmother. But he would tell me nothing without ten half-crown coins in his greedy fist."

"A small price. You paid him?"

The man nodded.

"Did he provide you a map?"

"No. He said he had to lead us there himself. He did show me what he purports to have taken from the place with his own two hands."

"He will take us there, then?"

"That was the agreement. But I warn you, he will double-cross us in a minute if he sees his opportunity. He may have to be killed once we know the exact location."

"Again," said the other, "a small price to pay. You made arrangements to meet again?" he added.

"He will wait to hear from me."

"Good. It seems the time has come for us to make closer approach to the owner of the land in question."

SIXTEEN

The Festive Board

*T*he atmosphere around the lavish dinner table that evening at Westbrooke Manor was noticeably cheerier than could be claimed as the normal custom.

Young people are notoriously skillful at moodily subduing meal conversation into irritable and sullen silence, invariably preferring anyone else's company to that of their parents and anyone else's conversation as well. On this occasion, however, the addition of Percival Drummond to the Westbrooke family *ensemble* promised amusement to his cousins and provided at least a slim potential of conversational interest for their parents.

All except the youngest were seated promptly at seven thirty as a staff of two began to ladle out a colorless cabbage soup. Florilyn entered a minute later and took the last remaining seat, which happened to be opposite their guest. She did not look at him, though Percy was starring daggers at her.

Percy waited, not quite sure what protocol would inaugurate the proceedings. When his uncle at the head of the table picked up his soupspoon, he assumed that no formal prayer would be forthcoming. A glance in the other direction, however, revealed his aunt momentarily bowing her head.

The same instant Florilyn looked up. Her eyes came to rest on his face. Percy observed the movement and turned toward it. The expression that met his was not what he expected. It was a sly smirk, not particularly subtle. Florilyn's glance flitted toward her mother then back again, as if making silent sport of old-fashioned religious predilections. The expression carried with it the assumption that Percy was of one mind with her in finding the private moment of prayer humorous—as if they mutually shared a slightly naughty joke.

Now whereas Percy would have been the first to ridicule the faith of his own father and mother, and that not merely in private for he had in fact been doing his utmost to *publicly* ruin his father's reputation along with his own, the slight against his aunt annoyed him. Whether he found himself taking his aunt's part against his cousin because of the incident earlier in the day or whether some unexpected remnant of the spiritual training of his formative years suddenly rose to the surface unbidden, Percy Drummond himself would have been the least able to say.

It is a well-known fact that, removed from the parental objects of their rebellion, many temporary prodigals find themselves not nearly so antagonistic to the faith of their upbringing as they thought. They surprise both themselves and their parents by growing closer to the parental tree than seemed possible at the height of their youthful independence. In the end, their roots extend deeper into the soil of their early years than anyone would have expected.

Though perhaps invisible forces might even now have begun probing his soul, however, Percy was aware of no sudden spiritual epiphany. He simply did not like his cousin making fun of his aunt. He understood the look perfectly, and it rankled him. He gave it no answering reception by sympathetic expression of his own. He would not, even by the subtlest passing glance, play his aunt false.

Detecting by his blank stare that she had been rebuffed, Florilyn was clearly not pleased. The expression that followed added yet more to the spirit of worldliness that was all too apparent, even at fifteen, dripping from her countenance.

All this passed in less than two ticks of the second hand on the giant clock on the wall behind Roderick Westbrooke.

Percy waited in respectful silence. As soon as he saw movement from his aunt out of the corner of his eye, he took up his spoon with the others.

"So, Percy, my boy," boomed the viscount from the opposite end of the table, entirely oblivious, as he was to most of the internal dynamics at work in his family, to the brief drama that had taken place between the cousins, "how did you find your first day in Wales?"

"Fine, sir," replied Percy, looking toward him with an effort at a smile.

"What did you find to occupy yourself?"

"Percy went for a horse ride, Daddy," chimed in Florilyn in a mischievous tone.

"Did he now? Good for you, Percy, my boy. Did you accompany him, Flory?"

"No, Daddy," answered Florilyn in a tone of affected injury. "He seemed to want to be alone. He galloped off before I had the chance to ask if he wanted some company. It hurt my feelings, actually. . . . After all the rain, I had been wanting someone to go for a ride with."

"Don't forget, dear, this is Percy's first day here. We must be patient and allow him time to get used to his new surroundings. What do you say, Percy. . .perhaps you can take your cousin along next time? I dare say she won't slow you down much."

"Yes, sir," replied Percy, smoke coming out his ears.

"I don't know, Daddy," said Florilyn. "I'm a little unsteady on the back of a horse. I might not be able to keep up with him."

A flinch of the eyes shot her way from her brother, accompanied by the hint of a sportive grin.

"Nonsense," blustered her father. "You'll find we're not so bad," Westbrooke went on to Percy in a jovial manner. "Perhaps not so sophisticated as your city friends, but you must give us a chance. How about you, Courtenay," he said, turning toward his son. "Good to be home from the university, I'll warrant. How did you spend your day?"

"Colville and I went shooting in the forest," replied Percy's older cousin.

"Any success?"

"Not much. A couple of pheasants and a rabbit."

"Ah, well—the big game have probably retreated into the mountains for the summer. You'll have to take Percy out with you next time."

Courtenay vouchsafed no reply. Instead he busied himself with his soup. What he thought of his father's suggestion, he kept to himself. As the meal progressed, however, he thought that perhaps his father had indeed hit upon something.

Though but a year and a half separated them, he had grown up considering his cousin a mere child along with his sister. The teen years had done nothing to convince him that he ought to modify that assessment.

Yet in one of the inane displays of the animal kingdom, the male ego is compelled—in ways often foolish and rarely revealing manhood's true strength—to demonstrate superiority over its fellows. Ironically this impulsion is stimulated all the more by insecurity. The greater the self-doubts, the more overpowering the drive to prove prowess. On the other hand, a young man with sufficient self-confidence that his budding manhood is not threatened by his peers, with nothing to prove, has little desire to strut the peacock's tail of his ego. Paradoxically, the more cocksure a youth shows himself, in all likelihood the less of a true man he is on his way to becoming.

The moment Courtenay Westbrooke learned that his cousin was coming for the summer, and why, an undefined resentment began festering within him. That Percy looked and acted like such a stripling—he was fully six inches shorter and two stone lighter than himself—yet had been in trouble with the police, had actually, if he had heard the thing right, once spent a night in jail, made him resent him all the more.

He had never run afoul of the law, thought Courtenay. He had never been in trouble, never been arrested, never been sent away for the summer. Part of him envied Percy the roguish reputation that preceded his arrival. Yet in a perverted way, he also despised him for it. Hardly having subjected his motivations to the scrutiny of logic, Courtenay was anxious to prove, to himself and to Percy, that whatever his exploits in Glasgow, his fair-skinned little cousin wasn't as tough as he might think.

"How are you with a gun, Percy, my boy?" asked Westbrooke, turning from his son to their guest. "I take it you know how to use one?"

"Yes. . .of course," replied Percy hesitantly. The fact was he had never held a gun in his life, much less pulled the trigger of one. Guns had not been allowed in the vicarage. To his knowledge, his father had never owned one.

"What did you learn in town about poor Mr. Drindod?" asked Percy's aunt as the soup was cleared away and steaming platters of beef, vegetables, and potatoes were carried in from the kitchen and set before them.

"Nothing," replied her husband. "No one knows a thing. The man was simply found facedown on the beach half covered by the tide."

"Did you talk to Mr. Lorimer?" asked Katherine.

"I did." Westbrooke nodded. "He knows no more than I do."

"What's it about, Father?" asked Courtenay.

"One of the old fishermen from the village—he was apparently killed on the beach last night."

"Oh!" squealed Florilyn. "A murder—how exciting!"

"Florilyn, goodness! What a thing to say!" exclaimed her mother.

"What's wrong with it, Mother? Nothing fun ever happens around here. I think it *is* exciting."

"It is dreadful. . .the poor man."

"We don't know for certain it was murder," the viscount went on. "There are no obvious signs of it, no clues, as it were. He was too far from the bluff to have fallen. If there was a struggle of some kind, the evidence was washed away long before the body was found."

"The *body*. . .I like that!" said Florilyn exuberantly. "It sounds like a mystery novel! Is it allowed to call it a *corpse*, Daddy?"

"Florilyn, good heavens!" expostulated her mother a second time. "We have a guest. He's going to think we are a family of heathens."

"I don't care, Mother. Besides, I *am* a heathen, so why shouldn't I talk like one?"

The viscount roared with laughter at the humorous repartee. He hardly paused to consider what his reaction to his daughter's uncouth tongue indicated of his sensitivity toward his wife.

Percy was also enjoying it. He could not help an inward smile. It was not that his momentary loyalty to his aunt had faded. But neither could it be denied that he found his cousin's irreverent and sassy manner more or less in harmony with his own. But he was still furious at her. He would not give her the satisfaction of seeing him smile at her antics.

"What are you going to do, Daddy?" asked Florilyn enthusiastically.

"There isn't much we can do," replied her father. "I wrote today and reported the matter to the authorities in Dolgellau. Whether they will send someone to investigate, I don't know. Otherwise, he'll be given a decent burial. God bless him and take care of his soul is about all there is to it."

"Oh pooh, Daddy," Florilyn said with a laugh, "you don't believe any of that."

"What are you talking about, Flory?"

"That business of God taking care of his soul. You just pretend for the sake of what people will think. You go to church and sit there and make a pretense of paying attention. But I know you're looking at your watch waiting for the boring sermon to end. The man on the beach is dead, and that's all there is to it, don't you mean? You don't *really* think he's still alive somewhere. Nobody believes that anymore."

She had finally gone too far even for her father. The viscount's superstitions toward matters of religion were deeply enough embedded that he dared not cross them. Whether there was anything to it all, he hadn't a clue. But like many an unbelieving man of so-called religion, he saw no reason to take any chances.

A brief shudder coursed through him at the words that had just echoed about his table, as if his daughter's audacity was tantamount to a curse against the gods and would bring retribution down upon them all. "Of course I do, Flory," he replied, unaccountably ruffled by her perceptive assessment of his usual outlook of a Sunday morning.

"Then where is he, in heaven or hell?"

"How in blazes should I know? I'm no priest. I didn't even know the man."

"What do you think, Percy?" said Florilyn, turning and staring across the table with large, inquiring, devilish eyes. "You're the son of a minister. You probably know all about such things."

Taken by surprise, Percy had no leisure to prepare himself for suddenly finding himself on the spot.

Glad to be off it himself, this time his uncle did not rescue him.

"What do I think about what?" he said.

"Whether the dead man will go to heaven or hell."

"I would say the same thing as Uncle Roderick—how should I know? I suppose it would depend on what he believed."

"Do *you* think there's a heaven and hell, Percy?" she asked, blinking her large eyes playfully several times with feigned sincerity.

"I don't know. I suppose I don't really know what I believe."

"Doesn't Uncle Edward preach about heaven and hell all the time?"

The question took Percy off guard. He found himself thinking a moment. "Actually," he said slowly, "now that you mention it. . .no, he really doesn't. I don't think I've ever heard him preach a sermon about heaven and hell."

"What does he preach about then?"

"I don't know. . .doing good, being nice. . . He's always talking about doing what Jesus said. That's one of his favorite phrases."

"What does that mean? How can anyone do what Jesus said?" laughed Florilyn. "Why would anyone even want to?"

"I don't know," replied Percy a little testily. "I'm not claiming to know what it means. I'm just telling you what he says, that's all."

He suddenly found himself in the uncomfortably weird position of beginning to defend his father against his cousin's nettlesome barbs. He didn't like it. He had no interest in pursuing this line of conversation or being on the receiving end of his cousin's irksome interrogation.

Without planning it, he turned to Florilyn's brother at his right. "Who's the chap you went hunting with?" he asked.

"Colville?" said Courtnenay. "He's our neighbor."

"Colville Burrenchobay," added the viscount, relieved to have the opportunity to wrest the conversation away from his daughter. "His father owns the land adjacent to mine, northward."

"I saw what looked like a castle when I was riding," said Percy, "about two miles away, I would say."

"That's it." His uncle laughed. "Burrenchobay Hall. Hardly a castle, but an imposing edifice indeed. Colville's a year older than Courtenay. His father represents Gwynedd in parliament. But we try to forgive Trevelyan his odd politics. The boys grew up together. I doubt there's a square inch between Blanau Ffestiniog and Barmouth you two lads haven't explored together, wouldn't you say, Courtenay?"

Courtnenay nodded.

"Well, if you're the horseman Florilyn seems to think, Percy my boy," the viscount went on, "I'm sure you will learn your way around the hills in no time. No better place in all the world to ride."

"I ran into a fellow today with a flock of sheep," said Percy. "But the horse didn't seem to mind them."

"You'll find sheep everywhere in the fields and hills," rejoined his uncle. "The horses ignore them. Who was he—did he tell you his name?"

"Yes. . .uh, let me see—Stevie. . .something like that, I think."

"That's Stevie Muir," said Florilyn. "A big, ugly oaf if you ask me."

"He seemed nice enough," said Percy. "He invited me to visit him."

"Oh, ick!" exclaimed Florilyn. "I wouldn't set foot in that filthy cottage where he lives! All those poor people are so uncivilized. Their floors are nothing but dirt! Can you imagine how dirty everything must be? Ugh!"

At the end of the table, Katherine Westbrooke hardly tasted the food on her plate as the meal progressed. Listening to what came out of her daughter's mouth was mortifying and humiliating to her sensitive mother's ears. She excused herself with the pretext of a headache when the meal was over, declining coffee and dessert, and apologized to her brother's son for her departure.

Seventeen

Westbrooke Manor

*P*ercival, only son of Edward and Mary Drummond of Glasgow, had visited Westbrooke Manor but once prior to this in his life. That was so many years ago he scarcely remembered other than hazy recollections of the place. The last time he had seen his Welsh relatives was five years before in Scotland.

Lord Snowdon's estate spread across the sloping incline up from the moorland plateau above the sea toward the inland hills. From the house, therefore, one could command a view of most of the region seaward, as well as north and south for some distance. Approaching the estate from the village, as one entered the front gate the great house could not actually be seen. A thick wood lay between the gate and the manor, comprised mostly of pine and fir, as well as magnificent specimens of ancient beech, oak, and chestnut.

The drive wound through these trees until it emerged suddenly into a vast clearing. This expanse spread out on both sides, still sloping gently upward. At the far end of it, the manor rose majestically, presiding over lawns and trees and hedges and gardens. A lovelier setting could hardly be imagined. As the drive approached the enormous house, it was lined with flowering ornamentals of plum and cherry and crab apple, at the bases of whose trunks grew all manner of bulbed and perennial flowers, low-spreading lithodora, and several varieties of heather.

Reaching Westbrooke Manor, the gravel drive widened into an expansive stoned elongated circle, around whose circumference exploded at this time of year a profusion of color, from roses and azaleas to multicolored pansies, alyssum, lobelia, violets, violas, daisies, and an abundance of other blooming things, scattered and planted among one another seemingly heedless of pattern. Their diverse colors and foliage mixed and flowed together in chaotic beauty. In the middle of winter, the sight would not have been nearly so inviting. But in early June, it was a sumptuous feast for the eyes.

The house itself—of gray stone and slate, intermingled with red brick from England, here and there with iron and copper work accenting the colorful mosaic of its design—stood as an impressively beautiful estate, whose draftsman must surely have enjoyed himself. Originally constructed in the late sixteenth century after union with England had reduced the defensive requirements of the castles and great houses of Wales, Westbrooke Manor represented one of the oldest and largest such structures where aesthetics and functionality replaced solemnity and starkness as the paramount architectural concerns.

The front face—opening southward and with columned entryway inset from the remaining plane of the building—and west wing boasted perhaps more windows, larger and of unusual design, than any mansion in Wales. These afforded magnificent views, when weather permitted, of the entire coastline. The architect must surely have cherished a particular fondness for the ornamental potential of the openings he set among the stone walls of the massive building. Its windows were the eyes into the soul, if not of Westbrooke Manor's present occupants, then surely into the man who conceived it. They were clearly the singular visual highlight of the place.

The manor's windows represented enormous variety of size, shape, and framing material. No more than three were alike. Even these possessed tiny crafted individualities that revealed themselves only to the most diligent scrutiny. While the primary object had been to give the manor's inhabitants a view outward, this unique architectural feature also granted the visitor a striking sight as he beheld the house upon approach.

Great double doors of solid oak planking three inches thick, each measuring four feet in width and eight in height, ornately framed and studded in black wrought iron, were overspread with a great stone plate upon which the Westbrooke coat of arms was carved. This was surrounded by miscellaneous heraldic symbols, swords, and roaring and leaping beasts from both the world of men and fairy.

Away from this entryway around to the left along the west wing and extending northward behind it, a rambling, curved mossy stone pathway led toward an area near the house, which from the position of the house relative to the sun, remained shady during most daylight hours. Among the trunks of spaciously placed sycamores, beeches, and chestnuts, grew a distinctive variety of ferns and other plants, mostly now showing off their thick foliage of green. This was the winter garden. Those of its contents that flowered—only perhaps a fourth of the whole—had been placed here for their wintry blossoms, which came into prominence when the deciduous giants above them dropped their leaves to let in the cold, thin light of the winter months.

The oak doors of the manor opened into a large hall of high ceiling. Around its tall wood-paneled walls hung guns, swords, stags' heads, a few faded tartans, and other similar ornamentation. The effect gave a visitor at first glance more the appearance of a hunting lodge in the Scottish highlands than a family home. Full-length suits of armor stood opposite one another as silent sentinels guarding the two far corners. Two corridors extended from this entryway, one to the right and one to the left. Directly ahead a wide stairway swooped down, slightly curved though not circular, from above.

Most of the family's more comfortable living quarters were located up this grand staircase and to the left, on the first floor of the west wing, whose windows overlooked the sea. There was no limit to parlors and drawing rooms in the west wing of the ground floor either. The kitchens and servants' quarters occupied most of the area to the right of the entry hall, comprising the remainder of the main south wing and the small east wing.

Two dining rooms, a great formal banquet hall outfitted in paneling and wainscoting to resemble the hunting motif, and a smaller room, warmer of atmosphere and of floral tones, sat directly to the rear of the entry hall. It was in this latter where the family's meals were taken. Both dining rooms looked out on the courtyard enclosed by the three wings of the manor, kept tidily manicured by the viscount's gardener, Stuart Wykeham. A breakfast room of immaculate white walls and ceiling and black floor tile also faced the courtyard.

The second floor of the manor sat mostly unused now except for a multitude of bedrooms and storage rooms, the viscount's private study, and an ancient armory in which he took special pleasure.

Roderick Westbrooke had not always prided himself in being master of the family estate. His father, the seventh viscount Lord Snowdon, was already old when Roderick was born and was dead before his only son reached his teen years. Whatever family fortune might once have existed, it had been unwisely invested, spent, squandered, and gradually used up in the generations prior to the present viscount's life.

Nor did young Roderick help matters with regard to his own financial future by leaving Wales in 1830 at sixteen as a pampered aristocratic heir intent upon seeing the world, ostensibly, he said, to seek what he called his fortune. In reality all he succeeded in accomplishing was to dry up what remained of the stipend guaranteed him by his father's will until he should come of age at twenty-five and inherit the title and property that went with it.

He was gone for five years—traveled extensively on the continent, remained a consequential year in Ireland, and returned under somewhat mysterious circumstances to Wales at twenty-one, virtually penniless and peculiarly dispassionate according to those who had known him before. At the same time, however, he was no more at peace with himself. Something ate at him. But he confided in no one.

One thing was clear upon his return—Roderick Westbrooke was a boy no longer, though still four years from becoming master of the estate. Whether he was older and wiser from his voyages, adventures, and amorous escapades or merely older would require the rest of his life to determine. His mother remained trustee of the estate until he inherited at twenty-five.

He met the wealthy daughter of the Glasgow earl in 1845 when in the northern seaport on a minor matter of business. On the surface, they made an odd match—he the thirty-one-year-old man of the world, she eight years younger, well-educated but untraveled, and the daughter of an earl whose chief reputation lay in his unconventional religious views. That the religious family possessed money added in no small measure to the attractive young Katherine Drummond's charm in Roderick Westbrooke's eyes. Yet in fairness to his motives, she did cause his heart to beat with something resembling affection again, and he persuaded himself that he loved her. Katherine, on her part, found the nobleman from western Wales more dashing than he really was. Like many young women, she did not inquire too deeply into his character beyond what appeared on the surface. She convinced herself that she was in love with him, which she probably was, however unwise that love may have been. They were married two years later.

Their two offspring—Courtenay, cut from the same cloth as his father, now eighteen, and Florilyn, fifteen—rather than infusing the bloodline with the spiritual tradition brought into it by their mother, appeared to be going to seed along with the former Welsh lineage of their descent.

Gradually the faith of Katherine Westbrooke waned under the constant pressure of her husband's unbelieving churchgoing religiosity. She held out hope during their early years of providing their two children *some* spiritual grounding. She discovered, however, that weekly church services were a singularly ineffective means of doing so, especially under the shadow of worldliness with which the viscount's outlook on life infused the home.

Katherine continued to love her husband and made of it a good enough marriage for both. Yearly, however, her grief deepened at the realization that though they continued to attend the Church of England socially as a family every Sunday, her son and daughter were growing into pagans of the first order. What heartache must surely follow, either from the grave or more eternal regions, for those scions of spiritual families who spurn the good soil implanted into them and choose the world's way instead.

Whatever evils might be laid at the charge of their paternal pedigree, Courtenay and Florilyn Westbrooke at least had the benefit of a maternal rootstalk of godliness to stand them in good stead as they developed. This bloodline, however, both were learning to despise. Their father's influence had certainly been formative. But scorn of spiritual things is entirely individual. Thus, the downward spiral of character was given most of its energy by the power of their own self-willed choices. None of the three—father, son, daughter—had the slightest notion that the demon called "playing with religion" had nearly entirely taken them over.

Katherine wept in her room for an hour after Florilyn's ridiculous exchange at the dinner table. How could they do Percy any good, she thought through her tears, with her own children adding to the problems of her brother's son with such dreadful ideas of unbelief?

What would Edward think of her if word reached him of what faithlessness reigned in Snowdonia!

Eighteen

The Generations

A cold front blew in off the sea, keeping most of the inhabitants of Westbrooke Manor indoors for the next several days.

As Percy walked up the main staircase, returning to his room at the distant end of the west wing's second floor, he glanced about him at the paintings on the walls. He realized for the first time that many of these people were in a way related to him, even if distantly and by marriage.

Who were they? he wondered.

He paused at the landing between the ground and first floors, his attention suddenly arrested by a penetrating look in the eyes of the portrait of one particular woman. She stood as if eternally gazing over the entry hall below with a mysterious expression.

"Having a stroll about the old place, eh, my boy?" came a voice behind him. Percy turned to see the viscount striding toward the base of the staircase.

"Yes, Uncle Roderick," he replied. "It has been raining so steadily all day I had no choice but to get my exercise indoors."

"Shrewd thinking," said his uncle, climbing the stairs toward him. "The rain here can be insufferable. But it always clears, have no fear. What do you think of the old woman, there?" he added, pointing up to the painting in front of his nephew.

"She has an unusual countenance," answered Percy. "Her stare stopped me cold as I passed. I felt like she was actually looking at me."

His uncle laughed. "It's my grandmother," he said. "Well her eyes *might* stop you in your tracks!"

"Why is that?"

Westbrooke lowered his voice mysteriously and leaned close to his nephew. "They say she possessed the second sight," he said into Percy's ear.

An involuntarily shudder swept through Percy's chest at the words. "What's that?" he asked.

"A Scotsman like you. . .never heard of the second sight, my boy? But I forgot, your family's religion probably disavows the existence of such fancies. It's the Celtic blood of the ancients that still lives in these hills. Surely you know of our great old Welsh ruler, Rhodri Mawr, and our warrior king who fought the English in the early fifteenth century, Owain Glyndwr."

"I've heard of them, that's all," replied Percy.

"Great men if you believe your history," rejoined Westbrooke. "Legends abound of their mystical powers. It's a power that lives on, especially here in the north in Gwynedd and Snowdonia. They roamed these very hills, you know—Mawr and Wyddfa. They say it occasionally gets into folks even today, the second sight, I mean. They say it enables them to see things other people can't see. Some say they can even predict the future. Runs in family lines, they say."

"Do *you* have it, Uncle Roderick?"

"Me—good heavens, no!" The viscount laughed with a shudder at the thought. "No one around here lays claim to such clairvoyance. Well," he added with a chuckle, "other than the old hag in the village. But then she's a different story altogether." He glanced away briefly, as if something had distracted his train of thought. "It's mostly all superstition," he resumed quickly. "Nothing to put stock in. But come," he added, "let me show you the armory."

He led the way up the main staircase to the second floor, then to the right and into a part of the house Percy had not yet seen. "Neither Courtenay nor Florilyn have any interest in the family's history," he said as they entered the room. "Perhaps I shall be more successful in arousing your fascination."

Percy glanced about. Every wall was covered with weapons and implements of battle of many diverse kinds—swords, guns, axes, knives, daggers, lances, coats of mail, leather jerkins, two more full suits of armor, ornately carved and painted shields, and a crossbow.

"It was something of a hobby of my grandfather's," said the viscount as they strolled leisurely about the room. "He was the husband of the lady downstairs with the probing eyes. Perhaps I have inherited his interest. What do you think?"

"It's fabulous, Uncle Roderick," replied Percy, gazing about at the walls.

"It's one of the largest collections in Wales. Look out here," he added, walking to the east window of the room. "If you are partial to mountains rather than the sea, this window affords the best view in the house."

Percy followed his uncle to the window. The two stood side by side, gazing out for a time.

"If I'm going to make a Welshman out of you, you will have to learn to love those hills," said the viscount at length. "Sometimes, on the clearest of days, I stand here and gaze on Mount Snowdon away up there to the north."

"Can you really see it from here?" asked Percy.

The viscount nodded. "It's eighteen miles and requires ideal conditions," he said. "On most days all you can make out is mist and clouds. It's then," he added, laughing, "when you definitely need the second sight!"

He and his uncle chatted easily for another ten or fifteen minutes as they moved about the room.

"Come and have a look about any time, Percy, my boy," said Lord

Snowdon at length. "Feel free to explore the whole place. My house is your house, as they say," he added, laughing.

"Thank you, Uncle Roderick. You have been very kind to me. I appreciate your generosity. Thank you."

"However, I am afraid I need to leave you for now. I was on my way to my study when I ran into you on the landing. There is an important letter I need to answer. I hope you don't mind."

"No, of course not."

Left alone, Percy wandered about a few minutes more. He then left the armory and drifted along the corridor toward the library. He had only been inside it once since his arrival and was not a great reader. But on a rainy day like this, what else was there to do but find a book to occupy the time?

He had no idea where his cousins were or how they occupied themselves when housebound. He didn't really care. Neither had shown much interest in him. He had the feeling Florilyn was avoiding him until his anger over the incident with Grey Tide simmered down.

He entered the library. It was deathly quiet. He assumed himself alone. Slowly he wandered through the shelves lined from floor to ceiling with books.

Suddenly a movement startled him. There was his aunt seated in an alcove reading. She laid aside her book and glanced up at his approach.

"Hello, Aunt Katherine," he said walking toward her.

"Hello, Percy."

"I didn't know anyone else was in here."

"A gloomy day, is it not?"

"I suppose I should be used to it. It rains in Glasgow all the time, too. Still, you're right, it is rather a depressing sight outside."

"A perfect book day, that's what I call days like this."

"What are you reading?" asked Percy.

"Actually, a book your father just brought me—a novel by one of your fellow Scotsmen whom he has been taken with in recent years."

"Not that MacDonald fellow?"

"Why, yes it is!"

Percy chuckled. "My father and mother are always talking about him. Now that you mention it, I recall hearing them say they were planning to send you something of his that had just been published."

"What kind of books do you like?" Katherine asked.

"I don't know. I don't really read much."

"Have you read any of MacDonald's?" she asked?

"No," laughed Percy. "I figure if my parents like them, I probably wouldn't! We haven't exactly been seeing eye to eye lately."

"You might surprise yourself and actually like them," suggested his aunt.

"They're huge, long novels, aren't they?" said Percy. "I have seen several about the house. They look boring. I doubt I would be able to wade through something like that."

"Your father and mother are terribly fond of him. They are constantly waiting for every new title. If you don't care for the novels, maybe you would enjoy his fairy tales."

"Children's stories!" laughed Percy. "You're right—that would probably be just the right thing for me."

"I said fairy tales, not children's stories," rejoined his aunt with a smile.

"What's the difference?"

"All the difference in the world when the author is George MacDonald."

"Well, maybe I should," chuckled Percy. "Got to have something to occupy my time on a day like this, I suppose. Perhaps you could recommend something for me."

"I will be happy to," smiled his aunt. She rose and walked across the room and disappeared between two tall bookcases.

Percy followed.

Ten minutes later, his aunt had resumed her seat in the alcove with her book. On the other side of the library, Percy was slouched in a small couch that sat adjacent to a window looking out north from the manor, one leg slung up over the side rest, reading a book of much different fare than he had ever dipped into before, that his aunt had selected for him to try.

Nineteen

Altercation

Lord Snowdon sat in his office perusing the letter that had arrived two days before. He had read it over at least ten times but still could not satisfy himself that he had gotten to the bottom of it. The thing seemed straightforward enough. His naturally suspicious nature, however, could not prevent him from wondering if it was as simple as it appeared on the surface.

The Right Honorable, the Viscount Roderick Westbrooke, Lord Snowdon, he read yet again.

My Lord,

I have the honor to request your indulgence on a matter of some importance to me, though perhaps to no one else. I can only hope that you will treat the fancy of an aging sentimentalist with confidentiality and will consider my request with the same seriousness with which I make it.

Having spent some of the happiest years of my life as a boy romping the hills of Snowdonia with my father, it is my desire at this late stage of my life to build a small cottage on a meadow that I particularly cherished which sits on the slopes of one of Gwynned's lesser peaks. Investigating the matter, I find that the property in question lies within and almost at the boundary of your own estate. I am hoping that its remote location and relative insignificance among your vast holdings will encourage you to consider selling it to me.

I can assure you that my plans would in no way encroach on your privacy. I would seek to gain access by obtaining a right of way eastward through public lands from the main road between Blaenau Ffestiniog and Dolgellau. To put the matter in its simplest terms, you would not even know I was there.

I would purchase whatever amount of land you would graciously consent to part with up to a thousand or more acres. However, if a transaction of such size is impossible, I could carry out the plans for my small cottage with as little as twenty.

I am a wealthy man and believe I can make the transaction well worth your consideration. I am willing to pay anything within reason.

I am,
Sincerely and gratefully yours,
Palmer Sutcliffe

Westbrooke set aside the letter, leaned back in his chair, and exhaled a long thoughtful sigh. *Who is this man?* he wondered.

He reached for the copy of *Debrit's Peerage* on his desk and flipped through it but found nothing. He would have Tilman Heygate institute further inquiries.

Was it possible that this letter had come to him as manna from heaven, to meet his ongoing financial need? His wife's refusal in the matter of the yacht he had hoped to purchase remained a burr under his collar. This fellow Sutcliffe's proposal could make him independent of his wife's miserliness once and for all.

The wheels of the viscount's brain began to spin with increased momentum. How much could he reasonably ask for twenty acres? Such land was probably only worth ten or twenty pounds an acre. Surely Sutcliffe was no fool. Perhaps he would pay double, even triple that. But a few hundred pounds would hardly relieve his dependency on his wife.

Five hundred pounds. . .a thousand pounds? Even that would but temporarily ease his financial straits.

But a thousand acres! The thought of parting with such a sizable chunk of his holdings brought almost a physical pain to his chest. And yet. . .if he could raise, say, ten thousand pounds, he would be sitting pretty. For such a sum, however, he would have to give up a good deal of land.

How much would he be willing to let go of? Everything depended on how determined this Sutcliffe was on obtaining the specific land he mentioned. . .*his* land. . .and how wealthy he really was. If he asked too much, the man could simply build his cottage elsewhere. Land was cheap in Snowdonia.

The viscount drew in another deep breath. He would have to handle the matter with delicacy so as not to push too hard. As onerous as was the thought of parting with any of the estate's ground, this was the opportunity of a lifetime to gain financial independence.

He rose and left his office in search of his factor.

⚜

As Westbrooke contemplated the potential change in his fortunes, outside the sun was winning a brief battle against several swirling gray clouds, aided in the contest by a stiff wind off the sea. It now emerged bright and, for the present, victorious.

Seeing the change, the viscount's son left the house for the stables, thinking of a ride. The rain had put him in a surly mood. It would doubtless be a miserable afternoon for whichever horse he chose to bear him to help ameliorate his inward vexation at the world.

The sun's rays sent their life-probing radiance through the windows and into the house and into souls that were more malleable than that of young Courtenay Westbrooke. Little bubbles of God-shaped joy burst from hearts of servants and gentility alike. Gladness returned, and with it an occasional song came to the lips of housekeeper, maids, and cook.

Percy Drummond felt it, too. On the couch in the library, he had begun to doze. The sudden warmth as the sun shown on his face through the window brought him back to himself. An afternoon nap is a much different thing to a fifty-year-old than to a sixteen-year-old, for whom the very thought of sleep when the sun is shining is an abhorrence. Percy laid down the book of fairy tales, which had nearly fallen from his hand, got up, and left the library. He had no definite purpose in mind. He only knew that the sun and fresh air drew him and he must be out in it.

He left the house a minute or two later and drew in a satisfying breath of the chilly, damp air. Almost the same moment, he heard the fearsome shriek of a horse. A dreadful mad frenzy had just erupted. Thinking that either man or beast must be in some terrible trouble, he broke into a run and sprinted toward the stable yard as the earsplitting whinnying rose in fury.

Percy flew through the door of the barn. After the brightness of the sun, it took several seconds for his eyes to adjust. He was aware of frenetic kicking and stomping and flying dust. Men's voices were raised in argument. Drowning them out, however, continued the horrifying screaming of a beast either in terror or tremendous pain.

Courtenay had come in some time earlier and, not finding the groom, had set about saddling his horse carelessly and in haste. The moment he mounted the nervous and highly strung Gelderlander, the horse began to back and rear. Courtenay gave him a vicious cut with his whip. The poor beast went wild, plunging and kicking.

Hearing the racket, Hollin Radnor hurried in from outside as the viscount's son was bringing his whip down a second time. "Don't punish him, my lord!" implored Radnor, hurrying forward. "You'll drive him madder than he is already!"

"Get back, Radnor," yelled Courtenay, "or you'll come in for your share with him!"

The viscount's son was a good horseman in the sense of being able to hold himself in the saddle in almost any circumstances. Yet he knew little about horses. He had not learned to love them as among the noblest creatures of the animal creation. To him, they were mere beasts of burden to be compelled into obedience. If it took cruelty to achieve that end, he would not withhold it.

One of his father's horses had been put down years before because Courtenay, at twelve, had ridden it to such exhaustion, whipping it beyond all hope of endurance, that the poor creature had simply collapsed and shattered both its front legs. Even then, angered at having been thrown, he withdrew his whip and attacked the animal as it lay dying. Alas, the intervening six years had taught him nothing about curbing his temper.

But Hollin Radnor did love horses, if not more than his own life, perhaps close to it. Ignoring the young lord's command, he ran to the horse's head and set about desperately trying to calm him.

Courtenay's rage as he looked down on the insolent servant overpowered good sense and common decency together. A series of blows from the whip descended on head of groom and horse together.

Almost the same moment, Percy rushed in.

"My lord, my lord," Radnor cried as the blows fell relentlessly on him, "the curb chain is too tight! The animal is suffering great pain. Please, my lord. . .hold off him and allow me to loosen it!"

Percy now ran toward them hoping to protect Radnor from further blows.

Seeing his cousin take the groom's side added contempt to Courtenay's dudgeon. The next blows from his whip were directed at Percy.

"Stop. . .stop, Courtenay!" howled Percy. "If you don't stop hitting Mr. Radnor, I'll—"

"You'll what?" cried Courtenay scornfully. "Get back. This is between me and him." Another whack fell from the whip against Percy's cheek and forehead.

A stinging pain on his face brought his blood to a boil as hot as his cousin's. "It's between you and me now!" Percy yelled. "Stop, I tell you, or I'll throw you from that horse!"

A peal of derisive laughter filled the barn. But it is unwise to laugh at an angry man. Percy rushed toward Courtenay, took hold of the nearest booted foot, and with a great shove pitched him backward over the thoroughbred's side. Taken by surprise at Percy's daring and strength, Courtenay did not keep hold of the reins. He tumbled to the ground with a great thud and groan.

Radnor led the crazed and terrified horse a little way off and struggled to slacken the twisted chain that had been biting into his jaw. The poor animal was dripping with sweat, his flesh quivering and trembling, still prancing and jerking his head about. Radnor gradually soothed him with whispered words and the gentle touch of his hand.

Percy stood above Courtnenay waiting.

Recovering his shock, his cousin leaped to his feet. "You will pay for that, you little rotter!" he cried, squaring off against Percy with fists in the air. "Do you really think you are any match for me?"

"Probably not," replied Percy, his gaze warily fixed on Courtenay's eyes and fists. "You may beat me to a pulp, but you will not touch that horse or Mr. Radnor again."

"You think you can stop me?"

"I *will* stop you."

Courtenay leaped forward with marvelous speed. The fist of his right hand smashed into Percy's forehead with such lightning force that Percy scarcely had a chance to blink. A second pounded into his cheek at the edge of his nose and drew blood.

Percy staggered back, dazed, and toppled to the dirt floor.

Seeing blood coming from his nose, and with Radnor leading the frothing horse outside, Courtenay thought better of pursuing the battle on either front. "Let that be a lesson to you," he said down to Percy where he lay. "You stay away from my horse. You stay away from everything of mine, or it will go worse for you next time!" He turned and stormed from the barn.

By the time the incident had passed, the sky had darkened again. The weather remained fitful for the remainder of the day.

TWENTY

Devious Invitation

*T*he conversation around the dinner table that evening at Westbrooke Manor was noticeably subdued.

No word had reached either husband or wife about the day's altercation in the barn. There had been talk among the servants, however, for Hollin Radnor had sought one of the maids to bandage his face and arms. Though he divulged nothing about the cause of his wounds, the girl who tended him came of a family that considered horses almost equal in the family to the children. Her father was universally regarded the most knowledgeable man concerning horseflesh in the region. She knew the mark of a whip when she saw one. Everyone at the manor knew the young master's proclivity with the leather. Speculation had run rampant ever since.

Some of this talk came within the hearing of Florilyn Westbrooke. She was a girl for whom secrets existed but for one purpose—that she might find them out, discover their source, and use the information gained to work mischief in the lives of those involved. This she would do by any and all means that lay open to her cunning and wiles. She was a pixie, a knave, an inciter of annoyance, what the French would call a *provocateur*. To disrupt, confuse, frustrate, sabotage, and irritate was the spice of her life.

The moment her cousin entered the dining room, she divined the truth. Percy's forehead and cheek were badly swollen and bruised. A thin cut extended along the opposite cheek up to and across half his forehead. She knew as well as Padrig Gwlwlwyd's daughter what the cut of a whip looked like. Her suspicions were all but confirmed when Courtenay came in a minute later, favoring one leg but without a mark on his face. Both boys wore serious expressions. Neither looked at the other throughout the meal.

"You must have had an interesting day, Courtenay," said Florilyn with a twinkle in her eye.

Her brother did not reply.

"I thought you were going for a ride earlier," she went on. "I was watching, but I never saw you leave the stables. Did you have some kind of trouble?"

"I decided not to go," said Courtenay moodily.

Florilyn turned to her cousin. "What happened to *you*, Percy?" she said. "You look a mess."

Percy shrugged and went on with his dinner.

"Did something happen, Percy, my boy?" now asked the viscount. For the first time, he seemed to take note of Percy's face.

"Just a little accident," answered Percy. "I fell in the barn."

His uncle did not press the matter, though Katherine appeared concerned.

Florilyn, however, was not about to let it go. She continued to bait both boys throughout dinner. But to no avail.

Later that evening in her room, Florilyn's lust to know what had happened between her cousin and brother gradually gave way to a yet deeper puzzle. Why hadn't Percy said a word about the incident? What could account for such behavior? If Courtenay had so much as spoken an ill word to her, she would have been ranting with accusations to their parents at the first opportunity, trying to get even with him.

She knew good and well that Courtenay had given Percy those cuts and bruises. Why his silence? Was he afraid of getting more of the same from Courtenay if he squealed?

Somehow she thought not. Percy was smaller than Courtenay, that was true. But she doubted he was afraid of him. Percy carried himself as one who knew how to handle himself in a tussle. There had to be more to it.

Did some twisted form of gallantry prevent him from blabbing? Twice now he had refused to blame either Courtenay or her. What was the reason for his silence? Did he possess some peculiar code of conduct that barred accusation. . .even when it was deserved?

Not knowing nearly drove her mad. She was determined to loosen Percy's tongue one way or another.

By morning Florilyn had made up her mind what to do. She needed to get Percy angry. Angry enough to retaliate. What was the fun of being mean to him if he wouldn't fight back? Even if it meant getting in trouble herself, making Percy lose his temper would be such a sweet victory it would be worth it.

The rain passed through Wales and the sun came out, gloriously and warm the next morning. By noon, most of the meadows and fields were dry enough to consider riding again.

Percy was surprised to hear a knock on his door shortly after he had returned upstairs from lunch. There stood Florilyn in her riding habit. "I know you probably hate me for what I did the other day," she said, dropping her eyes.

"I don't hate you," said Percy. "I would just like to know why you did it. What do you have against me, anyway?"

"I don't know. Sometimes I just get that way and can't help myself. But would you like to go for a ride today? I promise, I won't swat your horse."

Percy thought for a moment. It wasn't much of an apology. But he was dying to get out of the house, and he was leery of doing so alone lest again he encounter Courtenay, which he was not anxious to do.

"Don't worry," she added with a winning smile. "I'll give you the gentlest mount in the stables."

"All right," he said, forcing a smile. "Just let me change my clothes."

"I'll meet you at the barn," said Florilyn, turning to go.

The two met in the stable yard twenty minutes later. Florilyn led the way inside. Percy followed.

"Prynhawn da, Miss Florilyn. . .Master Drummond," said the groom. He turned to greet the two young people in the midst of the empty stall he was cleaning.

"We're going for a ride, Hollin," Florilyn said.

"Will you be wanting me to saddle two horses, Miss Westbrooke?"

"I will do it, Hollin," she replied. "You go do something else. Leave us until we're gone."

The groom did as instructed, though he ambled from the barn slowly. He glanced back every so often as if delaying until he could see which horses they planned to take.

But Florilyn, who had experienced the old man's interference before, waited until he was out of sight. She then proceeded to saddle two mounts while Percy looked on.

She led the horses out to the mounting block. After handing Percy the reins of a reddish bay mare that she introduced as Red Rhud, she herself mounted the mare called Grey Tide. Percy managed to get up into the saddle alone, a feat he pretended to take in stride without displaying his profound satisfaction at the accomplishment.

They left the stable yard. Quickly Florilyn led the way down a sloping path through the gardens and trees, continuing in the direction of the sea. A few minutes later, they emerged onto the uncultivated fields and open moorland east of Mochras Head. Already Florilyn was a considerable distance ahead.

Percy gave the mare a touch of his heels. She darted skittishly forward, her four hooves prancing over the grass as if the ground was red hot. Percy jostled about but did his best not to show his concern.

Soon, however, Florilyn slowed, waited for them to catch up. She then veered southward. In a huge gradual arc, she led the way across moor and field until they had come around 180 degrees and were bound on a course almost due east in the direction of Moelfre and Yllethr.

They rode for an hour or more into the hilly forested regions, skirting north of the two peaks, making many turns and changes of direction, uphill and down, along streambeds, following a good-sized river for a while, then through meadows, here and there entering forests so thick there was scarcely room for the horses to pass single file through the branches.

Percy had not an idea where they were or in what direction they had been going. For all he knew, they could have been anywhere in Snowdonia. Had he been asked to point in what direction lay the sea, he might have turned around in a complete circle and scanned his surroundings without being able to settle on any of the 360 degrees of the compass.

He was thoroughly and completely lost.

No words were spoken between them. Though Florilyn led at a relaxed pace, she never allowed Percy to draw alongside. This was fine with Percy. Despite the apparent change in her attitude, he had no particular desire to exchange small talk with his cousin.

In time they reached what appeared to be a small green valley that sat between two ridges of hills that angled together and met a mile or two farther on in front of them. Whether it was truly a valley or a high plateau somewhere in the depths of the Cambrian Mountains would have been hard to determine. It was so protected and out of the way, it was impossible to tell anything about the surrounding terrain beyond the two ridges and the thick forest through which they had come at one end of the expanse. Wherever the place was, it was so remote that not a living creature was to be seen.

Percy had seen no sheep or cattle for an hour, though plentiful deer and rabbits were hiding among the trees.

They began to cross the flat grassland.

Suddenly with a shout, Florilyn leaned forward in the saddle and burst into a gallop. Hair streaming behind her, within seconds she was fifty yards away.

Red Rhud required no encouragement. With a tremendous burst, she shot after Grey Tide.

A cry of terror escaped Percy's lips as he lurched back in the saddle. Frantically grabbing at the saddle edge, he held on for dear life. Tearing up clods of the soft turf with her hooves and throwing them up behind, his mount flew across the ground.

Florilyn persisted in the reckless sprint toward the far end of the grassy flat then reined in, laughing gaily as she threw her head around.

Percy rode up out of breath, white-faced and angry. His mare slowed, though still pranced with spirit. The brief gallop, far from expending the great creature's energy, had only excited it the more. "I nearly fell!" he exclaimed.

Florilyn did not reply, only smiled. Her coy expression gave away nothing. She turned in her saddle and rode on at a slow walk.

Percy pulled alongside about to speak again then judged it best for now to say nothing. Maybe she *hadn't* done it intentionally. It certainly wouldn't do to anger her when he was at her mercy and so far from the manor.

Percy's respite from the precarious gallop, however, was short-lived.

Even more rashly than before, again Florilyn shouted to her horse and burst with astonishing acceleration into another madcap gallop. "Race you to the ridge!" she shouted over her shoulder.

"I don't think—" began Percy.

It was no use. His words gave way to a piercing wail of terrified surprise. His own steed had again bolted, exactly as Florilyn knew she would. The two mares, so different in temperament, were actually twins. A great rivalry existed between them, a fact the viscount's daughter had decided to exploit on this day.

Looking behind her, Florilyn saw the response she had expected. She dug her heels into Grey Tide's sides and urged the mare to the full measure of her speed. For the gentle horse Radnor said she was, with her mistress on her back, few horses in all the region of Llanfryniog could equal her for raw speed.

Clutching reins and saddle as he was wildly tossed about on Red Rhud's back, Percy made a gallant effort to keep his seat. He might have succeeded, too, had their way continued on level ground.

But Florilyn had other designs. Unlike Percy, she was not a bit lost. She knew exactly where she was, knew the precipitous terrain that lay up the steep slope ahead. She knew, too, what must be the inevitable result with Red Rhud straining every muscle of her great flanks to overtake her twin.

Florilyn kept on, therefore, as fast as she dared, flew into the trees at the far end of the flat and up the incline that began almost immediately. Over fallen logs Grey Tide leaped without breaking stride, across a stream eight feet wide, and through another level of about fifty yards. There she swung the mare sharply left. If Percy behind her managed to keep in the saddle over the trees and stream, the steep path she followed for the next two hundred yards would surely prove too much for his novitiate equestrian skill.

She dared not look back. She would have to be able to profess innocence to her father that she did not know when she might have lost him. Therefore, she leaned forward, hugging her chest to Grey Tide's long neck to keep in the saddle herself and scurried the rest of the way up the near vertical ascent. Reaching the crest, she straightened again in the saddle and galloped along the top of the ridge for some distance.

Soon she heard Red Rhud behind her and gaining. She suspected the cause well enough—that the burden on the red mare's back had been reduced at some point along the way by exactly the weight of a sixteen-year-old Glaswegian.

Finally Florilyn glanced back over her shoulder. It was as she thought. Red Rhud was flying toward her riderless.

She laughed, thoroughly delighted with herself, and eased back on Grey Tide's reins. Red Rhud came alongside. Keeping up a swift canter, Florilyn now led the two horses on a slant down the opposite side of the ridge, thinking herself well out of sight of any human eyes, and then in a westerly direction that would take them back to the manor.

Twenty-One

Heaven-Sent Guide

*T*he final steep ascent had not been necessary to achieve Florilyn's end.

Percy had barely managed to cling to his seat as Red Rhud leaped the first fallen tree across her path. But repeating the feat when the mare went airborne a few seconds later, landing on the opposite side of the wide stream with a great jolting earthquake of a bounce, proved impossible.

Luckily the water flowed through a grassy section of wood or he might have been seriously hurt. As it was, when Percy looked up from the soft grass where he found himself after his inglorious tumble to see Red Rhud disappearing through the trees in the distance, though his back would feel it tomorrow, the chief injury he had suffered was to his pride—actually not a bad injury to sustain. As humility is its opposite, for a humble spirit to emerge within the human character usually requires that pride be dealt a series of painful blows by the hammer of circumstance, and Percy had just had one to his.

He took stock of himself, realized nothing was broken, then drew in a deep breath and climbed to his feet. He knew the general direction his mount had gone. He could still hear her hooves thudding in the distance as she made for the ridge. He had no doubt Florilyn would be waiting for him at the top with an insufferably obnoxious grin.

He set off trudging up the hill. It took Percy some fifteen or twenty minutes, after a much steeper climb than he had expected, to emerge into the clearing along one of the two ridges he had seen from the field below.

He stopped, breathing heavily, and gazed about. There was no sign of Florilyn. The entire world was still and quiet.

He turned around, looking back and forth and in every direction a second time. His initial bewilderment slowly turned to anger. The vixen had deserted him in the middle of nowhere!

Nor did he have the slightest notion in which direction lay the sea, the village, or the manor. Beyond the two ridges, which seemed more or less to join a quarter or half mile away, lay an endless series of forested hills, broken here and there in the distance by a few higher peaks. Had he known the the region better, he would have been able to identify these hills as sitting in a near straight line between Mount Snowdon in the north and Calder Idris farther south. From their relation to one another, it would have been an easy matter to tell whether he was looking north, south, east, or west. But as he was not familiar with the northern Cambrians, he had no idea. Nor, for the present as it beamed down from overhead, did the sun accurately suggest to Percy his bearings.

In every direction he looked, the outlook was identical. He was not high enough to see the sea beyond any of the ridges or ranges. He might walk for hours and only succeed in getting farther from home and more deeply into what could be dangerous mountains. He did not relish the thought of spending a night out here alone. Snow was not unheard of in June. And no doubt more wild animals came out after dark than he cared to meet.

An evil oath began to rise to his lips. But it never reached them.

A sound interrupted it, as if sent from heaven to answer the cry for help it did not occur to him to lift to the One who knew where everyone was.

"She's g–g–gone, M–M–Mr. Drummond," a voice said simply.

Percy spun around in terror, as if the preternatural silence had been broken by the roar of a lion rather than the gentle timbre of one of God's angels. But the stupendous relief of finding himself not alone rushed in to banish his fear.

There stood his stuttering young friend who gave bouquets of wildflowers to strangers!

"Gwyneth!" he exclaimed. "What in God's name are you doing here?"

Percy spoke more truth than he realized.

"I have been w–w–watching you and Lady F–Florilyn as you rode," she said, coming toward him with a smile.

"Where is she now?" asked Percy.

"She is gone, M–M–Mr. Drummond. She kept riding b–back down there." Gwyneth pointed down the hill.

Percy followed her arm but could see nothing.

"I knew you had b–been thrown, so I w–w–waited for you. Are you hurt, M–M–Mr. Drummond?"

He answered her with a smile. "I don't think so," he said. "Did Florilyn see you?"

"I would not have let her see me."

"Why not?"

"She would have said cruel things."

"Well," said Percy, his self-deprecating humor rising to the surface as he began to feel better about his predicament, "it would appear I am not much of a horseman."

"Y–y–you were riding my lord's w–w–wildest m–mare."

"You don't say," said Percy with significant tone. "His *wildest* mare?"

"R–R–Red Rhud throws everyone except L–Lady Florilyn."

Percy chuckled at the revealing information. Though calming under the mesmerizing girl's peculiar power, he was still irritated enough to find little humor in Florilyn's deception.

"How do you come to be so far from home?" he asked.

"It is not so very far. B–b–besides, I know every inch of these hills."

"Are you not afraid to wander them alone?"

"No, Mr. Drummond."

"Can you lead me back to the manor?"

"Of course. Come, Mr. Drummond," she said, walking to his side and taking his hand. "I will show you." She led the way down the hill, Percy followed as if he were a compliant child, laughing at the incongruity of it. She treated him as if he were a full-grown adult, yet she carried herself with the maturity and self-confidence of a fifty-year-old.

Who could not be charmed by such a one!

Before they had gone far, Gwyneth let go of Percy's hand, paused, shielded her eyes from the sun with one hand, and looked down in the opposite direction. An expression of question crossed her usually placid countenance.

"What is it?" asked Percy.

"Nothing," she replied thoughtfully. "I saw some men off there a few weeks ago. They weren't from around here. I did not like them."

"Were they so close you could see their faces so well as to know whether you liked them or not?"

"I was not close. But I could tell they were not good men."

"How?"

"I don't know. I could tell."

Intrigued, Percy did not press the matter. In another minute Gwyneth was scampering down the hillside with Percy beside her.

They descended the ridge and within minutes were surrounded by overspreading boughs of pine and fir. Percy saw no hint of a trail anywhere. "How do you know where to go?" he asked.

"Because I know where we are. I know the sea is this way," she answered, pointing in front of her. "I walk everywhere here. I cannot get lost."

"You have been in this exact place before?"

"Of course. This is near one of my special places."

"Your. . .'special places'?"

"Yes. I have many special places where I go to visit animals and visit God and visit my mother."

"I don't know what you mean," said Percy.

"My mother is dead, Mr. Drummond."

"I am sorry, Gwyneth. I didn't know that."

"She is with God. So at my special places, I go to be alone and visit them and talk to them."

"And one of them is near here?"

"Yes, would you like to see it?"

"I would, yes. . .very much. But isn't it a private special place?"

"It is *my* special place. So I can bring anyone to it. Remember, Mr. Drummond, you are my friend now, not a stranger. The flowers made us friends. So I can show it to you."

She continued to lead Percy through the thick wood. They came a few minutes later to a little brook. It was no more than a foot or two wide and could have been easily stepped across. Instead, Gwyneth turned and led Percy along the edge of it. They were still descending from the same ridge where they had begun.

The brook was swift and noisy, splashing over rocks and pebbles, creating tiny little waterfalls as it went. Its water was brown and foamy from the mountains and hills of peat through which it came.

They continued another ten or fifteen minutes. The downward slope grew less steep as they reached the bottom between this ridge and the next one westward. Through a dense growth of pines they went in single file, until it suddenly opened into a clearing.

In front of him, Percy beheld a secluded meadow in the midst of the wood. It was perhaps twenty yards wide and fifty long, flat and grassy. The brook they had been following flowed through the center of it, where it tumbled into a pond that was deep enough, because the water was brown, that the bottom was not visible.

Gwyneth stopped and gazed about. The smile of pleasure on her face said clearly enough that her heart was full of delight to share her discovery with a friend.

"It's beautiful, Gwyneth!" exclaimed Percy. The sound of his own voice almost startled him. Except for the gentle babbling of the stream, the place was so secluded that utter stillness reigned. "This must be your special place."

Gwyneth nodded.

"How did you find it?"

"I came upon it when I was exploring in the woods. So I kept coming here and made friends with the animals."

"Animals come when you are here?"

"Only deer and rabbits. I don't think they will come today because they don't know you. They will be afraid. It took them a long time before they realized they didn't need to be afraid of me. Come and sit by the pond. That's where I sit when I come."

Percy followed her across the grass, and they sat down.

After a minute or two of silence, Gwyneth spoke. "God, this is Mr. Drummond," she said simply.

Surprised, Percy looked over at her.

Gwyneth was staring into the pond. "I'm sure You know him already," she went on, "but he has not been here before. He is a good man. He is kind to everyone. He is visiting at the manor, but they are not kind to him. Mummy, I want you to know Mr. Drummond, too."

Percy listened spellbound. He did not want to intrude upon one of the most unusual one-sided conversations he had ever heard in his life. For one who had always associated prayer with his father's prayers from the pulpit or at the table, the simplicity of Gwyneth's conversation with God was almost too much to take in. Especially hearing her speaking to God about him!

This was, as Percy had said, Gwyneth's own private place. No one else in the whole world, or so Gwyneth thought, except now for Percy, knew of it. Sitting here, not necessarily thinking or praying about anything in particular, but *feeling* it, silently moved her with the invisible music of creation. She did not always talk aloud when she came to the pond in the wood. She spoke as she did on this day so that Percy could share in her thoughts.

When Gwyneth felt the silent mysteries of the world and felt the tunes of God's music inside her, all creation made her happy. At such times her whole being was at prayer, for she was swallowed up in the expansive presence of God Himself.

There are those who only associate what they call prayer with formality and words and churches and mealtimes and public worship. But from a young age, Gwyneth had intuitively known, though no one had taught her, that all motions of heart and brain sent heavenward were prayers, for they went into the heart of Him who treasured the uplifted thoughts of His children.

After some long minutes of silence, Gwyneth stood. "We should leave now, Mr. Drummond," she said. "We have a long way to go. I want to be home before my papa gets home from the mine."

They left the meadow on the opposite side from where they had entered it and started up the next in a series of several ridges that still lay between them and the sea.

"Your father works in the mine, does he?" asked Percy as they went. "A coal mine?"

"No, Mr. Drummond. The slate mine. There is no coal here, only slate. There is a gold mine, too, somewhere not very far away, but my papa works in the slate mine."

"There is gold in Snowdonia?" said Percy in surprise.

"Yes, but not as much as slate."

"Gold is more valuable."

"My papa says that, too. He says that much of the gold of Snowdonia lies under the hills where no one has yet found it."

"Does he know where? Why doesn't he look for it?"

"Papa says that dreams of gold cannot buy potatoes. But slate can because it is no dream. Grannie has seen real gold, though I have never seen it."

Before Percy could question her further about the remarkable turn the conversation had taken, they entered a dense grove of trees. They were occupied for some time getting through it with a minimum of scratches.

By the time they came near the crest of the final ridge an hour later, Percy was feeling the effects of the afternoon's ride and walk. He would definitely sleep well that night!

They had been climbing steadily through a rocky hillside of pine. Ahead they appeared nearly to have reached the top of the incline.

Gwyneth stopped. "We have come to another of my special places," she said.

Percy glanced about but saw nothing to distinguish the hill they had been climbing. "Where?" he said.

"Right there," answered Gwyneth pointing in front of them. "Just ahead, at the top of the hill, there between those trees. We will walk through them, and then it will be downhill the rest of the way."

"What makes this a special place?"

"You will see when we get to the top. Come."

Gwyneth had brought Percy along this particular route for the very purpose of the overlook that was suddenly about to present itself when their vision rose over the crest in front of them. She had discovered it years ago and never tired of the stunning revelation as her head came up slowly over the top of the hill.

With Percy beside her, having no idea what was coming, Gwyneth continued slowly. They emerged through the trees at the crest. Two or three more steps brought their eyes above it. . .and lo! There was the whole of the coastline spread out below them in the glorious splendor of late afternoon.

The great ocean seemingly stretched out before them to infinity from the Lleyn Peninsula ahead and to their right, into the distance where their vision finally failed somewhere in the direction of Barmouth Bay to their left. Below them the plateau of Mochras Head extended out into the deep blue of Tremadog Bay. From this vantage point of a mile or more from the shoreline, and so high above it, the sea and all the countryside inland was eerily silent. A gentle breeze off the ocean met their faces as they came over the rise. Faint reminders of salt spray were borne upon it. The wide panorama, so alive yet so silent, appeared as a painting rather than the resplendent reality it was.

The silence surrounding them was deeper than silence, a *full* silence because the whole of North Wales lay in front of them. It pulsed with the energy of being, of life, yet no sound, not even of the gulls soaring along the cliffs at the shoreline, reached them.

Percy had never beheld such a sight. As the view overflowed his senses, a sensation stabbed his soul with an almost physical longing for something he desired but felt he could never attain.

The reaction that followed was not what Gwyneth had expected.

He stood gaping for a few moments at the majestic overlook, slowly shaking his head in wonder and disbelief. Then suddenly he broke into laughter. "Gwyneth!" he exclaimed. "You did it. You brought me out of the wilderness, from wherever we were to. . .just look. . .to here! There's the manor! There is the sea—glorious, blue, radiant! I'm back. . .you brought me home!"

Without warning, he turned, grabbed her two hands, and began dancing and skipping about with joyful abandon.

Gywneth giggled with childlike happiness.

Round and round they danced in the clearing between the trees. Finally Percy let go, spun around one more time for good measure, then threw himself on what sparse dry grass grew at the crest of the ridge and stared out toward the sea.

Slowly Gwyneth lay down beside him.

It quieted again. Neither spoke. They lay side by side perhaps ten minutes. The dome of the sky overhead appeared to meet the edge of the sea at the horizon in an unbroken continuity of blue.

But the line between them was not as unbroken as it seemed.

"Can you see Ireland?" said Gwyneth after some time.

"No," said Percy. "Is it really out there?"

"Yes—straight across the ocean."

"Can you see it?"

"I think so," said Gwyneth a little hesitantly. "Sometimes I imagine I can when I really can't. But from here on the clearest of days I *know*

I see it. There is a tiny bit of haze today so I cannot be completely sure."

"Maybe you have the second sight," said Percy, more lightheartedly than serious.

But Gwyneth took in his words earnestly. "Papa says I do," she said. "I don't even know what it means. But look—surely you can see the tiny bumps of land out there. . .at the edge of the ocean."

Percy squinted and sent his eyes back and forth. "Yes. . .there it is," he exclaimed. "I do see it—you're right!"

"You must have second sight, too, Mr. Drummond."

Percy laughed. "I doubt that. So, that is Ireland across there?"

"Yes. My mother was from Ireland."

"Was she indeed?"

"Yes. My father married her in Ireland. He says she was really Welsh, though I don't understand about all that. I was born there. Then we came back here to Wales, though I was just a baby and cannot remember. There was a terrible storm at sea, and my mother died. So when we arrived here, my father and I were alone."

"I am sorry, Gwyneth," said Percy. "It must be hard not to have a mother."

"I don't know what having a mother is like. But I have the best father in the world. Perhaps God knew that I could do without a mother for a while. But I will see her again."

They lay a few more minutes in silence. The scents of the sea breezes continued to drift up the sloping moor to meet them. The peace of the world enveloped them in its embrace.

TWENTY-TWO

Gwyneth's Offer

*A*s Percy and Gwyneth romped down the ridge toward the plateau of Mochras Head, laughing and talking gaily, they were being watched.

Exulting in her supposed triumph over her cousin for the two hours since she had returned to the manor, Florilyn had been eagerly awaiting Percy's arrival. If he somehow managed to find his way home before dark, she could not wait to greet him face-to-face and watch him lose his temper with her.

She knew he would not hurt her. But if she could make him yell at her—or even swear aloud!—she would count the day a wonderful success. If she could somehow badger him into doing so in front of her father or mother, whose movements she was carefully watching for exactly that purpose, so much the better. A victory over a rival, in her opinion, was infinitely sweeter if he could be humiliated in front of witnesses. She never took out her revenge on her brother in private. She hoped to do the same with her cousin.

Seeing him now coming toward the manor with the tiny white-haired brat, Gwyneth Barrie, however, filled her with sudden uneasiness. Something didn't look right.

They were laughing! Percy didn't appear the least bit upset!

128

"Well, Gwyneth," Percy was saying, "I thank you for a most enjoyable afternoon. . .and for rescuing me! If you hadn't been watching out for me like a guardian angel, I would still be out there wandering around in circles. I shall be more careful in the future when Florilyn baits me into a race."

"Do you think you will race her again, Mr. Drummond?"

"I don't know. I hope not!" Percy laughed. "It's humiliating being trounced by a girl—no offense to you."

"Would you like to beat her in a race?"

"Would I ever!" Percy laughed again. "But that's easier said than done. As irritating as she is, she happens to be very good on the back of a horse."

"You *could* beat her."

"How?"

"I could teach you," said Gwyneth simply.

Percy stared back, wondering if he had heard correctly.

"You. . .could teach me to ride faster than Florilyn?"

"Yes, Mr. Drummond."

"You know horses that well?"

She nodded.

"I should say, you know how to *ride* that well?"

"Yes, Mr. Drummond. I could help you learn to ride like the wind."

Percy could not help himself. He broke out laughing at the delicious humor of the suggestion. The girl was such an innocent! But she had not yet said a word to him that was untrue. He had already come to feel a supreme confidence in whatever she told him.

What did he have to lose?

"You're on, Gwyneth Barrie," he said, still chuckling at the thought. "I accept your offer."

Gwyneth glanced toward the manor and realized they had come closer than she had intended. She thought she had seen Florilyn by the house watching them. She paused, suddenly nervous, then began to leave him.

"G–g–good-bye, Mr. Drummond," she said as she started walking away. "You can find your way from here."

"Where are you going all of a sudden?" said Percy.

"Home. L–L–Lady Florilyn will be angry with you if she sees you t–t–talking to me."

"Don't worry, Gwyneth." Percy laughed. "We won't worry about her. You may talk to me anytime."

"But she d–d–doesn't like me. I don't want her to g–g–get angry with you. G–g–good-bye."

"Thank you again, Gwyneth," said Percy after her. "Where will I find you so that you can give me those riding lessons?"

"Ask for G–G–Grannie in the village," replied Gwyneth. "She will t–t–tell you where to find me."

"What horse should I bring when I come to you?"

"Any of them, M–M–Mr. Drummond. I know all the horses. I can t–t–teach you to ride any of them f–f–fast. Mr. Radnor will help you. He is my friend. He will keep our s–s–secret."

As suddenly as she had appeared on the ridge in the wilderness, she ran from him and within seconds had disappeared from sight.

Percy did not see his cousin again until that evening. Her gloating turned to pique; she had walked back into the house in the huff of defeat. She was still filled with ire when dinnertime came.

Percy's spirits, on the other hand, remained high as he took his chair at the table, a fact that enraged Florilyn all the more. She had deserted him miles from home for the express purpose of making him angry. But he seemed happier than ever!

She made several juvenile attempts to bait Percy into tattling on her. But they only succeeded in making her look foolish. None of the other three had an idea what she was talking about. In truth, he had spent such a delightful afternoon with Gwyneth Barrie that he was actually thankful for the fall off Red Rhud's back. Florilyn's antics were beginning to strike him as more humorous than spiteful.

"You seem cheerful tonight, Percy," said his aunt as the meal progressed. "You must be enjoying the turn of warm weather."

"Very much, Aunt Katherine. I had begun to wonder if summer would ever arrive."

"Well, it seems it has. I am enjoying it as well."

"How did you occupy yourself, Percy, my boy?" said the viscount.

"Florilyn and I went out for a ride, didn't we, Florilyn—a *very* long ride."

"Splendid! There, you see—I knew you two would hit it off if you just gave her the chance. Florilyn is a dashed good horsewoman, you know."

"Yes, I have discovered that," said Percy with a wry grin. "Certainly out of my league! I'm not near the horseman she is, that's for sure."

"Where did you go?"

"Actually, I'm not altogether sure, Uncle Roderick," laughed Percy. "We headed off into the hills. I became so turned around I had no idea which way home was. I was completely lost! We were gone hours and hours. But luckily I wasn't left out there *alone*. That would have been frightening. Can you imagine, being out in the hills and not knowing your way back. . .and with night coming on?" He cast Florilyn a glance and a wily wink.

The expression on her face indicated clearly enough that she was not appreciating his humor. She did *not* like the tables being turned. Now it was *her* turn to feel the smoke coming out her ears.

"But 'all's well that end's well,' isn't that what old Bill Shakespeare says?" Percy added. "Here we all are, safe and sound. It was an extraordinary day. In fact, I can't think when I've enjoyed myself more."

"Excellent," said the viscount, obviously delighted that the cousins were all hitting it off so well. "Your father and mother will be pleased that the country air is agreeing with you. You shall have to write them, Katherine," he added to his wife at the end of the table, "and tell them that Percy is enjoying himself here with us."

Twenty-Three

The Draper's Shop

*T*he fair weather continued. At last, it seemed, perhaps summer had decided to grace North Wales with its presence for an extended stay.

The next days would have been spectacular for riding in the hills. But Percy had had enough of horses' backs for a while. He was eager to take Gwyneth up on her offer but needed to let his body recover from its bumps and bruises. By the morning following his adventure in the hills, his back was screaming from the fall. When he was ready to get on a horse again, he would sneak away from the manor alone.

He spent a couple of days recuperating, mostly indoors. During that time, he finished the book his aunt had suggested he read. One of the stories in particular had moved him in a way he could not explain. He finished it and felt tears rising in his eyes. He had to put the book down until he recovered himself, wondering what on earth had come over him. Unaccountably, for he had never done such a thing in his life, when he was done he immediately began to read the story over a second time.

On the third day, feeling better, he decided to walk to the village and acquaint himself a little more with his summer's surroundings. It was surely no Glasgow, but he was curious to feel the pulse of life in the place.

As he made his way down the entry from the house and thence along the road through the sloping plateau toward Llanfryniog, he stooped now and then to pluck a few wildflowers from the roadside. He smiled at the reminder of Gwyneth Barrie's endearing habit of greeting strangers. If he saw her today, he would return her kindness from three days ago with a bouquet of his own making!

He reached the village, by now clutching a good handful of wild daisies, bluebells, and assorted bits of color and walking with a jaunty step. He passed several villagers who nodded and smiled as they passed, though with the unspoken question in their minds—who was he? Percy returned their smiles. After so long in the city, the simplicity of their guileless country faces touched him with honest sincerity.

In the normal course of human relationships, it is to those older, wiser, more knowledgeable, more experienced to whom one looks with respect and honor as befit their years. Percy had never had what in any sense could be called a *mentor* in the things of life, mainly because thus far he had eschewed the mentor God had intended for him. Yet something very strange had slowly begun to infect him—that was the subtle influence of one *younger* than himself, and one in his view a mere child at that! The thing was absurd on the face of it, impractical, laughable, unheard of.

And yet. . .he could not deny that the forceful pressure of Gwyneth Barrie's outlook on life and the world had come to exercise a hold on him. She was like no one he had ever met—a mountain-nymph, a fairy-child, a tiny cherub of mystery who roamed fields and hills and ubiquitously turned up in the most unexpected places and said the most unusual things. Yet a fairy-angel with such a sensible streak to her whimsical nature that she asserted with perfect calm and confidence that she could teach him to ride a horse like the wind!

Percy broke out in a peal of laughter at the reminder of Gwyneth's offer. Two or three women glanced toward him from across the street. Young men who walked along laughing to themselves were best avoided. They hurried by, casting him skeptical glances.

Since his walk out of the hills with little Gwyneth, then with the haunting, tear-luring story he had read coming on the heels of it, everything began to *look* different—nature and the faces of humanity most of all. In some inexplicable way, Percy found himself seeing all about him through Gwyneth's fearless, trusting, unassuming pale blue eyes. He found himself wondering what *Gwyneth* would say to this, what *Gwyneth* would think of that, whether she would laugh at something he said or make one of her otherworldly comments that jolted new regions of awareness awake in him.

Percy had walked down to Llanfryniog on this day with neither specific purpose nor destination in mind, thinking simply to explore the town, perhaps walk to the harbor and along the shore. He was not yet a great friend of the sea as are most who live on the borders where water meets land in the daily dance of its tides. But he was *beginning* to love it because he knew from how she gazed across it that Gwyneth loved the sea. Seeing it through her eyes, what could he do but love it? And thus, almost without his realizing it, the sea subtly began to woo him with its hypnotic allure.

He passed several shops as he made his way casually along, looking absently into their windows. As he came to the draper's, he paused. A handsome buggy and single horse stood in the street tied to the rail next to it. In the window a display of brightly colored spools of ribbon caught Percy's eye. He looked down at the clump of flowers in his hand. He was seized with an idea, broke into a smile at the thought, and went into the shop.

The bell above the door rang as he entered. The shopkeeper was engaged across the room with a woman whose back was to him. Beside her, a girl about his own age turned at the tinkling bell. The smile, not yet faded from Percy's lips, met her glance. She thought it meant for her and returned it.

Percy came into the shop, saw a girl smiling at him—and a very pretty one at that—and walked toward her. "Hello," he said pleasantly, mistaking her look. "Are you one of the shopkeepers?"

"Oh, no," she said, laughing lightly. "I'm here with my mother."

"Oh, sorry."

He saw her eyes flit toward the bouquet in his hand.

"For a friend," he said. "I came in to get a piece of ribbon to tie it with."

"A friend. . .a *girl?*"

"How did you guess?" Percy said, laughing.

Now Percy Drummond, when he was not being surly to his father or mother, and though the lines of his countenance were still in the process of developing, was an extraordinarily good-looking young man. His features yet remained a little delicate, even, it might be said, bordering on the feminine. His face did not yet require the razor. A thick clump of light brown hair fell over a low forehead, on this day mostly obscuring the remaining evidence of Courtenay Westbrooke's whip and fist, though the bruise on his cheek was still prominent. His nose and lips and jaw were unremarkable but well-formed, not yet showing the pronounced angles that manhood would bring. In spite of the visible bruise, and in a way perhaps almost enhanced by it, the overall effect, accentuated by a winsome smile, was more than moderately attractive to a young woman of fifteen.

Rhawn Lorimer was exactly such a girl, herself prettier than she had a right to be. The fact that she knew every boy or girl for ten miles around but did not recognize Percy made him all the more interesting in her eyes. And that he was carrying a bouquet for some *other* girl immediately set the wheels of her inquisitive brain spinning about who the lucky recipient might be.

Before she had the chance to coax more information out of him, a tactic at which she was singularly skilled, her mother moved down the counter, occupied in the examination of something she had just been handed, and the shopkeeper behind it addressed an interrogative expression to Percy.

"Hello," said Percy buoyantly. "I saw some ribbon in your window. I would like to get some. How do you sell it?"

"By the foot," replied the woman. "It is over here," she said, leading Percy across the shop. "There are a number of colors. It is a penny a foot."

"Oh, I see. All right, then. . .I think I will take, let me see—" Percy dug in his pocket to see what coins he had. His father hadn't left him much money, but he certainly had enough for a few lengths of ribbon. "I think I would like three feet each of the red, the yellow, and the blue. And would you please cut off six inches from the red. I'll use it right away."

The woman went to find her scissors.

The magistrate's daughter approached Percy again. "That will be a lot of ribbon for such a little bouquet," she said.

"Oh. . .that," said Percy. "I decided to get some extra. The girl I am buying it for will love it."

"She must be a lucky girl."

"Actually, I think I am the lucky one!" Percy laughed.

Unknown to either Percy Drummond or Rhawn Lorimer, Courtenay Westbrooke was riding—calmly and on a different horse than the flighty thoroughbred—through Llanfryniog just about the moment the shopkeeper had spoken to Percy. He was on his way back from Burrenchobay Hall and had taken the long way through the village to check at the post office for his father. For several days the viscount had been impatiently expecting a telegraph from his factor, whom he had sent to London. Courtenay saw the carriage, recognized it, reigned in, tied his horse beside it, and went into the shop.

He came through the door just in time to hear the fading echo of Percy's laugh and to see the answering smile, which he took for one of fascination, on Rhawn Lorimer's face.

Courtenay strode forward but did not look toward the latter in greeting. A thundercloud gathered on his brow.

Percy saw him and turned away. But it was too late. Courtenay grabbed his shoulder from behind and spun him around.

"Hi, Courtenay," said Percy, trying to sound friendly. He had no idea what had caused the angry expression on his cousin's face.

"I thought I told you to stay away from what's mine!" said Courtenay heatedly.

"Uh. . .yes," said Percy in a confused tone. "You made that quite clear. I haven't touched your horse. I haven't so much as looked at it."

"I don't mean that. You stay away from my girl."

"Your. . .girl?"

"That's what I said. I don't want you looking at her any more than I do my horse."

Out of the corner of his eye, Percy saw the horrified look of mingled chagrin and indignation on the girl's face where she stood staring at Courtenay. Immediately he divined the truth. Irritated afresh at Courtenay's bluster and presumption, his calm demeanor left him. "You're not actually telling me that you are comparing *this* beautiful young lady to your horse?" he said, feigning innocence but with obvious sarcasm in his words. "She deserves better than that, Courtenay. I think you owe her an apology."

"What she deserves for talking to the likes of you," Courtenay shot back, "is between her and me, and it is certainly *not* an apology. I am telling you to stay away from her!"

Incensed to hear herself spoken of as if she were chattel, Rhawn Lorimer at last found her voice. "How dare you, Courtenay Westbrooke!" she said. "You have no right to call me your girl."

"What are you then?" rejoined Courtenay brusquely.

"Maybe I don't want to be called your girl any more than I want to be compared to your horse. You have no right to talk to him that way either," she added, glancing toward Percy. "We don't even know each other. He just came into the shop a minute before you. You can't go around yelling at everyone I meet. You owe *him* an apology!"

Momentarily ruffled by the stares of the two women and Miss Lorimer's rebuke, Courtenay realized he might have overreacted. But he was not sufficiently chastened to have learned his lesson. "Look, Drummond," he said, "if you know what's good for you, you will remember what I said. And you," he added, to the girl, "you stay away from him." He turned and stormed out.

Whatever dignity Courtenay Westbrooke may have entered the store with was certainly in tatters as he left. And he had accomplished the shredding entirely on his own. Jealousy is indeed one of the stupidest of demons. The louder it cries, the more it defeats its own ends. By threatening Percy in her presence, Courtenay only succeeded in elevating Rhawn Lorimer's interest in the handsome young stranger a hundredfold. Without his childish rant, she might well have forgotten the incident.

She was not about to forget it now!

Added to Percy's good looks was now the increased fascination of both underdog and forbidden fruit. Thus, as he left the shop a few minutes later with his bouquet and ribbon, her eyes followed him with keen attentiveness and feverish curiosity.

Who could he possibly be?

Twenty-Four

The Magic of the Sea

*P*ercy had planned to ask the shopkeeper who Grannie was that he might deliver his bouquet while it was still fresh. In the flurry of events with Courtenay, however, it slipped his mind. When he remembered, he turned momentarily again toward the shop. But as Courtenay was still in town and just walking into the post up the street, he thought better of it.

He set out instead in the opposite direction and continued on his course from earlier. He passed the chapel and school at the end of the village, followed the bend of the street seaward, and soon found himself approaching the small but serviceable sixteenth-century harbor that was now home to several dozen small fishing vessels.

A week ago, Courtenay's blustering threats would have filled him with anger. But now he could laugh them off. What did he care for his cousin's petty jealousy when there was a world to enjoy!

A few fishermen were about with their boats and nets. Small groups were clustered here and there talking among themselves. It was a small harbor, not in any sense a center for commercial fishing like the more sizable ports of the Wales west coast. But the local fishermen kept families, friends, and nearby villages supplied with fresh mackerel, salmon, and haddock. It therefore served its purpose bravely and kept the worst of the sea's storms from eroding the shoreline—as important a function as providing a home for the many-colored boats that rested in its protected waters when not being employed in the fish-laden waters.

Percy spoke to a few men as he passed. Their greetings were more reserved than those in the upper town, in keeping with the two women who had seen him laughing to himself. These fishermen were a rugged lot who remained wary of strangers considerably longer than did Codnor Barrie's daughter. They eyed him skeptically as he wandered on, all the more so that he was carrying a handful of posies bundled with a short red ribbon. It was not the sort of thing, in their opinion, that *men*, or even boys on the way to becoming men, did. Whoever he was, with that fair face and with flowers in his hand, the lad had sissy written all over him.

Leaving the harbor, men, and boats, Percy made his way along the sandy shoreline, walking southwest at the water's edge in the direction where Mochras Head protruded into Tremadog Bay. As he went, the shoreline rose inward gradually where he came again even with the village. As he continued, it rose to become a hilly bluff then gradually by degrees a sheer cliff that separated sea from the plateau above.

The sea was calm. Its wavelets splashed gently landward, foam-topped, and ran up the gentle incline of sand until, their momentum spent, they slowed and receded back toward their home to meet the next coming toward it in the endless ebb and flow that made the sea, wherever it met land, a *living* thing. The sensations of sound and movement and smell wove their subtly intoxicating spell over the minister's son from Glasgow.

The tide was probably halfway in. Percy walked along perpendicular to it, his shoes imprinting themselves in the wet sand in an uneven line behind him that might have been made by a wobbly drunk as he wandered in and out at the edge of the shallow foamy flow. The rhythmic resonance of the water to his right, the cries of the gulls flying overhead, punctuated by an occasional louder crash of waves on the distant rocks, made a music in his soul different than anything he had heard from the pipe organ in his father's church. It was the music of nature, the symphony of the universe, the sounds of whose instruments he had only lately begun to recognize. He was not merely seeing through Gwyneth's eyes, he was hearing the call of creation through her ears. The sights and sounds of the world were coming *alive* and stirred his heart.

Gradually the sand underfoot gave way to pebbles, then larger rocks, until the beach was no more. Ahead he saw clusters of larger rocks and boulders and seaweed-filled pools and submerged muscle-encrusted stones, with eddies of the tide swirling in and among them with unceasing motion and undulation, where lived a whole oceany universe of tiny creatures. Assuming his way blocked to further exploration, Percy was about to turn back when a sight arrested his attention in the distance.

In the middle of the cliff face that had risen on his left, perhaps half a mile ahead, a speck of white was moving down from the plateau above against the gray of the rocky cliff. At first glance, he took it for a gull. But the back-and-forth movement could surely be no graceful bird in flight. *It must be a sheep,* he thought. As he stared further, however, he realized it was too small for a sheep.

Suddenly he knew that speck of white!

He continued on, stepping carefully across the uneven rocks and stones and climbing around the increasingly difficult obstacles in his path. He slipped a few times as he worked his way through the boulders that filled the space between the water and promontory, doused his boots more than once in slippery tide pools, but finally succeeded in arriving onto the surface of another expanse of flat sandy beach.

By now the promontory on his left had risen to considerable height. Four hundred yards ahead the white head of his mysterious but delightful friend reached the shore.

"Gwyneth!" he yelled and broke into a run toward her.

In truth, Gwyneth's eyes, whether from the second sight or careful observation, had seen Percy on the beach almost the same moment she had begun her descent down the bluff. She was not certain it was Percy. From that distance the features of his face would have been more difficult to descry with certainty than the Irish coastline from the overlook where she and Percy had gazed toward it over the sea.

Her heart beat a little more rapidly at the sight, for she *hoped* it might be him. But she was not sure until he called her name.

Her young heart leaped again. But she did not run across the sand. Rather she continued walking slowly toward him. Her heart had begun to be stirred, too, but for different reasons than Percy's.

Percy reached her a few minutes later. He ran toward her out of breath and stopped. "I can't believe I found you!" he exclaimed. "I had hoped to. I was going to ask in town how to find Grannie, but I forgot. I brought you these." He handed her the bouquet.

Gwyneth blinked back something that sought to rise in her eyes. Flowers always moved her. To her they were tiny windows into the soul of God's creation and made her happy. But flowers exchanged between friends meant even more. She gave flowers all the time. But no one had ever given *her* flowers—no one except Grannie.

Her heart was touched to be on the receiving end of such kindness. "Thank you, Mr. D–D–Drummond," she said softly as she took them. "You are more k–k–kind to me than anyone has ever b–b–been. It is a pretty ribbon."

"Oh yes, I almost forgot!" Percy dug into his pocket. "Look, I bought you some more—three pieces in different colors. I thought you might like to use them when you make your bouquets." He held them out to her.

Gwyneth stared at the lovely gift in disbelief. Was she being given a bouquet and a gift besides?

"Here, take them, Gwyneth," said Percy. "I bought them for you."

"Thank you, M–Mr. Drummond."

"And about this *Mister* Drummond business," laughed Percy. "I thought we settled all that the first time I saw you in the hills. I told you that my friends call me Percy. Surely you qualify as my friend by now! I'm only sixteen—I'm hardly a mister yet. Don't you think you might call me Percy?"

"I can try, Mr. Drummond," said Gwyneth simply. "But it might be hard. You *seem* so much like a man."

Percy laughed again. "I suppose I shall be one someday. But not yet. Just promise me you will try."

"I promise," said Gwyneth. "Would you like to see the cave where I found the pirate's skull?"

The words slammed into Percy's brain as if he had been hit by a train. She could stop a conversation so abruptly with the most unexpected statements!

He stared back with a look of incredulity. "A. . .*pirate's* skull!" he exclaimed.

"That's what Grannie said it was when I told her. Papa didn't believe it. He thought I had seen a dead animal's head. But I knew it was from a man. I could tell. Come, I'll show you where I saw it."

She led him along the beach back toward Llanfryniog. Percy had run right past the cave's mouth only a few minutes before but had not seen it. Moments later they crept into the darkened opening.

"The water is almost too high," said Gwyneth. "I never go inside unless it is low because I don't want to get trapped inside."

"You found a skull in here?" said Percy, his voice echoing into the darkened chamber.

"It was buried in the sand."

"What became of it?"

"I don't know. I've never seen it again. I think the water washed it away. But I have been a *little* afraid to come here since. I have only peeped inside, just in case the pirate is still there. Grannie says there is pirate gold somewhere, if only we could find it."

Was there no end to this girl's surprises?

"Pirates. . .*and gold*!" said Percy.

"That's what Grannie says."

"How does she know?"

"I don't know. Grannie knows many things. But sometimes it is hard to understand what she means."

"Let's go inside and look!" said Percy excitedly.

"I am nervous about the water," said Gwyneth. "It will rise into the cave soon."

"The tide comes in so slow, it won't bother us."

"Sometimes a big wave comes in all at once. It is high enough now that that could happen. I am very small, and I have to be more careful about the water than bigger people. It is too dark to see inside anyway. And there is no gold in the cave. I have been all the way to the back of it."

"How do you see well enough to be certain?" asked Percy.

"When the sun shines exactly right at the end of the summer, it shines all the way to the very back wall. Then you can see everything. That only happens for a few days, when the sun is coming straight into the cave's mouth from the water. That's why I know there is no gold in the cave."

On this day the sun was too high in the sky for its rays to probe inside the cave more than a few feet. Having come out of bright sunlight, all Percy and Gwyneth could see was blackness.

"I think I want to go now," said Gwyneth, walking back outside.

Percy followed, turning the remarkable series of revelations over in his mind. "Where were you coming from," he asked, "when I saw you from back there? It looked like you were climbing down the cliff."

"A trail comes from the top," replied Gwyneth.

"Can you show me? I'll go home that way instead of walking back through the village."

Again they turned along the beach, continuing past the place where two lines of footprints coming from opposite directions still showed the place of their meeting in the sand. They walked past them toward the base of the trail.

"So, Gwyneth Barrie," said Percy as they went, "when will you begin teaching me to ride like the wind?"

"Whenever you like, Mr. Drummond."

Percy looked at her with a stern smile.

"Whenever you like...*Percy*," said Gwyneth shyly, her face reddening.

"That's more like it! How about tomorrow, then?"

"All right."

"Where shall I meet you?"

"On the beach there where you came from," said Gwyneth, pointing back toward the harbor, now probably a mile distant. "Between the harbor and the rocks. Lady Florilyn never walks along the sea. She will not see us there. I don't think she likes the ocean. I love the ocean."

"I know you do. I think you love it because of your mother."

Percy's statement made Gwyneth thoughtful. "I don't know," she said slowly. "I have always loved the water. Perhaps you are right and that is why."

"Then the beach below the village it is," said Percy. "I will be there as soon after breakfast as I can get away. I will ask Mr. Radnor to saddle a horse for me."

They made their way up the steep trail from the beach to the plateau above, then struck out across the open moorland in a direction that led toward Westbrooke Manor and finally parted.

TWENTY-FIVE

Secrets of Nature

*A*s soon as he had finished breakfast on the following morning, Percy slipped out of the house for the stables. He had never yet seen Florilyn in the breakfast room. She was not an early riser. To his relief this day was no exception.

Hollin Radnor was out with Stuart Wyckham pruning some of the hedges around one of the gardens after their vigorous spring growth.

Percy walked toward the two men. "Good morning, Mr. Radnor," he said cheerfully. "I think I am ready for another ride. Would you mind helping me saddle a horse?"

"Certainly, Mr. Percy," replied the groom. He set aside the shears. "I will be back in a few minutes, Stuart," he said.

Then he and Percy walked together toward the stables.

"Fine day indeed for a ride, Mr. Percy," said Radnor as they went. "Going out alone, are you?"

"For now," replied Percy. "Though I suppose you never know who might turn up, eh?"

"Which horse do you fancy, sir?"

"The gentle one you recommended before. Grey Tide, I believe she was called. I got on well enough that first day. I'm not keen on going out on Red Rhud again!"

"Yes, sir—I heard what happened. I would have prevented that unpleasantness if I had been able, Mr. Percy."

"Well, no harm done. I survived it. Still, I think a gentler mount will suit me until I am a little steadier in the saddle."

"Grey Tide is a wise choice, Mr. Percy. You will do fine on her back."

Fifteen minutes later, after a detailed lesson in horse saddling, Percy rode off in the direction of town. The morning was still chilly. But Percy was full of the jubilation of life, added to by the exhilaration of sneaking away from the manor without Florilyn knowing it. Exuberantly he even encouraged Grey Tide into a trot two or three times on the way down to Llanfryniog. He was still timid about allowing the mare to cantor or gallop. Hopefully before long, with Gwyneth's coaching, that would change.

He found Gwyneth walking along the shore south of the harbor waiting for him. He rode up beside her, reined in, and dismounted. "Good morning, Gwyneth," he said. "It looks to be another fine day."

"And the tide is low," she said, turning toward him with a smile. "It is good for riding."

"Do you ride here often?"

"We do not have a horse. I do not have many chances to ride."

"But you know how to?"

"Horses are my friends. I have always known how to ride."

"Well then, teacher," said Percy with humor in his tone, though he meant the word with an endearing respect, "how do we begin?"

"You must show me how you ride first," said Gwyneth. "I have seen you from far away. Now I want to see you close."

"I shouldn't have dismounted," Percy said, laughing. "I still have a hard enough time getting in the saddle." With some difficulty he climbed back up. "What do you want me to do?" he said.

"Can you gallop?" asked Gwyneth.

"I've never galloped on purpose," answered Percy. "The only time I've ridden fast was on Red Rhud, and she threw me off!"

"Can you try?"

"I will try."

Gwyneth stepped back.

Percy gave a few kicks into Grey Tide's flanks and flipped at the reins. Grey Tide eased forward into a gentle cantor then gradually, as Percy kicked harder, into a halfhearted gallop, with Percy bouncing clumsily about in the saddle. He reined back after a short distance, turned the mare around, and returned to where Gwyneth stood. He stopped and looked down at her.

"To ride fast," she said, "you need to lean forward. You sit up too straight. That's why you bounce around. If you are bouncing up and down, the horse knows you aren't secure. If it knows that, either it won't do what you want or you will fall off."

"I'm *not* secure!" Percy laughed.

"But you will be. When you are secure, the horse will know it. Then it will do what you tell it. So first you must lean forward. And sit higher in the saddle, with your knees bent. You must feel the horse with your knees, not your bottom."

Percy tried to adjust himself.

Gwyneth continued to suggest this or that until she was satisfied with his seat for the present. "When you want her to go," she went on, "press into her sides with your heels. Don't kick—just press in with your heels and knees and lean forward. Then talk to her, tell her to run, and stroke her neck."

"Why don't you show me?" said Percy. He jumped down.

"You'll have to help me get up," said Gwyneth.

Percy took her foot in his hand. She reached up for the saddle with her hands as he lifted her. She was so unexpectedly light that he nearly flung her up and over the top. But Gwyneth recovered and landed gently in the saddle with the grace of a cat. Her feet did not reach Percy's stirrups, but she hardly noticed.

She took told of the reins, then leaned forward, stroked the big mare's neck, and spoke a few whispered words into her ear. "Now watch, Percy," she said. "I will press in with my knees to keep me balanced.

I am hardly touching the saddle, you see. . .and give her a little nudge in the sides with my heels, and lean forward. . ." She spoke again into the mare's ear, "Dash on, Grey Tide. . .dash on!"

Though her command was soft, Grey Tide bounded with several steps into gentle motion. Quickly the pace increased. Within seconds she was at top speed and flying away from Percy down the wide sand glistening wet from the retreating tide. Huge clumps flew up behind her hooves as their echoes pounded through the morning air.

Percy gazed after her in astonishment that one so small could command such a powerful beast with so few words and movements. Until that moment, he had taken the proposed riding lessons more as a lark than that he really thought he could ever beat Florilyn in a race. Suddenly he realized, all things being equal, Florilyn would have no chance against Gwyneth. So why couldn't he learn to ride as fast as she?

Had it not been for the rocks and boulders enclosing the harbor portion of the beach to the south, Grey Tide and her tiny white-haired rider would have quickly disappeared from sight. As it was, while he stared in wonder, Percy saw them make a wide semicircular arc on the sand that, because of the tide, was fifty or seventy-five yards wide. Gradually they came flying straight back toward him again.

Horse and rider were truly one. The motion of Gwyneth's tiny frame flowed in a harmony of exquisite precision with Grey Tide's movement. Elbows out, knees flexed, her frame parallel with the horse's great neck, her body floated with fluid ease as if riding on a cushion of air. As they flew toward him, Gwyneth slowed the mare so gradually that Percy never once saw her use the reins.

A few seconds later, the huge horse stood panting beside him, great puffs of white pulsing from her nostrils in the chilly morning air. Gwyneth's face was flushed with animation, her eyes wide with joy, a smile of ecstasy on her lips.

"Gwyneth," exclaimed Percy, "that was marvelous! I had no idea you could ride so fast."

"I told you I could ride fast."

"Yes, but. . .*that* fast! I've never seen anything like it. How do you do it?"

"When you move up and down, holding by your knees instead of bouncing in the saddle, in exact rhythm with Grey Tide's back, she will scarcely feel you. Then you will be able to ride as fast as me."

"I can't imagine that," Percy laughed.

"Your motion must be smooth with hers," said Gwyneth. "She will not feel you. She will be free. When Grey Tide is free, there is no horse at the manor faster. Now you try it again," she added, swinging one leg up and around the mare's back and slipping to the ground.

Again Percy mounted.

"Remember, feel Grey Tide's motion," said Gwyneth. "Move gently up and down. Do not let her feel you bounce in the saddle."

For the next hour, Percy rode up and down the beach, sometimes fast, sometimes slow, trying to follow Gwyneth's instructions. She watched and told him this or that to try next. By the end of his first lesson, he did not feel much improvement. Although he had begun to know what she meant when she spoke of moving in concert with the rhythm of the horse, to achieve his goal would take much practice.

They parted, and Percy rode back through town. By now the morning was well advanced. The sun was high and warming the earth, luring from the grass and trees and shrubs and dirt and water the fragrances of the wonderful time of late spring that was the month of June. For the first time in his life, Percy felt relaxed and confident enough on the back of a horse to enjoy himself. It was still early. He was not anxious to return to the manor. Instead he struck out inland over moor and field toward the hills east. He was curious whether he could find Gwyneth's special high place with the spectacular view.

He rode slowly up the plateau. After a good deal of exploration along the ridge, he found the spot he had been looking for. He dismounted, tied the horse, and sat down looking out over the sloping plateau and coastline.

His mood grew thoughtful. His father came to his mind. With

it floated into his consciousness an unexpected sense of fondness. Poignantly Percy realized that things were changing within him. Thoughts of his father were no longer irksome in his memory. Instead they drew him with emotions he had not felt in years. It reminded him of how much he had once loved his father and enjoyed nothing more than being with him.

Where had these new feelings come from? What could be the cause of these strange sensations? Were they really *new*…or was he just feeling again sensations he had lost from long before?

A hunger after something beyond him, something he could not have described, had come awake in his heart. When it had begun, he could not have said. Once he was aware of it, he realized it had been there from his first week here. It was, in fact, the beginning of the greatest transformation in all the universe, though Percy did not yet know it as such. He had heard his father preach about such things. He had never dreamed that the very movements of soul his father described would one day come upon him.

Was Wales the cause of it—the walk through the hills with Gwyneth… lying on the top of the ridge, at this very place, overlooking the moor and sea and sky…walking along the sand at the water's edge…seeing the faces of humanity through newly loving eyes—or had it begun even before?

He came to feel a strange mystery in the world. It seemed full of meaning, yet a meaning he could not lay hold of. He perceived a whispering of unknown secrets in the wind that now came up the moor from the sea to greet him. He was stung with a consciousness of inexplicable rapture at the cry of a gull or the song of robin and sparrow. He took joy in every sunrise, felt a poignant sadness in the oranges and purples and reds of the sunset. He felt there must be something wonderful beyond and inside and above him. What could he do but ask, "What can it all mean?"

Wherever he turned, the bewitching loveliness in the face of the world met him. The scents the wind carried from field and forest and sea were sweeter than ever wind-borne scents from Glasgow's streets and lanes and the deserted alleys he had roamed during the darkest days of his prodigality.

He sat on the high ridge for perhaps an hour. When he remounted Grey Tide and started back down the hill, he was still not ready to return to the manor. He was too *full*. The last thing he wanted now was to run into Florilyn or Courtenay or his uncle.

He descended the ridge and made his way across the plateau, then struck out along the promontory of Mochras Head. By now the tide was well on its way in, the beach below where he had walked with Gwyneth yesterday almost covered. The splashing and crashing of the waves against the rocks below echoed up and met him and filled his consciousness with the undefined pleasure of being.

As he went, the breeze coming off the water braced his face with a welcome chill, as if it had something to say. The sea glistened below as if it knew something it would be good for him to know. Its waves broke on the shore with words in a strange tongue he could not understand. Their watery echoes plunged into his heart and made him both happy and sad.

Creation reveals itself in secrets, but as secrets that are outer cloaks of truths waiting to be discovered. All around, in leaf and grass and cloud and rain and flower, the world whispered into his heart. It said that life could be a good thing, and that somehow God was in it all.

The world suddenly seemed so full of joy. But in truth the joy he felt was within *him*. Something was coming awake in the soul of Percival Drummond, something that had lain as an embryo of God's creation, waiting to flex the seed-life of its being and break the sleepy shell of its chrysalis, that a new and higher form of being might emerge. What was it but *life* itself struggling to come awake within him.

He had begun to uncover the truths that lay beneath creation's secrets.

TWENTY-SIX

Secrets of Man

While Percy was riding along the headland, Lord Snowdon sat in his study perusing the telegram that had finally arrived from London the previous afternoon. He had been stewing over it ever since.

Not only had Heygate learned that Palmer Sutcliffe was business manager for mining magnate Lord Coleraine Litchfield, but he was a forty-two-year-old business manager at that. He was a young man in the prime of his career. The fellow was a Londoner, born and bred, had probably never been to North Wales in his life. . .and was certainly not on the verge of retiring so that he could spend his leisure time in some cozy little cottage nestled in the Snowdonian mountains!

The letter from Sutcliffe had been a ruse, a fabrication of lies from beginning to end!

Litchfield's interests, for such the fellow Sutcliffe was certainly representing, were in mining. Neither was Sutcliffe's boss anticipating retirement anytime soon. Whatever he was up to had profit at the bottom of it, not nostalgia for the bygone happiness of childhood.

What did they take him for—a fool whom they could scam into selling off a piece of property for a few shillings? Whatever it was they thought lay beneath his property—and the logical assumption was coal—he wasn't about to let some greedy Englishman waltz in and help himself!

It was time for a response. The viscount wrote:

Dear Mr. Sutcliffe,

It has come to my attention that you represent Lord Coleraine Litchfield in his business dealings and mining interests. I have only to assume, therefore, as you do not appear near retirement age yourself, that your recent letter expressing the desire to purchase a small portion of my land was sent on behalf of Lord Litchfield.

Is his motive personal, or do business pursuits make my land of interest to him?

I am,
Sincerely yours,
Viscount Roderick Westbrooke

A week later he received the following reply:

The Right Honorable, the Viscount Roderick Westbrooke,
Lord Snowdon.
My Lord,

Please forgive the subterfuge of our previous correspondence. I asked my manager and assistant Mr. Sutcliffe to draft the letter you received, expressing sentiments that are dear to my heart. Knowing the speculation my name invariably raises because of my extensive business interests throughout Britain, I told him to make the request in his own name. It was foolish of me. I see now that I was wrong not to be entirely candid with a man of your experience and good reputation. I apologize. Rest assured, however, that my motives are as stated, and my interest genuine.

Despite the fact that we have gotten off, as it were, on the wrong foot with one another, I hope you will consider this a new

beginning and will consider my request to purchase a piece of your
land as outlined in the previous letter with sincerity.

I am,
Humbly yours,
Lord Coleraine Litchfield

By now, however, having stewed on the matter for another week and having carried out further research, Westbrooke's suspicions had nowise been alleviated. Indeed, they were greater than ever.

As a result, Litchfield received a second and more pointed communication from Lord Snowdon:

Lord Coleraine Litchfield,
My Lord,

I am deeply appreciative of the straightforward manner in which you have explained the letter from Mr. Sutcliffe. While I can assure you that I am not on principle opposed to selling a small portion of acreage from my estate and would happily entertain an offer, I would have to know more details regarding your purpose in such a proposed transaction. The image of a cozy retirement cottage nestled in the mountains is appealing. My instincts, however, tell me that there must be more to it than that and that the candor you spoke of has probably not yet been entirely forthcoming.

I remain,
Sincerely yours,
Viscount Roderick Westbrooke

Litchfield swore lightly as he read; then his fist slammed down on his desk. This was not going to be as easy as he had hoped. He would have to consider his next move with care. To tell this provincial Westbrooke *everything* could spell doom to his whole scheme.

TWENTY-SEVEN

Shoes, Horses, and Friends

*C*odnor Barrie's daughter usually kept to the side streets when walking through Llanfryniog. Thankfully Grannie's cottage lay where she could easily reach it and keep mostly out of sight.

This girl of far-seeing eye but faltering tongue could welcome harshness from the elements of God's world with glee. But meanness from those of her own kind was a harshness far different that she could not understand. She was child enough to be hurt by the lashes of unkind tongues. She thus kept to herself within the shadows of the village, although this habit contributed all the more to her reputation among the more low-minded of its inhabitants.

She climbed, on this summer's day, from the grass and rocks down to the southern sandy tip of the Mochras Head beach, removing her shoes the moment she hit bare sand, and now wandered along it northward in the direction of the village. She climbed through the rocks halfway along more easily with bare feet than Percy had with his shoes. Before reaching the harbor in which the few boats were tied at the northeast end of the protected bay, she turned and scampered up the beach onto one of Llanfryniog's outlying dirt streets, still carrying her shoes. From there she ran in the direction of Grannie's cottage.

A few jeers and taunts came flying as she passed, mostly from school classmates, whose idleness led them to no good. But a friendly voice soon brought her swift barefoot steps to a stop.

"Hey there, young lady," it said. "Where'll you be bound in such a hurry?"

Gwyneth turned toward the wide doors of the blacksmith's shop, which stood open to the day's sunshine. "H–h–hello, Mr. Radnor," she said as she caught her breath. "I'm on my way to Grannie's."

"She's a fine woman, your Grannie."

"N–not everyone thinks so," replied Gwyneth, walking toward the Westbrooke groom, one of her few friends in the place.

"Not everyone has eyes to see people as they are," he rejoined with a smile. "But I know what she's made of. Are you taking your shoes to the cobbler?" he added, nodding toward her hands. "He won't be working today, I'm thinking."

"No. I took them off s–s–so I could feel the sand in my t–t–toes."

"The sand is one thing, hard streets are another."

"The shoes are more uncomfortable than the stones. I'd n–n–never wear shoes if I didn't have to!"

"The mare's done," said a voice behind them. The next moment appeared from the shadows the hulking form of the smithy. With a blackened leather apron tied around his thick waist, rippling muscular chest and arms bare and perspiring from his work over the fiery forge, leather reins held in his gloved hands, the huge man led the horse out into the street with a slow *clop, clop, clop* behind him. His great black eyebrows creased and his eyes darkened as he saw with whom his customer had taken up conversation. He handed the reins to the groom and turned inside without another word.

"You see you're not the only one concerned about shoes," said Radnor as he began walking along the street with Gwyneth at his side. "But I came to the horse cobbler to get a *new* set of shoes for Red Rhud, not get them taken *off* like you did yours. Would you like to lead her?"

"Oh, yes!" exclaimed Gwyneth. "M–m–may I really?"

With a smile, the groom handed her the reins.

Gwyneth dropped her two shoes on the hard-packed dirt then took the reins with one hand and with the other gently stroked the long face and nose and whispered a few unintelligible words to the mare.

Radnor picked up her shoes and resumed on his way.

Gwyneth followed, speaking quietly to the great beast at her side. Despite her occasionally wild behavior with a rider on her back, the huge mare gave every appearance of being perfectly content to be led by such a tiny girl. "W–why does Red Rhud need new shoes?" asked Gwyneth at length.

"To keep from picking up pebbles and getting bruises in her hooves."

"Don't the nails hurt?" said Gwyneth, who had watched the shoeing process many times at her father's side.

"Nay, lassie. The smithy-cobbler knows what's good for horses. He would never hurt them. It's like our own Master does—sometimes things that *look* like they hurt keep us from worse trouble in the end."

"That's like something Grannie would say."

"A fine and a wise woman," rejoined the groom. "She's one who knows the ways of the Master. And, young lady," he added, "it seems we're nearly to her door." He took several steps toward the cottage in front of them then called into its open door, "I brought you a visitor, Mrs. Barrie!"

An elderly woman appeared a moment later. She shielded her eyes from the sun as she emerged from inside. "Who's your great friend there, Gwyneth dear?" she said.

"Red Rhud, Grannie."

A smile spread across the old woman's face. She and the groom shook hands and exchanged a few words. "Won't you join Gwyn and me for tea, Mr. Radnor?" she asked.

"You sorely tempt me, Mrs. Barrie," he replied. "I fear my charge here would lose her patience. She'll already be wanting her oats, I'm thinking."

"Then you must come back another time."

"I promise." He nodded as he took the reins from the girl's hand.

"And here will be *your* shoes, young lady," he said.

"Thank you for letting me hold the reins, M–Mr. Radnor."

The groom chuckled, gave Grannie a wink, then continued out of town.

Gwyneth and the old woman went inside.

Twenty-Eight

Sabbath

*T*he day happened to be a Sunday, the Calvinist "Sabbath" for those attending the worship service at the Methodist chapel at the north end of town, and in the two houses of worship to the south, "Holy Day" for the Anglicans and "High Mass" for the Catholics.

Percy Drummond had been in North Wales three weeks. After declining two previous invitations, he had at last decided to accompany his aunt and uncle and cousins to church. Being of the aristocracy, they were staid and respectable members of the Church of England.

All the shops of the village were of course closed. But Kyvwlch Gwarthegydd, blacksmith and village atheist, made certain that he was vigorously and noisily at work in his blacksmith's shop every Sunday between the hours of ten o'clock and noon. Any home or farm for probably three miles north, south, or east, might set their clocks weekly to the 10:00 a.m. hour. At the very moment Big Ben began to strike in Westminster, the rhythmic *clank, clank, clank* of hammer on anvil likewise began to toll loudly from Gwarthegydd's shop. His choice of this hour was chosen because it was at ten o'clock that the first of the three church bells pealed out from the Methodist chapel, and he did his best every Sunday to drown them out. He was mostly successful, too, as he was at 11:00 a.m., when the two dissonant knells from opposing sides of the street at the opposite end of town announced the commencement of their services.

The clanking continued, on and off, for the duration of all three services, to the supreme annoyance of the more spiritually minded of the clergy and laity of Llanfryniog. They considered the sound to be the very drumbeat of the devil from hell itself standing in brazen opposition to the truth of almighty God, whose existence the heathen blacksmith so flagrantly denied. Not a few sermons through the years had used the background discord as a fitting object lesson to rail against those who openly mocked God and the fiery retribution of judgment that awaited them.

Neither did Hollin Radnor often spend his Sundays in church. He did not as a rule find God's presence much in evidence in any of Llanfryniog's three houses of worship. He visited them all from time to time, not so much looking for God, for the groom knew where *He* was to be found, but looking for kindred hearts that might know Him after the same manner in which he had himself grown to know Him. It was not an enterprise that had been crowned with much success through the years, but he remained hopeful of occasionally discovering such a one. No doubt that he was doctrinally fluid and nonsectarian in his acceptance of the men and women from all three congregations contributed in large measure to the fact that none of them accepted him as one of them. In such assemblies, it was always who was "one of us," not who was "one of God's."

In fact, there was no man to be found in all Snowdonia who *knew* God on the intimate footing of daily obedience more than did Lord Snowdon's humble groom. As is often the case in such instances of godliness, however, few recognized that fact. As he left Grannie's cottage and made his way back up the street and out of town on the back of the newly shod bay mare, he was surprised to see the manor's three cousins walking along toward him.

"Good day to you, Master Courtenay, Miss Florilyn, and Master Percy," he said, tipping his hat as he passed.

Percy greeted him warmly. A patronizing nod was all that came his way from the other two.

The appearance of the three youths a few minutes after noon on the main street of Llanfryniog was not difficult to explain. It being a warm day, as they were approaching the buggy at the conclusion of the morning's service, Percy announced that he was going to walk home. Having nothing better to do, and vaguely thinking that perhaps it might present her an opportunity to get back at Percy somehow for the grudge she was still nursing against him, Florilyn said she would join him. Inwardly chagrined at the thought, Percy could hardly object.

Instead of following the direct route home, it was Percy's intent to take the long way round along the beach and, if the tide was low enough to permit passage through the rocks near the cave, to continue on and up the bluff path. It only took a moment's reflection to cause him to relish the thought of Florilyn trying to keep pace with him over the rocks and through the tide pools in her Sunday shoes. He and Florilyn, therefore, set off toward town.

They were surprised a few seconds later to hear Courtenay's steps running to catch them. Upon reflection, he thought the day might present an admirable opportunity to visit the Lorimer home, *without* Percy in tow, and soothe whatever ruffled feathers might remain between himself and the magistrate's daughter.

Roderick and Katherine Westbrooke found themselves in consequence riding home in the buggy alone.

TWENTY-NINE

Homegoing

*O*n this same day in Glasgow, a faithful minister who had given his life in service to the Church of Scotland was struggling mightily to reach the end of the morning's service.

The day's reading had been taken from the fifteenth chapter of the Gospel of Luke. He had managed, with more than one throaty hesitation, to get through the poignant passage of scripture. But the sermon had progressed with increasing difficulty.

He had, of course, anticipated for some time that this Sunday was coming and known what would be the morning's text. He had agonized over it all week. More than once he had all but decided on the coward's way out of his intensely personal difficulty. He would have one of the church elders give the New Testament reading. That would keep him from having to utter the words in public that stabbed his heart with pain: "*I will arise and go to my father, and will say unto him, Father, I have sinned....*"

Avoiding the text itself, he would then dust off one of the stale sermons from his seminary days, written with the intent of impressing professors rather than moving hearts. Or perhaps he would follow the script in one of a half dozen volumes on his shelf of sermon outlines and notes. He would gloss over the powerful passage with a few dusty truisms. His words would thus be guaranteed to keep his own tears at bay and, at the same time, to put his listeners to sleep. One thing they would certainly never do was rouse so much as a flutter of homegoing, right-making conscience-movement in the heart of whatever unrepentant prodigals might be listening in his congregation.

He knew as well as any man who had asked God for insight into the human condition that prodigals of all ages were alive and well in his parish. He knew that thirty-, forty-, and fifty-year-old prodigals needed to repent no less than their younger counterparts, before the matter of their prodigality became of internal import. Some, it was true, delayed their homecoming until it was too late to say the healing words. How deep must be their grief and how bitter their tears before God to realize their fathers were no longer alive to receive them into a loving embrace.

Still...such must repent and arise...they *must* repent and go to their fathers.

Homegoing is imperative, whether in this life or the next. Homegoing is the eternal imperative, the overarching *must* of the universe.

How fortunate for those thirty-, forty-, fifty-, and even sixty-year-old prodigals, perhaps who have grown comfortable in their prodigality, who awake, alas, late in life, but not *too* late, thank God, with their fathers still alive. For they could go to their aging parents, hearts of young and old breaking together, and whisper the eternal words, "I have sinned." However late it comes, they have the opportunity to hear the father's long-awaited, "I love you, my child. You have always been forgiven. Welcome home."

Yet for most of his listening prodigals, those who bury the rebellion of youth in the deep recesses of consciousness as a blurry dream from long ago, it was easy to allow life simply to "go on" and not look back. These never face the heart-probing reality of what their words and actions inflicted into the hearts of those who sacrificed themselves on the altar of parenthood. Many indeed drift back into relationship with their elders on such a superficial foundation. In the presumed maturity of their own adulthood, the hostility of early years fading, they assume it enough to be on "speaking terms." But as long as the underlying schism remains unhealed, it is *not* enough. Relational drift cannot eradicate the roots of rebellion. Only repentance can accomplish that. Outwardly respectable, these never take account before God for the hubris of their early years with the words, "Father, Mother. . .I sinned against you. I am sorry. I want to be a true son, a true daughter to you for the years I have left."

The vicar knew there were such comfortable prodigals in his church, because they existed everywhere. As the consequences of this unseen prodigality swirled through his mind, the question rose in the heart of Edward Drummond: Could he, in good conscience, deny them the opportunity of being challenged to "arise and go" because of the frail tenderness of his own suffering father's heart? In the end, he had realized that the answer was no. He had to issue the challenge of Luke 15, whatever it might cost him personally.

And surely it *would* cost him. The image of father and repentant son was too personal, too close to his own breaking heart. Yes, it would *cost* him! But he could not shirk his duty. He could not shirk the truth. Thus he would not shirk the challenge.

With that decision came an even greater realization. He had to confront the reality of Luke 15 for *himself*. With his own son adrift in prodigality, did he, Edward Drummond. . .did *he* still believe in God's goodness, in God's infinite fatherhood, in the welcoming embrace of the Eternal Heart of Forgiveness?

He could only answer that question by confronting the Fatherhood of Luke 15 in all the anguish it might cause his own heart and in all the glory of its eternal resolution.

Truly no man nor woman can apprehend the full pathos of the prodigal story who has not stood as the waiting, praying, seeking, hurting, eager, long-suffering, grief-stricken, shattered yet patient parent of Luke 15—who has not stood on the road day after day, wept night after night, and gone out again morning after morning to stand on the road. . .waiting for the return of son or daughter.

THIRTY

Grannie

 *A*fter leaving church and passing Hollin Radnor on his way out of town, the three cousins from Westbrooke Manor made their way casually through Llanfryniog's streets. A few others were out, mostly young boys with nothing on their minds other than that favorite pursuit of the weak-minded—seeing what amusement might chance their way now that they had been released from the prison of Sunday morning.

Still not having seen much of the town, Percy struck off the main street with Florilyn trailing after him. Courtenay followed as well since they were moving in a general direction that would take him where he was bound. Soon they were lost in a maze of twisting and turning lanes and streets.

Percy paused to stare down a side street where an oddly shaped purplish building caught his eye. Brother and sister continued sauntering along. They came to an open door through which they heard the *whirrrrrr* of a spinning wheel.

"Look, Florilyn," said Courtenay. "The old witch is spinning."

A girl walked out the door. When she saw who was standing in front of her, she turned and hurried back inside. But it was too late.

"Hey, th–th–there, funny-looking little Gw–Gw–*Gwy–neth*!" taunted

166

Courtenay. "Visiting the old w–w–w–witch today?"

Florilyn laughed at what she supposed her brother's wit.

Gwyneth turned and planted her feet firmly. "G–G–Grannie's not a w–w–witch!" she said. "Y–y–you should be ashamed of yourself, M–M–Master C–C–Courtenay!"

"Did you hear th–th–that, Florilyn?" laughed Courtenay. "This little brat thinks I ought to be ashamed of myself! You know what I think?" he added, turning back toward Gwyneth and glaring down at her. "I think it's *you* who's the w–w–w–witch! Ha! Ha! Ha!"

By now Percy was approaching and saw who they were talking to. "Cut it out, Courtenay," he said. "She meant no harm. Hello, Gwyneth," he said, smiling down at her.

"She's just the little village idiot—that's what she is."

"Leave her alone," repeated Percy.

"What—is she a friend of yours now?"

"That's right—she's a friend of mine."

"So that's how it is! That explains everything," laughed Courtenay. "I'm hardly surprised. And she *is* a witch. Didn't you hear her stutter?"

"That doesn't make anyone a witch."

"Listen to the city boy!" Courtenay spat back. "Even if she's not a witch, she's a half-wit." He touched his index finger to the side of his head and winked at his sister.

"I tell you there's nothing wrong with her," said Percy angrily. "That's the trouble with cowards like you, Courtenay. You don't know how to pick on someone your own size."

"You're calling me a coward?"

"For making fun of a girl half your size—that's exactly what you are."

The words were unwisely spoken. Seconds later Percy found himself on the ground groaning. A little more on his guard after the incident in the barn, this time he managed to sidestep the quick jab from his cousin's hand. But Courtenay was not merely bigger than Percy, he was twice as cunning. Missing with his fist, he gave a lethal swipe with his foot. Percy's legs went out from under him, and the next instant

Courtenay's booted foot landed two well-placed kicks into the side of his ribs.

Brother and sister continued on their way laughing at the two fools behind them.

Percy rolled over and tried to sit up in the dirt of the street, while Gwyneth ran inside the cottage. A moment later she stooped beside him, this time with no fistful of flowers but holding a moist cloth. She handed it to him. He took it with a smile of gratitude and wiped at his dust-covered face.

His two cousins were not yet out of sight. Glancing back and witnessing the tender scene, they could not keep themselves from the temptation to add insult to injury. They walked back toward the cottage.

"Percy, Percy, baby Percy!" chanted Courtenay. "Witch girl taking care of baby boy from the city!"

Florilyn was laughing so hard by now that she could scarcely contain herself. This was sweeter revenge than she had hoped for!

Suddenly a great shooing and scurrying interrupted the laughter and taunts. A woman by appearances ancient beyond years ran from the cottage with a torrent of shouts. In truth she was but eighty-one, old enough to be wise yet still robust enough to hold her own against the viscount's troublesome brood. She held a great broom in her hand and came flying into the street like an old Celtic warrior from whose stock she had come. Heedless of their father's status in the region, she whacked and swatted at the two young Westbrookes, whose character she knew well enough. "Get away from here, you two troublemakers!" she cried, landing a powerful blow with the blunt handle of her weapon on Courtenay's head.

"Ouch. . .hey, you old witch!" he shouted, jumping back. "Stop it! I'll send my father down here after you."

"I'll give him the same," shot back the woman, "if he tries to harm a hair on another body's head!"

Wham! came another strike from the broom.

"Get on home! You two are no better than a couple of street urchins!

Whatever happened to gentlemen and ladies?"

"Come on, Florilyn," said Courtenay. Now that he had recovered himself, he found himself a little cowed by the rumors he had heard of the old woman. "Let's leave Percy to the two witches."

They ran off down the street, laughing again, though not quite so gaily. They were superstitious enough to be nervous about having a run-in on God's day with one of the devil's presumed workers of iniquity.

Gwyneth took Percy by the hand and tried to pull him to his feet.

"Goodness, goodness!" said the old woman, out of breath from the battle. "Come inside, the two of you. What you need, young man, is some strong hot tea."

"Grannie, this is my friend, Mr. Drummond," said Gwyneth as they entered the darkened cottage. "He's from Glasgow."

"Is he now! Well then, welcome to Grannie's house, Mr. Drummond," she said as Percy followed them inside. "You must have these violets I picked just this morning," she added. She set down the weapon-broom and took a tiny clump of purple from a water dish on the table. "No stranger comes to my house without flowers to make a friend of him."

Percy and Gwyneth glanced toward one another and smiled.

"Thank you," said Percy. He took the tiny bouquet and lifted them to his nose as he sat down on the straight wood chair the woman pulled toward him. "Are you Gwyneth's grandmother?"

"No, young man, I am Gwyneth's great-great-aunt. Her father is the grandson of my husband's brother. They're all gone now to their home with the Lord, all except the lad, Gwyneth's daddy."

The old woman set about the tea making. At her side, Gwyneth assisted with the familiar routine.

"I hear rumors," said Grannie as she worked, never embarrassed to speak her mind before either lord or peasant and especially before friend, "that in Glasgow you're not much better than your two cousins." As she spoke she glanced over her shoulder to where her guest sat holding the wet cloth to his face.

Percy was so shocked by the unexpected words that he did not answer at first. His only reply came in the form of the reddening of his cheeks.

"Sometimes the Lord must turn the tables on us," she went on, "so that we see ourselves as we really are." She glanced toward Percy again. This time she gazed deeply into his eyes. "No," she added with a knowing nod, "you are not one of them. The difference is not hard to see. You've just been a mite confused about some things. But there's the look in your eye of one who knows right from wrong. You are of the truth, I'm thinking."

Grannie sat down and said nothing more. Gradually she seemed to drift away to some distant time in the past.

Gwyneth quietly finished the tea preparations. She handed a cup to Percy then laid the tray on a small table beside Grannie's chair.

Percy remained thoughtful over Grannie's words. He *did* know right from wrong. The woman was right. He had been no better than his cousins. He deserved more than just a kick in the ribs. He deserved to be in the gaol right now. He would be, too, if his father wasn't a respected vicar.

Gwyneth had inherited Grannie's straightforward tongue as well as the Celtic clarity of her vision. "What's bothering you, Grannie?" she asked after a few more minutes. "Why are you so quiet?"

"Did you not hear about poor old Sean Drindod, dear?"

Gwyneth nodded. "Papa told me."

"He and I were two of the few left from the old century, you know," said Grannie. "When someone you've known all your life goes on to their next home, it makes a body thoughtful."

Percy detected from her tone and the faraway expression that had come over her countenance that there was more behind the old woman's mood than her brief explanation revealed.

Thirty-One

A God to Call Father

By the time Sunday came to Glasgow, the vicar doubted he would survive the morning without tears.

"My friends," his message had begun, "I would like to speak to you this morning about reconciliation. It is what the Bible calls *unity*."

He paused to allow the word to sink in. He was also trying to settle his own thoughts.

"I believe," Drummond went on, "that unity is what God cares about more than anything in the world. Jews the world over remind themselves daily that God is one.

"It is a mighty truth—God is *one*. God's nature is singleness, oneness. . .unity. For things to be one as God intends. . .for relationships within God's creation to reflect their Creator, all discord, all separation, all disharmony. . .these must be brought together, made *one*. Everything in life, everything in the world, must be made one, because God is one.

"Reconciliation is the goal and purpose of God's heart. He would have His created beings reconciled with His Father-heart. That is the ultimate oneness, the ultimate unity. Until this reconciliation is perfected between God and His created universe, all within that creation is at strife."

Drummond paused and drew in a deep breath. His eyes closed briefly then opened, and he continued. "But this unity is not a reconciliation that can take place in some grand and sweeping way between *mankind* and God. It is a reconciliation that takes place individually—one man, one woman at a time. It takes place in *my* heart, not mankind's heart. And it takes place in *your* heart, not the whole world's heart.

"If God is anything," he went on, "He is our Father. We have in this parable before us no mere story of a broken family. Our Lord here offers us a picture of the entire scope of the human drama. In a mere twenty verses, we are given a microcosm of the grand epic of the biblical saga. A loving father gives his children all they could ask for. Instead of being content with this provision, one decides to seek his fortune outside the loving abundance of this home. He squanders the inheritance that is his, at length returns to his father, repents of his foolishness, and is happily restored.

"This morning, however, it is not the son's sin that I want us to focus on, but rather the father of this wonderful parable. For if we can truly see into the heart of this man whom Jesus described, we discover a picture of God found nowhere else in the Bible.

"Look, my friends—see the parable with new eyes. How does *God* respond when we return to Him?

"The Lord's words tell us God's response upon the return of a single wayward prodigal to his father's home. They are more beautiful even than the son's humble repentance. They are among the most important words in the Bible, for they tell us what God is like. 'But when he was yet a great way off, his father saw him, and had compassion, and ran, and fell on his neck, and kissed him.'

"See the father of the parable! He is waiting with a great smile on his face, a smile of welcome, arms outstretched. He is not waiting to judge or punish his wayward son; he is waiting to embrace him and kiss him and love him and be all the home a father can be to him.

"The image makes my heart swell. God is waiting for us! He sees us coming even while we are yet far off! He runs *to* us. Can you grasp it—God running to us to throw His arms around us and kiss us in welcome!

"How different is this from the austere image of God presented by the old theologians. Does this sound to you like the God of the hellfire evangelists who rant about sinners in the hands of an angry God, about sinners being dangled over the flames of hell?

"Of course not. The Father of Jesus Christ does not demand that we repent in sackcloth and ashes before He will deign to look down upon us from His almighty throne, wielding thunderbolts of retribution if we do not. He is a *loving* Father, a *patient* Father, a *good* Father, a *forgiving* Father.

"Of course there are consequences if we refuse this reconciliation. But they are consequences we bring upon ourselves, consequences He observes with tears in His eyes. They are not the consequences of vengeance, retribution, and wrath. They are consequences of our own reluctance and stubbornness.

"In Luke 15 we are presented the Gospel in its fullness: Our Father is a good and loving and forgiving Father. He is the perfection of that broken and incomplete fatherhood that we all experience in our earthly families. Our earthly fathers are incomplete and broken. They have hurt us. We who are fathers have done a poor job of it and have been broken and incomplete examples of what God intended. We, too, have hurt our sons and daughters.

"But earthly fatherhood, in its imperfection, is intended as a reflection of what lies beyond. It is meant to lead us to our true Father. It is thus the human doorway to God Himself. In spite of its flawed nature, it is the most important relationship in the world for us to get *right*. We must make *our* hearts right with our fathers and mothers that we can be right with God.

"God is the *perfection* of the broken earthly image. He is everything we hoped our fathers would be, all we wanted them to be. He is the perfection of all that lies in your father's heart and mine to be to our children that which we were incapable of being. He is a God whom to call *Father*. Not Monarch, not Terror, not Judge—though He can surely be those to those who continue to refuse Him—no, nor Tyrant nor Despot. . .not even Holy, though He is that, not even Omnipotent, though He is that. . .but He whom Jesus taught us to call 'Abba, Father!'

"*He is our Father.* And He waits for our return. In the embrace of His love is our home. There only is it possible for us to find the home in which we were created to live.

"That is where unity originates—in my heart and yours. The words of the prodigal are the universal words of the reconciliation of the universe. They are the words by which we acknowledge our disconnection from our Life-Source. They are the words by which we return to oneness with God, who is nothing more nor less. . .than our *Father.*"

Drummond paused again and drew in a deep breath and closed his eyes briefly.

"It takes humility, great humility to seek reconciliation," he went on after a moment. "Yet *humility* is the doorway into reconciliation. The prodigal son, whose story Jesus told, looked around and realized he was eating with pigs! He had had such dreams! He had been so eager to claim his inheritance and to live life, as we of this modern age say, *on his own.* But where had it brought him in the end? What did he have?

"Only loneliness. He was eating with pigs!

"When he realized it and admitted it. . .then was born in him the *humility* that leads to reconciliation. That humility, that swallowing of pride, that recognition of what he had sunk to, led him home to his father. It is humility that leads us home.

"It is that same humility that leads us to reconciliation in our lives. Humility, my friends. The humility to say to one we have wronged, to one who has wronged us, to one with whom misunderstandings have separated us for whatever reason. . .to say, 'I no longer want to be disconnected. I do not want to be apart from this one whom I once loved.' In humility I am ready to say, 'I will arise and go to my brother. . .my sister. . .my mother. . .my daughter. . .my father. . .my son.' I will say, 'With all my heart I desire again to be in relationship with you. I am sorry to have failed in loving you, but I will try to love you again.'

"The humility to acknowledge, 'I do not want to be separated one day more. I will arise and go.'

"Humility, my friends. Humility to recognize that life is not what we had hoped. Humility to recognize that life is full of mistakes, that we have made our own share of them. Humility to apologize. Humility to arise and go to the one we have hurt. Humility to go to one who has hurt us.

"Humility is the doorway, my friends. It is the door to all healings, the door that leads to our brethren, the door that leads to our sons and daughters and mothers and fathers and our friends. . .the door that leads to the heart of God."

Drummond stopped. He glanced around for a moment and exhaled deeply. It was obvious he was spent. The church was silent.

THIRTY-TWO

Cryptic Words

*I*n the humble cottage of Llanfryniog, Codnor Barrie's great-aunt continued to stare into the fire. She had not yet poured out a drop of tea from the pot.

At length the old woman began to talk. Her speech was soft and faraway. "He wanted to take it from me," she said in scarcely more than a whisper, "thought he had a right to it. . .but I wouldn't give it to him. . . wouldn't tell him where I'd kept it this many a year."

The words were cryptic and strange. Percy asked no questions. Even after three weeks, he was still a stranger to this place. Nor could he keep from his brain reminders of his cousin's claim that the old woman was a witch.

As Grannie rocked gently back and forth, she continued to say odd things in an otherworldly voice. Percy could not prevent a certain sensation upon neck and arms commonly known as feeling one's flesh crawl.

Gwyneth busied herself around the cottage. She seemed to pay her aging aunt no heed. She had heard such oddities too many times to consider the words strange.

"Old man said it was *all* mine if only I could find it. . .out there, he said, though Sean always thought I knew more than I was telling. . . resented me having it. . .never know what fate your steps will lead you

176

to, the old pirate said. . .now look where Sean's have led him. . .dead on the same shores. . .just like the old sea dog we found."

The cottage fell silent. By and by Grannie came to herself. She glanced about, saw the tea, reached out her hand and touched the lukewarm pot, then gave a little chuckle. "Have I fallen asleep in my chair?" she said.

"You were talking about the old man again, Grannie."

"Ah," she nodded. "It's no wonder, after what happened to poor Sean. My mind's been turned toward that day ever since I heard the evil news. Shall I put on a new pot?" she added, rising again to her feet.

"I have to go home, Grannie," said Gwyneth. "I have to make tea for Papa."

"Don't forget the bread then, child," said Grannie. She rose and picked up a fine brown loaf from where it stood on the table.

Percy rose also. "Thank you for the tea," he said.

"The door of my cottage is always open to you." Grannie smiled. "I hope you will visit me again. Gwyneth, dear," she added, "here's the loaf for your papa."

By now Gwyneth's shoes were back on her feet, and she had both hands available for it.

Grannie's two visitors walked outside. Wondering if his cousins were still about, Percy glanced up and down the street. When he turned back, Gwyneth was already making her way homeward out of the village, carrying the large round loaf under her arm. Percy hurried after her.

"Where are you going, Percy?" she asked as he jogged up to her side.

"Home with you first."

"W–w–with me!" exclaimed the girl in delighted surprise.

"I'm going to make sure Courtenay and Florilyn aren't sneaking about somewhere waiting to hurt you. Once you are home, then I'll return to the manor."

"Thank you, Percy. N–n–no one's ever looked after me like that before."

"You've taken care of me twice now," laughed Percy. "Isn't it time I returned the favor?"

They continued out of Llanfryniog and up the rising plateau. Gwyneth felt safer with her grand knight beside her than she thought she had ever felt in all her life. She talked the whole way, explaining to Percy about every inch of the terrain about them.

THIRTY-THREE

Arrows of Prayer

*D*rummond concluded the remainder of his sermon quickly, endured the handshakes and smiles and well-wishes at the door, then escaped with his wife to the solace of the parsonage.

She felt the ache of his heart. She said nothing, merely slipped her hand through his arm as they walked home. The mother, too, shared the universal parental heartache of unrequited love.

"What do you think, Mary?" He sighed at length, still reflecting on his own message. "What were the father and mother doing the whole time their son was reducing himself to such foolish straits?"

Both pondered the question as they walked.

"Even as I was speaking," Drummond went on, "I found myself considering the parable from that light, wishing our Lord had spent more time on the *parental* side of the tale rather than following only the son. Now that we find ourselves in such circumstances, I am hungry for a specific example."

"What could the father and mother do but pray?" suggested his wife. "It seems all other means of parental influence were taken from them."

"Except keeping arms ready to open themselves," added the vicar with a sad smile.

His wife nodded.

They reached home and went inside. Mary put on water for tea. In ten or fifteen minutes, husband and wife sat down together with steaming cups in the parlor of the parsonage. Oddly, for this man and woman of God whom so many in the city looked to as pillars of spirituality, Edward and Mary Drummond were in truth lonely at such times. Their family was broken, and they knew it.

"Did we do the right thing, Mary," said Drummond at length, "by sending Percy to the country?"

"I truly believe so," she answered. "Here he was only becoming wilder by the day. A city's ways are not healthy for a rebellious spirit."

"The country can sometimes allow God's voice to get through more directly." Edward nodded. "I only hope our son will open himself to its influences."

"God has people everywhere," rejoined Mary. "Percy will come into contact with those the Lord will use to help his eyes open."

His wife's words caused the vicar to burst into spontaneous prayer. "Oh Lord, our Father," he said, "we ask You to bring our dear Percy into contact with Your people. May they touch his heart in ways even he perhaps does not see."

They fell silent for several moments.

"Your prayer reminds me of that wonderful sermon you preach from time to time about arrows of prayer," said Mary. "It is truly one of the profound truths God has revealed to you—how we can launch prayer arrows up into God's heart and then must trust Him to resend them down to earth where He will in His time, turn them into arrows of light and clarity in human souls."

"Even miraculously sending the answer arrows occasionally *before* the prayer arrows are launched." Edward nodded. "*Our* notions of time are nothing to God." Edward became thoughtful. "Your mentioning that...," he mused. "You know, I honestly don't know if I have prayed that prayer for our own Percy."

"Lord," Mary began almost immediately, "wherever our dear Percy is at this moment, whoever he is with, whatever he is thinking, we ask that You would be there beside him, inside him—speaking, wooing, luring him to Your heart. Send arrows of clarity into his thoughts, pleasant reminders and fond memories."

"Give us fortitude and courage to trust *You* to be Percy's Father in our place," added Edward. "Send piercing arrows of light into his heart. Accomplish Your perfect will and desire in his life."

"And in ours," added Mary softly. "As painful as this separation is, dear Lord, we ask You to perfect Your will in us through it. Bring Percy awake. Send bursts of revelation into his consciousness. Illuminate truth within him. Wake him to You, God—to the Father You want to be to him."

"Give us courage," prayed Edward, "to trust You and to believe that You love our Percy far more than we do. Remind us that *Your* arms ache more for him than ours."

"May we *keep* trusting You for him no matter how long it takes," added the mother.

"Help us believe more deeply than our frail flesh seems capable of that You are infinitely more Percy's Father than *we* are his father and mother. Help us, God our Father, to believe that You will not rest until he acknowledges himself the son he was created to be."

Mary kept her head bowed in silent prayer. When she heard a trembling sob escape her husband's lips, she laid down her cup and went to him.

The two wept together. Their tears accompanied the cleansing painful knowledge that they had truly given their son into the hands of the Father of them all.

What comfort it would have given them to know that their prayers were indeed already being answered. But God's comfort, like His arrows of clarity into the human soul, He sends in His perfect time, that heartache, too, may accomplish its appointed purpose in the hearts of His faithful ones.

THIRTY-FOUR

Gwyneth's Friends

Codnor Barrie stood in the door of his cottage waiting for his child.

The moment she arrived with Percy, Gwyneth told him excitedly of the events of the day.

"I'm very thankful to you, young man," said her father when Gwyneth paused for breath. "Surely you'll join us for tea."

"I only just had tea at Grannie's," laughed Percy. "I probably should be getting back to the manor. They may wonder about me—Sunday dinner and all. I mustn't offend my hosts."

"It sounds as if it is already too late for that, young man. That is if you consider the young brood your hosts as well."

Percy laughed. "I do not. I will offend the two of them anytime I can! But my aunt and uncle are very kind to me."

"The viscount is a decent man. I have no quarrel with him. But you'll not leave without a thick slice of Grannie's good bread to keep you company across the moor," added Gwyneth's father, taking the large loaf from his daughter.

"It smells peculiar," said Percy hesitantly. "I noticed it on the way. What kind of bread is it?"

"Laverbread—seaweed, oatmeal, and bacon fat."

"Hmm. . .maybe I should try it next time," said Percy.

"Percy, please don't go yet," implored Gwyneth.

"Why not?"

"I want to show you my animals."

"Your pets?" he said, glancing about for a dog or cat.

"My daughter has more than a few pets." Barrie laughed. "She keeps what can only be called a small zoo. Animals flock to her like to no human being I've ever seen. It's uncanny. I truly believe they see her as their master."

Already Gwyneth had taken hold of Percy's hand and was tugging him around toward the back of the stone cottage. Percy was surprised to see a large fenced enclosure extending far behind the cottage. In it scampered the most diverse array of creatures he had ever seen.

At sight of the girl at his side, they all scurried and scuffled and bounded and pattered toward them from inside, bursting into a cacophony of screeching, squealing, barking, chirping, meowing, and happy caterwauling. From somewhere a whirring of bird wings whisked toward them overhead.

Percy laughed at the wild and joyous greeting.

"Is it feeding time?" he exclaimed.

"They always greet me like this," said Gwyneth simply. "They think I'm their mother."

Percy later learned that the fence had been built merely to keep wild animals from the mountains *out* rather than to keep Gwyneth's friends *in*. Most would have remained near the dwelling of their mistress without any enclosure whatever.

To one side, a small cluster of pens and kennels served as hospital to those animals presently being tended for injury. If such a thing as communication between species occurred in the animal kingdom, surely Gwyneth's animal hospital gave credibility to the theory. Weekly it seemed some creature appeared with a gash on its side or with a wounded leg or broken wing or sliver in its paw, somehow knowing that this was the place where help would be given. Nor did the creatures flinch when Gwyneth approached to examine paw or wing and administer the nursing care so instinctive to her nature.

Around the outside of the pen, a half dozen deer grazed contentedly on the lush grass of the moor. Some would return to the mountains when night fell, others would leap over the fence into the compound, there to spend the night with racoons and rabbits and dogs and chickens and other of their diverse fellows of the animal kingdom.

In Gwyneth's zoo all creatures were at peace. No harm came to any. A spell of goodness lay upon the place. For they behaved in Gwyneth's presence as perhaps did the creature friends of that first man and woman in the garden so long ago.

"Don't you love all the creatures God made?" said Gwyneth as they walked back to the Barrie cottage.

"I don't know that I thought about it much before. When you live in the city, nature isn't something you think about."

"You're not in the city now. Maybe God sent you to the country to learn to see what He has made."

"God didn't send me to the country."

"Who did?"

"My father."

"That's the same thing," said Gwyneth.

"How do you mean?" laughed Percy. "God's not my father."

"Oh, isn't He?" rejoined Gwyneth, astonished that Percy would say such a thing. "What else is He then if He isn't your father?"

"I didn't mean it like that. I mean, of course I suppose God created everyone. I meant He isn't my *own* father, you know, like my *real* father."

"Grannie says I have two fathers. She says that Papa is my father so that I will learn to look up to know my real Father."

That night as he lay on his bed reliving the day's incidents, Percy's thoughts came to rest on young Gwyneth Barrie.

Meanwhile, across the moor in her own cottage, Gwyneth Barrie also lay awake, eyes wide, thinking about Percy. She would not have believed it had she been told that he was thinking of her.

New sensations filled her tender heart. That another person besides Grannie, Hollin Radnor, and her papa had befriended her, stood up for her—even been attacked for her! The very notion rose so mightily in her consciousness as to render sleep impossible.

And a young person besides! Someone not her own age, yet not so *very* much older, she thought. Percy was the same age as many of the boys and girls in the village who made fun of her.

In Gwyneth's eyes, the boy was not a boy at all, but fully a man, a giant eight feet tall, a prince, a warrior, a defender of the helpless. In the short time she had known him, young Percy Drummond had become Gwyneth's hero, her knight in shining armor.

She would never fear to walk Llanfryniog's streets again. She had as good a papa as ever lived. She had as kind and wise a grannie as ever it pleased God to give a girl. And now she had a new friend who had come from Glasgow and was afraid of nothing.

What Percy would have thought had he known himself viewed as the answer to a young girl's prayers would have been interesting to inquire. He had for some years been in the habit of scorning his father's spirituality. Now his new friend saw him as God's special gift just for her.

God, thank You for Percy! prayed Gwyneth simply, then turned over and, with a smile on her face, was soon asleep.

Thirty-Five

Conflicting Affections

*C*ourtenay had been so successful, he thought, in patching it up with Rhawn Lorimer on the previous Sunday that he pressed his advantage with an invitation to luncheon with his family at the manor later that week.

It was a spontaneous gesture. Only upon later reflection did the potential awkwardness, even danger, of the situation present itself to Courtenay's suspicions. But he could hardly retract it, nor could he tell Percy to get lost for the day without in all likelihood incurring the viscount's anger. His father had, to both son's and daughter's profound annoyance, developed a soft spot for his nephew. He and his sister had to be a little careful what they said in their father's hearing.

Courtenay's reservations would have increased tenfold had he divined Miss Lorimer's true reason for accepting the invitation so eagerly. Having successfully ascertained the identity of the mystery boy she had encountered in the draper's shop and learning where he was living for the summer, she was far more anxious to see him again than she was Courtenay Westbrooke, with whom the association, on her part, was more the result of proximity to her best friend than genuine affection.

Had Courtenay been a gentleman, he would have taken one of his father's buggies to pick up his guest prior to the luncheon. But he was of the school that said let the girl come to him. And as Percy showed no sign of disappearing, he was secretly hoping that maybe Rhawn might not make an appearance anyway. She was, however, like Florilyn, an expert rider. She arrived on horseback almost exactly as the hour of twelve began to strike on the clock above the stable yard.

Hollin Radnor heard her approach and went to meet her. He helped her dismount and saw to the horse while Rhawn walked to the front door of the manor. There, next to the door post, hung a bouquet of wildflowers, tied with red. She recognized the ribbon immediately.

So, she thought, *the young man's affections were closer to home than she had realized!* Was he really falling for his own cousin?

But what an odd place to leave a bouquet. Their rooms were so near one another, why not put them on her own bedroom door rather than out in the open where everyone would see them?

Courtenay had been watching the front of the house from an upstairs window. The moment he saw Rhawn riding up, he dashed downstairs to the front door. He wasn't about to risk her running into his cousin again without him around.

Even as the echo of the bell faded, he opened the door to greet her. The smile meant for Rhawn Lorimer died on his lips as his eyes fell on the bouquet hanging almost directly in front of him.

"What in blazes is that?" he exclaimed, hardly aware of his rudeness.

"It would appear that *someone* in this house has a secret admirer," replied Rhawn, more than a little surprised by the intensity of his reaction. "Hello, Courtenay—my goodness, you look like you've seen a ghost. Not exactly the greeting I expected."

"Oh. . .right, sorry—yes, hello, Miss Lorimer," said Courtenay, trying to recover himself, though continuing to stare at the bouquet out of the corner of his eye. "The impish little tramp!" he muttered under his breath. He grabbed the flowers and flung them across the stones of the entryway. "People like that need to mind their own business!" Again he struggled to regain his composure, laughed nervously, and led his guest inside.

"Not a very nice way to treat a gift to your sister," said Rhawn in a humorous though confused tone. She was both bewildered and amused by Courtenay's bizarre behavior.

"She needs no gift from the likes of *that*!" rejoined Courtenay. "And neither do I!"

Having no clue what he meant, Rhawn Lorimer followed Courtenay to the dining room. Florilyn and her mother were already present.

"Good afternoon, Rhawn," said Katherine. "I am so glad you can be with us today."

"Thank you, Mrs. Westbrooke," said Rhawn with a pleasant smile. "Hi, Florilyn," she added to Courtenay's sister.

Though Rhawn was dying to get Florilyn off to one side of the room to ask about Percy out of Courtenay's hearing, the far door opened almost immediately. Hope of further conversation was cut short by the entrance of the viscount and the object of her curiosity himself. Uncle and nephew were laughing and chatting like the best of friends.

"That's a good one, Percy, my boy!" roared the viscount. "I'll have to tell that to my friends in London. Nothing like Glasgow humor! Oh," he added, glancing about, "it would appear we are the last to arrive. All here, what? Ah, Miss Lorimer," he said, taking note of their guest, "welcome, welcome! How is your father?"

"Very well, sir. He sends his regards."

"Good, good—thank you. Give him my best, of course. You have, I take it, met our guest for the summer, my nephew. . . ," he added, gesturing toward Percy.

"I. . .uh," Rhawn began. With Percy's eyes staring straight through her, she suddenly found herself at a loss for words.

Percy quickly rescued her from the difficulty. "Miss, uh. . .Miss *Lorimer*, is it?" he said, "and I ran into one another in town. Courtenay," he added, turning toward his cousin with the hint of a smile, "you remember the day, I'm sure. Unfortunately, we were not actually introduced."

He turned now to face the young woman directly. "Hello," he said, extending his hand, "I am Percival Drummond."

"Hello, Mr. Drummond," said Rhawn, taking his hand and clinging to it an imperceptible moment longer than propriety demanded. "I am Rhawn Lorimer. I am extremely pleased to make your acquaintance. . . at last."

"The pleasure is all mine, Miss Lorimer," rejoined Percy, withdrawing his hand lest Courtenay get any ideas.

Indeed, Courtenay had been watching, though absently. He was still a little shaken from having been the recipient of one of the witch-girl's voodoo bouquets. He had actually been turning over in his mind whether tossing it on the ground had been a good idea. Weren't such things supposed to be burned or otherwise destroyed to mitigate their occultish power? Thus, the looks being sent toward Percy by Rhawn Lorimer uncharacteristically escaped his notice.

By the time they were all seated around the table, Rhawn's fluttering eyelids had calmed themselves. But her eyes remained busily glancing back and forth between Percy and Florilyn to see what kind of expressions passed between the two lovebirds. Observing nothing to titillate her interest, however, as opportunity presented itself, she tried to urge the conversation into the proper channels. "Do you come to Wales often, Mr. Drummond?" she asked, ignoring Courtenay's displeasure at her question.

"I haven't been here in years," replied Percy. "I can hardly even remember the last time—when was it, Aunt Katherine? I was just a wee lad, as we say in Scotland."

"I think you were about five," replied his aunt.

"What brings you here this summer?"

"That is. . .uh, a little awkward to explain. My father thought perhaps a change from city life would be good for me."

"Percy got in trouble with the police," chimed in Florilyn merrily.

"Goodness, Florilyn!" exclaimed Katherine. "Must you be quite so frank? Think of Percival's feelings."

"That's all right, Aunt Katherine," said Percy. "No harm done. Besides, Florilyn is right."

"There is no reason for her to air the family's dirty laundry," persisted Percy's aunt.

Rhawn Lorimer was enjoying the exchange immensely. She had apparently stumbled into the middle of a juicy family secret!

"I don't mind so much," said Percy. "No sense in trying to hide it. Yes," he added, turning to Rhawn, "I was behaving foolishly in the city. To keep me from getting into deeper trouble, my father asked my aunt and uncle if they would take me in for the summer. They agreed and have been very gracious to their wayward nephew."

He glanced toward the two with a genuine smile. His pleasant expression did much to ease Katherine's annoyance.

"Miss Lorimer's father is our local magistrate, Percy, my boy," boomed the viscount. "Better watch your step around her!"

"I will be very careful," Percy said, laughing.

As the meal progressed, Courtenay was anything but pleased with the direction the conversation around the table seemed determined to go, with Percy at the center of it. But he found himself unable to do much about it other than ask Rhawn if she wanted a ride after lunch. Even that, however, after her halfhearted consent, she foiled by asking Percy if he and Florilyn rode together. She was far too interested in the blighter to suit him.

When the two girls were alone in Florilyn's room later, the moment the door was closed behind them, Rhawn turned to Florilyn. "He's an absolute dream!" she said excitedly. "How did you get so lucky?"

"What are you *talking* about?" said Florilyn with a confused expression. "*Who* are you talking about?"

"Your cousin. . .Percival, of course."

"You must be joking!" Florilyn laughed. "Why would I be lucky?"

"To have someone like that fancy you, of course."

"Percy. . .fancy *me*? Ugh, what a sickening thought!"

"You don't like him?"

"I can't stand him!"

"Now it's you who must be joking."

"I'm not," insisted Florilyn.

"What about the flowers he left you downstairs?"

"Percy?" Florilyn's tone was more disbelieving than ever.

"Yes. A little bouquet tied with the very ribbon I saw him buying at the draper's shop. He had flowers with him that day, too. He said they were for a girl. I never dreamed it was *you*."

"When was that?" asked Florilyn a little more seriously.

"A week ago maybe."

"He never gave me any flowers."

Rhawn stared back at her in surprise. "Then who are the flowers downstairs for if he didn't mean them for you?"

"What flowers downstairs?"

"I told you—a bouquet hanging on the door outside. Courtenay saw them."

"What did he do?" asked Florilyn.

"He got really angry and threw them on the ground. He was acting very strange."

Florilyn did not reply. A brief shudder went through her as she recalled the incident in town after church.

But Rhawn took little notice of her change in mood. "Don't you think your cousin is good looking?" she asked.

"I don't know," Florilyn replied distractedly. "I suppose. I never noticed."

"How could you *not* notice?"

"Well, now that you know he's got no interest in me, if you're so sweet on him, you can have him. But what about Courtenay?"

"What about him?"

"What about, you know. . .you and him?"

"Oh, Courtenay's okay, I guess. But that was before I saw Percival. What kind of trouble was he in with the police? I think it's exciting! Was it something really awful?"

"I don't know. I doubt it was so bad. He's not very brawny. I can hardly imagine him being in serious trouble. But I did overhear my parents say that if they didn't take him in for the summer he would probably wind up in jail."

"*Jail*. . .that is exciting. He doesn't *look* like a criminal."

"He's still a boy if you ask me. Courtenay's already beat him up twice."

"Why?"

"They just don't like each other. Courtenay hates Percy even more than I do. If you even look at him, it will make him furious."

"So I found out at the draper's shop. I will just have to be careful."

"You'd better start now," rejoined Florilyn. "He's probably already waiting for you down by the stables to ride you home. If I know my brother, you are going to have a lot of explaining to do for the way you were fawning all over Percy at lunch."

Rhawn smiled. "I can handle your brother."

THIRTY-SIX

Market Day

Summer weekly market day began in Llanfryniog in July and would continue every Saturday until the harvests were in and the leaves of autumn began to fall.

It was still early for most produce, though strawberries were at the height of their season. Besides the strawberries, new potatoes, carrots, turnips, and homemade cheeses and jams, most of the featured items were handcrafts the village women had been making through the winter and spring months, as well as small trinkets and sweeties to tempt the children. Not that there was much money to be made. Barter was more common than cash. Nearly everyone grew their own potatoes and carrots.

But it was a tradition of long standing, more social than economic in the life of the community. No one for miles would miss the first market day of each new summer, when all manner of local wares were available on the grass in front of the chapel and school building. It was not unheard of for animal flesh to trade hands as well.

Nor would it be Wales without music! Though the school term had finished several weeks earlier, the children all came together on this day to sing from the school steps several songs they had practiced the previous spring. They would alternate throughout the day with choirs from the three churches and a dozen or more fiddlers and accordionists.

By noon of the first Saturday of July, the town was full with movement, bustle, and activity. Singing could be heard in the distance. A variety of aromas from fires and kettles tempted hungry stomachs to part with a few pennies in exchange for their lunch. Booths and tables and games and amusements and handcrafts and all manner of hand-knitted wool caps and socks and sweaters and scarves for sale were spread out everywhere.

At one end of the field were tied a few pigs, sheep, and horses to see what offers might be made. Already Kyvwlch Gwarthegydd and Padrig Gwlwlwyd and a handful of men were clustered about a pure white five-year-old stallion, examining teeth and legs, hooves and flanks.

As he felt more and more at peace with himself in the country and at home on his uncle's estate, Percy had taken to roaming the region with increasing freedom. His comfort upon the back of one or another of the viscount's horses, though he had not ventured out again on Red Rhud, had greatly increased. In Llanfryniog, he made acquaintance with a growing number of the villagers. Despite the fact that he was well known by the youths of the place as little Gwyneth Barrie's defender, that he was Lord Snowdon's nephew caused most of the older townspeople to give him the benefit of any doubts they may have had in regard of his peculiar relationship with the strange girl. A few, in fact, secretly admired his championing of Barrie's daughter. This general prejudice in his favor was aided by his cheerful disposition, as well as by the fact that he was so likable and unlike the viscount's two children, neither of whom had made themselves particular favorites with anyone.

Hearing about market day, Percy was not about to miss it.

As much as they gave every indication of despising him, for reasons difficult to explain, both Courtenay and Florilyn were reluctant to leave their cousin on his own. In actual fact, the lives of the two scions of the Westbrooke name had grown a little tedious of late. When Courtenay was not shooting or riding with Colville Burrenchobay or pressing his attentions on Rhawn Lorimer, he had very little to occupy himself during the long days of summer. He did not read, did not ride merely for enjoyment. The sea, the mountains, the village, the forests held no fascination for him. Much the same could be said of Florilyn. Both were too wrapped up in themselves to find delight in the world about them.

The three young people were therefore often found together more often than could be accounted for by cousinly friendship. Courtenay and Florilyn kept track of Percy's movements and, motivated as much from boredom as interest, almost followed him about. If he chanced on some amusement, they did not want to miss it. He found them a nuisance. But he could hardly tell the son and daughter of his hosts to leave him alone. So he went about his affairs, and not wanting to be left behind, they tagged along, sniping at him with derisive comments.

Percy, newly alive to the delights of the country, was eager to be out exploring and walking and riding, talking to the servants, meandering through the town, encountering new people, making friends, engaging the old fishermen in conversation as one by one they overcame their reticence toward him. To her great disgust, Florilyn had once even seen him helping Hollin Radnor cleaning out the horses' stalls, talking away to the groom as if they were old friends!

In spite of such revolting tendencies, Percy brought an energy and enthusiasm to life at the manor that slowly rubbed off on everyone, staff and family alike.

Both his cousins accompanied him into town on this day also because they knew that Colville, Davina, and Ainsworth Burrenchobay were planning to be in Llanfryniog after lunch. The five aristocratic youths of the two neighboring estates were capable of far more mischief en masse than singly. Davina Burrenchobay, at thirteen, was too young to interest Courtenay. But she idolized Florilyn, and the viscount's daughter found her attentions gratifying. They offered Florilyn, too, the occasional opportunity to try out her seductive wiles on Davina's nineteen-year-old brother, Colville.

They had not been in town long before Percy disappeared. By then neither Courtenay nor Florilyn cared. Half suspecting where he might have gone, they would not have followed him anyway. That Courtenay had managed to run into Rhawn Lorimer allayed his anxiety about Percy in that regard. From somewhere, Davina Burrenchobay came running excitedly toward them. Before she knew it, Florilyn had been deserted by both brother and cousin and found herself walking along with thirteen-year-old Davina chatting away and ten-year-old Ainsworth traipsing along behind.

"Where's your brother?" asked Florilyn.

"I'm right here!" piped up Ainsworth eagerly.

"I mean your older brother, you goose," rejoined Florilyn.

"I don't know," replied Davina. "I think he's over there somewhere looking at a horse. He's always looking at horses."

Meanwhile, Percy was enjoying a cup of tea with Grannie in her cottage. With every visit, he learned more about the village, about Gwyneth and her father and why Codnor Barrie had been in Ireland when Gwyneth was born. He also continued to pick up tidbits of interest about the family of his aunt and uncle with whom he was spending the summer.

"Will Gwyneth be here for market day?" he asked.

"She doesn't take to crowds," replied Grannie. "You know how people are to her, poor lass."

Florilyn and the two younger Burrenchobays continued to wander about aimlessly. In the distance, Florilyn saw Courtenay and Rhawn. She increased her pace in their direction. The two younger ones followed.

By the time Percy arrived at the festivities an hour later, the sheep-shearing contest was in full swing. A hundred or more spectators were cheering on their favorites. Percy moved toward the noisy commotion and was soon swallowed by the crowd.

"Hoy there, Mr. Drummond, isn't it?" said a voice at Percy's side.

Percy turned to see his sheep-herding acquaintance from his first ride into the hills. "Hello, Stevie," he said, shaking the other's hand. "Are you one of the contestants?"

"Aye, I am. How is your summer?"

"Good. . .very good."

"I am still waiting for that visit to my house."

"I haven't forgotten." Percy laughed. "Seeing you again. . .I will make a point of riding out your way next week."

He saw Stevie glance behind him. A serious expression came over the shepherd's face. Percy turned to see Florilyn walking past them at the side of a large youth. She pretended not to notice as they moved beyond the crowd. She was smiling and laughing and carrying herself with a flirtatious air.

"I don't like to see your cousin with the likes of him," said Stevie.

"Why, who is he?" asked Percy.

"That's Colville Burrenchobay," replied Stevie.

"Ah, yes. I've heard of him. He's a friend of my cousin Courtenay's."

"Not the sort of fellow I would want my sister or daughter keeping company with. I'm concerned only for Miss Florilyn, you understand. I don't know what my lord Snowdon is thinking to allow it."

"I don't think he pays much attention to what his son and daughter do."

"All the more reason he should."

"Is the bloke really so bad?" said Percy, watching the two walk off together.

"There are stories that find their way back from the university," replied Stevie. "That's all I will say. Oh, I just heard them call my name!"

"Best of luck to you!"

"Don't forget that visit." Stevie ran off.

Percy inched his way to the front of the throng for a better view. As he did, out of the corner of his eye he noticed Florilyn and Colville Burrenchobay moving out of sight behind the chapel. He was soon caught up in Stevie's performance with the sheep. By the time Stevie flung the coat of wool in a single piece away from the skinny little white body that emerged from beneath it, Percy was cheering and yelling with the rest.

"Well done, Stevie!" he exclaimed when Stevie approached at the conclusion of his effort. "Will you win, do you think?"

"Who can say? I was third last year. Some of the men have been at it decades more than me. It will take me years to catch them. If I manage to get in the top five, I will have had a good day of it."

"Is your father here? Does he participate?"

A sad smile came over the young shepherd's face. "No, I'm sorry to say," he replied. "He used to be the shearing champion of all Gwynedd. But he's not well just now, you see. He doesn't get out anymore."

As they were talking, Percy was surprised to see Rhawn Lorimer walking toward them. She was alone. "Hello, Percival," she purred. She glanced toward Stevie. Her nose crinkled squeamishly.

"Miss Lorimer," said Percy. "Quite a day, eh? Do you know Stevie Muir?"

"Everybody does," she answered, not attempting to disguise her repugnance. "Would you like to walk with me, Percival?" she added.

If she had thought to win Percy's affection by being brusque with Stevie Muir, the magistrate's daughter had misjudged her prey. Nevertheless, by that subtle art at which young women are so skilled and of which young men are so oblivious, in less than a minute Percy found himself cleverly drawn away from his shepherd friend and the sheep-shearing crowd together. He glanced back, but Stevie was already swallowed up by the activity.

"What are you looking at?" asked Rhawn.

"I was just wondering where Stevie disappeared to," replied Percy.

"Who cares about *him*?"

"I care about him."

"Florilyn says you're friends with the little witch-child, too. Are you friends with all the local riffraff?"

"Riffraff?" exclaimed Percy. "What are you talking about? They are people. God made them no less than He made you and me. Yes, I am friends with Gwyneth and Stevie. They are two of the first people I met here. I like them."

Percy hardly realized that the words out of his mouth might well have come from his father. Had he been paying closer attention, he would probably have wondered what was becoming of him. They continued to move farther from the crowd.

"What about me?" said Rhawn in a coquettish tone, moving close and brushing Percy's side.

"You're a nice enough girl, Miss Lorimer, I suppose," replied Percy. "But I hardly know you."

"Do you think I'm pretty?"

"What kind of question is that?" laughed Percy. "You don't go around asking people if they think you're pretty."

"All the other boys think I'm pretty."

"I am sure they do. All I am saying is that I want no trouble with Courtenay. He told us to stay away from each other. So I'm not exactly sure what you are doing. What if he sees us?"

"Do you take your orders from Courtenay?" baited Rhawn.

"No. But he's bigger and stronger than me, and with a temper I don't particularly want to upset. He's already put me on the ground twice. I'm no idiot. I'm not eager to experience it again."

"Wouldn't it be worth it. . .for me?"

"Honestly, no. Sorry. I don't want to hurt your feelings, but if you are Courtenay's girl, I have no desire to interfere. I certainly have no intention of getting beat up for you."

"I'm not his girl," rejoined Rhawn with the hint of a pout.

"If Courtenay thinks you are, then—"

What Percy had been about to say was interrupted by the scream of a girl's voice. It came from behind the chapel. Percy bolted toward it.

He rounded the corner of the stone church to see Florilyn struggling in the arms of the same youth he had seen her with earlier.

"Just a simple kiss, Florilyn," he was saying in a voice that revealed aggression. "I know you're in love with me!"

"No, I'm not! Colville. . .let me go!" cried Florilyn.

Obviously provoked, the young man pressed his advantage. He grabbed her tight and pulled her face to his.

Another scream sounded. Somehow Florilyn struggled to loosen herself sufficiently to free her arm. A great whack struck Colville Burrenchobay's cheek.

Florilyn was stronger than it might have seemed, especially when aroused to fury. Burrenchobay's eyes filled from the sting of the blow. "You little vixen!" he cried. "You will pay for that!"

However he thought to retaliate was preempted as Percy flew into their midst.

"Hey, what the—!" exclaimed Burrenchobay. In the torrent that followed, he forgot that he was in the presence of a young woman, if not quite yet a lady.

"Stand back, Florilyn!" said Percy in a commanding voice as he separated them. "Get away!"

Whether Florilyn had really been shocked by Colville Burrenchobay's advances, only she could say. The strength of his grip had, in truth, frightened her just a little. She, too, had heard the stories to which Stevie had alluded. But like many foolish maidens, she found playing with fire tantalizing, thrilling, and dangerous. She greatly overestimated her ability to keep from burning her fingers. She had been as much to blame in the clandestine affair as Burrenchobay, perhaps more so. Yet with a squire suddenly rushing in to protect her honor, as it were, notwithstanding that it was one whose interference she would have scorned had she taken the leisure to stop and think about it, what could she do but back away and see how the thing turned out?

"You will regret your insolence, whoever you are, you little cur!" shouted Burrenchobay in a rage.

He was not one who stood on ceremony, nor who cherished qualms of etiquette about taking on someone half his size. Charging like a wild bull, within seconds Percy yet again found himself on the short end of a brief but violent scuffle.

Florilyn saw nothing of it. She raced from behind the chapel, only stopping when she met Rhawn Lorimer coming around the side of the stone wall.

"What—" began Rhawn, seeing the look of fright on Florilyn's face.

Behind her she heard the yells and saw the fight well enough. It did not last long. A minute later, Colville Burrenchobay had disappeared.

The two girls walked slowly to where Percy was sprawled out on the grass.

"What happened?" said Rhawn.

"Colville tried to kiss me," replied Florilyn. "I screamed. Percy, like the nincompoop he is, ran in and tried to rescue me."

"That hardly sounds like the work of a nincompoop," said Rhawn. "No one's ever rescued *me*."

They approached. Percy still lay motionless.

"Is he. . .dead?" said Rhawn, her voice trembling at the word.

Slowly Percy opened his eyes. He saw the faces of the two girls staring down at him. "Ohhh!" he groaned in pain. "I definitely do not think I am cut out for country life." He groaned again and tried to move. "These blokes here are lunatics," he said. "They'll knock your block off at the drop of a hat. I'll never survive the summer."

Florilyn could not prevent an inward smile. He was always saying something funny.

So relieved that nothing appeared broken, both girls stooped down and tried to help him sit up.

"I'm all right," said Percy, drawing in a deep breath. He breathed in and out a few more times where he sat on the grass. "Whew," he sighed. "That was one big, strong guy. Remind me to keep out of his way."

Rhawn broke into laughter to hear Percy feeling good enough to make light of it. Florilyn joined her, but her laugh was mingled with anxiety for herself and what would be the upshot of the incident.

"You two can go," said Percy, struggling to his feet. "I don't want you to get in trouble on my account. That's all I need, to incur Courtenay's wrath now as well. Why don't you go and have fun and pretend this never happened. I'll find my own way home. . .like the proverbial dog slinking away with his tail between his legs."

THIRTY-SEVEN

Mixed Fortunes

Once again at dinner that evening, Percy's facial condition was the object of comment and question. He did his best to brush off the questions, but the viscount was noticeably concerned.

When his uncle began hinting at talking to Styles Lorimer about investigating the incident, Percy knew he had to come clean before it went any further. "It's really nothing, Uncle Roderick," he said. "I got into a row with Colville Burrenchobay, that's all."

"Oh. . .I see. Hmm. . .not a lad to tangle with, Percy, my boy," said the viscount seriously. "He's twice your size, I dare say."

"I will be more careful in the future, sir, believe me."

"What were you fighting about?"

Florilyn's face sought the table. She felt her cheeks redden and was afraid to look up without betraying herself.

"Nothing much," said Percy. "Just a difference of opinion. It was my fault."

"I can hardly believe that," rejoined the viscount.

"It's true, sir. I am sorry if I disappoint you."

"No, no, Percy, my boy—think nothing of it. Boys will be boys. Young Burrenchobay is well known to have a hot head."

The meal progressed. The mood remained subdued. Florilyn said almost nothing. For once Courtenay seemed to be enjoying himself more than the rest of the family.

Most of those attending the market day gala had gotten wind of the fight behind the church. Young boys smell a fight a mile away. Any scuffle to lads under twelve is like catnip to a cat. A few had managed to catch glimpses of the tail end of it, and the exciting news spread like a brush fire.

Not having discovered Rhawn Lorimer's treachery toward himself in the way of her advances toward Percy, Courtenay was delighted with the turn of events with regard to his friend and cousin. And he could not help but enjoy watching his sister squirm in hopes that her part in the incident, which he learned later from Colville, would not come out.

Later in the evening as he was walking slowly down the corridor to his room, one arm noticeably drooping at his side and very much looking forward to his bed at last, Percy was surprised to see Florilyn standing waiting for him. The expression on her face was one whose acquaintance Percy had not made before. In a strange way, he hardly recognized her. He approached and nodded in silent greeting.

Florilyn glanced down at the floor. She was clearly embarrassed.

He waited.

Finally she looked up at him. "Why didn't you tell my father it was my fault?" she said.

"I didn't know it was."

Again Florilyn glanced down at the floor.

"*Was* it your fault?" asked Percy. "It didn't look that way to me. He was behaving badly to you—certainly not like a gentleman."

"No one has ever accused Colville Burrenchobay of being a gentleman," rejoined Florilyn. She looked up. The gaze that met Percy's was earnest and sincere. "But I was flirting with him," she said.

Percy took in the information without comment. He was not surprised. "What would it have accomplished to blame you?" he said after a moment. "Your father doesn't need to know. . .that is, if you learned your lesson."

"I hope I have," said Florilyn, obviously uneasy. "Daddy would have whipped me if he knew. Well, thank you, I guess." She forced a smile, though the effort seemed to strain the muscles of her face to their limit.

She turned and left Percy at his door pondering the unexpected exchange with his cousin.

Percy remained out of sight for a few days, nursing his wounds for a third time and vowing to keep clear, whatever the circumstances, of his older cousin and his wild friend from Burrenchobay Hall. If he didn't find a way to keep out of the way of these two crazed young Welshmen, his father would have to come fetch him from the hospital!

Several days later he ran into Florilyn outside the house. He and she had not spoken since the previous Saturday night.

"Would you like to go for a ride?" she asked.

Percy smiled skeptically. "So you can get me thrown and ditch me again?" he said, half playfully, though not *entirely* playfully.

"No, I promise. You can lead the way."

She *sounded* sincere. Percy thought for a moment then nodded.

"I may regret this," he said. "But. . .all right. I'll take you up on your offer."

Twenty minutes later, the cousins rode out of the stable yard. True to her word, Florilyn allowed Percy to lead. They took the same two horses as before, but this time Percy was on Grey Tide, and not once did Florilyn increase her speed. They led the two mounts slowly down the entry drive side by side, and then Percy turned onto the main road and down the slope of the plateau toward Llanfryniog.

"You seem steadier in the saddle," said Florilyn.

"I've been riding quite a bit," said Percy. "I'm getting comfortable with it."

"That's good."

"We should have another race before I return to Glasgow. You did rather take advantage of me last time."

"That wasn't really a proper *race*."

"Maybe the next one can be."

Florilyn smiled. Her expression was difficult to read. "Do you really think you could keep up with me?" she said with a hint of playful banter.

"Maybe not. . .not now. But perhaps by the end of the summer."

"Is that a challenge?"

Percy did not reply. He met her coy smile with one of his own.

They reached the village and clomped leisurely along the hard-packed dirt street between the stone buildings lining it on both sides. Most of the people they passed, to Florilyn's surprise, greeted Percy by name. He led the way through town, past the chapel, all evidence of the previous Saturday's festivities gone, and down to the harbor. They continued onto the sand and a short distance along it then turned back up again into town. Returning through the village, Percy led randomly through several side streets and lanes where the two horses occasionally had to walk in single file.

"What is that strange building there," asked Percy, pointing to his right down a narrow lane, "with the funny roof and purple doors and windows and all the statues about?"

"That's Madame Fleming's house—the fortune-teller."

"A fortune-teller? You must be joking!"

"No, really," replied Florilyn.

Suddenly her face lit. "Percy!" she exclaimed. "Let's go get our fortunes told!"

"I don't—"

"Oh, let's. Can we, please? I've always wanted to. I would be afraid to go alone. But with you, I wouldn't be. Oh, let's do!"

Though he had never once spoken with them about such things, somehow Percy knew that his parents would strongly disapprove of his setting foot inside such a place as Madame Fleming's. His father would also remind him, as the man and the older of the two, that if it lay within his power, he had a responsibility to protect his cousin from harm.

Yet the youthful spirit of adventure proved an irresistible lure. For once Florilyn was being nice. He didn't want to snub her only request on the first day she had made an effort to have fun with him. He thus found it impossible to deny her.

They turned and made their way down the narrow lane. Suddenly the village grew quiet around them. To their ears, the *clop, clop, clop* of the horses' hooves echoed louder than Kyvwlch Gwarthegydd's anvil on Sunday morning. It seemed to announce to everyone within earshot what they were about to do.

Florilyn glanced around nervously. Her father would probably whip her for this, too, if he found out. But she was determined not to back out now.

Slowly they approached the house. Percy shuddered as he looked at the steeply slanted roof with its weird ornaments at the corners and the occult weathervane at the apex. All around the house, the assortment of statues of goblins and dwarfs and trolls silently seemed to shout, "Stay away; there is evil here. Come if you will, but leave the past behind. Here lies your future. . .and it may fill you with dread."

They came to a halt and slowly dismounted. Even the two horses seemed ill at ease and moved about with jittery feet. They tied them to a nearby rail.

Percy glanced along the adjacent street. He could just see one wall of Grannie's cottage a hundred feet away. He thought to himself that he would rather visit her. But it would take a more than moderate-sized miracle to get Florilyn into that house of light. Yet she was eager to visit this house of darkness in front of them and was already halfway from the street to the door. Reluctantly he turned and followed her.

They walked onto the porch. Percy glanced at the sign above the door, ornate with snakes and horrid-looking animals and faces. MADAME FLEMING, PSYCHIC—FORTUNES AND FUTURES FORETOLD, he read.

Florilyn rang the bell. "I hope no one sees us!" she whispered. "My parents would kill me if they knew I was visiting the old hag."

The door opened. A face appeared, shrouded in darkness from behind. Percy shivered at the ghostly sight. The woman's countenance was pale and wrinkled. Out of deep, dark sockets, eyes of black shone above lips painted bright red. A purple-orange scarf of silk covered the hair above the face. From the woman's ears hung gaudy ringlets of gold and silver.

A tingle of terror swept through Florilyn's body. "We have come to get our fortunes told," she said, her voice shaky. "May we come in? I don't want anyone to see us."

"Come in. . .come in, my sweets," said the woman. "Your fortunes told is it you're wanting? You've come to the right place." She opened the door just wide enough for them to squeeze through then shut it noiselessly behind them.

Peculiar aromas assaulted them, and sights too strange to be told. Candles flickered throughout the room. Burning incense was so thick as to hover over them like a visible cloud. It was not sufficient in itself, however, to completely overwhelm the smell of the old woman herself. The interior of the place was furnished with peculiar ornaments and statues and furniture such as surrounded the exterior. Silks and tapestries covered the windows and hung throughout in the dim light, along with beads and draperies and a few paintings. The only item of immediately recognizable design was a bookshelf that stood against one wall, filled with books of dubious origin and purpose.

"Come, my sweets," said the woman. "Come through and sit with Madame Fleming." Her voice was old and scratchy, thick with Bulgarian or Russian accent. That it was fake was a fact lost entirely on the wide-eyed cousins. The good Madame Fleming was as Irish as any self-respecting leprechaun, but she carried off the gypsy charade to convincing effect.

She led them into a small anteroom and waddled around a table that sat in the middle of the floor. A single candle burned in its center. She eased her plump frame into an upright chair on the far side of the table. "Sit. . .sit down, my sweets," she said.

As if they had been expected, two empty chairs awaited them. They sat down opposite her.

"So it's your futures and fortunes told, is it?" she said again.

Florilyn nodded.

"It will be a shilling each, then. . .in advance."

Even at the best of times, the good Madame Fleming's sign would never have read, FORTUNES TOLD AND FORTUNES MADE, for there was not great money to be had in her chosen line of endeavor. But she would do well for herself on this day. The quoted price was three times her going rate. Like a spider in her lair, she had seen the two innocents coming through a slit in the curtain hanging over one of her windows and knew well enough who they were. If the inmates from the manor up the hill intended to purchase her wares, she would make them pay as befitted their means.

Percy and Florilyn looked at one another. Neither had considered the practical aspects of the case. Florilyn had not so much as a ha'penny on her. Percy always carried a few coins, but two shillings was unexpectedly steep. Regretting his acquiescence to this questionable enterprise all the more, he dug into his pocket and took out everything he had. "I'm sorry," he said, looking over his meager resources. "It looks like I've only got one shilling sixpence." He began to rise. "Here, take the shilling. You can tell hers. I don't need my fortune told."

"Sit. . .sit, my sweet," said the woman. "I am feeling generous today. A shilling sixpence it is. You shall both leave knowing what your futures will bring."

Percy laid down the coins. Quickly they disappeared across the table away from him in the midst of a large fleshy palm.

Slowly Percy sat back down.

"Give me your hand, young lady," said Madame Fleming.

Tentatively Florilyn held out her hand. A tingle of electric current surged through her at the touch from the woman's leathery fingers. The psychic closed her eyes. Her lips began to move but remained silent. Florilyn stared with eyes as wide as saucers. The candle flickered and shadows danced on the walls and ceiling. There was no other movement, no sound.

After what seemed an eternity, the woman's lips stilled. Her eyelids quivered and slowly opened. She leaned forward and peered intently into Florilyn's hand. She began mumbling again to herself, running one finger up and down and across the lines of Florilyn's palm.

"I don't know who you are, young lady," she said at length. Her voice was thick from the East and full of exotic mystery. "But I see a great change coming to you. An inheritance that is yours will be taken away. Another will be given you in its place that is greater yet. Evildoers will try to take advantage of you and steal what is yours. But you will find love, and one will be faithful to you, though he is the least in your eyes. He will be your protector, and thus you will gain your inheritance in the end."

"What does it *mean?*" said Florilyn, trembling with the terrible thrill of mystic unknown.

"I cannot say," replied Madame Fleming in a voice of hidden wisdom. "The eyes of the oracle only pass on what they see and what secrets the hand divulges." Keeping Florilyn's palm clasped in the fingers of her own right hand, she reached toward Percy with her left. "And now you, young man."

Percy hesitated.

The woman's open hand stretched toward him.

"No," said Percy after a moment. "I don't want you looking at my hand."

"There is nothing to fear."

"I am not afraid. But I—"

His father's face rose before Percy's mind's eye. The expression was calm and purposeful. It steadied him. His father was staring into Percy's soul. Suddenly Percy realized that he *loved* his father and knew that his father was a *good* man and full of truth.

"No," he repeated. "I do not think my father would be pleased."

"Your *father?*" chided Madame Fleming. "Are you not your own man?"

"I am my father's son," said Percy. He rose. "Let's go, Florilyn."

"Wait," said Madame Fleming. "Even without your hand, I can see that though you are poor, you shall be rich, for you will find love and wealth together where you least expect them. Yet great pain will accompany the journey where you will discover—"

"That's enough," said Percy. "I will listen to no more. Florilyn, I am going." He left the anteroom and walked back through the large dark room toward the door.

Terrified to be left alone, Florilyn pulled her hand away, jumped up, and hurried after him.

Back in the sunshine of the street, Percy drew in a deep breath and exhaled. He felt as if he needed to rid himself of the spell of the place.

"Why did you rush out like that?" said Florilyn. "It was just getting interesting."

"She gives me the creeps. I didn't like being there."

"What about everything she said?"

"It means nothing. They just make that stuff up," said Percy. "Let's get out of here," he added as he took Grey Tide's reins and hastily mounted.

Inside the strange abode, Madame Fleming chuckled to herself as again she peeped through her window at her jumpy young customers. They would be back. She had given them enough to whet their appetite with all that nonsense about inheritances and evil people and wealth and love. She knew her words would worm their way into their minds, especially the girl's. The day would come when she would want to know more. Today's purpose had only been to bait the hook.

Her most lucrative profits were derived from repeat visits.

THIRTY-EIGHT

Below Stairs

A gentle knock came to the open stable door behind Westbrooke Manor. "I say, Hollin, my auld frien'," sounded a voice thick with accent from the north, "be ye ben?"

"Ay, is that you, Richard?" replied Radnor. "I'm inside—come in, come in!"

" 'Deed, 'tis me," said the visitor, Richard Hawarden, entering the darkened barn. "Ye maun hae kenned my tongue, I'm thinkin'."

"There's no mistaking the tongue of a Scot any more than there is that of an old Welshman," rejoined the viscount's groom. He walked out of the dark with a smile and a hand extended to his longtime friend from Burrenchobay Hall. "What brings you all this way from the Hall?"

"Jist yer ain stables. 'Tisna anither finer in all Gwynedd, as a'body kens."

"Lord Snowdon takes pride in his stock, that's the truth," remarked Radnor. "What is it you need?"

"A four-horse harness. Sir Armond has taen it intil's heid tae hae a jaunt aboot the coontryside the morn's morn wi' ane o' his Lonnen frien's frae parliament an' a' the rest o''em. He wants t' tak oot twa coaches wi' four, an' we haena but the ane harness."

"I think I have just what you'll be needing. But it's nigh eleven.

211

Come inside and join us for tea."

The groom led his counterpart from the neighboring estate out the door and toward the kitchen. Already the cook was pouring out eleven o'clock refreshment for the rest of the servants.

"You brought a guest, I see, Hollin," she said. "Welcome to you, Richard."

"Thank ye—and hoo are ye, Mrs. Drenwydd?"

"Well as can be expected," replied the woman in her customary fashion.

The two grooms sat down. Presently Broakes, the butler; Stuart Wyckham, the gardener; Mrs. Llewellyn, the housekeeper; and Deaken Trenchard, the viscount's footman, all entered. Greetings with the Burrenchobay groom were exchanged all around. They had just started on a loaf of sliced bread when Percy came through on his way outside.

"Tea, Master Percival?" asked the cook.

"Oh, that is very nice of you. But no, thank you, Mrs. Drenwydd," he replied, "I'm off for a ride." He shook hands with each of those present in turn.

She introduced him to their guest.

Hollin Radnor slowly uncoiled his lanky frame and rose from his chair, thinking to accompany Percy out to the stables.

"Stay where you are, Mr. Radnor," protested Percy. "I'll saddle her. I think Grey Tide is used to me now."

"I'm happy to—"

"Don't worry. I've watched you do it a dozen times. I'd like to try it myself."

The groom sat back down with a smile.

Percy left the kitchen and headed toward the stables.

"A muckle daecent chap, it seems tae me," remarked Sir Armond's groom.

Nods went around the room.

"A pleasant smile on the lad's face as weel. An' he gie me a fine grip o' his han'."

"I only wish the lad of the house were as interested in horses as his cousin," remarked Radnor.

"Or anything else for that matter," added Stuart Wyckham.

" 'Tis jist hoo things stan' at oor place," rejoined Hawarden. "Seems the yoong ones are the wairst o' it fer manners. I dinna like tae be aroun' when Master Colville comes wantin' a mount, though he comes searchin' fer me if I'm nae there. He'd ne'er dirty *his* fair hands saddlin' a horse! Luckily he's tae be off soon."

"To the continent, I hear," said Mrs. Drenwydd.

"Ay."

"The viscount and Sir Armond have spoken of a match between the two, I hear," now put in Lady Katherine's housekeeper.

"Master Colville and Lady Florilyn, you're meaning?" asked Trenchard.

"I'm not saying I approve," answered Mrs. Llewellyn. "But who else would I mean?"

"Never!" rejoined the cook.

"Dinna be so sure, Mrs. Drenwydd," rejoined their guest. "Talk aroun' the Hall is that they've aye ta'en a fancy tae ane anither. Mightna e'en need the father's tae show themselves in the matter."

"Meaning no disrespect to the Hall, Richard," persisted the cook, "but Sir Armand's eldest isn't fit to be husband to *any* woman, least of all our Lady Florilyn. We all know what happened on market day, though none of it's come within the ears of the viscount or Lady Katherine, poor woman."

Hawarden did not reply. In truth, he had more reason for agreeing with Mrs. Drenwydd's assessment of Colville Burrenchobay than any of the viscount's people knew.

"What about the two younger ones, Richard?" asked Broakes.

"Master Ainsworth and Mistress Davina—a mite better than their brither, I'm thinkin'," replied Hawarden. "But they're still carryin' the blue blood o' their kind. And ye ken what that means. An' they're yoong yet. Takes the teen years tae reveal character, ye ken. Canna say much afore the testin' o' pride an' independence rear their heads."

The butler nodded, joined by Mrs. Llewellyn. She knew the three Burrenchobay children well enough. She had served there some years before coming to the Westbrooke household. She had heard rumors of the proposed match for years, and she feared for Miss Florilyn.

" 'Tis the same here," remarked the cook. "Our young lady's already getting a long nose toward her inferiors, as she judges us. Though I can't think where she got it. Her mother's the kindest soul a body could meet."

"She got it from watching her brother, make no mistake," gruffed Broakes. "He's had the long nose of superiority since he could walk. He didn't need the teen years for *his* character to show itself. It was there long before."

"If she's not out riding," said Mrs. Llewellyn, adding her own critique of the young mistress, "it's every day she's wanting this dress pressed or her room cleaned or her bedclothes freshened."

"I daresay, what's to become of these young ones when their parents are gone?" sighed Wyckham.

"What do we care?" rejoined Llewellyn. "By then we'll be gone as well."

"They may be what they are," remarked Radnor, returning the conversation to their houseguest, "but the young man from Glasgow is a gentleman. It is nice to see in one so young."

"It is indeed," assented the butler. "The other afternoon he called me by name. 'Mister Broakes,' he said. And he's always got a kind, 'Thank you,' for me."

Nods and comments went round the room.

"Ay, he does the same with me," said the housekeeper. "He *thanks* me for doing up his room! Who's ever heard of such a thing?"

"Did you not hear him speaking to me just now in that respectful tone?" added the cook.

"I never saddle his horse without a kindly word of gratitude," nodded Radnor.

"His father's a preacher, you know," said Mrs. Llewellyn. "Lady Katherine's brother. That must be where he comes by such respect."

"I begin to wonder if the stories we heard of him be exaggerated," added Broakes. "I can't imagine the likes of *him* in trouble with the law."

"And why shouldn't they be exaggerated?" Mrs. Drynwydd nodded. "It's Courtenay and Florilyn we hear speaking about him. They're jealous of their father, if you ask me. It's clear the viscount's taken a fancy to the lad."

"Hollin says he knows how to talk to the horses," interposed the gardener. "That says a good lot about a man, young or old—isn't that right, Hollin?"

"Indeed so, Stuart," nodded Radnor.

"He was afraid of them at first, as I hear it," chuckled Trenchard.

"At first, maybe," said Radnor. "But a young man who can learn from his fear is on his way toward manhood. You saw yourself, he's not afraid of them now."

Tea completed, the little company gradually broke up.

Hollin Radnor and Richard Hawarden rose and ambled back out to the barn to finish the business that had brought the latter to the manor in the first place. They found Percy just completing his initial effort to saddle a horse by himself. Both grooms checked the straps, pronounced the job well done, and sent him off on his way with praise for his effort.

Thirty-Nine

The Tea Cake

The day dawned especially warm. Gwyneth had walked with her father to the slate mine early in the morning. She treasured every moment with him, even so simple an activity as walking him to work. Clouds over the mountains indicated rain, perhaps not that afternoon but surely by the next day.

Their conversation had been happy. Barrie kissed his daughter good-bye and turned to enter the quarry. Gwyneth's spirits were high as she stopped in at Grannie's for breakfast tea, her normal custom when accompanying her father to the mine.

No visit to town on Percy's part, whether to look in at any one of the half dozen shops or to pass through to the shore, there to chat with one of the friendlier fishermen or watch them coming and going from their trade, was complete without a visit to Grannie's cottage. There a warm pot always sat near the flame—awaiting the arrival of visitor, whether friend or stranger—with fresh tea leaves ready in the canister on a nearby shelf. Many days found Percy gone from the manor by midmorning and not returning until evening tea, chatting with Grannie, often with Gwyneth waiting on them hand and foot, exploring the town, or visiting with his widening circle of village friends.

Such associations, though ridiculed by his cousins, increased all the more his uncle's affection for his nephew. In truth, the viscount found it difficult to sympathize in heart with the humble folk of the region. Seeing how well the son of his wife's brother was received gave him a certain vicarious sense of satisfaction. It was as if, through the boy, he was a little more doing his duty by his people.

Gwyneth skipped and danced her way through the narrow lanes toward the east side of the village. Suddenly something pelted her from behind.

"Look, Eardley, it's the idiot-girl!" said the boy whose hand had just released the stick that had hit her back.

Percy's ride into town on this day was a little later than usual. Gwyneth was already on her way home from Grannie's as he rode between the two solemn church buildings at the south end of town. He heard a few shouts in the distance but thought nothing of it at first.

"Been to visit the witch, idiot-girl!" yelled a second taunter. "Ha, ha, ha! Let's get her, Chandos!"

The two boys, thirteen and twelve respectively and well known in the village for their pranks, sprinted after Gwyneth.

She might have returned to Grannie's, but that would only bring the trouble down on them both. And besides far-seeing eyes, Codnor Barrie's daughter had been blessed with two of the fleetest feet in all Llanfryniog. She could easily outrun the boys across the moor. She was confident they would not pursue her beyond the edge of the town.

Gwyneth turned and flew.

News of the incident outside Grannie's cottage between the cousins from the manor had spread among the youth of the town as rapidly as had reports of the fight behind the chapel on market day. Everyone for miles knew about the Westbrooke cousin, and the younger ones were wary of him. That he had been ready to take on the likes of Courtenay Westbrooke and Colville Burrenchobay convinced them that they would do well to keep clear of him.

Notwithstanding the account that both older boys had soundly thrashed the Scotsman, today's two young hoodlums had cast a few quick glances about to make sure Percy was nowhere near before commencing their attack against Gwyneth. Unfortunately, they hadn't looked closely enough.

Suddenly the sound of a galloping horse swooped toward the two boys. When he realized what was happening, Percy hardly stopped to consider whether he was capable of a fast ride through Llanfryniog's narrow streets. As it turned out, his practice had paid off.

He caught up to the boys, reined in, wheeled around, and leaped to the ground before they could flee. The two stood momentarily paralyzed as Percy walked toward them. Both thought of making a dash for it. But they knew that one of them would be run down by the big sixteen-year-old and that he would find the other soon enough.

"You blokes have a problem?" said Percy as he approached.

"No, sir," replied the younger of the two.

"What are your names?"

"Eardley White," replied the one who had spoken.

"And you?" he said, glancing toward the other.

"Chandos Gwarthegydd."

"Are you the blacksmith's son?"

"Yes, sir."

"Do you think your father would want me to tell him that you were trying to hurt a girl half your size?"

"No, sir."

Percy looked the two over a few seconds. "All right, then," he said, "I am going to tell you this once. If I hear that either of you have been bothering little Gwyneth again, I will come find you. Do I make myself clear?"

"Yes, sir," they said in unison.

"I will expect you to spread the word that anyone who even thinks of hurting her will have me to deal with. Do you understand?"

"Yes, sir."

"Then get out of here."

They ran off.

Percy returned to his horse and looked about. Though Gwyneth had glanced over her shoulder long enough to see Percy flying to intercept her pursuers, by this time she was nowhere to be seen. Percy's first instinct was to ride after her. But he knew the speed of her feet, as well as the rest, and that she was now safe. He was more concerned for her aunt. He did not trust the two scamps. Watching him leave town, they might retaliate against Grannie. He rode, therefore, to her cottage and spent the next hour there.

Rather than going inside when she arrived home, Gwyneth made her way behind the cottage to greet her friends for the day. She would never understand the meanness of her schoolmates. She did not fear them, at least too much. But she could not understand why people were not kind to one another.

In the large enclosure, her menagerie came bounding and romping toward her, each awaiting its turn as she sent a small hand probing through the fence to pet nose and head and speak to each by name. Two dogs came barking up from behind, eyes aglow, tails whisking back and forth, wet pink tongues seeking any part of her person to lick, jumping and whining impatiently for their share of the attention.

When she was able to free herself, Gwyneth walked to the smaller pens. Two orphans here were her special concern of the moment, a gull from the sea and a small gray rabbit. The gull had immediately allowed Gwyneth to hold and feed it. She had found it trapped in a bit of some strange kind of netting down on the shore. She managed to free it, though its wing was broken. Speaking gently, she had carried it up the steep path and back home.

The rabbit she had discovered one day at her doorstep, limping and with signs of blood on its coat. Unlike the gull, it had been skittish and afraid of her touch. Wearing his leather gloves, her father managed to capture the little creature and place it in a pen. Gwyneth had been feeding it daily ever since. After two days she was able to hold the timid little thing in her arms and feed it grasses and flowers from the meadow.

She opened the pen and gently removed the furry little rabbit who had by now been given a name. "You understand what it is to be afraid, don't you, Bunny White Tail," she said softly, walking about stroking behind its soft, furry ears. "I know you were afraid when you came here, weren't you? You know now that there is nothing to be afraid of, because I am here to take care of you. I am not afraid, either, for God has sent someone to take care of me, just like He sent me to take care of you."

Most of the larger beasts left for hours and days at a time, some by day, others by night, to feed and forage as best they could in the wild. Gwyneth's father could not afford to buy grain to feed all the small animals in her care. But he managed to keep a supply of corn or oats or meal on hand at least to prevent the starvation of the chickens and injured creatures. The former repaid them with a steady supply of eggs. As for the latter, he only hoped his generosity would somehow be credited to him in the eternal scales by which the world is sustained. He certainly could ill afford extra expenditures.

Barrie was on good enough terms with many of the local farmers that a decent supply of usable hay and grain came his way. He and Gwyneth visited the harvest fields every autumn to glean what they could when the harvesters had completed their work. On most such days they pulled a large cartload of broken stalks home at the end of each afternoon's effort. After threshing out what grain could be salvaged, they stored their own little harvest in the loft of the shed beside their cottage for use throughout the winter.

On this day, Gwyneth's thoughts were not on her animals. She was thinking instead of Percy. How could she repay him for his kindness? After she had come home from the village an idea struck her—she would bake him a fine sweet tea cake!

She set about almost immediately mixing the ingredients—just as she had learned from Grannie—and placed the tiny loaf in the coal oven to bake. An hour later it was nearly ready. She opened the oven door to check her creation. By then its aromas filled the cottage. Gwyneth patiently waited another ten minutes. Again she opened the iron door.

The top was a perfect golden brown.

With careful hand slipped inside a great padded mitten, Gwyneth removed it and set it on top of the stove to cool. Now she just had to find a way to get it into Percy's hands. She had sneaked onto the manor grounds without being seen to leave the forgiveness flowers for Master Courtenay and Miss Florilyn. But she could hardly leave a cake hanging from the doorpost!

She went to the front door, opened it, and gazed out across the moor in the direction of the manor. Rain clouds clung to the mountains. She would have to watch for him. If she didn't see him today on his way back from the village, perhaps he would visit Grannie's tomorrow.

Midway through the following morning, Gwyneth Barrie's keen eye was rewarded. She darted inside. The next instant she was dashing across the moor as fast as her legs could carry her.

Percy had emerged from the manor gate, on foot this time, when Gwyneth saw him. As he turned onto the Llanfryniog road, he heard a high voice calling his name. He looked around to see Gwyneth running toward him through the field of grazing cattle between himself and town, white hair streaming behind her appearing almost golden in the sunlight. He stopped and waited.

"Good morning, Percy!" she said sweetly then paused to catch her breath. "I baked you a tea cake!"

"Why, Gwyneth, thank you," said Percy. "What's the occasion? It's not my birthday."

"It's a friendship cake," she replied. "To thank you for chasing those boys away and for what you said when Master Courtenay and Lady Florilyn were laughing at me at Grannie's. Here, Percy."

"This is an unexpected pleasure!" he said as he took it from her hand. "I shall look forward to it—thank you!"

Slowly they left the road and began walking across the plateau toward the sea. In a few moments, they came to the stream that flowed down from the mountains westward across the moor and tumbled over Mochras Head into the sea. It had not much water in it now and was of no great depth, though was five or six feet in width. Percy paused, set the cake on the grass, then placed his hands on the sides of Gwyneth's little waist, plunged his feet into the water, and whisked her over to the other side.

"O–o–o–h!" she squealed with delight, "that was fun! But you've gotten your boots and trousers all wet."

"They will dry soon enough," laughed Percy. He recovered his gift and rejoined her.

Gwyneth led farther up the slope, and Percy was happy to follow.

"Come," said Gwyneth. "I want to show you the view from the top of the cliff."

They continued two or three hundred yards along the inland edge of the promontory.

"I have to stay back from the edge," said Gwyneth as they walked. "Papa knows I am careful. But he says I must always be cautious near the sea."

At length Gwyneth stopped, then threw herself on the grass and pointed her face out over the cliff edge. "Come, Percy," she said, "lay down beside me."

Percy laid his cake-gift on the grass beside him and did as she said.

"Scoot forward," she said. "Now, put your hands under your chin. . . like this. Look out—isn't the sea beautiful like this, so high above it?"

"Is this another of your special places?" asked Percy.

"Yes."

"So now I know about three. How many do you have?"

"I don't know. I've never counted. Probably six or eight."

They lay motionless for five or six minutes, drinking in the sea air. It was mingled with earthy aromas from the grass and moorland around them. Below, the waves splashed against the shoreline though the bluff-edge obscured the sight. In front of them, gulls played in the cliff-breezes.

"Papa says he will take me back to Ireland one day," said Gwyneth. "He wants to show me where my mother lived and where I was born."

They remained quiet as they stared out across the ancient waters.

At length Percy rose to a sitting position. "All this salt air has made me hungry," he said. "How would you like to join me for some tea cake?"

"Oh, but I couldn't, Percy. I made it for you!"

"So it's mine, is it?"

"Yes. I gave it to you."

"Then I can do anything I want with it?"

"Of course."

"Even share it with my friends?"

Gwyneth nodded with a smile.

"Then I want to share it with you!" Percy tore off a chunk of the soft white cake, split it in half, handed one portion to Gwyneth, then took a bite out of the other. "Delicious!" he exclaimed.

"It is supposed to be eaten with tea," said Gwyneth.

"I'll save the rest—I promise. Uh-oh!" he exclaimed, looking up. "I think I felt rain."

Within seconds huge raindrops were pelting them.

"O–ow—you were right!" cried Gwyneth. "Come, Percy! We'll run to my house. We'll have a fire and tea and dry out."

"And eat the rest of my cake!" Percy laughed.

They leaped to their feet and dashed across the moor as the downpour engulfed them. By the time they reached the stone cottage, though Percy had done his best to protect the tea cake inside his shirt, both were dripping wet.

With the promise to come back the next day if the rain cleared for another riding lesson, Percy returned to the manor late that afternoon. He was not yet quite dry but was happier than he had been in years. The humblest pleasures in life, simply lying on the ground looking out across the sea or getting caught in a rainstorm, gave him more joy than he ever could have imagined.

FORTY

Remote Cottage

*W*ith the basic principles of riding clearer in his mind and becoming more natural as he felt increasingly comfortable on the back of a horse, Percy had been out riding almost every day for the past several weeks. On several of those, his uncle had accompanied him. They had spoken of many things.

He often rode south through the gentle terrain of the coast and occasionally east. He was learning his way along the trails and roads in every direction. He had tried to replicate his lengthy precarious ride with Florilyn but turned back when he realized that he was in danger of losing his way. Whenever he wanted to practice his galloping technique, however, he went to the shore where it was level and the footing secure.

He knew he must eventually also learn to ride fast over bumpy grassland, even through wooded regions. It was for that reason that he had requested another lesson with his diminutive instructor.

The day after the downpour dawned fair though chilly. Percy waited until after lunch when he knew Florilyn usually went to her room. They had not spoken again about the incident at Madame Fleming's. After her strange friendliness of that day, he was afraid she might want to go riding with him again. But on the days of his lessons, he had to keep his riding secret. Once the door of her room closed behind her, Percy left the house for the stables to prepare for his afternoon's ride.

He set out down the drive and onto the main road. Instead of turning left on the village road, he continued north then veered onto the moor and through farmland until he was approaching the Barrie cottage.

Gwyneth saw him coming from behind the house. She ran excitedly to meet him. "Hi, Percy!" she cried.

"Hi, Gwyneth. . .are you ready to give me another lesson?"

"Let me just run inside and take the pot off the stove so it won't boil over."

She returned a minute later. "Shall I run to the beach?" she asked.

"Why don't you get up behind me and we'll ride together," said Percy. He reached down and took her hand. With a single motion as if he found her light as a feather, and with a high-pitched squeal of delight, Gwyneth flew up onto Grey Tide's back just behind the saddle. She stretched her arms around Percy's waist.

As Percy encouraged Grey Tide into motion, Gwyneth thought she had never been so happy in her life. Percy may have been only sixteen. But he was still a grown man in her eyes. She felt safer in his presence than with anyone other than her father.

"I would like to try galloping on grass instead of sand today," said Percy over his shoulder. "Florilyn will be sure to want to race someplace that won't be easy for me. Where can we go that is not *too* bumpy?"

"Go over there," said Gwyneth, "to the right and up the hill. I will show you."

They crossed the main road, continued through several fields full of grazing cattle. As the plateau rose away from the sea, the terrain of patchy moorland became less arable. They rode up and down several inclines, moving into the hills and toward the series of ridges they had been over together on the day he had lost his mount with Florilyn. On this day they were farther north than Percy had yet been.

"I thought you were going to take me someplace gentle and flat!" He laughed. "I wouldn't dare gallop here—I'd be thrown in no time."

"Don't worry, Percy," said Gwyneth behind him. "There is a flat meadow near the Muir cottage. I think you will like it. It is another of my special places."

"*Stevie* Muir?" said Percy.

"Yes, do you know Stevie?"

"I do indeed. I saw him shear a sheep in the market day contest. I didn't know you knew him—though I suppose you know everyone."

"Stevie is my cousin."

"Is he! What a coincidence! Well, it probably isn't that much of a coincidence. I suppose many of the families around here are related in one way or another."

"There is my aunt's house...just there. Can you see it?" said Gwyneth.

"I think so... Ah, yes, there in the little hollow between the slopes."

They continued toward it. As they came closer, all at once a clustering mass of sheep came bounding toward them. Without waiting for Percy to stop, Gwyneth leaped to the ground and went running toward them. They baaed in a frenzy, nudging and sniffing and waddling around her. Gwyneth giggled in delight as she ran her hands through their woolly, greasy, dirty, matted coats while they pressed close around her. Percy reined in and stopped, his way blocked by the mass of sheep.

A minute later Stevie Muir appeared behind them. He waved and called out in greeting. "Hoy, Gwyneth!"

"Hi, Stevie. I brought Percy Drummond."

"So I see. Welcome to you, Mr. Drummond. So you came for your visit along with a wee friend!"

"I had no idea the two of you knew one another," said Percy. "Gwyneth tells me you're cousins."

"We are indeed. Let me run back and tell my mum to put the kettle on. It's not many visitors we get out here. She will be eager to show you the hospitality of the Welsh. She's heard about you, you see." He turned and ran toward the cottage.

"Come with me, Percy," said Gwyneth, leading the way slowly through the sheep. "They will stay out of Grey Tide's way."

Percy followed. As they came near the cottage, several barking dogs bounded to greet Gwyneth. The sheep did not seem concerned. Percy dismounted, and Gwyneth led him inside.

A woman of some fifty years stood at a black cookstove. Her partially graying dark hair fell down over a forehead and cheeks dappled with perspiration. In a word, her countenance looked *tired*. Stevie was nowhere in sight.

She turned toward them as they entered. In spite of her fatigue, her eyes lit up. "Ah, Gwyneth, my dear. How are ye the day?"

"Well, Auntie. This is Mr. Drummond."

"Welcome to ye, young man," said the woman, drying her hands on the apron tied around her waist. She extended a strong hand whose appearance indicated close acquaintance with hard work.

"Thank you, Mrs. Muir," said Percy. "Your son invited me for a visit several weeks ago. I am sorry to say I have been negligent. But Gwyneth finally got me up here. She says you are related."

"Ay. Her daddy's my brother."

Just then Stevie reappeared.

"Daddy's fine," he said to his mother then glanced at Percy. "My daddy's sick, you see, Mr. Drummond," he said. "He's forgotten most things and gets agitated when there's a commotion. I was just in telling him we had a guest so he wouldn't be confused. Come. . .I'll take you to him."

Percy followed into the adjacent room. There sat a man by appearance at least a decade older than Mrs. Muir. What thin hair he had left was pure white. His face was pale and drawn as he sat in an overstuffed chair staring vacantly ahead out of sunken eyes. A blanket of faded red wool lay over his knees and legs.

"I've brought you our visitor, Daddy," said Stevie. "This is Mr. Drummond."

Percy bent down with a smile. "Hello, Mr. Muir," he said. "I am happy to make your acquaintance." He took the man's hand where it lay in his lap and shook it gently. Stevie's father did not seem aware of Percy's presence.

Stevie led him across the room, and they sat down. A few minutes later, Gwyneth and Mrs. Muir appeared with a tray of tea things.

"I'm sorry I didn't know you were coming, Mr. Drummond," said his hostess. "I would have baked some scones. I'm afraid I have nothing to offer you other than buttered bread."

"And nothing goes quite so well with tea, Mrs. Muir," rejoined Percy cheerfully. "That is. . .would it be *laver bread* you are speaking of?"

"No," she said, laughing. "Not quite to your taste, I take it?"

"I have to admit, the idea of eating seaweed has been difficult to get accustomed to."

"Have no fear—my bread is nothing but thick dark rye and wheat."

"Then I will enjoy it heartily!"

"Ye be an easy young man to please. 'Tis not every day we get a visitor from the manor in our wee cottage. What am I saying? We have *never* had anyone from the manor set foot past our door, much less sit down with us for tea. We are right honored, sir."

Percy laughed. "I doubt my presence is worthy of such praise, Mrs. Muir. I am but a friend of Stevie's and Gwyneth's who is answering a long overdue invitation. But I thank you for your hospitality and kind words."

"We get the viscount's factor calling, Mum," said Stevie.

"Ay. Every six months like clockwork coming for his rents. Yet he never darkens the inside of my door, but just waits outside for me to bring it to him."

"Manor. . .what's that you say about the manor?" suddenly said the old man from across the room. "I worked at the manor, you know. The viscount treated me right well when I was a lad. Did odd jobs and ran errands for him, I did."

"Yes, Daddy," said Stevie. "We have a visitor from the manor."

"The viscount's come, you say? He'll be wanting me." He folded back a corner of the wool blanket, though it seemed too heavy for him to get off his knees, and struggled to rise.

"Nay, Daddy," now interposed Mrs. Muir. "The viscount's not here."

Bewildered and disappointed, her husband relaxed back into his chair. He continued to glance about the room, as if looking for someone. Slowly by degrees, he drifted again into silence.

"I can hardly imagine him working for the viscount," said Percy. "I would guess him to be quite a bit older than my uncle."

"He is speaking of the old viscount, Mr. Drummond," said Mrs. Muir. "It's your uncle's father he's thinking of. His mind's about gone, ye see, but his memory of his early years is as clear as the water in the lake up yonder on the far slopes of Rhinog Fawr. Much of the time he doesn't even know who I am, poor man. I have to watch that he doesn't wander off. He won't know how to get back home."

"I am sorry, Mrs. Muir," said Percy. "I had no idea. Can nothing be done for him?"

"Nothing but what the good Lord Himself can do. My dear man is in His hands now."

A few moments of reflective silence fell as they sipped at their tea.

"Is there anything he needs?" asked Percy at length. "Medications or the like, anything I might be able to obtain for you?"

"That is very kind of ye, Mr. Drummond," replied Stevie's mother. "With my man the way he is, we do struggle a bit to keep up with the garden and what things we are able to grow. The work's a little much for just the two of us now, and Stevie's got his hands full with the sheep and cows and chickens. But my brother helps us now and then, as he is able. That's Gwyneth's papa. With my daughter gone, Gwyneth comes and helps me clean the house. Don't you, darling?" she said, turning to Gwyneth with a smile. "We do right well, don't we, Stevie? We are more blessed than we can imagine. Stevie's sister, ye see, is a servant at Burrenchobay Hall. It isn't much Sir Armond can pay her, ye see, for he isn't of old money like Lord Snowdon. But what my Gracie gets she brings home to us, and we've mostly got all we need."

"If there ever is anything I can do," said Percy, then glanced toward Stevie, "you come to the manor, Stevie. You find me."

Stevie nodded. They chatted for another fifteen or twenty minutes.

At length they finished their tea and Percy glanced at Gwyneth. "Actually," he said, "Gwyneth and I came up here for what I must confess is an ulterior motive. Gwyneth has been giving me riding lessons."

"Has she now?" said Mrs. Muir.

"Galloping lessons, actually. I'm not so good on the back of a horse. Florilyn took me out a few weeks ago and succeeded in getting me both thrown and lost. Gwyneth told me she could teach me to ride fast enough that I could beat my cousin in a race. She said there is a place nearby where she wants me to practice."

"The meadow on the way to the lake, Stevie," said Gwyneth.

"Are you really going to race Miss Florilyn again?" asked Stevie enthusiastically.

"That is my plan," answered Percy. "She doesn't know it yet."

"I would love to see that!"

"Then you will definitely be notified of time and place!" Percy laughed. "But bring your bandages and smelling salts in case I end up on the ground again."

"You will win, Percy," said Gwyneth confidently.

"How can you be so certain?"

"I have seen you both ride. You are almost as fast already. You will win."

"I didn't know you were such an expert teacher, Gwyneth," said Stevie. "May I go with you? I might learn something myself."

The three young people rose.

"Thank you for the tea and bread, Auntie," said Gwyneth.

"Yes, thank you," added Percy, shaking the hand of Gwyneth's aunt. He walked across the room and again took Mr. Muir's limp hand. "Good-bye, Mr. Muir," he said.

"Are you the one from the manor?" asked the old man faintly. He glanced up but could not quite focus on Percy where he stood before him.

"Yes, sir."

"Did the viscount send you?"

"No, sir. I came to visit your son and wife."

"I have a son?"

"Yes, sir. Stevie."

He mumbled a few unintelligible words, and then his eyes glazed over again.

The three young people left the cottage.

"I will run ahead," said Stevie. "It's only about a mile." He turned and broke into a gentle loping stride away from the cottage.

Percy and Gwyneth remounted Grey Tide and set off at a leisurely pace after him. They arrived at the meadow ten minutes later.

For the next hour, both Stevie and Gwyneth coached Percy as he galloped back and forth over the grassy terrain. He was eventually comfortable enough to try jumping a tiny stream and did so several times without incident. Whenever he glanced over at Gwyneth, she reminded him, by extending her elbows and gently rocking them up and down, to feel the motion of the horse beneath him and to move in oneness with it.

When they were through, Gwyneth pronounced him ready, though Percy was still not altogether convinced.

FORTY-ONE

Picnic in the Hills

*R*hawn Lorimer had not been pleased with Percy's rebuff on market day. She had been stewing and scheming ever since how she might try her wiles on him again. That Courtenay's sister was so obviously uninterested left the field wide open for her to pursue him.

There remained the mystery of the strange floral bouquets to get to the bottom of. She still had not made the connection in her mind between Percy's bouquet in the shop and the village witch-child. But whoever the secret girl was for whom Percy had bought the ribbon, Rhawn had no doubt that he could be enticed to forget her. But she had to get him *alone*.

And she couldn't help it—she was jealous of Florilyn. After what he had done in the village, what a goose not to see that he was crazy about her. Percy's words still annoyed her that he wouldn't risk a fight for *her*. It made Rhawn all the more determined to win him over.

She did not lose much sleep speculating on what would be the result to Percy from Courtenay if she was successful, *Boys had to be able to take care of themselves* about summed up her thoughts on the matter. Alongside Courtenay's view that girls ought to come to him, the two were ideally matched for one another in conceit.

Thus Rhawn Lorimer's machinations continued. Every time she

went near the manor, however, ostensibly to see Florilyn but keeping an eagle eye out for her cousin, there was no sign of him. And Courtenay always insisted on hanging around.

One day late in July, with high summer abroad throughout North Wales, Rhawn Lorimer decided that she would lure the rivals out for a ride. She would use Florilyn as the pawn for her stratagems. From certain comments from her friend, she gathered that the animosity between she and Percy had begun to wane. That fact concerned her more than a little. She had to act before it went too far and Florilyn took it into her head to return Percy's attentions.

Rhawn appeared at Westbrooke Manor midway through the morning. "Florilyn," she said excitedly, "it is a gorgeous warm day. I'm going to ask Courtenay to go for a ride toward the mountains. I haven't been into the hills for longer than I can remember. Do you want to go? Let's take a picnic lunch!"

"Why would I want to go with you and Courtenay?" replied Florilyn. "I don't want to tag along with the two of you. Haven't you heard about three's a crowd? Courtenay would hate me."

"It would be more fun with you along."

"Maybe for you!"

"Well. . .perhaps it wasn't such a good idea," sulked Rhawn.

"Why don't you just go without me?"

"I don't know," rejoined Rhawn hesitantly. "Courtenay's been, I don't know. . .a little funny lately. I don't know if he would be such good company by himself."

They were silent a moment. Rhawn was clearly disappointed.

"I've got an idea," said Florilyn. "I could see if Percy wants to go. . . that is, if you don't mind."

"Oh. . .okay—that sounds all right. Then we would each have someone to ride with. Do you think he would?"

"I'll ask him. He went to his room after breakfast. I think he's still there. He reads a lot," she added, as if the idea of reading a book was repulsive. Florilyn bounded out of the room and ran down the hall.

Percy's initial reaction when Florilyn appeared at his door was not promising.

"Courtenay and Rhawn are going for a ride—do you want to go?" Florilyn asked.

He met her words with a blank stare. "Why would I want to go riding with *them*?" he asked.

"You'll go with me. I'm going, too."

Percy shook his head. Rhawn Lorimer was dangerous. He wanted nothing to do with her. . .especially with Courtenay watching him like a hawk. "I'm sorry," he said, "but the book I'm in the middle of will be better company than those two."

"Please, Percy," said Florilyn. "It will be fun."

"Look, Florilyn, I don't want to do anything to irritate your brother. When it comes to Rhawn Lorimer, Courtenay is very edgy. Believe me, he *won't* want me around."

"I won't let him do anything to you."

"How will you stop him?" smiled Percy sardonically.

"He's not going to beat you up again with the two of us there."

"You're probably right."

"Come on. . .please!"

"All right." He nodded. "But you'd better keep Courtenay off me!" he added with a laugh.

It was soon arranged. Within half an hour, the four horses were saddled, Mrs. Drynwydd had packed a lunch and they set off.

Rhawn was in high spirits. It was obvious from the beginning that she intended to pay as much attention to Percy as to Courtenay.

Percy regretted his decision before the roof of the manor was out of sight behind them. He did his best to keep as far away from her as possible. He was hampered in this effort in that he was still not as skilled on uneven ground as the other three. But his skills had improved sufficiently that he mostly managed to keep one of his cousins between himself and Rhawn as they made their way eastward into the hills. The girls chatted away. Courtenay remained silent. Percy was content to follow his example.

As they went, he recalled a rumor that had come within his hearing in the village of a strange creature that haunted the lake regions of Snowdonia. It was said to walk on two legs and be the terror even of wolves and bears. He could not deny that he was curious to see what substance there was to the stories. He had no reason to trust what the village urchins said. Yet the fact that the younger of them, from reports pressed with great exaggeration upon the ears of their imaginations by older brothers and sisters, were terrified to venture much beyond the north-south road made him wonder what truth might exist in the tales.

A narrowing forced the girls to ride ahead. Percy found himself side by side with Courtenay.

"Is there any truth to the rumors of a lake monster in the mountains?" he asked his cousin.

Courtenay glanced to his side without much expression. "There is talk of it," he replied. "I've not heard it called a *monster*. Most of the people who claim to have seen it say that the thing is tiny."

"People have seen it?"

"People have *claimed* to see it."

"What do you think?"

"That it's nonsense. Colville and I have been riding in these hills since we were so high. We've never seen anything. That reminds me. . . we were supposed to take you hunting."

"No thanks!" Percy laughed. "I don't think your friend much cares for me. I'm not sure I want to go out in the mountains with him toting a rifle."

Courtenay smiled wryly. "I see what you mean," he said. "Yeah, he's not too fond of you. But I still think the creature talk is rubbish."

The girls ahead had been listening.

"Don't be so sure, Courtenay," said Florilyn over her shoulder. "What about Gwberr-niog?"

"What's *that*?" said Percy.

"A water-kelpie who lives in the mountain lakes," replied Florilyn.

"We all grew up hearing about it."

"Come on, Florilyn," insisted Courtenay, "you know as well as I do that it's all nonsense."

"Who says? I would never ride out here alone at night."

"I would," said Rhawn, making sport of the whole thing. "That is. . . if I could get someone to come with me."

Neither of the young men was inclined to take the bait.

"You'd be safe enough around here," said Courtenay. "Gwberr-niog only lives in the lakes farther north."

"I thought you didn't believe in him."

"I don't. I'm only saying that's where he is *supposed* to live."

"He eats humans, you know," said Rhawn. "And only comes out at night. That's when his hunger for human flesh is greatest."

"Rhawn—ugh," said Florilyn. "Don't talk so! You're going to make me afraid. You'll ruin our picnic."

"Nothing can hurt *us*, Florilyn," said Rhawn, turning to smile over her shoulder at Courtenay. "We have two brave men to take care of us." As she turned her head slowly around, she allowed her eyes to linger on Percy's face with an expression whose meaning was impossible to miss.

Percy glanced hurriedly away and did his best to ignore it.

The route before them widened again. The girls eased back. Again the horses continued along four abreast. They came to a long level pasture.

Suddenly Rhawn bolted. "Race you to the far side!" she cried galloping ahead.

Florilyn on Red Rhud was after her like a flash, with Courtenay, who did *not* like to be bested on the back of a horse by any girl, at her side.

Percy urged Grey Tide into an easy gallop. Even after his time with Gwyneth near the Muir cottage, he did not care about trying to keep up with the others. In seconds they were thirty yards ahead.

It was exactly as Rhawn had planned it. She knew what the other three were likely to do. As quickly as she bolted, she now abruptly reined in. Florilyn and Courtenay sped by, not immediately apprehending her intent. They were too caught up racing one another to look back.

Rhawn slowed, and Percy drew alongside. She cleverly kept Grey Tide at her side, gradually easing back until both horses had slowed to a trot and finally resumed a comfortable walk. Ahead, the other two sped on.

"So here we are," said Rhawn, "alone at last."

"I don't want us to be alone," said Percy.

"But I do."

"I thought you were going for a ride with Courtenay."

"That was only so I could be with you."

"You don't care what Courtenay thinks?"

"No. Why should I? Courtenay's a bore."

"That may be," laughed Percy, though without humor in his tone. "But he's a bore with a temper."

Percy realized that it was time he put into practice everything Gwyneth had told him a few days earlier. He dug his heels into Grey Tide's sides, leaned as far forward as he could, and eased into a gallop.

Rhawn laughed merrily and caught him within seconds. Percy saw he was not about to outrun her. But at least he could make a pretense of trying to keep up with his cousins. They rode up side by side two minutes later to where Courtenay and Florilyn sat waiting.

"I guess I'm not ready for that rematch quite yet, eh, Florilyn!" laughed Percy, trying to divert attention from Courtenay's suspicious glances.

"You kept in the saddle at least," she said. "That is an improvement!"

"What's this about a rematch?" asked Rhawn.

"Nothing," replied Percy. "Just a private little contest between Florilyn and me, isn't that right, Florilyn?"

"Percy has challenged me to a race," said Florilyn in fun, never one to keep anything to herself.

"Which I am obviously not yet ready for!" rejoined Percy.

For the rest of the day, as they ate their picnic lunch, and throughout the entire ride back, Percy remained more on his guard than ever. It was now he who watched Rhawn's every move like a hawk. She knew what he was doing and enjoyed the cat-and-mouse game immensely. As a result of it, Percy was forced to attempt more conversation with Courtenay. He kept to his side like a twin.

"Is it true that you were in trouble with the police?" Courtenay asked as they rode along.

"I'm afraid so," replied Courtenay.

"What was it for?"

"Nothing serious. Petty theft. I was stupid. I broke into shops and stole things."

"Why—I thought your parents were well off."

"They are. Like I said, I was stupid. It was just for the adventure of it. But it was to the point where my father couldn't protect me any longer. I was close to getting thrown into jail."

"You were actually. . .*arrested?*"

"Not exactly. Most of the policemen knew my father. They usually brought me home with stern words and warnings. But for my father's sake, they let me off. You know how it is. I imagine if you got in trouble, Rhawn's father wouldn't send you up for a stretch in Dartmoor."

Another smile creased Courtenay's lips. "Don't be too sure," he said.

Percy laughed. "What do you mean?"

"You know fathers—no young man is ever good enough for their little girls."

"I see," chuckled Percy. "Well, I suppose it is to your advantage that your fathers are friends."

"Maybe. . . Now all I have to do is keep her away from you!" said Courtenay with a significant smile.

"Believe me, you have nothing to worry about."

"So *you* say."

"It's true!" Percy laughed. "Besides, I'll be gone in a couple of weeks."

From high in a tree, the four riders were being watched as they went. Gwyneth had in truth been following for some time, running ahead, circling around, taking shortcuts up the steepest of the hills while they rode around them. She could not keep from curiously wondering what Percy was like when with the three older youths. It felt funny in her stomach to see her friend with them. Was he really the same person with them? As the afternoon progressed, she crept ever closer, hoping to catch sight of his face or hear his voice as they passed.

Suddenly Rhawn Lorimer looked up and let out an ear-piercing shriek. "Look, it's the witch-girl!" she cried, pointing up in the tree ahead of them. "She's right there. She's spying on us!"

Courtenay followed her gaze and saw the little miscreant. Filled with rage and immediately assuming his role as presumptive heir and future viscount, he kicked his horse forward. "Come down from there this instant!" he yelled up into the tree.

Trembling to have been discovered, Gwyneth did not move.

"I demand that you come down."

Still Gwyneth did not flinch.

He realized that she was calling his bluff. Unless he was prepared to climb up the tree after her, he would come off looking impotent. So Courtenay changed his tactic. "This is my property," he said. "You are on the Westbrooke Manor estate. You are not allowed here. Perhaps you wandered here by mistake, so I will let it go this time. But if I find you trespassing again, I will not be so lenient. I hope I have made myself understood."

"Watch yourself, Courtenay," said Florilyn. "You don't want to get any more bouquets."

Rhawn's ears perked up at the mention of the mystery of the flowers.

"It's all right. Let's go," said Courtenay, still a little ruffled. "The sooner we get away from here the better."

The others continued on their way.

Percy rode toward the tree, stopped, and glanced up. "Hello, Gwyneth," he said. "What are you doing so far from home? You're not lost?"

The merry laugh that met his ears rang out louder than he had imagined her voice capable of.

"Come down and join us. I'll give you a ride home."

Gwyneth scampered down through the branches as if she were a tree lizard. In less than a minute, she was standing beside Percy's mount.

He reached down with his hand and again pulled her up and behind him on Grey Tide's rump as if she were weightless.

The other three watched with mixed reactions to see their foursome suddenly turned into a fivesome, and an unwelcome one at that. For the rest of the way back, they kept their distance.

The remainder of the ride was subdued. Had he dared, Courtenay would have given Percy a tongue lashing for interfering. The two girls kept their own counsel as well, but for very different reasons.

Gradually Percy's horse, with Gwyneth hanging on behind him, moved farther ahead. Their companions could hear Gwyneth and Percy laughing and talking. The very sound of it irritated two of them almost to distraction.

Courtenay's brief thaw toward Percy had thoroughly frozen over. He was profoundly annoyed to have his rebuke of Gwyneth so completely ignored.

The incident had also seriously tarnished the luster in which Percy stood in Rhawn Lorimer's eyes. She had done everything but kiss him, and he had as good as laughed at her. Yet now he was falling all over himself to give the little witch a ride home. She was more jealous of Gwyneth than she had ever been of Florilyn.

How could she be jealous of a mere child? The whole thing made her furious. She was more than a little afraid of Gwyneth, too. She knew the rumors as well as everyone else. But there was nothing she could do.

As they rode, however, Florilyn found herself filled with odd and unexpected reactions that were strangely sympathetic toward Percy. She didn't dare say anything to the other two. But as she listened to Courtenay and Rhawn grumbling angrily, she found herself wondering just what was so despicable about his being nice to one of the village children.

Not so very long ago she had been intentionally cruel to him, trying to bait him and make him angry. Yet he had been stubbornly insistent on being nice to her, too. She didn't deserve it, but he had persistently paid back her meanness with kindness. How could she fault him for being nice to someone else?

Percy treated everyone the same, whether rich or poor, boy or girl, young or old. After a summer in his presence, she had begun to realize what an unusual, and perhaps even wonderful, quality that was.

FORTY-TWO

Lake Creature of Gwynedd

The first days of his summer had been so tedious and slow. Suddenly Percy realized that his summer in Wales was flying by so rapidly that it would soon be at an end. What had begun as an incarceration had turned into the experience of a lifetime. It was with a poignant sense of melancholy that he realized he would soon be saying good-bye to all this.

Late in the morning of a brilliant warm day of early August, Percy set out on horseback for the hilly region northeast of Westbrooke Manor. After his ride with the other three, it had come into his mind to venture even farther into the mountainous inland region, where Stuart Wykeham, the gardener, told him several small, high, cold crystal lakes lay tucked between the peaks and offered a spectacular sight of the sort one never forgets.

Percy made his way through the east gate of the estate in high spirits, continued in the same direction through an ascending valley between two flanking ridges, then cut northward into the high hills. No trail marked his way underfoot, but he had been given rough directions by Wykeham and Hollin Radnor. He was confident enough in his sense of direction by this time that he almost wanted to get lost for the sheer pleasure of finding his way back out of the mountains.

A tremendous downpour had drenched the whole of Gwynedd the night before. Today's sun made the earth shine as though it had been sprinkled with diamonds. From its grasses and shrubs and trees gently rose a fragrance sweeter than the most costly perfume. The melody of Wales infected Percy as he rode happily along. He found himself occasionally breaking into some song or other he had heard in town, though he didn't even know the meaning of half the words he tried to sing.

The climb steepened steadily the farther inland he progressed. In two hours, Grey Tide was breathing heavily. As they descended into valley or dell, losing sight temporarily of mountains ahead, a quiet sense of isolation stole over him. Percy felt that he was entering a fairy-tale world disconnected from Wales and England altogether. Scarce breeze could be felt, no sound heard other than the occasional call of a hawk high overhead.

Rising out of these fairy hollows as he pursued his trek upward, the eastern mountains rose again into view. Once more Percy felt the gentle winds on his face. Pausing at the highest of each successive summit, he turned to behold the coastline spread out in the distance behind him, the deep blue of the sea stretched as to the very horizon. Then again he descended down the eastern slope, and all sense of being near the sea again vanished.

Midway through the afternoon, growing tired but with the weary pride of accomplishment, Percy approached what he hoped, if he had followed the landmarks indicated by the manor's two men correctly, would be the first of several lakes. He was leading Grey Tide through a wooded region of pine and fir. On his left rose a steep, rocky hillside, almost cliff-like and impassible, the opposite slope of which was supposed to overlook the tiny body of blue.

Making certain of his bearings, he worked his mount around the base of this small mountain as he continued to move gradually upward. At length he came to a jagged opening to his left where the shoulder of a projecting ridge opened between this hill and the next, extending down almost to Percy's level. Turning into this pass, Grey Tide scrambled with some difficulty up the rocky surface. Around several large boulders, Percy arrived at the overlook he sought.

Cresting the summit of the narrow opening between the higher hills, Percy saw below him, surrounded on all sides by jagged rocky hills and peaks, a tiny lake of the most gorgeous blue imaginable. Not a ripple disturbed its surface. In size it could not have been more than three or four hundred feet across. The blue of its surface shimmered with the richest shade he had ever seen, growing almost black at the center, indicating great depth. Around the edges, the hues lightened to pale shades of turquoise, so still and pure as to make what could be seen of the bottom near the shoreline absolutely sparkling in clarity.

Percy dismounted and stood as one transfixed. Trees surrounded most of the lake's circumference, broken on one side by cliffs and boulders rising straight up from the glistening surface in the direction of the overlooking peaks. Directly across from this cliff face, among the trees, a grassy meadow stretched away from the water's edge perhaps a hundred and fifty feet before giving way to the slopes of granite. Near the water's edge stood a dozen or more deer gently drinking from the lake and nibbling at the grass.

As he gazed, a sound began to invade Percy's ears. Faint at first, it gradually increased. He realized he was listening to some faint, strange, far-off kind of music. It did not sound human. But he had never heard bird or other animal make such a call. The crooning tone was melancholy, like the lamenting howl of wild dog or wolf. A faint hint of melody could be detected in the repetition of its ethereal notes, hovering ever and about some unknown minor key, never quite resolving itself, yet mysteriously satisfying and peaceful.

Suddenly Percy remembered the rumored lake creature of the mountains.

The strange, otherworldly, melodic crooning grew. Was this how the beast lured its victims into its lair, with sweet spells that wove a seductive enchantment over the senses, bewitching the unsuspecting to their eventual death? Was it perhaps a great bird of prey? The sound almost resembled the lonely cry of a hawk—peaceful, mesmerizing, terrifying. He knew great mountain birds existed, capable of killing animals many times their own size. Was it trying to lure him closer with the hypnotic beguilement of its music?

The sight below him was truly lovely. Was that part of the bedevilment itself? Yet the sound floating over mountains and forest was not one he could fear.

The strange crooning kept him riveted where he stood. It now seemed to be coming from the lake itself. He felt his feet moving forward, down the incline before him. . .toward the sound.

Suddenly from behind the trees beyond the meadow, a figure appeared, a white-clad child-figure from whom the haunting melody came.

Percy stopped and stood motionless.

Here was no mountain bird, nor lake creature nor kelpie. It was *Gwyneth* singing to the animals!

Even from this distance, under the crown that appeared reddish gold in the sunlight, he could almost see the two eyes of heaven's blue, behind which dwelt something whose light and life came from another world altogether, and from Him who made heaven and earth together.

A great joy rose in his heart as a smile rushed to Percy's lips. His first instinct was to call out and rush down to her. Yet some power restrained both feet and tongue.

Gwyneth held out her hand. Several deer slowly approached to nibble something from it. Around her feet scurried squirrels and chipmunks and rabbits and what looked to be a family of quail. Overhead swooped sparrows and robins. The melancholy crooning continued. Percy knew it was not meant for him.

By and by the melody ceased.

Gwyneth turned and retreated into the wood beyond the meadow. The rest of the small herd of deer lifted their heads from water and grass and followed her. So, too, did the smaller creatures.

Knowing that he had been chosen to witness something holy, with careful step Percy returned up to the overlook. He took Grey Tide's reins and led her on foot for five or ten minutes, then remounted and quietly retreated the way he had come.

He had been to Gwyneth's most special place of all. But it was one he could never tell her he had seen. This secluded corner of heaven had to remain hers alone.

FORTY-THREE

Cousins and Friends

*I*t was early August. In two weeks, Percy would return to Glasgow. He had been revolving many things in his mind, especially about his future, about his father and what he would say to him when he saw him again. He knew there was much he needed to make right.

Before that time came, however, he had one thing he had to take care of *here*.

After several more days of intense riding, he judged himself as ready as he would ever be. He found an opportunity when Florilyn was alone outside. "Hey," he called, running to catch her.

She turned. "Hi, Percy," she said, greeting him with a pleasant smile.

"I'll be returning to Glasgow before much longer," he said, falling into stride beside her.

"Is it that soon already?"

"I'm afraid so."

"It won't be the same here without you."

"Glad to get rid of me at last, eh!" Percy laughed good-naturedly.

"That's not what I meant."

"I know. Just teasing. You have to admit that your brother will be happy to see me go."

"Maybe so—but Courtenay can be an old poop. He didn't learn

to—" Florilyn hesitated. "I've. . .I have enjoyed having you here," she said after a moment, glancing toward him with an awkward smile. "I know I wasn't very nice at first—"

"Aw, forget it," said Percy. "No harm done. You know what Bill Shakespeare says."

"I remember," she smiled. " 'All's well that ends well.' Do you really know your Shakespeare that well?"

"Are you kidding?" Percy laughed. "I was a terrible student in school. I'm sure you know more Shakespeare than I do."

"I doubt that. I wasn't the shiniest apple in the barrel either."

Percy laughed again. "That's a good one! No—I just throw around a quote or two once in a while to pretend I know what I'm talking about."

Florilyn laughed. "You are too funny, Percy! You've always got a comeback. Is there *anything* in life you take seriously?"

"Probing the Drummond psyche, are you now?"

Florilyn smiled. "I suppose I'm interested in what makes you tick."

"That's a switch."

"You've got to give a girl a chance to change, to see things more clearly. That's only fair, don't you think?"

"You're right. I suppose we've both done some changing this summer. Why are you interested in what makes me tick?"

"I don't know. Isn't it natural for people to be interested in one another?"

"Maybe so. But I don't think anyone's ever said something like that to me before. I'm not sure I know what makes me tick myself!" Percy laughed.

"There you go making a joke again!"

"It wasn't really a joke. It's the truth," rejoined Percy, then grew quiet. "Yes—there are things I take seriously. Knowing that I will see my father in a couple weeks is enough to make me somber in a hurry."

"Why?"

"My father and I haven't exactly been on the best of terms for the last several years."

"You're not eager to see him?"

"That's not it exactly. It's more. . ." Percy paused and drew in a thoughtful breath. He remained quiet for several long seconds. "I'm not sure I want it to continue the way it's been," he went on at length. "You say you've changed. I'm changing, too. I am beginning to realize that my father is a good man, an honorable man, a man of character and principle. Maybe it's time I owned up to that fact. I *want* to own up to it. I want to know him man to man, not as a pouty, spoiled, self-centered boy."

Florilyn took in Percy's words without reply. They struck a chord in her heart as well.

"But I didn't come out here to talk about all that," Percy added with a smile.

"What then?"

"You and I have some unfinished business."

Florilyn returned his look with a confused expression. "What do you mean?"

"Our rematch," said Percy, eyes gleaming in fun. "I want another chance to race you."

"Ah!" exclaimed Florilyn, her eyes now also lighting up. "A glutton for punishment, are you?"

"You are assuming the outcome before we saddle the horses," chided Percy playfully.

"It's *your* pride on the line," rejoined Florilyn with equal humor.

"I will risk it. My pride is equal to the task."

"Then you're on, cousin!" Floriyn laughed. "Just name the time and place."

"You are going to let *me* pick the place?"

"Why not? I'm so much faster than you, I ought to give you *some* advantage."

Percy roared with delight. "You wouldn't care to place a small wager on the outcome?" he asked.

Now it was Florilyn's turn to break out in a peal of laughter. Her merriment could be heard throughout the manor grounds. "If you are so anxious to lose your money," she said.

"I wasn't thinking of money."

"What then?"

"I don't know—what about the loser waits on the winner for a day. She obeys his every command and wish with good humor and without complaint."

Florilyn could not stop laughing at the delicious prospect. "Don't you mean—*he* obeys *her* every command?"

"My dear cousin Florilyn, I fear you seriously underestimate your opponent."

"You are on!" giggled Florilyn again.

"Then I propose as our appointed venue," said Percy, "the harbor beach at low tide."

"Why there?" said Florilyn.

"That would make it a race of pure speed," replied Percy. "It is flat, straight, no streams or logs or obstacles for you to trick me with."

Florilyn smiled. Her mood grew subdued. "That was mean of me, wasn't it? I won't do that again. All right then, the beach it is."

"Tomorrow?"

"Agreed."

"And horses?"

"Obviously, as you are the serious underdog, it is only right of me to let you select your mount."

"Then I will ride Grey Tide. And you?"

"I will have to think about it. But probably Red Rhud."

"I will check with one of my fisherman friends this afternoon," said Percy. "I will let you know the exact time of low tide."

Forty-Four

The Race

*A*t two o'clock on the following afternoon, just south of the Llanfryniog harbor, a strange scene had begun to unfold. A small gathering had formed on the wide glistening sand comprised of what might be considered an odd assortment of individuals. That Lord Snowdon's son and daughter and nephew appeared at the center of the commotion might seem to indicate some kind of aristocratic sport in progress. But that the shepherd from the inland hills, Stevie Muir, stood talking to Percy Drummond, while his tiny cousin, Gwyneth Barrie, held the reins of one of the prized horses from the manor's stables, spoke of wider involvement than merely the region's blue bloods.

Somehow through that mysterious osmosis by which news and gossip circulates about a small community, word had spread that there was to be a horse race that afternoon when the tide of Tremadog Bay reached its lowest. It did not take long for the news to become the chief topic of conversation.

Thus, from the village a steady stream was now walking toward the beach. It was comprised mostly of the younger element, led by Eardley White and Chandos Gwarthegydd, who, presuming upon their encounter with Percy, let it be known to their friends that they were now personal acquaintances of the young Scot and that he had taken them into his confidence. Whatever may have been his stern words to them, they could not help liking a man of the people such as Percy had proved himself to be.

Rhawn Lorimer was, of course, on hand with Courtenay as Florilyn's moral support. After what had happened a few days before in the hills, Rhawn hadn't quite made up her mind about Percy. But on this day, owing to her fear of Gwyneth, she kept close to Courtenay's side.

A few fishermen wandered in from the harbor. The bluff at the outskirts of the village was lined with spectators who, from a higher vantage point, would command the clearest view of the proceedings.

When everything was ready, Percy gestured to Florilyn. The two walked down the beach side by side apart from the others.

"This has turned out to be a bigger shindig than I imagined," chuckled Percy. "So much for our private little race."

"How did they all find out?" asked Florilyn.

"I thought you must have told them."

"Me?" Florilyn laughed. "I thought it was you!"

"Well, no matter. They're here now. So. . .are we agreed? We'll ride south and around the stake Stevie drove into the sand at the end of the beach where the rocks begin and back here. . .then again. Down and back twice."

"Agreed." Florilyn nodded.

Percy looked his cousin in the eye then gave her a wink and a smile and extended his hand. "Good luck," he said.

"And to you," rejoined Florilyn as she shook it. "You'll need it!"

"My, but you are confident!" Percy laughed. "So. . .shall we get under way and give these people what they came for?"

They turned and walked back. While they were talking, Stevie had run a long line in the sand with his staff, stretching from water's edge up to the soft sand.

"Well done, Stevie," said Percy. "Our start and finish line— impossible to miss."

The two contestants took the reins of their horses from Gwyneth and Courtenay and mounted.

"All right, then," said Percy, "from this line down the beach and back twice. We will each have someone stand here on the line as our turning points to begin the second leg. Gwyneth, would you stand on the line for me?"

"Yes, Percy," she replied.

"Courtenay?" said Florilyn.

Her brother looked with disgust toward Gwyneth but nodded.

The contestants gently eased their mounts to the line about ten yards apart. Both horses sensed the air of excitement. Percy and Florilyn looked over and smiled at one another.

"Ready?" said Percy.

"I'm ready," replied Florilyn.

"Courtenay," said Percy, "why don't you do the honors and start us off?"

"All right," said Courtenay. "To the line then. All right. Set. . .go!"

The shout of his voice and Percy's excitable kick in her flanks sent Grey Tide rearing slightly. Percy barely managed to keep his seat. By the time he had Grey Tide up to a gallop, amid frantic yelling and shouting from every side, Florilyn was twenty yards ahead and flying down the beach away from him.

He bolted after her, trying desperately to remember everything Gwyneth had taught him. He raised himself in the saddle, tried to feel Grey Tide's side with his knees, and leaned forward and stroked her neck.

Florilyn glanced behind, hair flying, eyes on fire. A great laugh sounded. Percy saw the gleam in her eyes and couldn't help laughing himself to see his cousin so full of joy.

Within seconds the cries and cheers from behind them were gone. The only sound remaining was of two sets of thundering hooves flying down the hard-packed sand, throwing great wet clods up behind them.

The distance to the stake and the first turn was some six hundred yards. Florilyn reached it first. As she turned Red Rhud sharply around, she was surprised to see Percy so close behind her that Grey Tide's nose was in danger of being brushed by her rival's out-flying tail and wicked feet. Florilyn had assumed herself pulling away. But so close was she to her twin that Grey Tide needed no guidance from Percy, mud splattering his face, to negotiate the tricky turnaround. She kept her position and spun sharply around.

They emerged from the turn with but a single length separating them. Florilyn glanced around a second time as they flew back toward the harbor, filled with the exciting terror of knowing that her cousin had learned his skills well. For the first time she realized that it would take all her prowess to keep him at bay.

By the time they were halfway back to the harbor and the shouts and yells came again into their ears, Grey Tide, her front splotched with wet sand from following so long, had drawn alongside Red Rhud's midsection. The twin mares and rivals matched each other stride for stride, sharp short gasps of white air pulsing from their flared nostrils, hooves thudding in perfect rhythm, a hurricane of sand flying behind them.

On they came. Slowly the spectators backed away. As the riders came more clearly into view, with Florilyn's long auburn hair flying in a tumult around her head on the bay mare beneath her, visible on the high side of the beach, with Percy on the gray toward the sea, Gwyneth and Courtenay took up positions on the finish line some twenty yards away from one another. Still no one, save those villagers lining the bluff above, could tell who was in the lead as the two riders slowly separated and made for their human turning posts.

With the yelling and cheering at a frenzy, they reached the line in a dead heat.

But Florilyn's experience told in the turn. She wheeled Red Rhud so tightly around Courtenay where he stood that he gave the mare's rump a swat as his sister flew back the way she had come.

Percy came in too tight to Gwyneth and could not hold the turn. This time Grey Tide had no one to follow and swung much too wide.

Unable to correct his error, Percy and his mount drifted many yards past Gwyneth and toward the water line. By the time he recovered and was bearing again southward, Florilyn had widened her lead again to fifteen yards.

As he circled around to straight, Percy glanced back to where Gwyneth stood unmoved. Her face was calm, placid, serene in the midst of the roar around her.

His eyes met hers. The sounds around him ceased. Though a hundred shouting spectators were screaming and exhorting him on, Percy heard nothing.

With Grey Tide thundering beneath him, he entered a dream world. . .a world of silence. Out of its center, two tiny orbs of deepest blue drew him into themselves.

The lips of his tiny friend were moving. And he knew what she was saying to him. *"Be one with Grey Tide. . .feel her rhythm. . .relax and let her run."*

She brought her hands together and held out her elbows as she had shown him a dozen times. Gently she rocked up and down with the fluid motion she had explained to him so often.

He had forgotten the most important principle of all—be one with the horse, let the rhythm of his body flow into hers. The movement of her arms and elbows reminded him that Grey Tide must feel nothing.

Then he saw on Gwyneth's lips the words, *"You will win."*

He glanced to the front. Suddenly his brain was again assaulted by the urgency of the race. There was Florilyn increasing her lead!

His instincts were to kick and yell and try all the harder. But Gwyneth's words remained. He forced himself to remain calm. He leaned forward, relaxed, and felt himself beginning to rise and fall in harmony with the powerful beast beneath him.

Moving lightly and rhythmically, immediately Percy saw the gap between them begin to shrink. Grey Tide again came even with Red Rhud's tail.

Percy had learned the lesson from his ill-fated turn around Gwyneth.

He glanced ahead. The stake was some two hundred yards away and slightly up the beach from their present heading. He guided Grey Tide gently to the left then urged her alongside Red Rhud's flank.

Florilyn glanced to her left with a grin full of competitive fire. But intent merely to keep ahead, she did not perceive Percy's strategy until it was too late.

The two horses reached the stake side by side. This time, however, it was Percy who clung to the post. Having thoughtlessly allowed him to overtake on the inside, Florilyn was forced to swing wide.

Keeping some reserve of power for the last, Grey Tide came out of the turn and thundered for home with Percy half a length in the lead. He did not relinquish it.

To exultant cries from the watching throng, Percy crossed Stevie's line two and a half lengths in front of his cousin.

FORTY-FIVE

The Accident

*E*xultant and smiling, Percy reined in and wheeled around as Gwyneth, Stevie, Eardley White, and Chandos Gwarthegydd, and half the youth population of Llanfryniog came running in jubilation to surround him with congratulatory shouts and cries. Whatever some may have thought of him two months before, he had reached exalted status now. Suddenly the young Scot, who had so recently come into their midst as a stranger, had, in a few exciting minutes, become a folk hero who had bested the daughter of the viscount.

No one was left to console Florilyn in her defeat but Courtenay and Rhawn Lorimer. And it was true that Florilyn had begun to change. It was equally true that such a beginning was admirable. Those of the village who considered her snooty and arrogant would in time come to alter their opinion.

Alas, it would not be on this day they would do so. For the demon of pride is neither easily nor permanently exorcised. As long as one remains in the flesh, it may rear its head, and violently, at a moment's notice.

The instant Florilyn realized that Percy had stolen a march on her at the far end of the beach, grabbing the post and forcing her wide, all the former antagonism toward him surged back upon her in a wave.

Seeing the back of Grey Tide's powerful haunches pulling away down the beach had enraged her. The pleasant banter between cousins and friends from minutes earlier vanished in the wind.

Crossing the line and realizing that she had been soundly trounced in full view of the entire community, the rage of her brother came rushing to the fore as if it were a familial curse. It possessed her with the evil spirit of anger and revenge.

By now a considerable crowd had gathered on the beach in a tumult over the exciting finish. Hardly slowing as she flew into its midst, Florilyn wheeled recklessly around. Heedless of whoever might get in her way, she powered her way toward Percy, breathing fire and shrieking irrational accusations. Men, women, and boys scurried from her path, for the glint in her eyes was dangerous.

A moment later, only Percy and Gwyneth remained on the sand ahead of her. Stevie was leading Grey Tide away, sweat pouring from her flanks, to calm her down.

Percy was gazing down with a tender smile of affection for his teacher. He had just thanked her for the reminder at the halfway point.

Florilyn saw the look that passed between them and apprehended all. The treachery against her had been Gwyneth's doing!

She flew toward them in a white fury. "You little urchin!" she cried. "What business is it of yours to interfere?"

Startled and shocked, Percy leaped aside.

Thinking Percy in danger, and for once in a position to help *him*, Gwyneth stepped in front of the horse's path. What had she to fear? All the horses at the manor were her friends. She stood calmly then lifted her hand to the charging animal. "Hello, Red Rhud," she said in a quiet voice. "It's your friend, Gwyneth. You don't need to be afraid."

Seeing the tiny girl in its path, the horse reared. Florilyn screamed and pulled back on the reins. She managed to keep herself in the saddle, but not without a frantic rearing and pawing and whinnying from the excitable and terrified horse.

When Florilyn found herself again secure on Red Rhud's back,

Gwyneth lay unconscious on the sand, blood dripping down the side of her forehead onto her cheek where one of the flailing hooves had grazed her above the ear. Staring down at what she had done, Florilyn's eyes widened in shock.

Percy came yelling toward her and pulled her from the horse in a rage. She hardly heard a word of the dreadful things he screamed in her face. He could only be kept from hitting her by Courtenay hurrying forward and pulling him away.

Meanwhile, Stevie rushed in, scooped Gwyneth into his arms, and ran for Grannie's cottage. She would know best what was to be done.

FORTY-SIX

Grannie's Cottage

*T*he crowd, so recently jubilant, was dead silent. No sound was heard as they watched Stevie bear the limp form in his arms, the white-haired head drooped bleeding over his elbow.

When Percy came to himself in a cold sweat, tears streaming from his eyes, the crowd was slowly moving away from the scene. Courtenay had had the presence of mind to secure both horses and was leading them away with Florilyn clinging to him like a child.

Percy staggered away to Grannie's. Stevie was already inside when he arrived. Gwyneth lay on Grannie's bed and was being tended by the only hands in the village to which the imperative ministration of love would be added to whatever physical succor they could provide. Someone had gone to the doctor's, but he was away and his wife did not expect him till after tea that evening. Someone had also run to the mine to find the girl's father.

The crowd slowly and silently followed through the streets, with many quiet murmurings and shaking of heads and clicking of tongues. None dared venture too close, though the cluster of curious onlookers gradually filled the lanes nearest Grannie's.

A pall set in over the entire village. Talk gradually resumed. Much quiet conversation hinted that something like this had been bound to happen to the girl because of her peculiar ways. No good came to those who dabbled in witchcraft.

On the other side were abundant speculations on the part of those who said that the viscount's two offspring had never been any good and that this was the inevitable result. *Would his daughter hang?* wondered not a few. Not with Styles Lorimer as magistrate, shook the heads of others. As everyone knew, he and the viscount cared more about their reputations than the law.

Eventually even Courtenay and Rhawn, with Florilyn stumbling between them in a daze, followed, though the talk about their fathers did not come within their hearing. They did their best to keep Courtenay's disconsolate sister from breaking down altogether. As they passed, the crowd parted noiselessly. Whatever may have been little Gwyneth's acquaintance with the forces of evil, there were a hundred eyewitnesses to what Florilyn had done. She was suddenly a pariah in their midst. They backed away with looks of revulsion, as if she were a leper.

In truth, it is doubtful that Florilyn meant to harm anyone. She was full of mischief and petty jealousies. But she was not an evil girl, only an immature and feisty one. It now remained to be determined what her outburst of temper was capable of making of her.

After some time, Grannie had Gwyneth comfortable and was wiping her face with a wet cloth. The wound was bandaged and the bleeding stopped. Grannie was speaking and singing softly to her with unintelligible words. Percy and Stevie sat at the bedside.

The time since the accident had calmed Percy from his fierce explosion on the beach. With Gwyneth's life hanging by a thread, in a vicarious sense, sixteen-year-old Percival Drummond's brief existence had also passed before the inner eyes of his soul. In the short time that had elapsed, he had grown still inside. Inexplicably, again the image of his father rose before his mind's eye. He knew his father's profession often required him to sit as he was sitting now, beside bedsides where death approached.

How did his father handle it? What did he say? What did he do?

Percy knew the answer. His father would pray. His father would speak to the grieving loved ones about God's fatherhood, about God's goodness, telling them that God's love covered all, even those things they could not understand. One of his favorite sayings was, "God is immeasurably more the lover of our loved ones than we are. And because He is their Father, He sometimes takes one of His children into His heart before we think it is time."

Some impulse caused Percy to glance toward the door where it stood open to the street.

There stood Florilyn in the light of the doorway. A look of abject horror was on her face. Tears stained her pale cheeks. As if in a trance, she slowly stumbled into the darkened cottage where none of the other villagers would have dared venture.

At the sight of her eyes, again rose the image of his father in Percy's mind. His father not only spoke of God's love, God's fatherhood, God's goodness, but he spoke of God's *forgiveness* and healing. He was always talking about reconciliation, between mankind and God, between friends, between parents and children. Reconciliation and healing—they were his father's constant themes. "If God's forgiveness is total," he had heard his father say, "can our forgiveness toward one another be less?"

In the second or two that passed as Percy stared into Florilyn's forlorn, desperate, tormented eyes, he knew that *this* was a moment for the healing and forgiveness his father spoke of. He knew exactly what his father would do at such a time. It was a moment to let the fatherhood of God bathe the wounds of a broken humanity with the balm of its forgiving love. Slowly he rose.

"Percy," whimpered Florilyn like a lost child, beginning to crumble. "I am so sorry. . . I didn't mean—" She began to collapse.

Percy hurried to her as she fell into his arms. She burst into sobs of bitter remorse. Percy held her tight, and she wept like a baby.

FORTY-SEVEN

The Vigil

Codnor Barrie arrived an hour later.

By then, much of the crowd had returned to their homes. Percy went outside to see if Courtenay was anywhere about. Finding him, he asked him to bring a buggy from the manor for his sister. She was resting, he said, but he doubted she would be able to walk further than to the cottage door.

Barrie went back to his home to get a few things then returned to spend the night on Grannie's floor. Stevie also returned home. The way was considerably longer and the dusk was well advanced by the time he again walked into Grannie's where he also intended to remain for the night.

It was nearly dark by the time Percy and Florilyn were again at last in their beds at Westbrooke Manor.

Percy slept but fitfully and was on his way back to the village the next morning shortly after dawn. He arrived at Grannie's cottage to find no change.

Under the circumstances, it was the best news they could hope for.

Florilyn did not leave her room for three days.

Dr. Rotherham examined Gwyneth and said that there was not much he could do for her beyond wait. He did not exactly couch it in such words, but the gist of his report to Codnor Barrie was essentially that his daughter would eventually wake up in the presence of her earthly father or her heavenly Father. No one at this point could tell which.

The bedside vigil of the small praying family continued.

On the fourth day, eyes drawn in spite of so much sleep, Florilyn accompanied Percy to Llanfryniog. She had hardly eaten since the race. Her cheeks were sunken, her whole face haggard and pale. The others received her kindly. Like true Christians, they knew that Florilyn's suffering was even greater than their own. Their compassion went out to her, and they took the suffering, foolish, immature girl to their hearts. When Codnor Barrie took her in his arms and stroked her hair as if she were his own daughter, Florilyn wept great tears of cleansing such as had never flowed from her eyes all the days of her life.

Thereafter, Florilyn insisted on sitting as much as she could at Gwyneth's side with the tiny white limp hand resting in hers. On and off she wept. At first her tears rose out of the well of her own guilt. As time went on, however, they became tears of repentance. The change may not seem like much to those who understand neither guilt nor repentance. But there is all the difference in the world in the eyes of Him who would have people's tears turn them to Him, that they might grow into His humble sons and daughters.

In a strange way, being at Gwyneth's side gave Florilyn hope. She began to eat and drink and regain her strength.

Then came a day when Percy could think of nothing but that he was soon scheduled to leave on the northbound coach. All day he and Florilyn took turns at Gwyneth's side, helping Grannie with tea and food for the small band, for Gwyneth's father and Stevie remained with them when not at their work.

A few of the more stouthearted and compassionate villagers began coming by, reminded of old friendship and at last laying aside foolish aversions. They remembered how Gwyneth always returned good for evil and how often Grannie had come to the aid of one or another in time of sickness. Some of these, as women do, brought food. Before many days, there was more on hand than would have been needed to feed twenty people.

As the day came closer, the burden of his impending departure weighed heavier and heavier on Percy's heart. How could he leave without knowing whether Gwyneth would live or die?

Evening came. Still there was no change.

After a simple supper, knowing that Gwyneth was well looked after, Percy went out into the warm evening. He walked through the village, up the plateau, and slowly made his way along the promontory toward Mochras Head.

How quickly the two months had flown by, he thought. He had changed more than he would ever have dreamed possible. What different thoughts and emotions floated through his brain as the still and peaceful evening settled over him.

He recalled his first night here, how angry the peacefulness of the country had made him. Even the crickets had angered him, he recalled with a smile. It was earlier now than on that night. The multitude of crickets had not yet taken over the moonglow of the countryside, though a few could be heard warming up for their nightly concert.

The sky over the sea showed radiant from horizon to apex in the fiery shades of gold, magenta, and violet he had come to associate with the Welsh coast. Perhaps the same colors radiated over the slate rooftops of Glasgow, but he had never noticed them. Never again would he look at a sunset and not recall this place with longing reminders of these weeks now drawing to a close.

Thinking of Gwyneth, he continued over the stream and to her special place at the edge of the bluff. Forgetting her father's three-foot rule, he sat down and let his legs dangle over the edge of the promontory as he stared out to sea. Slowly but inexorably, the giant yellow orb sank into the distant waters then sent up its flaming aftershoots far into the fading blue of the sky. He was still sitting unmoved half an hour later, until all shades of the gorgeous display had turned to purples and blacks and the rising moon began to exert its strength over the coming darkness.

At first he thought the changes had been caused by his new appreciation for the natural world that Gwyneth had helped him to see. Then he wondered if it was simply being away from the city, away from his parents and the unspoken pressures of youth and school and peers. Then he found himself thinking it must be the country itself. Everything was different here, the people, customs, sights, smells, foods, language, song.

Slowly a deeper truth began to dawn on his consciousness. He saw that the changes did not originate from any of these. Nature and the country and Gwyneth and new experiences were all but echos of *another* Voice speaking into his heart.

At last he knew whose that voice was. All these influences had come speaking to him from the voice of his father's God. And he knew by his father's example how to approach the Father of them both.

Percy backed away from the edge of the bluff and slowly sank to his knees in the soft grass.

Thank You, God, he prayed silently, *for bringing me here that You might speak into my heart. Thank You for the many ways You revealed Yourself and for opening my ears to hear. Thank You for Gwyneth,* he added as his voice choked, *and for all the ways she helped open my eyes to see You.*

He paused. *And thank You for my father, too,* he added. *Thank You that he did not give up on me either. I know now that he loves me. Give me the courage to keep growing, even back home, where it may be most difficult of all.*

Slowly he rose and set off back down toward the village.

He was at peace with himself. But he knew he could not leave Wales with Gwyneth's condition in doubt.

FORTY-EIGHT

A Dream and a Prayer

*B*y the time Percy returned to the cottage, it was nearly dark. Stevie had gone home to be with his mother for the night. Grannie and Gwyneth's father were sitting at the table in the kitchen. Florilyn dozed in the chair beside the bed.

All the way down from Mochras Head, Percy's thoughts revolved around little Gwyneth Barrie. He recalled every conversation he had had with her through the summer. He remembered fondly all her special places. Over all hovered the ghostly, mystical, otherworldly image of her singing to the animals beside the lake in the mountains.

He had not put it into so many words before this night. Suddenly it occurred to him that her peculiarities, her mysterious origins, her utter simplicity and humility—did they all have an astounding yet somehow plausible explanation? Perhaps she truly *wasn't* of this world. . .

Might she actually be. . .an *angel*?

Had she always been an angel? Perhaps she was now simply being called back to the true home of her origin.

With such thoughts swirling through his brain, Percy entered the cottage. He walked through the kitchen, nodded with a smile to Codnor and Grannie, then continued to the bedside.

Florilyn heard his step, woke, and looked up with a wan smile.

"Any change?"

Florilyn shook her head.

Percy sat down in the empty chair beside her. With the mood from his walk still imbuing him with a peaceful sense of presence, Florilyn glanced over in astonishment as he broke into audible prayer. "Oh God," he said aloud, "wherever she is right now. . .bring Gwyneth back. If she is truly one of Your angels, let us have her yet for a little while longer."

Florilyn saw that he was weeping. One of her hands still on the bed with Gwyneth's, she reached across and gently laid the other on Percy's arm.

A few minutes more they sat in silence. Percy recovered himself and breathed in deeply. He glanced at Florilyn and smiled an embarrassed smile.

"I've never heard you pray before," she said.

"I never have prayed out loud before." Percy smiled. "Well, except when I was a boy at bedtime. I've never done anything like that in my life."

He grew thoughtful. "Do you remember that first night when I was with your family at dinner, when you asked me if I believed in heaven and hell?"

Florilyn nodded.

"I don't know about that," said Percy. "But I think maybe I believe in God more than I realized at the time."

Slowly he rose and stood at the bedside gazing down at the pale face that was even whiter than the pillow it rested upon. All at once the features did not look so young or childlike. The expression on the face was ageless. . .like an angel's. Percy bent down and gently kissed the white forehead.

A moment more. . .

A gasp sounded from Florilyn's lips.

"*Percy!*" she breathed, her voice soft, hopeful, frightened, and full of wonder. She began to rise from her chair.

He saw it now. A tiny movement around the eyes. . .then a fluttering.

Slowly the lids began to open. Out from between them again peeped the eyes of heaven's blue!

"Percy," whispered the tiny lips from the bed as Gwyneth gazed up at the face staring down at her. "I hoped it would be you I saw when I woke up."

Heart pounding, head exploding for joy, Percy struggled desperately to remain calm. "You knew you would wake up?" he said with great effort, his voice husky and blinking hard.

"Of course," replied Gwyneth simply.

"Were you dreaming?"

"No, I was with my mother. She is everything I knew she would be, Percy. But I couldn't wake up until you prayed for me."

"You were waiting. . .for me to pray for you?"

"I'm not sure. It was dreamy. Maybe I was dreaming, because it was like being surrounded by a cloud of white. I think God was waiting for you to pray for me so I could wake up. But He was waiting so that your praying for me could wake *you* up, too."

For the first time, she now saw Florilyn standing at Percy's side. "Hello, Miss Florilyn," she said. "What are you doing here? I thought you were afraid of Grannie."

"Not anymore," Florilyn sobbed, sniffly and teary.

"I am sorry I made your horse rear," said Gwyneth. "I hope you were not hurt."

"Oh, you dear girl!" exclaimed Florilyn, able to contain herself no longer. She bent down and kissed Gwyneth on the cheek.

"Why are you crying, Miss Florilyn?"

"I am just happy that you are awake."

The voices from the bedside had been soft, but gradually their increasing volume and animation drifted into the hearing of the father and great-aunt in the kitchen. They realized that three voices were coming from the adjacent room, not two. They jumped up and rushed to the bedside.

FORTY-NINE

End of the Summer

*T*he morning came early.

Percy readied himself, said good-bye to all the servants, then, in as cheerful a manner as he could manage, to Courtenay.

Florilyn had been hanging back.

Percy walked toward her. "You will check on Gwyneth?" he said.

"I promise—every day."

"Let me know if there is any change. I think she will be fine. She already seems her normal self again."

Florilyn nodded. She smiled at her cousin with an expression that contained a world of meaning then stepped forward to hug him.

He returned her embrace affectionately.

"Good-bye, Percy," said Florilyn. "There is too much to try to say, so I will say nothing. I will never forget this summer."

"Nor I," rejoined Percy.

His aunt Katherine gave Percy a tender hug. "I hope you will visit us again," she whispered softly in his ear.

"I would like that," replied Percy, stepping back with a smile.

To his astonishment, he saw tears in the woman's eyes. She smiled, but it was a smile tinged with sadness.

"Well, let us be off, my boy!" boomed the viscount, trying with a little too much effort to counter the emotionally dense atmosphere of the occasion threatened by the faces of his wife and daughter and two or three of the servants. "We don't want that coach leaving without you, or you'll miss your train!"

The two left the manor for Llanfryniog. By the time they arrived, the thrice-weekly coach stood in front of the small inn, its four horses snorting and prancing impatiently.

There also stood Gwyneth, hanging back in the shadows of the building. She looked none the worse for wear. The only lasting reminder of recent events was a bandage between her ear and forehead, mostly covered by her wild crop of white hair.

Percy caught her eye.

Her lips parted in a radiant smile of innocent love. She would cry, too, but not until he was out of sight. In the event he never saw her again, her friend from Glasgow must remember her with a look of happiness on her face.

Percy's two bags were hoisted above. He and his uncle shook hands. The viscount managed some stiff words about his being welcome any time.

Percy climbed inside the coach and closed the door.

Only after the viscount stood back did Gwyneth now run forward.

"Get back, girl!" yelled the driver as he climbed up onto his box. "Don't you see these great horses? They'll trample you to death!"

"They won't hurt *me*, sir," she said sweetly.

Even at the sound of her voice, the agitated horses calmed. The driver muttered something and grabbed the reins.

Gwyneth walked calmly to the side of the coach where Percy sat looking out the window. She held up a small parcel wrapped in paper. "I baked you another tea cake, Percy," she said. "I didn't want you to get hungry."

"Thank you, Gwyneth," he said. "I shall think of you with every bite. If we stop for tea," he added, "I shall eat it with tea. . .as it is supposed to be eaten."

"Good-bye, Percy," she said. Her eyes seemed bluer than he had ever seen them.

"Good-bye, Gwyneth."

She stepped slowly back.

The driver gave a shout, and the coach lurched forward. Percy continued to wave through the open window.

There stood the receding forms of the great man of the region with his hand in the air. Several paces in front of him a girl with hair of white waved her own tiny hand. Slowly the coach disappeared from their view.

Viscount Lord Snowdon cast on the child a curious look.

Gwyneth smiled at him then walked away along the street as Westbrooke returned to his buggy.

Now at last came tears. Gwyneth did not even stop at Grannie's but continued the slow walk up the moor to her home, alone with her thoughts. She spent the afternoon with her animals.

Gwyneth's friends felt her sadness. Their mood remained subdued for two days.

FIFTY

Home in Glasgow

*E*dward and Mary Drummond saw a different look on their son's face the moment he stepped off the train when they greeted him on the platform of the Glasgow station. They little suspected the cause. They had to admit, however, that his pleasant and cheerful manner was a welcome surprise.

Percy had been due home for the fall session of school. It would be the last session expected of him. What would become of their son when it was completed, neither mother nor father had any idea. When his plans began to become more apparent, they would be in for the shock of their lives.

They had received but one curious note during their son's absence, from Edward's sister, saying that Percy's presence was full of unexpected surprises. What exactly Katherine meant by the odd phrase, they had no idea.

Being a few days later to arrive than previously planned, as he had notified them by telegram, Percy set about his studies in earnest almost the next day. He subsequently remained home every evening buried in his books. No mention was ever made of his former friendships or activities on the streets.

About two months later, shortly after his seventeenth birthday,

Percy sought his father in his study. He had been thinking through the interview ever since arriving home. But it had taken time to collect his thoughts and summon the courage to do what he knew he had to do. . .and *wanted* to do. He also had wanted to wait long enough to be certain he would not fall into old patterns.

"May I talk with you, Father?" he asked. His voice betrayed anxiety. Gone entirely was the arrogance he might have displayed a short time earlier.

"Of course, Percy," replied his father. "Come in. . .have a seat."

"If you don't mind, what I have to say I think is best said on my feet."

The vicar nodded.

Percy glanced toward the ground, then looked up again and drew in a deep breath. "I, uh. . .I don't exactly know how to say this," he began. "It's not an easy thing to do, but. . .well, I've come to apologize."

Still his father waited, listening patiently and with deep love in his eyes for this son who was about to become a man.

"I, uh. . .I've been nothing more than a fool these past couple of years," Percy went on. "Now that I look back on it, I can't imagine what I was thinking. You once asked me what kind of evil spirit had taken over inside me, and I can't think of any other explanation. When I try to recall exactly *why* I was so angry and full of resentment, I cannot think of a single good reason. You and Mother are the best and kindest and most loving parents I could hope to have. You gave me everything. You trained me well. You are good and godly people. What I was thinking to allow myself to become so alienated from you, I cannot imagine. I am embarrassed and sorrier than I can say for what I must have put you through. Yet you kept loving me, even in your occasional outbursts. You were only angry for what I was doing to myself. I see that now. You would have been wrong not to be angry for what I was doing. You saw how destructive it was to me."

The father's eyes filled. His breath grew shaky.

"When you sent me to Wales," Percy continued, "I began looking at things differently. A new set of eyes opened inside me—maybe a little like the second sight Uncle Roderick would tell me about on our rides together," he added, chuckling briefly. "I suppose being around Courtenay and Florilyn caused me to think about what kind of person I was becoming. In all honesty, Father, Courtenay just isn't very nice. He wasn't nice to me. He isn't nice to his mother. Maybe I saw more of myself reflected in him than I wanted to admit. Florilyn was the same at first. But the most curious thing happened. It was almost as if she began to change along with me. I still don't quite understand it exactly. But by the end of the summer, we had actually begun to form a friendship. We had an unfortunate row at the end. But that got patched up before I left. I actually think I miss her."

He paused, and his lips parted in a thin, reflective smile. "I had my ups and downs," he said. "At first I hated the country. I vowed not to let myself change. But in the end, the summer helped wake me up to the fact that I was making myself into a person of a certain sort, too, just like Courtenay, and that maybe I ought to give the matter more serious attention."

Again he paused. Another smile came across his face. "And I met a precious little girl there who helped me notice things I hadn't been in the habit of seeing before, a girl who loved animals and loved nature. She was tiny, almost fairylike, yet completely normal in every other way. Actually she wasn't so very much younger than me—three or four years, something like that. But her size made her appear younger than she really was. And she possessed such an astonishing maturity to see God's world in wondrous ways. I almost thought at times that she might be an angel."

"She sounds like a remarkable girl," said his father softly.

"She was. She cared about me, too. I know you and Mother care about me. But I suppose it sometimes takes somebody new to make you see what a wonderful thing that is and how grateful we should be when we are loved. She helped me see God's creation in new ways. I know you have taught me many of the same things through the years. I am embarrassed now to realize that it took somebody else to open my eyes to them, but. . .well, I suppose that's how it was."

He paused and exhaled a deep sigh then resumed. "Anyway, one of the things I feel I need especially to say to you, Father," Percy continued, "is that I respect and honor you for the man you are, for what you give to the people of the church, and for what you gave to me all those years that I was too blind to see until now. I am sorry. I ask you to forgive me. I don't think I will be quite so blind ever again."

Before Percy finished speaking, the poor vicar was on his feet, tears streaming down his face, covering the distance between them in two great strides. The next instant, father and son were in one another's arms, Percy weeping freely and without shame.

"I'm so sorry, Father. Do you forgive me?"

"You have *always* been forgiven, Percy, my son," whispered Edward. "The forgiveness has existed within my heart all along. Yet to complete the transaction, it was necessary for you to *ask*, that I might give it to you. So I *do* give it to you now. Of course you are forgiven for anything and everything. I love you."

"Thank you, Father," said Percy softly. "I love you, too."

A moment more they stood then gradually fell away.

"There is one more thing I need to say," said Percy. "Or, I should say, something I want to ask."

"Anything," replied the father, taking his chair again as he fumbled with his handkerchief at his eyes.

Percy took the seat his father had previously offered. He leaned forward then took a deep breath. "I have been thinking about my future," he began. "I have squandered the years when I should have been working and studying. I realize it is a great deal to ask. . .but might you be willing to help me catch back up on my studies and make up for my poor marks and help me prepare for the university? When we were out on our last ride together, Uncle Roderick suggested I try to make a go of it. I think I'd like to try."

"Of course, Percy. Nothing could delight me more."

"I know I will be a year, maybe two behind others my age. As it stands now, I could not even get into the university—"

"I know people that might be able to make a difference in that regard."

"I don't want strings pulled for me, Father," said Percy. "I want to work hard and improve my marks—"

"We shall find you a tutor."

"Perhaps I might enroll in one of the grammar schools to prepare for the bursary competition. I do not want to attend university until I have earned that right and until I am ready."

"What is it you think you want to study toward?" asked the vicar, having no idea what was coming.

"I haven't really settled on anything definite yet," replied Percy. "I don't have to make any hasty decisions."

He paused. An almost sheepish expression came over his face. "I know it may be hard for you to believe," Percy added after a moment, "but actually. . .I have been thinking of possibly following *your* own footsteps."

"Well, Percy," replied Drummond, whose heart swelled with pride and his eyes filled with tears to hear his son speak so, "in answer to your question—yes, I shall do all that is in my power to help you. . .if it means tutoring you myself!"

PART TWO

Return Visit

1870

FIFTY-ONE

The University of the North

*T*ime is a curious commodity for the young. No clock's minute hand moves more slowly than one being watched by a bored and listless youth with time on his hands.

For the youth in love, however, or the young man filled with dreams and vision and energy and plans, time races by, and never a glance is sent toward the clock on the wall. The chimes of its hours seem to ring out every five minutes with the pressing reminder that there is not *enough* time. Caught up in the moment, hours, weeks, months race by in a blur.

Truly for the young at heart, a day is as a thousand years, a thousand years as a day. Youth's present stands as an eternal now of existence— there is no past, no future.

Percival Drummond's suddenly altered outlook on life was all-consuming. Quickly the eventful months in Wales receded as a dream into his memory. He did not *forget*. He would never forget. It was a good dream, a wondrous dream. Scarce an hour, certainly not a day passed that he did not think about Wales and smile with the reminder of those individuals who had made it such a pivotal time of new focus for him.

But as a result of those brief months, he now had new goals and dreams. Those ambitions drove him in a way he had never been driven before. He had no leisure to dwell on the past. The future beckoned.

Within a year of his return home from Snowdonia, he had applied himself so diligently to his studies that, with a little of his father's influence, but no more than Percy was comfortable with, he had so rapidly advanced ahead of his peers and beyond all expectations of his incredulous instructors, that shortly after his eighteenth birthday, having spent the summer of 1868 in an intensive preparatory program, he had been accepted to continue his studies at the University of Aberdeen the following year. His acceptance for the fall term, however, was predicated on yet another summer of hard work, in the great northern seaport itself, in a rigorous program for incoming Bajan, or first-year, students whose educational resumes were not quite as thorough as the university preferred to see.

Edward, Mary, and Percival Drummond traveled to Aberdeen together in May of that year to get Percy settled into his new lodgings for the summer and following term.

He still had not settled on a career. His initial enthusiasm for the pastorate had, if not waned, been tempered by the very practical question whether he would indeed be temperamentally suited, as he had said, to follow in his father's footsteps. Nothing could have pleased Edward Drummond more. Yet he desired the best for Percy over whatever gratification he might feel by having a son in the ministry. He therefore encouraged Percy to explore a wide range of options. He put to him the very questions he had forced upon himself at the same crossroads of his own life—*Is this truly what God wants me to do?* and *Is this how I can best serve Him with my life?*

Father and son continued to discuss the matter at length. Many thoughtful and personal letters passed between Aberdeen and Glasgow.

Percy's studies in the great northern university began in earnest in the fall of 1869. They remained so demanding that he hardly had time to think of anything else. By the end of the term, he and his father were discussing both law and engineering as alternate potential career choices. Percy found both possibilities intriguing ones.

As he began to contemplate his prospects for the upcoming summer prior to his second term, the first in two years in which he would not have required schooling to look forward to, reminders of Snowdonia drifted into his consciousness.

The song of Wales crept out of hiding and began singing again to his soul.

FIFTY-TWO

Westbrooke Manor Again

*I*t hardly seemed possible that three years had passed since Percy Drummond's eventful visit to North Wales. Life-changing it had indeed been.

At nineteen, as he now looked back on his existence leading up to that fateful time, his heart overflowed with gratitude for his father's courage to take such strong action on his behalf.

As he sat on the coach bouncing over the countryside toward Llanfryniog, how very different were the thoughts going through his brain from that day three years earlier when he and his father had jostled along this same road in chilly silence.

He remembered that first awkward encounter with his aunt Katherine and uncle Roderick. He thought he would be so bored in Wales. As it turned out, his memories of the coast of Gwynedd were among the most wonderful of his life.

He did not have as long this time as before—a mere three weeks. Then he would have to hurry north to begin a tutoring assignment in Aberdeen. But he determined to make the most of what time he had.

It would be interesting to see whether his cousins had changed. Reports had reached them that Courtenay had just completed his second year at Oxford and had not been home in all those two years. He

had only preceded him to Wales by a couple of weeks. And Florilyn—
he hardly knew what to expect from her. Would she be the old Florilyn
or the new Florilyn, the tempestuous and self-centered girl of his first
meeting three years ago or the girl who had begun to show signs of
sensitivity and compassion?

Actually the invitation from his uncle a month ago, coinciding
with Percy's own thoughts of another visit south, came as something
of a surprise. He should think having his son home would be sufficient
diversion for the viscount. As he fell to reflecting on his uncle Roderick,
however, Percy realized what an enigma the man was. It was not until
he was home in Glasgow after his previous visit—of course by then he
was beginning to see *many* things differently—that he began to realize
that he had grown genuinely fond of his uncle during his sojourn in his
home.

Perhaps he felt sorry for him. It was not difficult to see that he
was more or less alienated from many of those around him—wife, son,
daughter, tenants. The origin of the tension that existed within the man
was difficult to identify. At one moment he could be so impulsive, the
next indecisive. Nor did closer inspection fail to reveal some lingering
mystery that seemed to hover over his uncle's countenance like a far-off
dream that nothing in his present circumstances appeared sufficient to
account for.

Perhaps all these factors explained why Percy occasionally had the
odd sensation, though he had been young at the time of his visit, that
his uncle was attempting to reach out to him more than he was capable
of to his own son or daughter.

Percy stepped from the coach in front of Mistress Chattan's inn and
glanced around with an enormous feeling of satisfaction. It was all so
familiar again!

He hardly had a chance to reflect on the sight of the main street or
fill his lungs with the crisp, tangy sea air before a jubilant cry pierced
his eardrums.

"Percy!"

He turned to see his cousin Florilyn rushing toward him from a waiting buggy across the street. She flew squealing to him, nearly knocking him over by her embrace.

"My, oh my!" laughed Percy, hugging her tight. He took a step back, placed his hands on her two shoulders, and looked her over from a considerably higher vantage point than before. "That is the most affectionate greeting I've had from anyone in years! Is it really you, my little Florilyn? When did you become a woman? Gosh, you are beautiful!"

Florilyn laughed in delight, though her face reddened with the compliment.

In truth, as Florilyn sat in the buggy with her mother and had seen the southbound coach roll up and stop in front of the inn, a sudden wave of timidity swept through her. What if Percy didn't remember her?

That was absurd, she told herself—of course he would remember! But what if he was. . .*different*. . .aloof. . .sophisticated? What if he had no use for her now? Courtenay had been *so* changed when he arrived two weeks ago. He hardly spoke to any of them, just sulked around moodily and acted as if he were better than everyone else. Being away at university had changed him. What if it had changed Percy? What if he—horrible thought!—was like Courtenay? She didn't think she could bear it.

As such reflections swirled through her brain, she saw a great lanky youth step onto the street. For a second or two she wasn't sure she recognized him. The young man was so tall! He appeared much older than she expected. He looked so dashing in the dark blue suit. Was it really. . .*him*?

Florilyn hesitated.

Then came a slight turn of the head. A breeze caught the corner of the light brown crop of hair in just the right way. It was all the recognition she needed.

Florilyn was out of the buggy bounding toward him the next moment. With the sound of his voice, all uncertainty vanished. He was still Percy!

True, the voice was deeper, more self-assured, no longer the voice of a boy on the threshold of manhood but of a youth well advanced toward it. But it was a voice that had lost none of its humor.

"I almost wasn't sure it was you," she said, "until I heard you speak. You're so tall!"

"What about you?" rejoined Percy. "You've put on two or three inches."

"You must have put on four or six! I think you're taller than Courtenay now. He will be so jealous."

"That's all I need!" Percy laughed.

"And you're just as funny as ever!"

"I'm still waiting for an answer to my question," said Percy.

"What question?"

"When did you become so stunningly beautiful?"

Again Florilyn laughed. This time she could not hide her embarrassment. "Maybe at the same time you became such a handsome man," she replied.

"Touché! A good one—you got me there." He laughed. "I can see that I had better not pester you about being beautiful, though I must say. . .you really are! Is that your mother with you?" he asked, glancing across the street.

"Yes, it's her."

Percy ran across and poked his head inside the covered buggy. "Aunt Katherine!" he said, leaning in and giving her a warm hug. "It is wonderful to see you again. You look well."

"And you, Percy," said his aunt. "Welcome again to Wales! Roderick would have come as well but got tied up with something or another. He will be so pleased to see you. He has been talking about your coming every day."

Inwardly Percy hoped his uncle wasn't doing so around Courtenay. "Just let me get my bags," he added and ran back to the coach.

Five minutes later they were bouncing out of town, Florilyn at the reins, Percy seated between her and her mother.

"I can't believe I am really here again!" said Percy. "Everything looks the same. I can't wait to explore everywhere—go riding and walk the beach. . .everything!"

Katherine laughed at his enthusiasm. "Are you sure three weeks will be enough?"

"No, it won't! Unfortunately, it's all I've got. The opportunity to tutor two young boys for the summer came up in Aberdeen. The pay was too good to turn down."

"Then we will go riding every day," said Florilyn.

"That sounds good to me."

"You will be interested in Roderick's latest project," said Katherine. "He is building new stables."

"*He* is building them?" asked Percy in surprise.

"He is having them built, I should say. He designed the structure and is supervising the construction."

"What is the purpose? Have you added more horses?"

"Daddy's going to raise race horses," said Florilyn enthusiastically.

"Really!"

"That is his dream," said Katherine. Her voice betrayed skepticism. She had been through too many of her husband's schemes to have much optimism concerning this latest one. . .especially as her husband's schemes could not budge an inch beyond the dream stage without *her* money. She was already beginning to regret allowing herself to be talked into funding the stables project. She would certainly think twice about letting him use any of her money to buy expensive thoroughbreds from Spain or Arabia. Let him find investors to go in on it with him. She had no desire to see her money go down a rat hole.

They rattled onto the cobblestones of the grounds and toward the great mansion. Behind the barns and stables, Percy immediately saw and heard banging and hammering from the work in progress. They had no sooner come to a stop than he was running off toward the scene.

"Percy, my boy!" boomed his uncle as he saw him running up. "You've become a big strapping fellow since I saw you!"

"Hello, Uncle Roderick!" said Percy as the two shook hands warmly. "Wow, this is some project you've undertaken."

"I plan to make them the finest stables in Wales," rejoined his uncle boisterously, "with horses capable of competing for the largest purses in Britain. Right now, as you can see, we're in the process of hoisting up the roof timbers."

"Do you need some help? I'll get into a different set of clothes and you'll have another set of arms." He hurried off.

His uncle watched him go with a fond yet wistful expression. Courtenay had shown not the slightest interest in the project, nor since his return even once offered to help. Percy hadn't been here two minutes and was already eager to pitch in with the laborers.

That evening the talk around the dinner table was more animated and spontaneous than the festive board at Westbrooke Manor had been in a very long time. That fact was due to two related but opposite facts—Percy's presence and Courtenay's absence.

"Do you remember when I was here before," Percy was saying, "on that first night? Florilyn, you were trying to bait your father and me into divulging ourselves closet atheists."

"I was not!" laughed Florilyn.

"You were, too," rejoined Percy. "You were chiding your father for not paying attention in church and trying to get me to say I didn't believe in heaven and hell. You were terrible! Aunt Katherine, you were having a fit."

By now Percy had his aunt and uncle and cousin in stitches at his depiction of a meal they all remembered very well.

"By the way," he went on, "as I recall, that whole conversation was prompted by the discovery of a body on the sand by the harbor. Was the murder ever solved?"

"Actually, no," replied the viscount. "The curious thing is that there continue to be occasional reports of strangers in the village asking about the man, unsavory characters by the sound of it, though I've never had occasion to be present at such times."

"Why don't you and I disguise ourselves and go down to Mistress Chattan's for a pint or two?" suggested Percy, looking at his aunt with a twinkle in his eye. "Maybe we could learn something."

"Goodness, Percy—what an idea!" she said, though she could not help smiling.

But her husband seemed to take the suggestion seriously. "Not a bad idea," he mused. "Though we would never pull it off. They would be certain to recognize me."

"We'll wait two or three weeks, of course," said Percy, feigning the utmost seriousness. "I didn't mean immediately. We'll grow beards and pull caps down to cover half our faces. . .and wear old grungy clothing, of course."

The viscount continued to mull the idea over as if seriously considering it. "I shall have to talk to Lorimer about it. He is baffled about the affair as well."

"Speaking of the magistrate, Florilyn," said Percy enthusiastically, anxious to get off the subject of an idea he had simply made in jest, "how is my old friend Rhawn Lorimer? Are she and Courtenay engaged yet?"

He was surprised as the atmosphere around the table went suddenly quiet. A few silent looks were exchanged.

"I must have stumbled into some uncharted waters," laughed Percy nervously.

"She and Courtenay have not exactly been on the best of terms since Courtenay got home," said Florilyn.

"Oh, yeah. . .why not?"

"Rhawn has been playing around," replied Florilyn bluntly.

"Goodness, Florilyn!" exclaimed her mother. "Must you be quite so outspoken?"

"It's true, Mother. Everyone knows it. When we were in London for the season last year," she went on, turning once more to Percy, "there were all kinds of stories. After we returned to Wales, the next thing we knew she had taken up with Colville."

"I thought it was you who had eyes for Burrenchobay," said Percy.

"Me?"

"You can't have forgotten the incident at market day where I got pummeled to save your honor."

"That was Colville's doing, you know that."

"And you told me that there was more to it."

"What's all this?" interjected the viscount. "Is there something about your row with Colville we haven't been told, Percy, my boy?"

"Oops, I forgot!" said Percy. "Sorry, Florilyn, old girl. It just slipped out."

"That's all right. Percy got into a fight with Colville that day, Daddy," she said, turning toward her father. "Colville tried to kiss me. I slapped him. And Percy came to my rescue. I later told Percy it was my fault, which it was."

"So you and Burrenchobay are no longer seeing each other?" said Percy.

"Good heavens, no. He and I parted brass rags ages ago, even before he began showing Rhawn his attention. Or, I should say, she began showing him hers."

"Ah. . .at last Courtenay's situation clarifies." Percy nodded significantly. "A little rivalry between friends! When the cat's away, eh? But I thought Burrenchobay was at university, too."

"He took a year off," said Florilyn. "He has been around for the past year, and Courtenay's been at Oxford. But. . . ," she added, then paused and gave Percy a wicked look of fun, "Rhawn is very anxious to see *you*."

"Oh boy! That's just great! Maybe I should just shoot myself now and get it over with. But after what you say about her escapades in London, what could she possibly see in a country bumpkin like me?"

"She has never lost her fascination for you. I think part of it is that you were the only boy in the world who didn't fall all over her."

Percy laughed briefly. His expression then faded into an odd smile. Quickly he recovered his aplomb. "So what about you, my dear Florilyn?" he said. "You are so beautiful—and I don't just say that to flatter my favorite cousin—after a glamorous coming out in London, where I'm sure you caught the eye of every eligible young bachelor between twenty and thirty. Surely you must have a stream of suitors lining up at the door outside to ask your father for your hand."

Florilyn threw her head back and laughed with abandon. "Percy, you *are* too funny!"

"I would wager ten gold sovereigns that you have had at least two marriage proposals since I saw you last. What about it, Uncle Roderick?" he added to his uncle.

"You will not find me taking your bet, Percy, my boy!" rejoined the viscount. "In truth, she has had three."

"*Three!* There—I knew it. Young men from all over England and Wales are no doubt asking one another even as we speak for directions to Westbrooke Manor in Snowdonia."

"And I will tell Papa to tell them the same thing he told the others," said Florilyn. "That is that I am not interested."

"You don't want to marry? What. . .is there something you are keeping from me, Florilyn? Are you considering taking holy orders and joining a convent?"

Florilyn could not help laughing again. "It's not that," she replied. "Of course I want to marry. I am just waiting for the right young man."

FIFTY-THREE

An Old Friend

*D*inner concluded, Percy rose to excuse himself. "I am sorry not to be better company," he said. "But suddenly I realize that I am very tired. I suppose the trip—and that work on the stables, eh, Uncle Roderick!—took more of a toll than I realized. I may read for a while and get an early start on a good night's sleep. Oh, Aunt Katherine," he added, turning to his aunt, "my father and mother let me bring along their copy of the new MacDonald. I started it on the way down on the train."

"Which one?" asked his aunt eagerly.

"It's called *Robert Falconer.*"

"Oh, I have it, too. I read it several months ago. I consider it his best so far. What masterful characterizations."

"I'm just at the part about the kite. What about you?"

"I am reading a new one of his called *A Seaboard Parish*. It's the sequel to *Annals of a Quiet Neighborhood.*"

"I didn't know *Annals* had a sequel!" exclaimed Percy. "My dad *loves* that book. Ministers are alike, I suppose. He says, 'How could MacDonald know exactly what I am thinking?' I wonder if he knows there is a sequel."

"And now you are at Aberdeen," rejoined Katherine. "What is it like knowing you are walking the same cobbled streets and byways and halls that MacDonald probably walked twenty-five years ago?"

"I hadn't thought of that." Percy nodded. "It's rather an amazing thought. Well," he added, turning to his uncle and Florilyn, "good night to you all." He paused and smiled. "I cannot tell you how good it is to be here with you again," he said. "I have really missed you!"

The two women smiled in return.

The viscount seemed a little discomposed by the depth of Percy's sincerity. He offered a few awkward comments about the feeling being mutual and their being delighted to have him again.

Then Percy left them. As he crossed through the entryway hall on his way to the central staircase, he glanced absently down the corridor leading toward the east wing.

A girl he took for one of the servants was walking toward him, a stack of linens in her hands. Halfway down the corridor at a distance of some forty or fifty feet, at sight of him she stopped abruptly.

Percy arrested his movement at the same moment. He paused as his foot fell on the first step of the staircase. His eyes had just drifted up to the painting on the landing of his uncle's grandmother then back again. The lines of his forehead wrinkled as his head cocked in question. For two or three seconds he returned the girl's stare then slowly brought his foot back down to level. Something about the girl was oddly, wonderfully, confusingly familiar. His brain was racing.

Why was she standing so still? She had turned into a gold-haired statue.

Percy's eyes squinted imperceptibly. *Was* her hair gold? Or was the thin light of the corridor playing tricks on him? Was it actually a lighter shade of. . .nearly *white*!

The next moment his steps were hurrying along the tiles. "*Gwyneth?*" said Percy as he slowed and approached, in mingled recognition and disbelief.

She looked down shyly then up into his eyes.

The moment he saw their blue, all doubt vanished. There could be no mistaking the eyes he had once taken for those of an angel.

Her countenance was still timeless! And yet. . .she *had* aged. Hers was the ageless countenance of a child no longer, but the delicate agelessness of the woman-child that had grown up since he had last seen her.

"Is it really *you?*"

She smiled. "It is me, Percy," she replied in a bashful voice.

"But. . .but what are you doing *here?*" said Percy. "Oh, this is brilliant! It is terrific to see you!"

"And you, Percy," said Gwyneth. The voice had changed. If possible, it was yet more serene, slightly deeper of timbre, and surely no longer that of a child. "To answer your question," she said, "I am Lady Florilyn's maid."

"I can't believe it. That is wonderful!"

"Lady Florilyn has been very kind to me."

"I am so glad!"

"I knew you were coming," said Gwyneth. "But I did not know when. You have grown so tall. You are a man now, Percy."

Percy laughed with delight. Gwyneth had not changed! And now that he saw it close, her hair was indeed more tinged with hints of red and shades of gold. Her eyes were of yet deeper and more translucent blue. She had grown several inches, though that was hardly to be compared with what had been added to his stature. Though still very short, she was no longer abnormally tiny. Percival Drummond had indeed blossomed into a fine-looking young man. At the same time, young Gwyneth Barrie—though in all the village only her great-aunt and father beheld what was taking place before everyone's eyes—had become a girl poised on the threshold of becoming a young lady.

Gwyneth had arrived at that wonderful and delicate age hovering precariously between childhood and womanhood, showing one moment the past and, to the keen-eyed observer, the next instant the future. As yet her dawning personhood remained dormant except to the most discerning of eyes. In Percy's mind she would remain for yet a little while the simple, kindhearted girl who had handed him a humble nosegay and called him her friend. . .and through whose honest heart he had learned to appreciate the God of his fathers. In truth, the nymph of Wales was no more the child of his imagination. As his eyes had been opened to nature, they would soon open likewise to the mystery of womanhood. When they did, he would see all that he was meant to see.

Percy, however, did not appear a great deal different in Gwyneth's eyes, though she had to look up a little higher toward the sky to find his face. Because she had always seen inside the people she met, the changes that took place to their outside appearances meant less to her knowing of them than such externals meant to most people.

"Grannie will be so happy that you are back," said Gwyneth.

Percy smiled at the delightful thought of more cozy talks in front of Grannie's fire. "Will she remember me?" he asked.

"We talk of you often. But I should go, Percy," said Gwyneth, glancing around, Percy thought, a little nervously. Slowly she resumed her way along the corridor.

"Do you still. . .stay with your father?" asked Percy, falling into step beside her. "Or do you now live here at the manor?"

"I still live at home," she replied. "Only Mrs. Drynwydd and Mrs. Llewellyn, and Mr. Broakes and Mr. Radnor live in the servants' quarters. I work here three days a week, alternating with the other girls who come from the village. But we are not to talk to guests."

"I'm not a guest!" laughed Percy. "I'm just me."

"To Lord Snowdon and Lady Katherine, you are an *honored* guest, Percy."

"You must be joking!"

"No, Percy. The whole manor has been abuzz over your coming."

Percy laughed at the thought.

"As soon as I take these linens to the breakfast room," said Gwyneth, "I will walk home."

They reached the stairway. Gwyneth turned to the right, Percy toward the stairs.

"Good-bye, Percy," said Gwyneth.

"I will see you again soon, I promise," said Percy. "I will come visit you and Grannie tomorrow. Do you work tomorrow?"

"No, not tomorrow. Only Tuesday and Thursday and Saturday."

"Then I shall see you as early as I can get away."

FIFTY-FOUR

The Promontory

*P*ercy returned to his room and sat down on the edge of his bed. The book he had intended to read sat on the desk. But his thoughts were too full of the changes in Gwyneth to think of Robert Falconer's kite. He rose again and strode to the window and gazed out over the countryside. It was about seven thirty. The sun was still high over Tremadog Bay to the west.

He stood for some time, absorbed in his thoughts. He had of course anticipated seeing little Gwyneth, as he still thought of her, probably more than anyone else other than Florilyn. But though logic told him that everyone aged at the same rate, somehow he had expected Gwyneth to remain the same. He had not actually said such to himself. Yet he had expected to find her still the tiny child he had known three years before. It was clear, however, that though she was still not yet five feet tall, she had *grown*. And not merely in stature. Her countenance was—there came the word again—ageless!

Was she an angel after all? He chuckled to himself at the thought.

Out the window, far below the manor toward the sea, a small figure was walking toward the promontory of Mochras Head.

He watched for some moments then turned and strode across the floor of his room. He did not pause until his hand was on the latch.

After having said his good nights and professed himself too tired for further company, he was hesitant to be seen going out again.

He crept from his room and glanced down the corridor toward Florilyn's door at the far end. He felt oddly like a sneak. It reminded him of his prodigal past, creeping furtively through the darkened streets of Glasgow. Those were unpleasant memories. Yet the compulsion to follow was too strong. But he did not want Florilyn to know he was leaving the house. . .or why?

He stole softly to the far end of the west wing, down the back stairway, and out by one of the side doors. Still conscious of not wanting to be seen, he made his way through the garden, around behind the stables, and onto the open moor leading down the slope toward the village and Mochras Head.

Probably when he reached the open plateau out from the cover of the wood surrounding the manor, he thought as he hurried along, the figure he had seen from his window would have disappeared further in the direction of the village. If so, he would retrace his steps back to the manor and spend the rest of his evening with Falconer and Shargar. It was too late for a visit to the Barrie cottage. But if by chance he *should* meet someone out for an evening walk in that wonderful, quiet, fragrant, peaceful time of the evening his native Scots called "the gloamin'," that was a different matter altogether.

By the time he crossed the stream and was approaching the promontory, he knew he would not turn back. There she was, in her white maid's dress, seated two hundred yards ahead of him at the very tip of the cliff face. Her back was to him, as she sat staring out over the sea in the direction of the setting sun.

Percy continued on across the soft grass with noiseless step.

She did not turn her head.

He approached from behind.

"Hello, Percy," said Gwyneth softly without turning.

"So you *do* have the second sight after all," he said, easing to the ground beside her.

"Why do you say that?"

"Because you knew it was me without looking."

"I would know your step anywhere, Percy. Besides, no one else knows this place."

"Your special place," said Percy. "Do you have any new special places?"

"No. Some of them are just more special now because I once shared them with a friend. Those are now my *most* special places."

It fell quiet a few minutes. With a sunset, the sea, and miles of open moorland behind them, no words were needed. What was to be said, both felt without words.

"You've changed, Percy," said Gwyneth at length.

"In what way?"

"I haven't completely decided. You are older."

Percy broke out in a peal of laughter. "I am indeed. So are you, my dear Gwyneth."

"I know. But I meant older in a different way. It is a good older. I could see it in your eyes the moment I saw you at the manor. I hope my older is a good older, too."

"I am sure it is."

"Not everybody's older is a better older. I do not think Master Courtenay has become a better older."

"Does he still make fun of you?"

"He does not even speak to me. I think he disdains me. But Lady Florilyn is a better older. And she is *very* fond of you, Percy. She has been talking of nothing but your coming for weeks."

"I am fond of her, too. She has changed from the first time I came to Wales. And you are right, so have I. You did not know me before I first came here, Gwyneth. I was very foolish and wasn't very nice."

"I know, Percy. I heard Grannie's talk. She knew all about you. But I didn't care what anyone said. You were my friend, and you were kind to me."

"How long have you worked at the manor?" asked Percy.

"A year. Miss Florilyn was so nice to me after you left. She came to visit me, and even Grannie learned to like her. She came to our cottage once to see my animals. Then one of the maids at the manor left and she asked me if I would like to work for her mother and be paid. My father said he thought I should, so I did."

"Do you like it?"

"It is not so very hard work, though it is tedious. I do not have as much time with my father and my animals as I would like. But we have more money now. And Grannie says that I am not a little girl anymore and that when people get older their lives change. Grannie is very wise. I know that a girl like me must think of what she will do when she is older."

In that, Gwyneth's great-great-aunt was right—she was no longer a little girl. The quietness of Gwyneth's spirit was even deeper than before. One moment would the child burst into a laugh of glee, the next withdraw into her private solitary refuge of peace she shared only with those she loved. Because of the faraway gaze of her countenance, many of the villagers were now even more apprehensive of her than before.

Little did Percy realize how changed she was, and how beautiful she was on the verge of becoming. It takes far-seeing eyes to apprehend into what another is growing. Changed as he was, Percy had not yet become so wise as that. But the day of his own internal second sight was fast approaching.

"How old are you now, Gwyneth?" Percy asked.

"Sixteen," she replied.

"*Sixteen*—goodness, are you sure you didn't grow more years than me while I was gone?"

Gwyneth giggled, suddenly a girl again. "I was thirteen when you were here before. Some people thought I was young because I was so tiny. My father is a small man, and I am small, too."

"You are not so tiny now."

"Lady Florilyn is many inches taller than me."

"But her father and mother are both tall."

"How old are you, Percy? I forgot how old you were before. I have tried to remember because I know you told me."

"I was sixteen. I am nineteen now."

"You are a man, Percy," said Gwyneth softly. There was a world of meaning in the gentle expressiveness of her voice.

"Not quite, my dear Gwyneth! I am only on my way to becoming one, with a long way yet to go. I had the misfortune to have gotten a late start. How is Stevie?"

"You should ask him yourself."

"I intend to—very soon."

"His poor father is not well. Grannie says the Lord will take him before the summer is out. I hope she is right. It will be a relief to Auntie for her to know that he is healthy again."

"Perhaps you and I might ride up there for a visit tomorrow."

Gwyneth nodded. "Perhaps Lady Florilyn will want to ride with you somewhere else," she said.

"You might be right," said Percy. "We shall see. But I will definitely come to the village tomorrow. There are so many people I want to visit."

"Grannie is anxious to see you, too."

Fifty-Five

Cottage in the Hills

*I*n spite of his long train ride followed by the southbound coach of the day before, and the fact that he lay reading in his bed by candlelight until past eleven, Percy awoke early and was downstairs to the breakfast room not long after seven. He knew Florilyn would not make an appearance for hours. Still, he was guiltily relieved to find the room empty.

To all appearance, Mrs. Drynwydd had only just brought out the covered silver pots from the kitchen, for they were steaming and fragrant. He ate in haste and was just finishing a second cup of tea with a last piece of toast when his aunt came in.

"Good morning, Percy," she said cheerily.

"Good morning, Aunt Katherine."

"Did you sleep well?"

"Very."

"How did Robert get on with his kite?"

A confused look met her question.

"Robert Falconer."

"Oh, right. . .of course!" Percy laughed. "Right—the kite. I moved a good way past that before falling asleep." He rose and began making his way toward the door.

"Where are you off to?" asked Katherine.

"I've been so anxious to ride in Wales again, I thought I would get an early start."

"Florilyn will be sorry to miss you."

"She and I will have many chances, I'm sure," laughed Percy.

As he left the house for the stables, he felt pangs of the same guilt that had come over him the previous evening—that he was being less than honest. Yet somehow he felt a gnawing uncertainty about what Florilyn would say to his being off so soon without her.

That Florilyn was changed, there could be no doubt. But the incident the day of the race three years before remained lodged in his memory. She had a temper; there was no denying that. He wanted to do nothing to rouse it again. But neither was he going to avoid visiting Gwyneth and Grannie and Stevie Muir and his other village friends for fear of her reaction.

Percy arrived at the Barrie cottage a little after eight. Codnor was already off for the mine. Gwyneth had not accompanied him. Percy saw her at the back of the cottage feeding her animals.

"Hey, Gwyneth!" Percy called out from atop Grey Tide while he was still a good way off.

She turned, waved, and waited for his approach.

"I thought I would ride in to see Grannie then out to Stevie's," he said as he cantered up. "Why don't you join me?"

"Do you want me to?"

"Of course! How could you even ask? Come on!" he said, reaching down and extending his hand. "Jump up behind me."

Though Gwyneth was at least four inches taller and fifteen pounds heavier than before, Percy was stronger in equal proportion. He took hold of her hand and whisked her up behind him as easily as before. Again sounded the girlish giggle Percy loved. She came to light behind him and stretched her arms around him.

Ten minutes later they were walking into the darkened kitchen of Grannie's cottage in Llanfryniog. A joyous reunion followed with hugs and exclamations of delight. Within moments the tea was on while Grannie continued to make over the giant of a man Percy had become in her eyes. In truth he did not quite yet measure a full six feet and was as slender as the trunk of a birch tree, though solid and strong.

"The last time I saw you here," said Percy to Gwyneth as they walked into the inner room of the cottage, "we were all praying for you. We didn't know if you would live."

"God was taking care of me," rejoined Gwyneth simply. "I was not afraid. And have you noticed, Percy—I do not stutter now."

"That's right! I hadn't stopped to think about it."

"I haven't stuttered since the accident on the sand. So you see, Lady Florilyn and Red Rhud did me a favor."

"I've often heard my father say that all things work for good. It must be true."

"My, oh my," said Grannie, turning toward Percy again, "you are tall for a Scot laddie! What your mama must be feeding you!"

Percy laughed again. "My dad still has an inch or two on me," he said. "And I've been away from home for a year, Grannie—at university in the north. But my landlady feeds me as well as my mother."

In Percy's eyes, Grannie, too, was much changed. A little shorter, he thought, stooped and more bowed in the back. Her eyes still sparkled with the vibrancy of what life remained. But it was clear that it would not be many years before Life itself would call her to the home of its origin. Now that Grannie was eighty-four, Percy could not but wonder how much longer she would be able to take care of herself, even with Gwyneth's help. And with Gwyneth now at the manor, the old woman was more on her own than ever.

Percy found himself thinking of his own grandparents. They were still spry, though they were probably a dozen years younger. But they were aging rapidly as well.

After tea and an hour's happy reminiscing, the bonds between the three were securely retightened as if no more than a day had passed, as is always the case when true friends meet again after an absence.

By ten o'clock, with the sun warming the earth beneath them, wooing from it the myriad fragrances the month of June is so uniquely capable of producing, Percy and Gwyneth were riding up into the hills on Grey Tide's back.

To sit so close to Percy, her arms around his great strong waist, knowing that he had not changed in three years except for the better, sent Gwyneth's spirits soaring. But her thoughts were for her alone. Like Mary of old, she kept them hidden where they would be safe and treasured them quietly in the depths of her heart.

Percy was in no hurry. For three years he had dreamed of being in Wales again. He did not rush Grey Tide along. Neither spoke much as they went. As much as their relationship was the same, both sensed, though differently, that much was new between them. They would never go back to how they were before.

There is a great difference between the motions within the heart of a thirteen-year-old girl and one who has reached sixteen and has arrived at the threshold of womanhood. Though she would always be childlike, Gwyneth would never be a child again.

They encountered Stevie and his flock of sheep well before reaching the house. Percy leaped from the saddle, leaving Gwyneth perched precariously on the back of Grey Tide's rump. The two young men ran forward and greeted one another like old friends, with sheep scattering and bleating in every direction around them.

"You've grown, Percy!" exclaimed Stevie. "Suddenly you're half a head taller than me!"

"But not half so strong!" rejoined Percy. "Look at you—you've added inches to your arms and shoulders. Goodness man, you look like the blacksmith!"

Stevie laughed. "I'm not quite so burly as that. Kyvwlch Gwarthegydd is the strongest man in two counties. His young Chandos shows signs of being the same one day."

"Your sheep look fine, Stevie," said Percy. "How's your mum?"

"Middlin'," replied Stevie. "Papa's doing poorly. It's nearly taken the life out of the poor woman."

"We are on our way to see her."

"She will be happy to see you. But I must get these lads and lassies up to their pasture, so I'll not be joining you."

"I shall see you again, then," said Percy, returning to Gwyneth where she sat waiting patiently on Grey Tide.

They reached the Muir cottage ten or fifteen minutes later. One look at Adela Muir told the story. She was worn and haggard. It appeared she had hardly slept in weeks.

"My poor Glythvyr's in a bad way, Mr. Drummond," she replied to Percy's inquiry about her husband. "He won't know you. He won't even know you're here. He doesn't know me or Stevie now either. That's the heartbreak of it. We're strangers to him, you see."

Percy nodded. "I would still like to see him, Mrs. Muir."

She led them inside.

Percy could smell the change even before his eyes adjusted to the dim light of the sick chamber. It was the stale stench of life slipping away.

He approached the makeshift bed. The thin form on it lay motionless and pale. The face staring up off the pillow was gaunt, almost as if its skin had been stretched over a skeleton's skull. That life remained was clear from the faint mumbling of the lips and the fumbling of fingers with the edge of the blanket. Percy could make out nothing of what he was saying. He glanced at the man's wife.

She shook her head. "It's just nonsense, you see," she said. "No one can make out a word of it."

Percy stooped down and gently laid a hand on the bony white arm. "Hello, Mr. Muir," he said. "It's Percy Drummond again. I'm here from the manor. I'm Lord Snowdon's nephew."

He thought he detected a faint increase of the man's muttering and a flicker of the eyes. But there was no other response.

After a moment, he pulled away, stood, and smiled sadly. "I am so sorry, Mrs. Muir," he said. "I cannot imagine how difficult it must be for you."

Gwyneth's aunt nodded. "I won't deny it," she said. "But it's the way of womanhood, isn't it, you see? I am just praying the Lord will take him soon, for his sake not mine, though Stevie will sorely miss him. He loves his daddy, you see."

They returned to the kitchen. After another hour, with tea and a few simple oatcakes, they said their good-byes.

They returned to Grey Tide, who had been waiting patiently and refreshing herself with grass and water and a few oats. Percy and Gwyneth began the ride back in silence.

Glythvyr Muir's condition sobered Percy. He thought of his father and realized anew the important role he played in so many lives. His only regret was that he had not begun to see his father for who he truly was while he had been at home. It was now too late to be part of it with his mother and father. The memory of his youthful blindness stung him anew with regret.

Absorbed in his thoughts, suddenly at a distance of three or four hundred yards, Percy saw six or eight horses of varying color gallop into sight, crest a small ridge, then disappear over the other side. "What was that?" he exclaimed. "Did you see it, Gwyneth?" he cried, turning around where he sat. "It was a band of horses. There was nobody with them!"

"It's the wild horses of Snowdonia," said Gwyneth calmly.

"*Wild* horses! There are wild horses here?"

"Oh yes, many more than that."

"Who do they belong to?"

"Nobody. They belong to themselves."

"Where do they live?"

"In the hills."

"Do you know where?"

"Yes."

"You know *exactly* where?"

"Of course. I know all the animals."

"Are the wild horses your friends, too?"

Gwyneth hesitated. "Not really my friends," she said after a moment. "They know me. But they are a little wary of me. They don't let me get close like the other animals do. Do you want to see where they live, Percy?"

"*Yes!*" exclaimed Percy.

"Then ride that way," said Gwyneth, pointing to her right and away from the direction they had been going."

"That's not where I saw them running."

"I thought you wanted to see where they lived."

Percy nodded and led Grey Tide to the right. He should know better by now, he smiled to himself, than to doubt Gwyneth!

She directed him back toward the hills, bearing north from the Muir cottage. Gradually they moved eastward in the direction of Rhinog Fawr where it loomed ahead of them. Not once again did Percy see any sign of the horses. He had begun to doubt whether he would see them again. But his trust in Gwyneth was so great that he said nothing.

They kept on. Gradually the strange sensation came over Percy that he recognized some of the terrain and landmarks about them. They continued to climb steadily into yet higher hills.

All at once as they came around the shoulder of a hill, before him rose a great cliff face of granite. He knew beyond any doubt that he had been here before. Gwyneth was leading him near the blue lake where he had seen her singing to the animals.

Almost the same moment, as if she had been reading his mind, Gwyneth's voice interrupted his thoughts. "We are close to the place now, Percy," she said. "But we must go very quietly. Horses frighten easily, you know. This is a very quiet place. It is one of my special places. I think I should lead the way now."

Percy stopped Grey Tide and climbed to the ground. Gwyneth scooted forward into the saddle. Percy placed his foot in the stirrup and, with a little more difficulty than getting Gwyneth behind *him*, managed to climb up behind her. Now it was his turn to stretch his hands around her waist. She was small enough that he could reach all the way around and take hold of the front of the saddle. Sitting tall, he could see straight over the top of her blond head.

Feeling his chest against her back and his arms around her midsection gave Gwyneth a feeling of happy power as she took the reins. She urged Grey Tide forward. Within minutes they were descending steeply. Percy still caught no glimpse of the lake.

Gwyneth led down through a rocky narrow wooded ravine. The cliff of granite loomed higher and higher above them as they descended into what was obviously a deep valley, though the trees and boulders surrounded them so closely on all sides that they could not see the bottom of it.

Finally Gwyneth stopped. "We must go no closer," she whispered. "They will hear Grey Tide's hooves and will know she is not one of them. We will walk the rest of the way."

Carefully they dismounted. Percy tied the reins to a tree. Gwyneth crept forward, making not a sound. Percy followed. After eight or ten minutes, the trees began to thin in front of them. Finally Gwyneth stopped. Percy drew alongside.

In the distance, some fifty yards away in a clearing beyond the trees, spread over with a carpet of lush green grass, ten or fifteen horses grazed peacefully. A few deer were also about. Rabbits occasionally scurried by. In the distance, Percy could just make out a glistening surface of translucent blue.

Neither said a word. They watched in silence for ten minutes.

Percy knew that alone, and crooning the otherworldly melody he had heard before, Gwyneth would have been able to make a closer approach. But he would never see these magnificent beasts closer than he was beholding them now.

It was a holy moment of oneness with creation that comes for most but once or twice in a lifetime. Yet Gwyneth Barrie seemed to live within that oneness all the days of her life.

FIFTY-SIX

Invitation and Ride

*P*ercy did not arrive back at the manor until midafternoon.

By the time lunch was concluded and still with no sign of him, Florilyn had retired to her room, a little perturbed, it is true, for she suspected that Percy had gone to the village. Every hour that went by demonstrated more clearly than ever that he was more eager to visit his peasant friends after three years than spend time with her. She had tried to read but was agitated. With the afternoon sun streaming through the west-facing window of her room, she had finally dozed.

When she went downstairs and outside again some time later, she found Percy atop her father's new stables, bare-chested and perspiring freely, holding one end of a massive roof timber in place while two laborers secured it at the ends.

She approached and looked up, shielding her eyes from the sun with her hand. "Percy, what are you doing up there?" she called out.

"What does it look like?" Percy yelled down. "We're putting the roof on."

"But why you? You're not a laborer. You don't get paid."

"I'm not doing it to get paid but to help your father. Besides, this is great fun! I haven't enjoyed myself so much in years."

"But. . .your hands—what if you get hurt or something?"

"A few blisters and a scrape or two—who wants lily-white hands that don't know how to work? Not me!"

"Where were you all morning?"

"I went for a ride."

"Where?"

"Up to see Stevie Muir," said Percy. In the time since he had left that morning, he had decided to be completely straightforward. "Gwyneth told me that his father is seriously ill. I wanted to visit them without delay. . .just in case, you know."

"When did you see Gwyneth?"

"Last night as she was leaving. I was amazed to find her working here! That was so kind of you to arrange for her to have a job, Florilyn. I am proud of you! She and I rode up to see the Muirs this morning."

"Oh. . .I was hoping to have a ride with you."

"So was I," said Percy. "But I thought it important to go to the Muirs as soon as possible. Now we've got to get these roof timbers set today. Maybe we could go with lunch tomorrow. Let's take that same ride from last time. . .you know, our first long ride together—but with me staying in the saddle this time!"

His enthusiasm mollified Florilyn's feelings that might, had the conversation gone differently, produced an outcome more reminiscent of the Florilyn of former days. No one had ever said the words "I am proud of you" to Florilyn Westbrooke in her life. She didn't know how to react, whether to receive them with quiet gratitude or take offense that one whom the pride of her past might have considered her social inferior could be proud of *her*. To her credit, she swallowed her perplexity, agreed to Percy's suggestion, and returned to the house.

On the following morning, as Percy and Florilyn were getting ready for their ride, a messenger arrived from Burrenchobay Hall.

Florilyn recognized the man on horseback as Richard Hawarden, Sir Armond's groom. Seeing an envelope in his hand, her natural curiosity was aroused, and she walked toward him as he dismounted. "Hello, Mr. Hawarden," she said, approaching from behind.

The groom turned. "Good mornin' tae ye, Miss Florilyn."

"What do you have there?"

"An invitation, my leddy—tae Mistress Davina's birthday party." He handed the envelope to Florilyn.

"Thank you," she said.

"Very good, Miss Florilyn," he said and returned to his horse.

Florilyn opened the envelope and read the engraved card inside. Percy walked up behind her.

"It seems we've all been invited to an event at Burrenchobay Hall," she said. "You are specifically included. If I didn't know better, I would think that scheming little Davina has eyes for you, Percy."

"What are you talking about?" he asked.

"You are quite the topic of conversation around here, you know. . . the handsome mysterious stranger from the north. Davina must have asked me ten times when you would be back."

Percy laughed again. "She's just a kid."

"Not anymore! She's sixteen next week. Believe me, she could go to London next season, no questions asked, and easily pass for eighteen. You talk about marriage proposals—she could scoop them in like flies to honey."

"Then maybe I should turn down my portion of the invitation," said Percy. "That family and yours. . .it's too complicated! I don't want to get in the middle of it. I'm not much for high society stuff anyway. I'll leave all that to you aristocrats."

Now it was Florilyn's turn to laugh. "We'll worry about Davina later. Let me take this invitation inside to my mother," she said. "Then we can be off."

Two hours later, the cousins arrived at the same level meadow that Percy recognized from their ill-fated ride three years earlier.

"I would never have found my way here alone," he said. "But I know this place well enough now that I see it. Ah, the memories come flooding back! Maybe it's my turn to challenge *you* to a race to the top," said Percy playfully.

"No, thank you. My racing days are over," said Florilyn in a quieter tone. "After what happened on the beach, the memory is too painful. I wouldn't mind if we rode *together* to the top. Then we can have lunch there."

"Sounds good to me. Let's go!"

Percy dug in his heels and galloped off across the grass. Florilyn followed and soon drew alongside. She looked across at him with a happy smile, eyes filled with fun, but without the twinkle of challenge she might have thrown him before. Both were content to ride beside one another. For the rest of the distance across the flat, they pushed their mounts but remained side by side.

"When we reach the wood," Percy called out, "you take the lead. I'm not sure I know the way."

Florilyn nodded.

Five or ten minutes later, stopping briefly at the stream to water the horses, and after navigating the woods and steep incline without incident, they crested the ridge.

"That was great!" exclaimed Percy as they eased the two mares to a gentle walk, looking about at the familiar sight. "It is nice still to be aboard after that climb."

Though the ridge was mostly rocky, they found a patch of tolerably soft grass where the twin mares could graze. They dismounted, tied the horses to the nearby shrubbery, and set out the simple lunch things they had brought.

"It is so quiet here," said Percy as they sat together. "I wouldn't know which direction the sea lay. In fact. . .I *don't* know!" He laughed.

"It's there," said Florilyn pointing, "straight west."

"How would I know which way is west?"

"I don't know. I've been out riding these hills for so long, I just know."

"It must have been wonderful to grow up here," said Percy, taking a bite out of an apple. "Not that I'm complaining. But the city—especially a place like Glasgow—it's nothing like this."

"And now you've traded one city for another."

"I suppose you're right. Unfortunately that's where they put the universities. So if you want an education, to the city you must go."

"How many years do you have left in Aberdeen?" asked Florilyn.

"Three. I've only got one year under my belt so far."

"Do you like it?"

"It's hard work, but yes—I do. I love studying and learning."

"What will you do. . .I mean when you've graduated?"

"I'm not sure yet. I am looking into engineering. I had thought about being a minister, too, like my dad."

"The *Reverend* Percy Drummund," said Florilyn slowly, trying out the sound of it. "Somehow it doesn't quite have the right ring. I think it would have to be the Reverend *Percival* Drummond."

"You're right." He laughed. "*Percy* isn't exactly right. What about for a solicitor? I'm also thinking of studying law, if God doesn't lead me into the ministry."

"I think you'll definitely need the *Percival* on the door of a solicitor's office."

"What about you, my dear Florilyn?" asked Percy.

"What about me?"

"You've turned into such a lady since I saw you. What are your plans?"

"Women don't have *plans*."

"Some do. Women making their mark in the world are all the rage these days. At university, some are saying that women will even vote in the not too distant future."

"*Vote*. . .women?"

"That's what they say."

"I can hardly believe that."

"Maybe you're right. It may never go that far. Nobody can see the future. Still, don't you have any plans?"

"There we are back to what I said before—women don't have plans. Men have plans, women get married."

"Bluntly put!" Percy laughed. "I guess you're right. So what does a pretty young woman like you do—just wait around until, like you said at dinner the other evening, the right man comes calling at your door?"

"I suppose that's about it."

"What if the right man never comes along?"

"Then a girl's got a big problem. She either gets more desperate as the years go by, or eventually she settles for second best."

"I was under the impression three years ago that you had every young man for miles wrapped around your little finger."

Florilyn smiled almost wistfully. "Maybe I did." She nodded reflectively. "I probably could marry several of them even now. But I've changed since then. I'm not so anxious to see a ring on my finger."

"You *are* changed. I saw it immediately. There is a quietness about you now. You seem content with yourself."

"I suppose I am. . .mostly. But aren't all girls a little insecure deep inside, wondering what people think of them?"

"I don't know. I'm not a girl."

"That is undeniably true!" Florilyn laughed. She paused and seemed to be thinking whether to say what had come to her mind. She glanced away.

Percy could tell she was embarrassed. He waited.

"Percy," she said after a moment, "do you—what you said before—do you really think I'm pretty?"

"Yes, I do. You are very attractive. Why?"

"I don't know. A girl never *really* knows what she looks like to people. You can look in a mirror for hours, but you don't really know. Everyone *wants* to be pretty. But you can't really trust what boys tell you. Half of them are such liars, and the other half are so shy they're afraid of their own shadows."

Percy laughed to hear such a characterization of his sex.

"All those young men you said had eyes for me. . .they were just trying to get me to like them and pay attention to them. Colville Burrenchobay—what a big oaf. All he wanted was to touch me and kiss me. Ugh! It makes me sick to think of it! How can I believe anything someone like that tells me?"

"So why did you ask me?"

"Because you're different, Percy. You say what you mean and mean what you say. You would never toy with a girl. I don't think you would even know how to. You're too real, too honest."

"I guess I never thought about it one way or another."

"Once I began to see you for who you were, you know. . .once I was through being nasty to you, I realized how shallow all the other young men were. I got tired of the games, of them trying to impress me and telling me I was pretty. I got tired of trying to impress them, too. Their words meant nothing. But coming from *you*. . .it means a lot. Thank you."

"Sure." Percy smiled.

"It was your coming here that changed me, you know, Percy. Like it or not, it's all your fault!" she added with a grin.

"That's quite a burden to put on a chap! So. . .you said you were waiting for the right kind of young man. How will you know?"

"I don't know." Florilyn smiled thoughtfully. "Do you ever really know ahead of time?"

"Probably not. I see what you mean."

"It's not as if you can prepare a form and ask them to tick all the boxes. It's not so cut-and-dried as all that."

"What *are* you looking for, then?"

Florilyn hesitated before answering. "Honestly?" she said at length.

"Of course."

"Say what I mean and mean what I say?"

Percy nodded.

"I suppose I am looking for someone. . .not so very different from you, Percy."

Now it was Percy's turn to grow thoughtful.

"You are considerate and fun to be around," Florilyn went on. "But you have a serious side, too. I can talk to you *and* laugh with you. You can't do that with everyone. No matter what happens, I know that you will be a gentleman."

"No one has ever called me a gentleman before."

"Well, you are. You can take it from a young woman who has met dozens of young men who aren't."

Again it grew silent.

"So, I will turn the question around—what about *you*?" said Florilyn. "Do you see lots of young women in Aberdeen—bonnie Scots lassies... parties and socializing every night?"

"I'm afraid not," replied Percy. "There are a few young ladies in the church I attend."

"Anyone special?"

Percy smiled. "No," he answered. "They're nice enough. But no one special."

FIFTY-SEVEN

Interlude

Several days had passed since Percy's arrival.

He had gone to the village every day, visited with the men at the harbor, been in all the shops, gone into Mistress Chattan's for several pints, and talked and laughed with the local fishermen and farmers and miners. He never went to Llanfryniog without tea with Grannie.

He ran into Chandos Gwarthegydd at his father's blacksmith's shop. As Stevie had said, Chandos showed signs of becoming as muscular as his father. The lad, now fifteen, was well capable of wielding his tools and keeping the fire in the forge glowing hot with coal. He could fashion a shoe for a horse as well as any blacksmith in Wales. He and Percy quickly formed a great friendship.

Seeing Gwyneth, however, was not so easy as before. Percy longed to walk and ride with her out on the hills and along the beach and to listen to her delightful, simple, humble talk about nature and God and animals and her special places.

But that became more difficult now that she was working at the manor. He couldn't simply drop in on her anytime as he had before. Nor did he so often find her at Grannie's. Neither could he interrupt her in the midst of her work. She had responsibilities now. He was on holiday. Gwyneth was not.

Even so, there were other demands on his time, too—as he quickly became one of the regular workers on the new stables. He was not obligated to maintain the work schedule of the hired men. But he enjoyed the project. Besides learning new skills, he was enjoying enormously working beside the humble Welshmen. He had only seen Courtenay two or three times, and then briefly.

He encountered Gwyneth from time to time as she went about her duties. She always glanced shyly away or greeted him simply as she passed.

Finally toward the end of one day, Percy saw her carrying a stack of towels on her way up to the family living quarters.

He had been lingering on the landing of the first floor, absently staring at the dozen or so portraits lining the walls of the main staircase. His eyes had again been arrested by the compelling expression and penetrating eyes of the woman his uncle had commented on during the first week of his previous visit. Every time he looked up at the image of her face, the woman's gaze drew him as if she were veritably *alive*. He found her gazing down at him every time he ascended or descended the stairs.

Hearing a step on the ground floor below, even as he was looking at the face of Lord Snowdon's grandmother, Percy glanced toward the sound. There was Gwyneth walking up the stairs. She was staring straight into his eyes.

For a moment, Percy gazed back stunned, then quickly looked back at the portrait. His face drained of color. The next moment the shocking revelation of what he had seen was interrupted by Gwyneth's voice.

He turned toward her as she approached with a smile. The brief expression was gone from her face. The trance that had come over him was instantly broken.

"Hello, Percy," she said. "You are standing there looking like you just saw a ghost!"

"Oh…yeah, sorry!" He laughed, shaking his head. "I was just…But, Gwyneth—I was hoping to run into you."

She reached the landing.

"I've hardly seen you at all," Percy went on. "I miss our talks."

"So do I, Percy," she said softly.

"Do you work tomorrow?"

Gwyneth shook her head.

"Then let's meet for the day."

"What about your work at the stables?" said Gwyneth. "All the rest of the servants are talking about what a big help you are. They say they have never seen Master Courtenay dirty his hands like you do."

"Just so long as they don't say it around him!" laughed Percy. "But the workers can get by without me. The roof is nearly done. They are just humoring me anyway. I don't really know what I am doing."

"That's not what Mr. Radnor says."

"Well, he has always been very nice. So what do you say about tomorrow?"

"If you really want to, Percy."

"Want to? I've been waiting for the chance."

"Would you like to come to Grannie's for breakfast tea?"

"That would be great!"

"Then I will walk my father to the mine at seven and be to Grannie's by eight."

"I'll be there."

The next morning, Percy left the manor on foot at seven thirty, just about the time Gwyneth was saying good-bye to her father for the day and returning to walk back to the village from the mine.

After breakfast tea with Grannie, Percy and Gwyneth left the cottage and walked through the village toward the harbor.

"Do the village people bother you much anymore?" asked Percy.

"Not so much," replied Gwyneth. "They don't talk to me, but at least they don't say cruel things. It is a great relief not to go to school. Grannie always taught me to return evil with kindness, and I tried to. One of my earliest memories is of Grannie's voice saying, 'Good returns fivefold. Secret good returns tenfold. Return good for evil—God never forgets.' But it is not so pleasant to have people make fun of you. I am glad not to be taking so many bouquets around as I once did."

They reached the beach. Percy paused to untie his shoes and take them off along with his socks. Gwyneth did the same. Before she was through, Percy had gone running off, yelling and laughing as he darted in and out of the incoming tide like a frolicksome dog. Gwyneth laughed with delight. Out of breath after a few minutes, he came running back to where she stood, still giggling to see him having so much fun.

"There is nothing like walking and running barefoot in the sand," he said as he picked up his shoes and they walked away from the harbor. I think this beach is one of my favorite places in the whole world. I think I will claim it as *my* special place! I wonder if you can see Ireland from here, too."

"Only on a very clear day, I think," said Gwyneth.

"The tide is out today," Percy went on. "Have you found any more spooky skeletons in the cave?"

"No," laughed Gwyneth. "I am still a little afraid to go there by myself."

"I've got it! You wait here." said Percy excitedly. "I'll run back to Grannie's and borrow a candle and matches. We'll explore it!"

He dashed off. As soon as he left the sand, he remembered his bare feet. He sat down and began to put his shoes and socks back on.

Almost the next instant Gwyneth ran past him. "*You* wait here!" she laughed. "I don't need shoes. I will get the candle and matches."

She was back almost in less time than it would have taken him to tie up his laces. Soon they were scampering over the rocky end of the beach toward the cave. Five minutes later they were inside.

Percy struck a match and lit the candle. With the flame flickering and sending its light and shadows dancing off the walls and roof of the perpetually wet rock, they ventured slowly inside.

"I've never seen the cave so bright," said Gwyneth, gazing all about. "It looks so different."

The cave was larger than Percy expected, easily forty or fifty feet to the far end where the downward slope of the roof met the walls at the sand. No dangerous protrusions or hidden stones were visible, and the sandy floor was smooth. The bottom sloped up markedly from the cave's mouth. If one did happen to get trapped inside by a sudden incoming tide, it would indeed be difficult to get out.

"Where did you see the skeleton?" asked Percy.

"I think about here," said Gwyneth, glancing about. "It is hard to tell. But it was only the head."

"You've never seen anything since?"

Gwyneth shook her head.

They reached the far end. Percy knelt down in the wet sand, feeling about with his free hand as he sent the light from the candle into every crevice and recess of the irregular rock of the walls. "It almost seems that it might go farther back," he said. "Look here, the rock angles farther in except that it is blocked up by sand. Waves must have constantly pushed the sand farther in and up against the rock. I wonder if there is another small chamber behind this pile of sand."

"I would be afraid to find out," said Gwyneth. "There might be spiders and crabs and scary little creatures. I would never come in here again if I thought there was a place where things like that were hiding!"

Percy laughed. "I thought you loved animals!"

"I do. But not spiders and bats and beetles that live where it's dark."

"Well, if there is more to this cave, we're not going to find it without a spade."

They crawled back away from the inner end of the cave until they could stand again, then left through the cave mouth and continued along the south portion of sandy beach. Soon they had their shoes on again and were climbing the trail up to the promontory of Mochras Head. They sat down at the top, gazing across the water.

"Can you see Ireland today?" asked Percy.

Gwyneth squinted. "I don't think so. Maybe. I can't be sure. Are you going to the party at Burrenchobay Hall, Percy?" asked Gwyneth abruptly.

"You heard about it, did you? I don't know. . . I suppose. Though I would rather not."

"Why, Percy?"

"Oh, you know. . .all those highfalutin society people. I'm not cut out for all that. I'd rather be having a pint with the fishermen than get dressed up for a party."

"But you have to go."

"Why do you say that?"

"Because Miss Florilyn is expecting you to be her escort."

"Is she? Hmm, well I suppose I shall have to go, then."

"I saw you and Miss Florilyn leaving for a ride yesterday. Did you have fun?"

"Yes, we had a good time catching up since seeing one another during my last visit."

"She likes being with you, doesn't she?"

"I suppose."

"Where did you ride?"

"Where you met me three years ago way out in the hills, remember? You had to lead me home."

Gwyneth smiled but then grew quiet, even a little withdrawn.

They sat awhile in silence.

"Do you have any new animals?" he asked at length.

"A few.

"I would like to see them."

They rose and walked slowly away from the promontory and toward Gwyneth's home. The mood that had come over her passed. She was soon herself again.

FIFTY-EIGHT

Burrenchobay Hall

*T*he big day of the party finally came.

Florilyn spent all afternoon getting ready. Gwyneth and one of the other maids spent most of the day waiting on her. By five o'clock she was ready, every hair in place, her long lavender dress perfect. Mother and daughter had at last attached the final ribbon at the waist to the expensive dress they had purchased in London some months before.

"You look lovely, dear," said Katherine as she adjusted the bow in her daughter's glistening black hair.

"Do you think Percy will like the dress?" asked Florilyn.

"I am sure he will."

Outside a large brougham with Deaken Trenchard at the reins stood ready to transport Lord and Lady Snowdon, Florilyn, and Percy the four miles to Burrenchobay Hall. Courtenay had made his own arrangements and had left some time before.

Percy came down the central staircase looking stunning in a dark blue suit with a white shirt, vest, and red tie. Florilyn stood waiting at the bottom of the stairs. The sight nearly took her breath away. It was the same suit he had been wearing on the day of his arrival. Yet something about it on this day was especially stunning.

Gwyneth, too, had been watching for Percy's appearance. She stood out of sight along one of the corridors, hidden around a corner of the wall. She knew she was neglecting her work. But she could not help herself. The compulsion was too strong to set eyes on him before a grand event the likes of which she had been listening to Florilyn describe all day.

Her reaction was exactly like Florilyn's. At sight of Percy as she peeped around the corner, Gwyneth felt a tightening in her chest. Could that really be *her* Percy. . .her friend of the seashore and hills. . .the same Percy who sat in Grannie's cottage day after day as if he were a simple villager. . .her sharer of the special places? She could hardly believe it!

Then the familiar laugh echoed down the hall in response to something Florilyn had said. The sound fell into Gwyneth's ear with a pang even as it sent her heart leaping. It was Percy!

Yet how could Percy be two such different people? How could he walk and talk with her like a friend, run along with bare feet on the sand, laughing as he dashed in and out of the incoming waves like a jubilant boy, and now be so dazzling and handsome?

As she crept away and returned to her final duties of the day, many confusing thoughts rushed through the brain of Gwyneth Barrie. How could one like her, so small, so slow of speech, a simple peasant girl who kept animals and took care of her Grannie and her papa, ever be worthy of one like Percy Drummond?

The sight of him had been a revelation, a wonder. Yet it was also a crushing blow. In that moment, Gwyneth had also seen herself. She knew she had allowed herself to build foolish castles in the sky and to dream dreams that could never be.

⟨✦⟩

The brougham with its four passengers left Westbrooke Manor and arrived at its destination forty minutes later.

The scene at the Burrenchobay estate as they approached was bright and festive. In the distance could be heard strains of music.

A servant led them in at the front door with the stream of guests who had been arriving for some time from the best homes throughout North Wales. The sounds grew louder, accompanied by laughter from behind the house. The butler continued before them through a wide hall decorated with medieval replicas, not unlike those in Westbrooke Manor, and out to the garden. There a hastily assembled choir of male voices was raised in resonant harmony to the strains of "God Save the Queen."

Always singing in Wales! Percy laughed to himself. He heard music coming from every cottage in Llanfryniog. Fishermen at their nets might spontaneously burst into song without warning, two or three together, and within minutes be joined by voices from boats out on the water. The servants around the house were constantly humming or singing to themselves.

The anthem ended with rousing applause from every quarter as the fifty or so guests broke into smaller groups.

The young lady for whom the occasion had been planned had purposefully delayed her appearance for maximum effect. . .and, most important, until the contingent from Westbrooke Manor arrived.

Davina Burrenchobay reached the bottom of the stairs, slowed and tried to calm herself, pinched both cheeks to make sure they were pink, then continued through the central hall and toward the gathering outside.

Several of her friends scurried to meet her.

"Has anyone seen Percy?" asked Davina.

"He's here!" said one of her friends excitedly. "He's over there with his uncle and your parents. . .*and* that Florilyn Westbrooke."

"Don't worry about her," said Davina. "Once he sets eyes on me, he will forget his cousin."

"Do you think he'll ask you to dance?" asked one of Davina's fawning friends.

"I intend to make sure of it, Iola. If he doesn't, I shall ask him!"

She continued through the crowd spread out on the expansive lawns to the side of the house, an entourage of four or five young ladies following her about just as she had once followed Florilyn.

"Ah, Lord Snowdon," said a distinguished-looking gentleman approaching the viscount and Katherine with outstretched hand, "how good of you to come."

"Thank you, Armond," replied Westbrooke. "And greetings to you, Lady Arial," he added, smiling to the woman at Burrenchobay's side.

The wives exchanged greetings along with their husbands.

Sir Armond Burrenchobay and Roderick Westbrooke had virtually grown up together on the north coast of Wales, both from old Welsh families. They had pursued different interests through the years, with the result that Burrenchobay had risen through the political ranks into its highest echelons.

"I would like you both to meet my nephew, Percival Drummond," said Westbrooke. "Percy is in Wales for a few weeks."

Handshakes followed.

"I've heard about your visit," said Burrenchobay to Percy. "You were here some years back, were you not? I believe my eldest son knows you."

"Yes, we. . .uh, ran into one another during my previous visit," replied Percy.

"That's fine—good. Perhaps you shall have a chance to renew your friendship."

The adults gradually moved away, talking among themselves.

"Hello, Percy," said Burrenchobay's daughter, slinking forward in the wake of her father's departure, dropping her eyes for just the right effect.

"Hello, Davina," replied Percy with the humorous poise of an adult speaking to a child. "Finally leaving the awkward age of fifteen behind, eh. Happy birthday."

At his side, Florilyn smiled inwardly at Percy's wit. She could not help enjoying the chagrin she saw in Davina's eyes at the reminder of how young Percy considered her.

"Thank you," said Davina recovering herself. "I'm so glad you could come. I am hoping you will dance with me. It *is* my birthday, you know."

"If Florilyn will allow me," rejoined Percy, casting a grin to his side, "I suppose it might be arranged. Wouldn't be right to disappoint the birthday girl!"

At the far end of the garden, Colville Burrenchobay came out of the house with Rhawn Lorimer at his side. Neither appeared happy. A perceptive observer would have seen that they had been arguing.

Percy was stunned by the change that had taken place. Both looked older than three short years could account for. If possible, Rhawn was even more beautiful than before, yet her face had a hard look, and she had done considerable filling out. Though her profile would still have been capable of making grown men swoon, she no longer boasted that willowy figure of youth that was still evident in Florilyn and young Davina.

As for Colville Burrenchobay, his expression and demeanor was, for lack of a better word, threatening. To call it evil might have been going too far. Still, Percy shuddered at the sight. He would not need to be reminded to keep well clear of Davina's older brother.

Soon the dancing was in full swing to the sound of a string sextet. Thinking it best to get the inevitable over with as quickly as possible, Percy had consented to Davina's entreaties. She was thus enjoying a second waltz with the young man, as she supposed, that she was about to steal from Florilyn Westbrooke. A few of the other girls, following Davina's example, had succeeded in enticing a handful of single youths in the direction of the music. Gradually the dance area filled with couples of all ages.

As dancing and discussions continued, servants moved silently among the guests bearing trays laden with tea, coffee, and for the most special of guests, samples from Burrenchobay's private reserve of thirty-year-old whiskey imported from the Scottish highlands. Several tables at one end would be heavily laden with a lavish spread of food within the hour and were now set with cups and saucers, milk and sugar, and additional steaming pots of tea.

Wives from twenty to sixty clustered about the grounds chatting about husbands and children and everything else wives and mothers talk about. These included several newly married young ladies, suddenly transformed from girls to matrons. One or two of these cast about distracted glances toward the dancers, accompanied by inward twinges of envy to think that they had married so young and would never more know the gaiety and freedom that Davina Burrenchobay and their former friends still enjoyed.

But the vortex of the gathering, as in all such events from London to Inverness, was reserved for the unmarried young men and young women who had been fortunate enough to receive invitations. Among them stirred budding affections to pluck a hundred invisible heartstrings that would result in many individual dramas of hope and heartbreak, triumph and disappointment.

Swirling and twirling with flourish, those young women were engaged in the wily art practiced since time began, of attempting to attract the eye of every young man on the premises. Some flirtations were modest, others bold, a few outright brazen. But all had the same end in view—to be *noticed*. . .then to draw a lingering shy smile, from some handsome boy, to be followed, whether in ten minutes or an hour, by the bashful invitation to the dance floor.

The most eligible of the young men, on their parts, carried out with exquisite perfection their own portion of the timeless rite, which was pretending *not* to notice. All the while they spoke of hunting and horses and guns, to all appearances oblivious to the giggles and fluttering eyelashes of the fairer sex.

The older and more handsome among them knew well enough that every smile, every laugh, every gesture was capable of causing one or another of the girls to go weak at the knees. Young men knew how to flirt, too. Thus, they chose exactly when to allow a grin, how wide to make their smiles, and where to direct them toward some vulnerable heart.

This was the centuries-old ritual of the British "coming out," practiced on the yearly stage of London's social season. Tonight's event had been planned merely as Davina Burrenchobay's warmup for the main event a year hence.

To have seen this undercurrent of coquetry on the part of the young ladies and roguery on the part of the young men and to have witnessed the self-preoccupied interplay among the youthful generation would have made the skin crawl on the arms and neck of Edward and Mary Drummond of Glasgow. That many of today's charms from the girl who swirled at the center of attention had been specifically designed in this case to lure and fascinate their own son would have broken their hearts. But they would have been proud to know that his reaction, after ten minutes at Burrenchobay Hall, was substantially the same as theirs would have been. None of the wiles directed at him exercised the slightest movement of either his heart or his ego. Already Percy was anxious to have the evening done with. For the sake of his aunt and uncle, however, he tried to enjoy himself.

At long last, having observed the machinations of the younger girls long enough, Rhawn Lorimer decided to show them how it was done. She left Davina's brother and prepared to move in for the kill.

As the drama of the social elite of Snowdonia was playing out its subtleties, on a hill overlooking Burrenchobay Hall, a lonely figure sat watching from a distance of some four hundred yards. The lights gleamed, and the music drifted up from afar and stung her young heart with longings she had never felt in the brief span of her sixteen years. After reaching home, consumed by thoughts of the celebration someone like her would never attend, Gwyneth had run over the hills, like a moth to the flame, and now sat watching and listening in silence as the dusk of evening closed around her.

"So, young Drummond," purred Rhawn Lorimer, sidling through the group of juveniles and squeezing Davina aside, "it would appear that you are the hit of the evening with the *younger* crowd."

Her emphasis of the word was lost neither on Percy nor the listening girls. But they had idolized Rhawn for a long time and were in truth a little afraid of her.

As she spoke, Rhawn gradually steered Percy away from the others. Unconsciously he followed, glancing about as if looking for Florilyn. A tingle of excited terror surged through him as he felt Rhawn's hand slip through his arm. Soon they were alone.

"I've been hurt that you haven't come to see me," she said seductively. "I hear you have been back for weeks."

"Not that long, really." Percy laughed, trying to make light of it. "I just arrived."

"Don't lie to me, Percy. You've been here almost two weeks. I keep track of you."

"I'm only here for a short visit anyway."

"All the more reason you should have come to see me. You will be leaving in a matter of days. We have much to catch up on."

Again Percy laughed, but nervously. He was feeling like a fly caught in the web of a very clever spider.

"Come, Percy. . .let's dance."

"I would really rather not, Rhawn," replied Percy. "I heard that you traded Courtenay for Colville, and I don't want to make *either* of them angry. I saw you with Colville, and he doesn't like me. Surely you know that. I think it would be best if I—"

"Percy, *please*," Rhawn interrupted. Her tone could hardly be mistaken. "I *want* to dance with you. If you don't, I will make a scene and tell Colville that you tried to get too friendly with me. I don't think you want that, do you, Percy? Whereas. . .if you give me what I want, I will make sure he keeps away from you."

Percy sighed. He knew when he was beaten. "I guess you win," he said. "So. . .may I have the honor of this dance?"

Rhawn smiled with her victory, gave a slight curtsy, and extended her hand. As if he were reaching for a cobra, Percy took it. They moved toward the rest of the dancers while Davina Burrenchobay looked on with helpless envy.

If Percy had hoped to placate Rhawn Lorimer in whatever game she was playing with a single inauspicious dance, he soon realized how mistaken he was. He found himself flying about among the other couples, wondering who was leading and who was following. Rhawn was loud and boisterous, laughing gaily as if intentionally trying to draw attention to herself. Percy wondered if she had been drinking.

The first dance was followed by a second, then a third. Between dances Rhawn clung to him like wallpaper. She continued to laugh and talk loudly. The eyes of everyone in the place followed them about. Mercifully, Colville Burrenchobay was nowhere to be seen. Percy had not seen Courtenay the whole evening.

After five dances, to Percy's profound relief, Rhawn excused herself, saying she was suddenly not feeling well. She disappeared inside the house.

Percy immediately glanced about for his cousin. He located her by the refreshment table almost the same instant he saw Davina Burrenchobay making a beeline toward him. He hurried toward Florilyn.

She saw him approaching and waited, a humorous smile on her lips. If she had been bothered that Percy had been thus far monopolized by her two former friends, she showed no sign of it.

Percy raised his eyebrows and shook his head as if overwhelmed and bewildered by what had taken place with Rhawn Lorimer. "I fear I have been neglecting you, my dear cousin," he said for the benefit of those standing nearby. "I hope you have been having a good time." He led her away, one eye roving to keep out of the way of the birthday girl, then put his arm around Florilyn's waist as the music to the next dance began.

As they moved together, he bent to her ear. "Why didn't you come rescue me? That Rhawn is too much!"

Florilyn's tinkling laughter sounded over the music. "It didn't appear to me that you needed rescuing," she said. "Besides, I've learned not to tangle with Rhawn."

"Do you think she's tipsy? She was acting really weird!"

"I don't know," replied Florilyn more seriously. "She is so changed, I hardly know her anymore."

"All I know is that I was in over my head. You just stay on my arm and don't let any of these conniving girls near me! And that includes little Davina. What is with her anyway?"

"She has a crush on you, Percy," laughed Florilyn. "She and all her friends. Isn't it obvious?"

"I thought I was supposed to be *your* escort. Fight them off with a stick if you have to! I'm yours for the rest of this evening—no one else's."

"If you say so." Florilyn laughed. "But if Rhawn comes back, you're on your own. I'm fond of you, Percy—but not fond enough to fight Rhawn for you."

"Hey—I fought for you once. Remember?"

"How could I forget? But Rhawn Lorimer is more dangerous than Colville Burrenchobay."

Meanwhile, the conversation between the two most powerful men in the region was progressing along different lines.

"I must say, Roderick," remarked the host, "what do you think of all this new money flooding into Wales on the heels of industry?"

"Good for the economy, I suppose," replied Westbrooke.

"Yes, but is it good for Wales?" rejoined Burrenenchobay. "Everywhere we've got *nouveau riche* industrialists buying up land, pretending they're something they're not."

"Where's the harm, Armond?" queried his neighbor.

"It's the idea of it I resent. I can't but think they're going to ruin the country in the end."

"You don't deny that the money is good for Wales."

"It may be her ruin as well. Look at what the slate mine has done to the land between our two estates."

"It gives people work."

"Perhaps, but I don't like to see the land cut to pieces. And if coal ever comes north, I hate the thought of it. Men like you and me must do our best to preserve the land of our heritage from such development."

"Men like *you*, don't you mean. I have no power to change the march of events. You do."

"I am but a humble back bencher, Roderick. I've got no more power in parliament than a fly on the wall."

Taking a break after several dances with Florilyn, and still keeping his eyes roving for any sign of danger, Percy wandered in the direction of his uncle and host.

"Ah, Percy, my boy, enjoying yourself?" said the viscount as he approached.

"All this dancing is a bit much for me, Uncle Roderick."

"You're young—enjoy it while you can. My friend Sir Armond here is a MP. Any complaints you have about the country, just bring them to him."

Burrenchobay laughed. "It is not quite so simple as that, young Drummond, I fear," he said. "So, you're a Scotsman, eh?"

"Yes, sir. My father is a vicar in Glasgow."

"A vicar. . .I see. Are all Scots as religious as they say?"

"I really don't know. What *do* they say?"

"That you Scots are all canting revivalists."

"I hope I am not a canting revivalist, as you say, Sir Armond. I thought it was you Welsh who were famous for revivals. In any event, my father is not a revivalist, I can assure you."

"Do you follow his ideals in matters of religion?"

"I would say so, yes. More than that, however, I hope I am simply a young man who tries to do what God gives him to do."

Burrenchobay stared at him blankly. "What exactly do you mean?" he asked after a moment. "I am not aware of ever being given anything by God to do myself. The phrase is new to me. I assume you mean something by it."

"Only that I try to order my life by the commands of Him who said He came from God to show us how to live."

Again, a stupefied stare met Percy's words. "I must say, if I didn't know better, I would think you were drunk. I know you Scots love whiskey and religion. Have you been partaking from my stock of Glen Grant over there at the refreshment table?"

"No, sir. I never touch it."

"Then I cannot imagine where a young man like you came by such notions. I've never heard the like from someone so young, nor from *anyone* outside the pulpit. Is that where you got it, from your father's pulpit?"

"Not from his pulpit, but from his character," replied Percy. "I wasn't a very good learner for most of my life. I am finally remembering much that my father taught me, the foremost teaching of which is to obey God and let Him order my steps so far as it lies within my power to do so."

"You'll have to excuse my nephew," laughed the viscount. "As he told you, his father, my brother-in-law, is a minister. Runs in families, I suppose." Even though his natural inclination was to explain away Percy's outspokenness to his friend, as he listened, the viscount could not help feeling a strange respect for his nephew. He had never considered himself a religious man and had always tended to look down on Katherine's brother. Yet what father would not be proud of a young man of such principle and moral character as Edward Drummond's son?

Gradually the dusk of the June evening enveloped the Wales countryside. Dancing and music, eating and drinking continued. As a chill slowly descended, some of the party moved inside to the parlors and drawing rooms of Burrenchobay Hall.

When Gwyneth finally rose to walk home from where she had been watching on the hill overlooking the hall, it was after ten and growing dark. She would almost have been able to find the way back to her cottage with her eyes closed. But the occasional tears that rose in her eyes made it more difficult to see the path beneath her feet. She had never cried for herself in her life. She knew she was crying for herself now, and she was ashamed.

Most of the guests who were not spending the night were gone from Burrenchobay Hall by eleven fifteen, aided in their homegoing by a near full moon and the dying remnants of a spectacular sunset in the west.

The carriage bearing the Westbrooke and Drummond contingent passed through the gates of Westbrooke Manor a few minutes before midnight.

Several days later it was all over the region that Rhawn Lorimer was in a young woman's worst trouble and that Percy was the cause of it.

FIFTY-NINE

Death Visits Snowdonia

*T*hree days after the party, Gwyneth was due for work at Westbrooke Manor. By ten o'clock she had still not made her appearance.

The rumors regarding Percy Drummond and Rhawn Lorimer did not drift so quickly up from Llanfryniog to Westbrooke Manor as they had circulated through the village. A few whispers, however, had begun to circulate among the servants and staff. As Lady Florilyn's best friend for many years and a frequent visitor to the manor, and then for a time as Courtenay's young lady, every one of them knew Rhawn Lorimer. Most had formed some opinion about her in recent years. They were only too happy to voice them in the servants' quarters or when Mrs. Drynwydd poured out eleven o'clock tea for the staff.

When Olwyn Gwlwlwyd finally carried the fully formed report from the village that Rhawn Lorimer was in a family way, whispering to Mrs. Drynwydd and Mrs. Llewellyn that their own Percy, whom they loved as if he were one of them, was the father-to-be, the women went into a flurry of denial, demanding where she had heard such a scandalous lie.

It happened that Florilyn chanced by the open door of the laundry room at that very moment looking for Gwyneth. She retreated swiftly and noiselessly along the hall, ears burning and eyes stinging from what she had heard.

It could not possibly be true, she told herself in a frenzy of girlish emotion. Percy wouldn't do that to her. Percy *couldn't* do that to her!

Yet in that irrational reaction to which youth is especially vulnerable, as her thoughts swirled in a turmoil of confusion, she took her vexation out on the nearest target.

Her emotions furious at Percy for stringing her along when he had been in love with Rhawn from the beginning—though she still didn't believe a word of it!—Florilyn stormed into Percy's room without benefit of announcing herself. "Where is she?" she exclaimed angrily.

Percy glanced up from the desk where he was writing to his father. There stood Florilyn, red-faced, eyes full of an expression he had never seen in them before. He gazed at her with a confused expression. "Where is. . . ? I'm not sure what you mean," he said.

"That little Gwyneth is late—two hours late! I've a good mind to tell her not to come back."

Percy rose and walked toward her. "Calm down, Florilyn," he said. "I'm sure there is a reasonable explanation."

He was shocked by the look on her face. She backed away as he approached, as if he had the plague.

"Tell you what," he said. "I'll ride down and find out what is going on."

Ten minutes later Percy was on Grey Tide's back galloping across the moor.

Florilyn watched him go from the window in her room. She then f on her bed, crying in earnest at how ridiculously she had just beh She was frightened and furious and hurt all at once by the d rumor. She was angry at Percy for being so nice to everyone, ; Gwyneth and Rhawn and everyone. At the same time, she v herself for acting like a featherbrain.

Percy reached the cottage of Codnor Barrie and / He remounted and rode in haste into town. There ¹ agitated. Percy said he had come looking for G hadn't turned up for work at the manor and he v

"They won't find her at the manor today," said Grannie. "She's up at her auntie Adela's."

"Why there?" asked Percy.

"Little Gwyneth, bless her, awoke in the night with premonitions. She couldn't sleep. Thinking I was in danger, she came to me while it was yet dark, the dear girl. I was already awake, for I had been roused by the same fears. I felt death all around me. I was trembling, wondering if it was coming to me. But Gwyneth said that it was her uncle, not me. She crept into bed with me, but neither of us slept another wink. At dawn she set out for Adela's. Oh, if only I was there myself!"

"Do you think the old man is dying?" asked Percy.

"I have no doubt in my mind," replied Grannie.

"Could you ride that far, Grannie?" asked Percy. "That is, if I had a buggy?"

"Aye, I could, though it's been many a year since I was so far into the hills."

"Then wait for me and be ready. I will return as soon as I am able."

Percy left the cottage and raced back to the manor. He went in immediate search of his uncle. He found him in his study. "Uncle Roderick," he said, "I have a favor to ask."

"Anything, Percy, my boy."

"May I borrow one of your smaller buggies for the day?"

"Of course. What's the occasion?"

"I want to take Grannie Barrie up to the Muir cottage. It appears that Mr. Muir is dying."

"I cannot have that old witch in one of my buggies," said his uncle.

"It would mean a great deal to me, Uncle Roderick."

"Simply out of the question, Percy," said his uncle, shaking his head. "When I said anything, of course, I meant nothing like *that*. Anything else I can do for you?"

More annoyed than disappointed to see how widespread the nsense about Grannie truly was, and still having no idea what hief was circling ever closer to his own reputation, Percy left the house. Without hesitating, he went to the barn and immediately set about hitching the oldest buggy in the place to one of the most reliable horses, an old mare of some twelve years. It was a buggy that, to his knowledge, had not been used in years and a horse that was not taken out but once in six months, if that.

Fifteen minutes later he was on his way with both into the village. He found Grannie on pins and needles with excitement at the thought of a ride into the beloved hills that she had never expected to set eyes on again. Percy helped her up into the seat with the grace of one taking a young lady to a ball then climbed up beside her.

The way was rough, for the road, if such it could be called, had not been repaired in years. No buggy had traversed it in more years than anyone could remember, as Grannie told Percy while they bounced along. Percy found himself wondering if they would make it at all. If so, would he be able to return his uncle's buggy in one piece without the wheels being reduced to splinters?

Gwyneth heard their approach. She and Adela and Stevie Muir ran from the cottage, unable to imagine what could possibly bring a buggy to their door. They were amazed to see Grannie seated on the open bench beside Percy.

"Grannie!" exclaimed Adela. "How do you come here?"

"See for yourself, Adela. Gwyneth's friend Percy. How's the laddie?"

"He's fading, I'm thinking," replied Stevie's mother. "But it's the Lord's mercy to be taking him home at last."

Percy leaped down, then offered Grannie his hand and helped her to the ground as if she were a young woman again. Then they all went into the cottage together.

SIXTY

The Charge and Its Answer

*I*t was well after dinner that evening when Percy rode slowly back into the precincts of Westbrooke Manor, still having no premonition of the vortex of sordid controversy that was soon to engulf him.

He was weary from the long day, and his heart was full of its events. He had never witnessed death in his life. The experience had sobered him, not for the least of reasons the peace of those involved as they watched their beloved father and husband and uncle and friend go to his waking on the other side of the eternal sunrise.

Far from being sad, the experience was beautiful to behold. Tears had accompanied it. But they were tears of fullness not emptiness, tears of gratitude for a life well lived rather than those of sadness and regret. It was a day that would remain in his memory forever.

By now the last thing on his mind were the circumstances of the early morning. He had almost forgotten that he had taken the buggy without his uncle's permission. Nor had he an idea that, since learning of it, his uncle had been watching for his return all day, his anger seething hotter with every passing hour.

Percy was completely unprepared for his uncle's reaction as he stormed out of the house. Percy had just climbed down and was leading the horse into the barn when his uncle strode up behind him.

"What do you mean by stealing my buggy and taking it for the day?" said the viscount in a loud voice.

Percy turned. "I'm sorry, Uncle Roderick," he said. "I really needed to use a buggy, and I had no time to explain. I didn't think you would mind my using this old thing."

"Its age has nothing to do with it. That happens to be my buggy, and you stole it."

At last realizing that his uncle was truly angry, though still perplexed as to what could be the cause, Percy shook his head in confusion. "I don't quite know what to say, Uncle Roderick," he said. "It wasn't like that. Surely you aren't seriously thinking I *stole* it?"

"What else would you call it?"

"I would say that I borrowed it. I hoped you wouldn't mind."

"Well, I do mind! I specifically told you no."

"I didn't think it would be that serious to you. I apologize."

"And you expect me to accept your apology, just like that? Pretend it never happened, is that it?"

"I don't know, Uncle Roderick," sighed Percy, tired and in truth growing a little exasperated. "I am confused, that's all. I must say I did not expect this kind of reaction from you. Do whatever you want— throw me out. . .charge me a day's rent on buggy and horse and I will gladly pay it. . .send me home if you want. All I am saying is that I am sorry to have upset you. Again, I offer my apology."

Still huffing, but with the wind taken out of his sails by Percy's soft tongue, the viscount turned and strode back to the house.

Under the circumstances, when he had the buggy put away and Hollin Radnor had taken charge of the horse, Percy slipped into the house through the servants' entrance and went straight to his room without seeing any of the family.

He met only his aunt at breakfast the next morning. She was quieter than usual and seemed behaving oddly. The servants, too, throughout the day looked at him with peculiar expressions. He saw nothing of Florilyn.

By early afternoon, great black clouds were rolling in from the north, accompanied by a precipitous drop in temperature. Having by then judged that he would surely have cooled off, Percy again sought his uncle. He found him subdued and not particularly talkative. Whether he was embarrassed by what had taken place or still angry, Percy could not tell.

"Could I talk to you, Uncle Roderick?" asked Percy, standing at the open door.

An affirmative wave of the hand beckoned him in.

"I am sorry about the buggy incident," Percy began, "mostly for taking it behind your back. That was wrong of me. But it has occurred to me to wonder whether you are at all curious about my reasons."

"You told me you wished to take that old woman in the village to visit some peasants in the hills."

"Yes. If I recollect, you called her a witch."

"What of it?"

"She is not a witch, Uncle Roderick," rejoined Percy. "I happen to be on very friendly terms with Mrs. Barrie, as, I am happy to say, your daughter is also. She is one of the finest women in all Llanfryniog. You would know that yourself if you took more interest in your tenants."

"How dare you accuse me of. . .of. . ." The viscount hesitated. He didn't quite know *what* he was being accused of.

"Of not being interested in the lives of your people," added Percy, finishing the thought for him. "What would *you* call it, then?" he went on. "*Are* you interested in them, Uncle Roderick? One of them lay dying in his bed yesterday. One of his closest relatives wanted to see him before the end. Yet all you could think of was a dilapidated old buggy that was gathering dust in your barn that you will never ride in again as long as you live. Your people would love you if you gave them half a chance, Uncle Roderick. But you never go near them."

A heavy silence hung in the air. Percy's words stung all the more in that his uncle knew they were true. His anger of the day before had sufficiently spent itself so that whatever defense might have risen from his old Adam died before it reached his lips. "And. . .what of the old man?" he asked after a moment, making a stab at expressing a modicum of concern.

"He died late yesterday afternoon," replied Percy. "His family was around him. His hand rested in Grannie's as she prayed right up until the moment God took him. His wife and son were at his side, as were Gwyneth and myself. His passing was peaceful. It was one of the most extraordinary days I have ever spent, and I will never forget it. So while I am sorry to have upset you and for acting behind your back, I cannot be sorry that I was there or for making it possible for Mrs. Barrie to be there. When I last saw her, Florilyn was angry with Gwyneth for not coming to work. If you have any influence with your daughter in the matter, I hope you might speak a word to her on Gwyneth's behalf. I think she was perturbed at me as well. She was behaving irritably and strangely. I am not sure why. I doubt my influence will carry very far with her just now."

"Don't be too sure, Percy, my boy. You may discover that you carry *great* weight with Florilyn, more than you know. However, you're right—she tends to be impulsive. Family trait, you know. I will see what I can do."

"Thank you, sir."

"However, there may be reasons having nothing to do with what happened yesterday to account for my daughter's change of mood," the viscount said. "She has been devastated by the news, as we all have. She spent much of the day yesterday crying, as my wife tells me. For her brother's sake, your aunt shed a good many tears of her own as well. I did not hear of the affair until a short time ago. Maybe they tried to keep it from me, knowing that I was already angry with you. They probably thought I would send you away, which I may have to do anyway."

"I am sorry, Uncle Roderick," said Percy, "but I must confess I have no idea what you are talking about. What reason does Florilyn have to be angry with me and cry all day? And why would you send me away? Is it really over my use of that old buggy?"

"Tut, tut, my boy. It is more serious than that. I am talking about you and Miss Lorimer."

"What about us—that I danced with her the other night? Gosh, I am sorry if that hurt Florilyn's feelings. But the girl was most insistent. She threatened to make a scene if I did not dance with her. Under the circumstances, I thought it best—"

"By heavens, man!" thundered Lord Snowdon as his fist slammed down on his desk with a sudden resurfacing of his anger. "Stop playing innocent with me. Out with it! Is it true? That's all I want to know."

Percy stared back at his uncle dumbfounded.

"I told you. . .yes, I danced with the girl. I have never denied it. Everyone saw us. *You* saw us."

"Are you intentionally trying to act like an imbecile? I don't mean the dancing. I mean the rumor—is it true?"

"What rumor?"

"About you and the Lorimer girl! Her father came to see me this morning demanding to know what I intended to do. Are you or are you not the father of her child?"

Percy stared back speechless again. The words slammed into his brain like an ongoing locomotive. "Her. . .*child*!" he repeated slowly.

"She says you are the father."

Percy broke out laughing. "I know I'm not the most worldly wise young man in the world," he said, still chuckling, "but, Uncle Roderick. . . I've only been here three weeks."

"Stop making light of it, you young fool. This is a serious matter with grave consequences. She claims that you and she had a liaison in Glasgow."

At last his uncle's words silenced him. Percy exhaled slowly and stood for some time in silence. "I see," he said at length. "Yes, you're right, it is serious. I am sorry for seeming to take it lightly. I had no idea what was being said."

Again he drew in a deep breath and let it out slowly. No wonder Florilyn had been so strange yesterday morning. Then came an even more horrifying thought—what if the rumors had reached Gwyneth's ears?

His uncle's voice interrupted his reflections. "You still have not answered me," he said. "I must know. Is it true?"

Percy stood in silence. He was thinking hard. He was remembering many things he had heard and been taught through the years.

"I think, Uncle Roderick," he said at last, "that I would prefer not to answer."

"That is as good as admitting it is true!"

"Only in the mind of one who does not understand silence."

"I demand that you answer the charges!" the viscount shrieked.

"I am sorry, Uncle Roderick."

"Do you refuse me?"

"If you demand that I answer. . .yes."

"Then at least tell me *why* you refuse," rejoined his uncle, calming slightly.

"Jesus says not to worry about how to defend yourself. When accused, He did not defend Himself."

"What does that have to do with anything?"

"I try to follow His example."

"There you go preaching at me again!"

"I am sorry. Nothing was further from my mind."

"What was on your mind then?" asked the viscount sarcastically.

"That you are going to have to decide for youself whether you think I am capable of such a heinous thing as is being said. You have to decide what you think of my character. But I will not defend myself. Nor will I stoop to answer the charges."

At last the viscount was silenced, even if momentarily. "A noble sentiment," he said after a few seconds. "Idealistic, though naive. Would it not be easier to put all doubt about the matter to rest and simply to say yea or nay?"

"It would not put the matter to rest," said Percy.

"What makes you say that?"

"Because those inclined to believe the rumor would go on believing it even if I denied it. The stronger my denials, the surer they would be I was lying. One of the few Shakespeare quotes I happen to know concerns protesting too much. There are certain kinds of charges, Uncle Roderick, that can *only* be countered by silence—and those are charges against one's character and veracity as a man. I am not much of a man yet. But I am enough one to know that this is such a time. The only way you will be able to arrive at the truth in this matter, as you say, is for you to arrive at that truth within your *own* heart. Nothing I say will help you or convince you one way or the other. I alone must bear the burden of the doubts that may hound me as a result of this. But the burden of proof, for *you*, Uncle Roderick, must rest with you."

Percy turned and left him. Even as he walked down the corridor to the stairway, hoping he would encounter no one before reaching the sanctuary of his own room, his eyes filled. How many people would be hurt before this was over he could not begin to imagine. He hoped it could be kept from his parents. He had hurt them enough already. He also prayed the ugliness would not reach Gwyneth. Yet he saw no way she could not be drawn into a knowledge of it.

In his study, Lord Snowdon rose and walked to the window and stared out at the turbulent gray sky, alone with his thoughts. The young fool was made of stern stuff, he thought. Better stuff than his own son, he sighed wistfully. The boy had courage—courage to confront an ugly rumor calmly like a man. . .and courage as well to confront him to his face about his treatment of his tenants.

By jove if the young son of a minister wasn't right. He *did* avoid his tenants. He couldn't help it. Poverty made him uncomfortable.

If only he could find a young man like *that* to marry his daughter! That is, if the thing wasn't true. Young men like Percy Drummond didn't grow on trees, thought the viscount as he continued to reflect on the interview that had just taken place.

Already Percy's silence in the face of the accusation was beginning to accomplish its work. In his heart of hearts, Roderick Westbrooke was all but convinced of the falsehood of it.

By day's end, almost as a judgment against all of North Wales for the ease with which its gossipmongers were able to spread a lie, and the readiness of its inhabitants to believe it, a tremendous storm broke over the region. The wind battered the coastline. Rain poured down in sheets. No one who did not have business outside ventured into it.

SIXTY-ONE

The Power of Mistress Chattan's Brew

*T*he fishermen of North Wales were an independent breed who kept both friendships and compliments close to the vest. Young Percival Drummond had cultivated an association with several of the more liberal-minded among them. Whether he would even now be considered a *friend*, however, was doubtful. That he had come closer to it in a shorter time than any other visitor to Llanfryniog in memory, especially one so young, was certain. As far as compliments went, about the best that could be hoped for was a nod of the head as he walked away from the harbor and a mumbled aside, "Not a bad sort. . .for a Scots laddie."

They made their living in the hardest of all possible ways—at sea. They did not give the hand of friendship to one who was not worthy of the honor.

There was one consumable item of commerce, however, capable of lubricating geniality and accelerating the bonds, if not of true friendship at least of the laughter and free-flowing conversation that often passed for it among men who knew no better. That one thing was Mistress Chattan's ale. Everyone knew that she did not brew it herself. Yet to a man, the male inhabitants of Llanfryniog swore that it was unlike any beer in the world—light or dark, Irish or English, lager or ale.

And thus when a man such as Rupert Wilkes stood beers at Mistress Chattan's, he was a man granted unusual privileges of access and conversation. None of the locals knew anything about him or where he came from. He appeared periodically, was generous to one and all at the inn, and always seemed particularly interested in the old times. He was most curious about those who had been alive before the turn of the present century. His questions always got around eventually to old Sean Drindod and his friends who might have known one another in those bygone days.

After Drindod's death, the fellow had disappeared for a long while. The fishermen of Llanfryniog began to think they had seen the last of him. Then he began showing up again and gradually with increasing regularity. From Drindod he had heard the mysterious name "Bryn." Since that time, Mistress Chattan's ale had not sufficiently loosened the tongues of the village's oldest citizens to reveal more. Whether anyone knew who it was, he had not been able to discover. And he had to make his inquiries with care.

It took three years. But at last the drunken tongue of an old fisherman, long retired, who rarely frequented Mistress Chattan's establishment, divulged a name—Branwenn Myfanawy, as she was known as a child.

Wilkes took in the name with greater interest than he allowed himself to show, bought the man another pint, and continued to shrewdly ply him with questions that eventually led him to a description of the location of Grannie's cottage. Whether she was the same woman, he didn't know. But he would search the place and find out. If the old woman caused him trouble, she could join her friend Drindod.

Sixty-Two

Grannie's Tale

*M*ortified about what was being said about him, Percy kept to himself. He found the writings of MacDonald a great solace in his trouble. But his aunt and uncle were distant. The servants avoided him. He did not see Florilyn for an entire day. She did not appear at dinner. The greatest humiliation, however, was having to imagine what Gwyneth must think.

Gwyneth had indeed heard the rumors. She could scarcely avoid it among the other servants. Gwyneth Barrie had rarely known anger in her life. But what she heard filled her with righteous indignation. She kept her thoughts to herself but went about her duties with smoke coming out her ears. She may have been small, but this was enough to ignite the fire of indignation in her young heart. It would not have gone well for the magistrate's daughter had she dared pay a visit to the manor and encountered the righteous wrath of Codnor Barrie's daughter.

Gwyneth saw Percy from a distance two or three times. She could tell from the way he walked that he was downcast. She knew he was avoiding her. He was avoiding everyone. And she knew the reason. As furious as she was at the snake Rhawn Lorimer, she knew that Percy's pain must be far deeper to be falsely accused of something so disgusting.

She was burdened for Grannie, too. The old woman had not been herself since Glythvyr Muir's death. She had been talking to herself and behaving strangely ever since the simple funeral, which had been attended by less than a dozen people. Percy had been one of them, though he left quickly afterward. Gwyneth's heart was sore for her two best friends in the world besides her papa.

She asked her father if they could invite Percy and Grannie for supper at their cottage the next evening. It would be a good-bye supper for Percy. Maybe it would make Grannie feel better as well.

And so it was arranged. As she did not have to work, she spent the whole next day in preparations. She bundled up tightly and went out that morning in the driving rain. Her first visit was to the manor, where she left a brief note of invitation for Percy. Then she walked to Grannie's in town, telling her that her father would come for her with their cart after work. At last she went home, chilled to the bone, changed out of her wet clothes, added new coal to the fire, and got busy with preparations for the evening's meal.

Percy was delighted for a reason to miss another silent meal at the manor. He was eager to get away, storm or no storm.

Thankfully, the rain temporarily spent itself by midafternoon. Percy left the manor, bundled against the wind but not thinking that the rain might resume by the time he was on his way home. When he arrived at the Barrie Cottage about six o'clock that evening, Grannie and Codnor were just clattering up the lane. Above them the sky was black and menacing. Percy and Codnor helped Grannie to the ground, and they hurried inside amid a tumultuous wind.

"You will be leaving soon, Percy," said Gwyneth as the three walked in.

"Yes, tomorrow is my last day," he replied. He was relieved to find no one any different toward him. In truth, the rumors had not come within hearing of either Grannie or Codnor Barrie.

"My little girl will miss you, Percy," said Gwyneth's father, helping Grannie to a chair at the table.

"I know," sighed Percy. "I will miss everyone here, too. I almost feel that this is my home now."

The conversation between the four friends flowed freely. For the first time in two days, Percy managed to forget the weight hanging over him.

When supper was over and they retired to the sitting room, Grannie seemed to grow quiet.

"How is Mrs. Muir?" asked Percy, addressing them all. "And Stevie?"

"I have seen them only once since the funeral," said Gwyneth. "They are sad but relieved. The house seems empty without Uncle Glythvyr. But they know he is in a better place."

The reminder of Glythvyr Muir's death plunged Grannie deep into thought. "It is the way of all flesh," she said, leaning back in the rocking chair where she sat. "My own time is not far off, I'm thinking."

"What are you talking about, Grannie?" asked Gwyneth.

"The good man's passing has made me thoughtful, Gwyneth, dear. I am old. I cannot wait longer to tell what I know. The Lord could take me any time. I must tell my tale to them I can trust."

"What tale, Grannie?"

"Get your tea and sit with me. You, Gwyneth child. . .you, my dear Codnor. And you, too, Percy, for you are a good young man, and Grannie knows she can trust you."

In a few minutes they had gathered round her.

"It was like this," Grannie began. "I was walking on the beach as a child." The moment she began, her voice took on an ancient and mysterious tone. The time of which she spoke was seventy-nine years before, in the previous century. "I was out on the white sand below the bluff," she went on, "white and as pretty to a child then as it is now. It was early in the morning. Most of the village still slept. But there'd been a fierce storm all the previous day and most of the night, worse than this one around us now, worse than any storm I've ever seen. I'd felt forebodings in my young heart all night. I heard voices calling out of the wind, wailing in the midst of the storm. I didn't know what I know now, that I had been both blessed and cursed with the ancient eyes that see what a body sometimes wished she hadn't seen.

"I rose early. It was a still dawn. The wind had died down. All about outside was deathly calm, yet still I thought I heard voices, eventually only one voice. I don't mean with my ears, but I heard it inside. And with that voice wailing somewhere in the wind, I couldn't sleep. I'd always been a free kind of child, like yourself, Gwyneth, and my mama and papa seldom worried about me.

"I set out in the morning light. There was a chill over the coast where my feet were leading me—straight to the sea, for throughout the storm I knew the wailing was coming from its waves. I climbed down the path. By the time I reached the sand, the sun was creeping up from behind the mountains in the east, though the promontory kept the beach in darkness for many hours. There was no breath of wind. But the waves still pounded the shore as if reminding me what business they had been about the night before. The tide was brown and gray from the storm, menacing with the color of evil tidings.

"I glanced about, then began walking along the shore like I had a hundred times before. Only this time there was fear in my heart for what I might see. Above me two eyes were watching me. They were the eyes of another youngster in the village, though no friend of mine. He was on top of the cliff. I didn't see him yet. But I would see him before long.

"Halfway down the beach, what should I see but the very thing I knew I'd half expected—the body of a man lying at the water's edge. I ran toward him trembling and knelt down. He looked dead. I reached my hand slowly out to touch his arm.

"Then suddenly it moved! A groan sounded. My heart leaped to my throat in terror. I'd never seen a pirate, but that was surely what the man was. He was fearsome as any man I'd laid eyes on. That he had just come back, as I thought, from the dead made him all the more terrifying. Sensing that I was near, he rolled over. Slowly he opened his eyes and gazed into my face. He tried to speak but couldn't. Then he seemed to gain strength. Finally he spoke." Grannie stopped and took a sip of her tea.

Gwyneth's eyes were huge as she listened. "What did he say?" she asked.

"He said they'd been shipwrecked by the storm, that the great and mighty *Rhodri Mawr* had gone down with all its treasure aboard."

By now Percy's eyes were wide as well.

Grannie's voice took on an eerie sound as she relived the scene from days long gone by. " 'It's all there,' " she went on. " 'It's all out there,' the dying man said, trying to point behind him to the sea. 'The fools wouldn't listen to me. I told them to put in. But they wouldn't listen. Lifeboats no better than sticks in them waves. When the lifeboat broke up and the others went down, I laid hold of a piece of the keel that was floating nearby. It kept me afloat long enough, just long enough. I made it, I tell you. I made it here. . .and I'm giving it to you, little girl,' he said, now grabbing hold of my arm, 'I'm giving it all to you—the treasure of Dolau Cothi.'

"I stood listening in terror. I hardly heard what he was saying. 'Don't believe me, little girl? I tell you, I saw it. . .saw it all, helped dig it out of the ruins, a whole chestful—and it's all out there now. It's yours. Look, I'll prove it,' he said. He let go of my arm that he'd kept clutching. I was too terrified to run away. He tried to sit up but fell back into the shallow water, fumbling about in some pocket of his water-soaked clothes. Then his eyes lit up as with fire, and he exclaimed triumphantly. He turned toward me again and thrust in front of my eyes a round gold coin he had pinched between his thumb and forefinger. 'There, little girl—you see! I tell you the whole treasure's there. . .and it's *yours.*'

"Then a spasm seized him. He coughed and choked and fell backward. His eyes rolled back into his head. Now I was certain he was dead. But then he groaned again, and tried to get up, but still lay on the sand. He opened his eyes and motioned me closer. 'Little girl,' he said, 'you take this coin. It's valuable enough, but I tell you there's thousands of them—down there.' Again he pointed out to sea. 'You take it. You never know what fate your steps will lead you to. Yours led you to me. It's yours now.' He grabbed my hand and pressed the coin into it."

As the three listened to Grannie's spooky tale, suddenly the heavens erupted, and the rain again poured down. They had no idea that at that very moment, had she been at home, Grannie's premonitions about her own fate might well have come to pass.

For as the wild and stormy night advanced, Rupert Wilkes crept to her cottage. No light shown inside. There was no sign of life. He tried the latch on the door. It was not locked. He went inside.

But fate did not order Grannie to die that night by the hand that had murdered the very youngster of her story. And she went on with the tale. "Suddenly I heard footsteps running up behind me," Grannie continued. "I turned, and there was a little boy named Sean Drindod, a little village troublemaker, as I thought. And I was right, for he caused me trouble all his life till his untimely end three years ago."

" 'What's that?' he cried, for he had seen the old pirate give me something. He grabbed at my hand and caught a glimpse of the gold. Seeing it, he struggled all the harder to take it from me. 'Give it to me, Bryn!' he cried.

" 'The man gave it to me,' I said, squeezing my fingers tight. I knew that if once little Sean got his greedy hands on it, that was the last I would see of it. He fussed and ranted, but being four and I was five, I was stronger and faster than him, and he could do nothing to get it from me.

"I ran back to the village, little Sean on my heels still trying to get his hands on the coin. I told my father everything that had happened. He and some of the men went down to the beach. They found the poor old sailor on shore and pulled him up out of the water and buried him in the town cemetery where you see the marker to this day.

"Word spread quickly up and down the coast. Bits of wood and rope and sail and rigging were gradually found over the next few weeks, confirming that there had indeed been a shipwreck that night. I told everyone what the man had said about the treasure that had gone down with it, though most of the grown-ups laughed because they were already finding out that I saw things other people didn't see. Most of them didn't believe half my stories. And Sean Drindod was known as a mischief maker and liar throughout Llanfryniog. So his tale about the coin, which I repeated to no one, not a soul believed.

"All the rest of his life, Sean tried everything he could to get his hands on that coin. I think he thought it would lead him to the *Rhodri Mawr's* treasure where it had gone down with the ship. But I kept it where no other person ever saw it, though I know he told people of it, and I think he died because of it. And now my own life's in danger just like his."

"How do you know that, Grannie?" asked Codnor Barrie. His voice was serious.

"I can feel it, my boy," she replied. "I can *feel* it. There's those that are looking for me—I can feel their eyes upon me. Maybe it's only death itself that's stalking me. Whatever it be, it is time I passed the coin on, as it was passed on to me. Whether there ever was any box of treasure that went down with that ship, I don't know. But there is this one coin. And it shall be mine no longer." Slowly she untied the gold coin from the inside of her dress. She held it a moment in her hand.

None of the others had ever seen actual gold in their lives. Their eyes widened as they saw the gleam from the ancient coin glitter in the light of the room's lanterns.

She looked at each of the three in turn. "But who is meant to watch over it now?" she said. "I would give it to you, Codnor, for you're a good man, but trouble is bound to follow it, and whoever would find me could find you. But none would think to look for it from a child. So you, Gwyneth—you will take it and keep it safe. It shall be yours, for maybe you will need whatever it might bring you sometime in your life." Grannie handed the coin to Gwyneth.

Gwyneth stared in awe at the bright shiny thing in her palm.

"But be careful," Grannie said. "I fear more than one's been killed for it already. Put it somewhere it will be safe. Tell not a soul about it."

"Was the man who gave you this the same man I saw in the cave, Grannie?" asked Gwyneth.

"It couldn't have been him, Gwyneth, dear. The old pirate who gave me the coin was hauled up and buried with his head still attached to him."

A deep silence fell. The hour had grown late, and dusk was descending. It was nearly dark, and Percy knew he needed to be on his way. It had already been arranged that Grannie would spend the night in the cottage because of the weather.

"It doesn't appear the storm is going to let up," said Percy, glancing out the window. "If I am going to run back to the manor in the rain, I had better get started. Thank you for an enjoyable evening. And, Mr. Barrie, if I do not see you again before I go, good-bye until next time." The two shook hands.

Gwyneth walked with him to the door. When they were alone, she handed Percy the coin. "I want no part of it," she said. "It frightens me. You take it, Percy. You keep it."

"It is yours, Gwyneth."

"Then you keep it for me. Please," she said, with pleading in her eyes.

"I will keep it for *you*, then. But it will always be yours."

Finally launching himself through the door and out into the storm, Percy sprinted for the road then up the hill. When he arrived at the manor ten minutes later, he was drenched to the skin.

Sixty-Three

Uncle and Nephew

*T*he stormy night passed fitfully for Roderick Westbrooke, viscount Lord Snowdon.

The previous night he had slept like a baby, relieved as he grew more and more convinced in his mind that Percy was innocent of Rhawn Lorimer's charges. But gradually the other topic of the conversation that had taken place in his study returned to haunt him.

Percy's words from a day before played themselves over and over all night in his brain. *Your people would love you if you gave them half a chance. . . . But you never go near them.*

The young blackguard had put his finger exactly on the nub of his discomfort with his position. He avoided the very people who depended on him, and upon whom he was likewise dependent for what meager income their rents provided.

The boy's manliness in refusing to defend himself. . .it had enraged him. Yet what a stout show of character!

In spite of his sleeplessness, yet also because of it, the viscount rose early. He felt that it was a day of new beginnings. He made an unexpectedly early appearance in the breakfast room.

The storm had passed and the day dawned cloudless and bright. The danger to Grannie's life had passed, and with it so had the tumult.

Percy and his aunt were the only others present, chatting over their tea and eggs and toast. Things seemed to be gradually returning to their former ways. There was still no sign of Florilyn.

"Ah, Percy, my boy. . .your last day in Wales, what?" said the viscount as he entered with unusual bounce to his step.

"Yes, sir. I am already feeing the sadness of departure coming over me."

"What do you have planned for the day?"

"I don't know—say my farewells, I suppose."

"How about you and I going for a ride together?"

"I would like that, Uncle Roderick."

"And, er. . .about that matter we discussed—the Lorimer girl. I told Katherine what you said. We are both in agreement—we *do* know you are innocent. You have proved yourself, and we know what mettle you are made of. You are right—sometimes silence is the best defense. I am sorry I doubted you."

"Thank you, Uncle Roderick. I appreciate that very much."

"After lunch, then?"

"I will look forward to it."

The ride that afternoon was not what Percy had expected. The apology seemed to have filled his uncle with new energy. He was in a rambunctious mood in the saddle, galloping with abandon, jumping streams recklessly. He was a skilled horseman, and Percy could hardly keep up with him.

"Easy, Uncle Roderick!" Percy laughed more than once as his uncle wobbled and nearly lost his seat. "Now I know where Florilyn gets her nerve in the saddle."

"I never felt better in my life, Percy, my boy. I feel like a young man again!"

On their way back, the viscount slowed, and they rode side by side together. They were still a good distance northeast of the manor.

"You know, Percy, my boy," said his uncle, "it has been a genuine pleasure to have you here this summer. Even more so than last time."

"Thank you, Uncle Roderick. I have enjoyed it, too. I appreciate your hospitality."

"I know my daughter has taken most of your time, but I have greatly enjoyed your company. I would say that I got the better half of the bargain—all your help with the stables—wouldn't you?"

"I had a great time. I wish I could stay longer. But I have a job waiting for me in Aberdeen."

"You are a responsible young man. I'm sure your father is very proud. And," he went on, clearing his throat, "I must repeat my apology for doubting you in the matter of that unfortunate business with the Lorimer girl. I knew better, of course. I was far too hasty to judge you."

"Think nothing of it, Uncle Roderick."

"But I feel bad about it. I had no right. Nevertheless, 'all's well that ends well,' as you are fond of saying."

"One of the two quotes from Shakespeare I know!" Percy laughed.

"What do you think of my daughter, Percy, my boy?" asked the viscount abruptly.

"I don't know, Uncle Roderick. In what way?"

"As a girl, you know—a young woman."

"I am very fond of her. We got off to a bit of a rocky start three years ago. But she and I have become the best of friends. I think a great deal of her."

The viscount took in his words thoughtfully.

Again they rode for a while in silence.

"You were right, too, Percy, my boy," the viscount began again, "about what you said about my contacts with the local peasantry. I have been far too distant. It took courage for you to look me in the eye and tell me that. You have helped me see the thing clearly. Isn't the Muir place around here somewhere?"

"Why yes? Uncle Roderick. It's probably a mile or two."

"Will you take me there and introduce me to the woman, the widow. I would like to see her."

"You will hardly need an introduction."

"Still, it might be awkward. I would feel better if you eased the way into it for me."

"Then I will be happy to." Percy veered off slightly to the left from the course they had been pursuing and led the rest of the way until the familiar cottage came into view.

They rode up. Stevie did not appear to be about, though two dogs ran barking toward them. The viscount appeared concerned.

"Don't worry, Uncle Roderick," said Percy, jumping down. "These lads know me. . .don't you, boys?" he said, stooping and roughing up the backs and heads of the tail-waggers with his hands. "Of course they'll have to take a little sniff of you," he said as his uncle dismounted. "It's their way of introducing themselves."

Moments later they were approaching the open door of the humble cottage.

As he began to duck down and walk inside, Gwyneth's aunt appeared.

"Why, Percy," she exclaimed, "what brings you—" Her words died on her lips as she saw the man walking up behind him.

"I've brought you a visitor, Mrs. Muir," said Percy. "He wanted to meet you. This is—"

"I know well enough who it is," interrupted Adela. "Welcome to you, sir. . .Lord Snowdon, sir."

"Percy has told me about your husband, Mrs. Muir," said the viscount a little nervously but with genuine feeling. He removed his riding cap and attempted an awkward smile. "I am sorry."

"Thank you, sir," replied Adela, her initial shock now giving way to her natural hospitality. "Won't you come in for a cup of tea?"

"We, uh. . .I don't think—" began the viscount.

"We would love to," said Percy.

"I'm sorry I don't have any fancy cakes or the like to offer you, sir," said Adela, leading them through the door into her kitchen.

"Mrs. Muir, your oatcakes are the best in Wales," said Percy. "I would have nothing else with tea even if you offered it to me."

They sat down at the table. Adela bustled about in a veritable panic of excitement to have the viscount under her roof. "How I wish my Glythvyr could have been here. He would have loved to see you, sir."

"I am sorry," replied the viscount. "I should not have waited so long to pay you a visit."

"Bless you, sir. He used to work at the manor as a lad, you know. For your father. He was fond of your father, he was." She poured out tea.

Stevie arrived a few minutes later, with equal astonishment to see who was sitting in his kitchen. The conversation continued to flow pleasantly.

After about thirty minutes, Percy judged that sufficient initial spadework had been done in his uncle's heart for one day. He rose and said that it was time they were leaving. He had much to do to prepare for his departure on the morrow. Hugs, handshakes, and tearful farewells followed. Who knew when Percy would visit the beloved cottage in the hills again?

"I know it will be difficult for you, losing your husband," said the viscount as they prepared to return to their horses. "You may consider your rent for the following term canceled, Mrs. Muir. I shall notify my factor."

"Bless you, sir!"

They mounted and rode off. Percy glanced back with a final wave to Stevie and his mother where they stood beside their cottage.

They rode most of the way back to the manor in silence. The brief encounter had penetrated deep into the soul of Roderick Westbrooke.

"That was a very kind gesture of you, Uncle Roderick," said Percy at length. "I know it meant the world to her. I honor you for it."

SIXTY-FOUR

Final Evening

*P*ercy had just finished dressing for dinner when a soft knock came to his door. He answered it and was surprised to see Gwyneth standing in the corridor. "Hi, Gwyneth!" he said.

"I know you are a guest and I am a servant—" she began.

"Gwyneth!" He laughed. "I'm me, remember?"

She smiled and glanced briefly at the floor before looking up into his face. "I know you are leaving tomorrow," she said a little bashfully. "Everyone's been talking about it. Since you'll be at dinner when I leave tonight, I wanted to say good-bye."

"Oh, right," said Percy. "Yeah—it's come up faster than I expected. . . much too short a visit."

"But you will be back to Wales," said Gwyneth, trying to sound cheerful.

"Of course. . .absolutely. Actually, I had planned to come down to see you this evening after dinner."

"You did?"

"You didn't think I would leave without seeing you?"

"I knew you wouldn't do that. But I heard Lady Katherine saying they were having a special dinner tonight. I thought I should come see you. . .in case you were busy."

"Oh. . .right, I see. I didn't know Aunt Katherine had plans." Percy thought a moment. "I've got an idea—let's meet tomorrow morning!"

"But you are leaving!"

"I mean early. The coach comes through at nine. That's when I have to be at the inn. Meet me before breakfast. I'll get there as soon after sunrise as I can."

"Where, Percy?"

"At our special place. . .where the sea and land meet and the waves crash, and we look across to see the sun set at the horizon, and if we are lucky all the way to the land of your birth. It will always be the most special of all the special places."

Gwyneth nodded. "When the sun comes up?"

"Right. I'll see you there!"

"But if for some reason you can't, Percy—"

"I will be there. I promise."

Though the dinner was lavish, and even Courtenay was relatively friendly, there was still no sign of Florilyn. It was hard for Percy to enter into the spirit of the evening knowing that he was the cause, even if indirectly, of Florilyn's not wanting to see him. It was at least gratifying that Courtenay extended his hand when he departed for the evening. It had come late in the game, but he hoped that at long last his cousin might be warming to him.

"I guess I haven't seen much of you this time, old man," said Courtenay, shaking Percy's hand. "But best of luck, and all that."

"To you as well, Courtenay. When do you return to Oxford?"

"August."

Percy nodded. "Right, well. . .hope it goes well. It's a lot of work, isn't it?"

"You know it! So. . .cheers then!" added Courtenay and left the sitting room where the four of them had been chatting since dinner.

Percy turned back into the room where his aunt and uncle sat.

"I am sorry about Florilyn, Percy," said his aunt for probably the fifth time. "I just don't know what's got into her. I know she is dreadfully embarrassed."

"She was angry with me," said Percy. "I understand that. Really, it's all right. She will get over it. When she does, you can assure her there are no hard feelings. All's forgiven and fine."

"I told her what you said to Roderick about not defending yourself. I'm sure she will come around and understand in the end."

"I know she will." Percy smiled. "Please don't worry about it, Aunt Katherine."

At length the conversation flagged. Everything that was to be said had been said two or three times. Percy excused himself, saying he would see them in the morning, and retired to his room.

SIXTY-FIVE

Where Land Meets Sea

*G*wyneth did not sleep well.

Her mental anxiety was caused by no premonition such as had awakened her during the night prior to her uncle's death, nor even anxiety about what had happened to Grannie's cottage. But she was anxious lest she oversleep and miss her farewell rendezvous with Percy. Every time she fell asleep, her subconscious brain jolted itself awake, and she looked toward the window to see if there was yet any sign of light.

Thus it went, on and off fitfully all night, until the faint imperceptible gray of first light began to hint that the sun was creeping slowly back around the earth in the direction of Snowdonia.

Gwyneth lay with her face to the window, watching the dawn approach slower than any watched pot that never boiled. There comes a moment, however, when all pots eventually boil. But with the coming of dawn, no such moment exists. *When* does dawn arrive is a question as much for the world's philosophers as for girls in love.

When at last Gwyneth could stand it no longer and judged that the morning had sufficiently arrived for her purposes, she crept quietly from between the blankets and dressed in silence. With nearly as many layers on as she would have donned had it been snowing, she found the bouquet of flowers she had picked last evening then stole noiselessly from the house into a morning heavy laden along the coast with a chill white mist.

Percy slipped out of the manor shortly before six o'clock.

He was ready for the journey. His bag sat on the floor of his room.

Hoping to disturb no one, he left as he often did by the side entrance, walked around the house and down the drive through the main gate and to the moor. Twenty minutes later he was approaching the promontory of Mochras Head.

It was a cold morning. A thick fog had settled over all of Tremadog Bay during the night. The white mist seemed clinging to the promontory itself, rising two hundred feet in the air. But it had not drifted inland from the water.

As Percy approached, he entered a world of whiteness. He could scarcely see the edge of the promontory in front of him. When he reached Gwyneth's special place, though there would be no sight of the ancient waters below on this day, he was surprised to find himself alone. There was no sign of she whom he had come to meet.

Percy sat down at the familiar place where he and Gwyneth had enjoyed the view so many times. The ground was wet. He would have to change into another pair of trousers before leaving for the coach. He heard the waves, muted by the thick fog, beating against the rocks far below.

He waited for twenty minutes, then forty. When an hour had passed, he began to grow concerned. He checked his watch and continued his wait. Why hadn't she come?

Suddenly a horrible thought occurred to him. Was it possible that she had only just now heard of the rumor? Was she, like Florilyn, unable to face him?

Gwyneth had not actually expected Percy to be at the shore at such an early hour.

But she did not mind arriving first nor waiting for hours if she had to. She only did not want to miss him. So she would be at the beach early.

It was, in fact, a few minutes before five when she passed Grannie's through a fog so thick she could scarcely see across the narrow lane. After the discovery that her home had been ransacked, Grannie was staying with her great-nephew. Nevertheless, Gwyneth said a brief prayer for her and continued on. It was the first time in memory she had not stopped in at the beloved cottage now sitting silent and cold and empty.

She walked down to the harbor in the white cloudy soup. She was all but certain Percy would come to the beach through town, not along the promontory path. The tide was coming in. To climb across the rocks by the cave, especially as he might be wearing his traveling clothes, would be all but impossible. He would have to come through town and pass close by her to reach the sandy beach that he called his *favorite place*.

She sat down on the concrete quay of the harbor and set the bouquet she had labored over with such care in her lap. It was tied with two pieces of the colored ribbon Percy had given her. This was no forgiveness bouquet but a gift from the depths of one human soul to another, speaking as flowers were created to speak, in the language of the heart.

There she waited. It was cold. But Gwyneth was warmly dressed, and the incoming and outgoing waves were of endless fascination.

An hour passed.

A few fishermen began to be about but paid her no heed.

Another slow hour went by. Still there was no sign of Percy.

⚬❧⚬

By eight o'clock Percy could delay no longer. He looked at his watch one final time and let out a long sigh. They would be waiting for him at the manor to take him to the coach, no doubt wondering where he had disappeared to.

He stood, walked carefully to the edge, and gazed over the promontory. Still he could see nothing but white. "Gwyneth!" he yelled. His voice seemed lost in the fog.

The only reply was the sound of the tide far below.

"Gwyneth!" he cried a second time, louder than before. Sadly he turned, chilled to the bone, and ran across the moor in the direction of the manor.

By now he realized he had waited too long. He should have left the promontory sooner. Now he had no time to run by the cottage to see her. He pulled out his watch and glanced down as he ran, suddenly annoyed with himself. He should have left sooner!

He hurried up the hill and along the entryway, into the house, and to the breakfast room. He gulped down a hasty cup of tea and egg, then ran up to his room to fetch his bag and change his clothes, and returned along the corridor. He paused at Florilyn's door. It was closed. He hesitated a moment but then continued to the stairway.

He found his aunt and uncle downstairs with a buggy waiting.

"Don't want to be late, Percy, my boy," said his uncle with watch in hand, twiddling the chain nervously. "It's coming on to quarter till the hour."

Sixty-Six

When Young Hearts Part

Florilyn Westbrooke had cried more in the last two days than she ever remembered crying in her life. Certainly she had never cried so much for being hurt by a boy. She had never cared enough for anyone to be this hurt.

A *boy!*

What was she thinking? Percy was a *man*...and a wonderful young man. What had possessed her even to *think* he could be involved with Rhawn Lorimer? She knew it was another of Rhawn's lies. Why Rhawn had blamed Percy for her troubles, Florilyn couldn't imagine.

She had behaved like such an absolute fool. She didn't deserve someone like Percy. She had been too embarrassed to face him. Like a baby she had kept to her room, unable to look him in the face. Yet with every day that passed, desperately longing to see him, the impossibility of looking into those honest, strong eyes mounted. Finally she had created for herself an imaginary barrier too great to overcome.

And now he was gone!

She stood at her window and watched the buggy leaving for town with her father and mother. They were taking Percy away. If she ever saw him again, it would be with a Scottish wife on his arm. He would never know what he had meant to her, never know how much she had loved him.

Tears filled her eyes at her childish foolishness. She would, as she had said to him, have to settle for second best and marry some boring, unmanly youth from North Wales.

Suddenly Florilyn's eyes shot open. *Why* was it too late? Why could she not put an end to her idiocy. . .and right now?

The next moment she was bolting from her room and down the stairs. She flew outside and across the stones to the stables.

"Hollin. . .Hollin!" she cried. "Saddle Grey Tide. Saddle her faster than you have ever saddled a horse in your life!"

◌⌇◌

Gwyneth had no watch. But she could tell from the activity at the harbor and the sounds from the village that the day was coming to life. The fog was still thick, and she was chilled. Surely it was well past eight o'clock by now. Her father would already be at the mine wielding his hammer against the stones.

Where was Percy? Had she dozed without knowing it? Had she missed seeing him in the fog? *Why hadn't he come?*

Could the horrible rumor be true? Had he gone to spend his last hours with Rhawn Lorimer? She could hardly bear the thought.

What was she to do? It was too late to go looking for him at the manor.

In the distance, the vague sounds of galloping horses, with jingling and clanging and bouncing and an occasional yell of driver, intruded into her hearing. But she was too absorbed in her thoughts. The sounds did not register in her brain.

◌⌇◌

The coach bounded to a jostling stop in front of Mistress Chattan's inn. Percy took his bag from his uncle's buggy and walked across and set it on the ground beside it.

He returned to his aunt and uncle. "Well. . .thank you again," he said. "For everything. This is truly a second home for me."

"Percy...," began Katherine, then for lack of words stepped forward and hugged her nephew with tender feeling.

Percy stepped back and smiled. The affection between them was mutual.

"Well, Percy, my boy," said the viscount, never at his best at such moments, "looks like the coach is about ready for you. You're welcome anytime, of course—goes without saying, what? Give your father my best."

The two men shook hands. Percy turned and walked toward the coach.

⚘

Suddenly Gwyneth realized what she had heard. It was the northbound coach on its way into Llanfryniog!

Something must have detained Percy from coming to the beach. But she could at least say good-bye to him and give him her gift.

She leaped from the quay and dashed for Mistress Chattan's inn.

⚘

As Percy's foot reached for the step to climb inside, at the far end of the street between the two churches, the sound of galloping hooves thundered toward them. He paused and looked toward it.

A smile crept over his face as they came into view from out of the mist. It was a horse and rider, hair flying behind her, that he knew well.

Florilyn reined in dangerously and jumped to the ground and ran to him. He turned away from the coach door to meet her as she threw her arms around him.

"Percy, Percy!" she blubbered, beginning to cry all over again. "I am so sorry! I knew it wasn't true, what they were saying. Can you ever forgive me? I am so sorry!"

Percy returned her embrace and whispered a few words into her ear.

⚘

At the opposite end of the street, hurrying past the chapel and church from the harbor, Gwyneth sprinted into view of the inn.

Suddenly her feet came to a stop, and she stared in horror. Through the fog she saw Florilyn stepping back from Percy's arms. Then she quickly leaned forward again, tiptoed high, and kissed him.

A gasp escaped Gwyneth's lips. She turned away. The bouquet of a broken heart fell from her hand. Her eyes burned with hot tears as she ran into the nearest lane to keep from being seen. The moment she was out of sight, Gwyneth stopped, crumbled against the stones of a windowless wall, and wept.

When at last she was able to continue on her way, out of sight through the back alleys and lanes of the village to the safety of the moor, the tears continued to flow.

A few minutes later, the coach bounded into motion. His face at the open window, waving back to his aunt, uncle, and Florilyn where they stood together, Percy's eyes fell on a smattering of color lying in the dirt of the street. It was a small bouquet of flowers. . .tied with red and blue ribbon!

A pang seized his heart. Frantically he leaned from the window of the coach and hastily turned his head about in every direction. "Gwyneth!" he called. "Gwyneth!"

But his voice was lost in the thundering of hooves along the hard-packed dirt street. The coach clattered past the chapel, turned toward the harbor, and disappeared in the morning mist.

6≈9

Far behind her as she sped across the grass outside the village, the rumbling of the coach and four receded in the distance as it returned to the main road north of town.

Gwyneth paused in her flight and turned toward it. She could hear it but saw nothing. Her eyes were swimming in a blur of liquid, and the fog still lay thick all about her.

"Good-bye, Percy," she whispered.

PART THREE

Changes

1872

SIXTY-SEVEN

Changes

*A*gain time sped and crawled by, depending on who was looking at the clock.

In Glasgow, the ministry of Edward Drummond thrived, in large measure, though indirectly, because of his son. Estrangement between any of the human family acts like a great dam preventing the rivers of God being able to flow. Reconciliation demolishes those obstructions, and those waters again gush through their channels, and God is able to work.

Meanwhile, the vicar and his wife, Mary, kept careful watch in Glasgow's bookstores for every new title to land on their shelves by Aberdeenshire native George MacDonald. These they passed back and forth by mail and discussed in letters with Edward's sister. Of the three MacDonald devotees, however, only Edward had the appetite for the weighty volume entitled *Unspoken Sermons* that was released. The sisters-in-law confessed themselves more fond of the Scotsman's novels than his theological works.

In Llanfryniog, Kyvwlch Gwarthegydd continued to pound his anvil against religiosity every Sunday morning, while his son Chandos became burlier and wielded the blacksmith's hammer with increasing authority. In one thing, however, the son did not take after the father.

Through a friendship with the man's son, young Chandos fell under the influence of the new minister of the Methodist chapel at the north end of town. He had in consequence taken to reading with great interest a New Testament the minister had given him.

Mistress Chattan continued to do a brisk trade on the reputation of her ale.

Madame Fleming had *not* made closer approach to the Bible that sat with the books on her bookshelves. She kept it almost as a talisman to insure that no aspect of the spiritual and occult was omitted from her repertoire of hidden knowledge. In truth, she was a little afraid of it. She had not opened it in fifty years. But she was terrified at the thought of discarding it. With every year that passed her soul grew darker.

When things were put back in order, Grannie eventually returned to her cottage in the village. She still sensed that her end was near.

Codnor Barrie made slates and prospered in the greatest commodity of life, his own character.

Rhawn Lorimer, who had *not* paid sufficient attention to the growth of her character, continued to decline. The soil was being tilled, however, in preparation for that greatest of all invisible seed-birthings deep within the human garden. She gave birth to a baby boy. Though speculation ran rampant about whom the father might be, none was man enough to step forward to claim either a wife or a son. She remained under the roof of her parents. The magistrate and his wife were mortified at the disgrace that had befallen them.

At Westbrooke Manor, Roderick Westbrooke, viscount Lord Snowdon, completed his stables but quickly grew restless again. His dream of racing horses withered for lack of funds. His wife remained unwilling to finance the venture. Her tenderness toward her husband grew as she observed many changes that seemed taking place within him, including an increased attentiveness toward the people of the region and a new warmth and affection toward her. Nevertheless, she did not feel it right to allow him to squander money on vain pursuits like yachts and race horses. It would do him no good to pamper such indulgences.

She had always known that he was running away from something, that there were memories haunting him from his life before she knew him. She had sensed it even when, as a young woman, she had fallen in love with the sensitive and quiet Welsh aristocrat eight years her senior. His grandiose schemes through the years, she was certain, were but attempts to flee from that past. She hoped that his new awareness and tenderness toward those around him signaled that at last he was finding the peace within himself that had so long eluded him.

Meanwhile, Katherine Westbrooke, like her brother and sister-in-law, continued to read every new book released from the pen of the Scotsman. Her recent readings had included the otherworldly tale *At the Back of the North Wind* and a new fantasy called *The Princess and the Goblin.*

The viscount and his wife took to visiting a few of the villagers. They also rekindled their love of riding together in the hills. On one such ride, the viscount led his wife to the cottage he had visited with Percy and introduced Katherine to Mrs. Muir and young Stevie. A warm and unexpected friendship sprouted between Katherine and Adela Muir, with whom Lady Snowdon began sharing her MacDonald books. The two women found within one another kindred spirits of the heart that completely transcended differences of station.

The viscount also took to walking in the village, visiting with the villagers as he went, even enjoying an occasional pint of Mistress Chattan's ale. More and more in consequence his wife accompanied him to town and visited the shops and made as many of her purchases for the manor as she was able to from them.

Courtenay Westbrooke returned to Oxford. His studies interested him less and less. He managed to struggle through another year. As he began his fourth year in the fall of 1871, however, knowledgeable parties questioned how much longer he would last.

In the hills, Stevie Muir tended his sheep and other animals, cared for his mother, took seconds in the next two shearing contests, and was touted as the young man to watch in coming years. In consequence of their occasional visits, both Lord and Lady Snowdon took a liking and developed a great fondness for Stevie's gentle spirit. The viscount was especially taken with his skill with animals. The result was the offer of a job at the manor—for two days a week only owing to the distance he had to travel and the extra work required in the matter of his own animals—as an assistant and apprentice to Hollin Radnor, whose step had begun to slow.

At Burrenchobay Hall, unable to land the Scot of her dreams, young Davina Burrenchobay was now engaged to the eldest son of Baronet Rasmussen of Blaenau Ffestiniog, a devilishly good-looking youth of twenty-two years, rich and as full of himself as Davina was of herself and destined for triumphant mediocrity in all things to which he set his hand.

Not much was heard about Colville Burrenchobay. He was still unmarried, though rumors about his entanglements continued. He returned to university, graduated without distinction, and had taken to traveling a good deal.

Young Ainsworth Burrenchobay took his brother's place in the gossip registers, was reportedly even better with a gun and with young women than his brother, and was preparing to enter Cambridge. To what purpose, however, would have been interesting to inquire.

Rupert Wilkes, the occasional visitor to Mistress Chattan's inn, was still no nearer the discovery of the treasure of Dolau Cothi.

And on the moor rising behind the village, Gwyneth Barrie took care of her father, Grannie, and her animals, in that order, while continuing to work three days a week at Westbrooke Manor. Her outward growth continued, albeit slowly. If she would never attain the stature of her peers, her late start had the advantage of keeping her adding an inch a year long after most of them had reached their final height. In that far more important kind of growth, that of *inner* stature, the life of grace and quiet peace within her continued to deepen and expand, adding not mere inches but cubits to her character.

Walking in Llanfryniog one day, the viscount saw approaching him a young woman of indeterminate age. She was short enough to be a child, but her countenance and the features of her face were those of a woman. He was arrested by the sight.

He grew more transfixed as she came closer. His steps came to a halt. He continued to stare at the face and snowy white hair as she walked toward him.

Slowly his face went pale. It was almost as if. . .but it could not be. . . not here! He shook his head, as if trying to wake from a dream as she stopped in front of him.

"Good morning, Lord Snowdon," she said sweetly.

The voice brought him once more awake to the present. But the smile that accompanied it nearly undid what little equanimity remained in the man's carriage. "Yes, uh. . .hello, er. . .what are, I mean. . ." He fumbled, as if he were the stutterer and she some princess that had stepped out of his dreams—as well she might be. "You, uh. . .I believe. . . that is, I know you, don't I? Your face is unaccountably familiar."

"Yes, sir," smiled Gwyneth. "I work for you, at the manor, Lord Snowdon. For your wife and daughter, that is."

"Ah, yes, of course. . .that explains it," he said. His voice revealed profound relief. "For a moment my brain was playing tricks on me. I knew there had to be some reason why. . .that is—but it is not important. So how are you this fine day?"

"Well, sir. . .very well."

"You are not working today?"

"No, sir. I work three days a week."

"Ah, right. . .I see. . .very good, then. What is your name, young lady?"

"Gwyneth Barrie, Lord Snowdon."

"Barrie. . .ah, right. Capital! Barrie, is it, then?" he replied. Again he appeared relieved. "Well then, Miss Barrie, good day to you." The two parted, though the viscount glanced back a time or two as he continued down the street.

Gwyneth stood staring after him for a few moments. She had found the interview almost as strange as he found it unnerving.

For days after, the incident haunted Roderick Westbrooke.

From his factor he discovered what he could about the name and learned all he could about Codnor Barrie, the girl's father. Barrie was a local man who had gone to Ireland seeking work as a young man. No one knew other than that when he returned to his native Snowdonia some years later, he had a daughter with him. It was rumored that the girl's mother had been tragically lost at sea, but no one knew more than that. There had at one time been suspicions about the girl, Heygate added, associating her with nature's darker side, rumors that had possibly originated with an old woman in the village, Barrie's great-aunt. They had largely died down in recent years, the factor said. No one had any charge to bring against any of the three.

The viscount took in the information with interest. Eventually came a day when he knew he must pay a confidential visit to the Barrie home.

All this time, Florilyn Westbrooke grew quieter, if possible more beautiful and stately. She seemed oddly content with the domestic life of the manor. She took on the increasing countenance of a woman, resembling her mother more and more. She mixed with the maids and staff far more than she ever had early in her life, even helping them with their duties from time to time.

The relationship between her and Gwyneth blossomed into a full, rich friendship, such as only two young women can share. That they once loved the same young man—the one openly, the other secretively—in no way interferred with their friendship. Their affection for one another was too selfless to let anything come between them, even a man.

The alternate days when Gwyneth did not come to the manor seemed drab and dull to Florilyn. The tedium had this benefit, however, that those were the days she learned for the first time in her life to love books. Many afternoons found her in the library. She had even begun to discover the stories of MacDonald, a fact that delighted her mother and gave mother and daughter endless opportunity for lively talk together.

In Aberdeen, meanwhile, after a rewarding remainder of the summer of 1870 tutoring two young boys, Percival Drummond was soon caught up again in his university studies. By the end of the school term, he and his father had all but settled on law as the profession most suited to his temperament and interests. When an opportunity arose the following summer to apprentice as a clerk in one of Abereen's prestigious law firms, he leaped at the chance to get a foot into the door of the legal community of Scotland.

Thus it was, as before, that he was prevented from returning to Wales as soon as he might have liked. The same position was made available again the following year, his Semi and Tertian terms behind him as he prepared to embark on his fourth and final Magistrand year at the university. But, he told the solicitor who had taken such an interest in him, he could not let the summer pass without a visit to Wales. If it meant giving up the opportunity, it was a price he would have to pay. There were friends he simply had to see, and one or two personal situations he had to resolve in his own mind, before any more time went by.

The man understood. He said his post would be waiting for him when he returned.

And so it was, in late June of 1872, after three weeks with his parents in Glasgow, that once again Percival Drummond prepared to travel south to Wales for a visit of undetermined length.

For reasons of his own, he told no one in Llanfryniog of his plans.

SIXTY-EIGHT

Inns, Anvils, and Special Places

*P*ercy Drummond again returned to North Wales by train, followed by the southbound coach to the small coastal village of Llanfryniog on Tremadog Bay.

Three years in the university were behind him. At the age of twenty-one he was preparing to embark on a career in law. It was his hope to follow in the footsteps of his father, though with different letters behind his name and through distinctive professional means but with the same end in view—to open the eyes of his fellows to the love of their Father-Creator.

A flooded stream caused several hours' delay in his journey. Wales, like his homeland farther north, could have *weather* any time of the year!

By the time he arrived in Llanfryniog, the afternoon was well advanced toward evening. He could walk to the manor and easily be there in time for dinner. One of the reasons he had decided to come unannounced, however, and had enjoined his parents to hint at nothing by letter, was in hopes of getting the lay of the land, as it were, with regard to how things stood in the community. If there was information it would be well for him to possess, he hoped he might get wind of it at the inn or with a visit either to Grannie or Chandos Gwarthegydd.

He chastised himself the entire journey for not keeping in closer touch with those he loved. But his studies and apprenticeship at the law firm had proved so demanding that even the deep spiritual correspondence with his father, which he treasured, had suffered. And he still had at least two, perhaps three more years ahead of him before certification as a solicitor would be possible.

In spite of this, however, he had in recent months begun to ponder and pray about his personal future, not merely his professional career. With such thoughts making themselves more importune on his heart, how could Wales not beckon him again? He knew this was where that personal future must begin. He had not been in a position to declare himself openly before. It would still be a good while before he would be capable of supporting a wife and family. But at last he was ready to begin making plans, even if still distantly. . .*if* she would have him. Before that, however, he must know how things stood.

He walked into the inn with his bags, wondering if he would be recognized. He now stood a full inch over six feet, with all the features of a man, lanky but filled out in shoulders and chest, his face showing strong lines above a firm chin, with a forehead overlooking both that spoke of wisdom developing behind it. If anything, his brown hair had lightened a shade and was full and thick as it fell around his ears. His smile was just as eager to brighten a room and his laughter no less spontaneous, though perhaps slightly more bass when it exploded from his mouth. His eyes were the same hazel, but their visage shown with a far-seeing light that had only been foreshadowed in his youth but whose potential was now becoming fully realized in his young manhood. His study of law and justice, along with mercy, had done much to deepen the intensity of his eyes.

A few heads glanced toward the door as he entered. Most paid him little heed. In truth he only recognized about half the men gathered for their late afternoon pint. But Mistress Chattan knew every customer who walked through the doors of her establishment, if not by name certainly by sight. And Percy had been in often enough that, notwithstanding the changes that had taken place upon his outer man, she knew him instantly. "Well, young Drummond," she said. "You're back, are you?"

"Hello, Mistress Chattan," said Percy with a smile. "I don't suppose there's any slipping into town unrecognized by you!"

"I heard nothing about your coming."

"No one knew."

"You didn't let those up at the manor know?"

Percy shook his head.

Mistress Chattan nodded with significant expression but revealed nothing.

"Why. . . ?" said Percy slowly. "Is there something I should know?"

"Nothing to speak of. Nothing for *me* to speak of. So you don't know about your cousin?"

"Florilyn?"

"The young man—Master Courtenay."

"No, what about him?"

"Came home from the university in midyear. There was talk of a scandal. Expelled is what I heard."

"What is he doing?"

"The same thing rich young men always do, sponging off his father waiting until his time comes to inherit."

"He will have a long wait!" laughed Percy.

"Not as long as most young men in his position," said Mistress Chattan in a cryptic tone.

"How do you mean?"

"Just that his father's older than most fathers of twenty-three-year-olds."

"Ah, I see. . .but not *that* old. My uncle is still in the prime of his life."

"It all depends on what you mean by the prime of life," remarked Mistress Chattan. "I'll warrant you'll notice more gray on his crown than you expect. And his shoulders are starting to sag. He's not far off from sixty, I'm thinking."

"What are you talking about!" laughed Percy. "My own father is only forty-five."

"That's as well may be," rejoined the innkeeper. "But I'm telling you that Lord Snowdon is nearly old enough to be your grandfather rather than your uncle."

She paused, glanced about, then leaned over the bar separating them and reached out with a fleshy hand and pulled Percy toward her. "You do know, don't you?" she whispered in a conspiratorial tone.

"Know what?"

"About your uncle's past."

"No, what about it?" said Percy, unconsciously lowering his voice in response to Mistress Chattan's suddenly peculiar manner.

"Just that the sins of the fathers follow the sons, as the Book says."

"What sins? What are you talking about?"

"Sins of the *flesh*, young Drummond. What other kinds of sins do young men commit? There was another woman. . .before your aunt."

"You have been drinking too much of your own ale, Mistress Chattan," said Percy, though suddenly he felt very cold.

"I'm only telling you what they *say*, though I never laid eyes on her," the woman went on. "No one around here ever laid eyes on her, for it wasn't here that it happened. Across the sea, they say. When he came back, he was lovesick but alone. There was a child, they say. Now do you see why I say that the sins of the sons follow the sins of the fathers?"

"Why are you telling me all this, Mistress Chattan?" asked Percy. "Not that I believe a word of it," he added with a laugh that betrayed more anxiety than humor. "You are the most tight-lipped woman in Llanfryniog. Why suddenly confide in me?"

"I don't know, young Drummond. Maybe because I like you. Maybe because your fortunes may be more linked to that family on the hill than you realize, and you ought to know who you are involved with. *Someone* ought to know the truth because none of them do except the man himself, and *he'll* never tell. Maybe because I figure that you will do right by me one day. Maybe because I've taken a liking to the old blighter since he began coming around. Maybe because I figure he deserves a better friend watching over him than that no-good son of his. I don't know why I told you, young Drummond. There's your answer."

"Fair enough." Percy nodded. "Are you saying that my uncle has been in here?"

"He has indeed. After you left last time, something peculiar seemed to get into him. He comes to the village now, visits with people, comes in and buys pints for the fishermen and talks to them just like you always did. If I didn't know better, I'd think he'd got religion. He talks to me like we're old friends."

"I am glad to hear it. And speaking of the manor, do you mind if I leave my bags with you for a few hours?" Percy asked. "I'll walk up to the manor and be back for them this evening or tomorrow morning."

"Not at all."

"But I will have a pint of your special ale first."

Carrying his glass, Percy walked toward a table where a few of his fishermen acquaintances were seated. They greeted him *almost* as they might a friend. He visited with them for half an hour or so and caught up on village news. He learned nothing of note other than confirming that they, too, had seen a change in his uncle. At length he bade them good afternoon.

Without his bags, Percy walked briefly about the village and looked in at several shops, always receiving the same warm greeting from the shopkeepers. Two or three made the same comment. "Oh, won't Lady Florilyn be excited to see you!"

At length he approached the smithy. The familiar pounding of hammer on anvil could be heard from a long way off. He saw the father at the forge and the son at the anvil as he walked toward them. The sight brought a sharp intake of breath to his lips. The two were nearly the same size!

"What ho, Percy!" cried Chandos as Percy came into sight. He dropped his hammer and bounded forward with outstretched hand. The great hulking seventeen-year-old nearly crushed his hand in his grip.

"My, oh my, Chandos!" exclaimed Percy. "What a brute of a fellow you've become. It wouldn't go well for me *now* if I tried to order you around like I once did. You would thrash me!"

"No worry of that, Percy. You did me a great favor that day."

"How so?"

"You made me see what I was becoming. I didn't like what I saw. I wanted to be like you—a *good* young man. You helped set me on that road."

"I am more than a little amazed to hear you say it," rejoined Percy. "But pleased, nonetheless. Hello, Mr. Gwarthegydd," he said as the blacksmith came toward him with a smile and a black outstretched hand.

"So you're back, are you, laddie?"

"For a while—just a visit. I am still at the university. I've a year to go, then law school after that."

"I always said you would make something of yourself. Too bad the same can't be said for that high and mighty cousin of yours."

"I heard he had some trouble at school. What about Florilyn?" he asked. "I've been out of touch with everyone. Is she married yet. . .or engaged?"

He spoke matter-of-factly, though in truth he knew the answer to his own question. His mother kept him closely enough informed that if a change of that magnitude had come along, he would know about it. But he hoped to get Chandos talking.

Both father and son stared at Percy with odd expressions.

"She's not married, Percy," said Chandos at length. "Why would you think that?"

"Well, she's twenty now. Many young women are married by twenty."

"She's waiting."

"For what?"

"What do you think, man?" exclaimed Chandos. "For you! There's not a bloke in two counties who even looks at her now. Everyone knows how things stand."

"Everyone, it would appear, but me," said Percy. He had hoped for news. But this was more than he had bargained for.

By the time Percy set out from Llanfryniog, with much on his mind, it was a few minutes before seven o'clock. As he left town, he cast a glance inland to the cottage he longed to visit more than any other. But it was late. That was a visit that could not be rushed. To try to see Gwyneth now would delay him beyond a reasonable hour to arrive at the manor. They had much to talk about, not the least of which was why she had not come to meet him on the morning of his previous parting. He had been haunted ever since by unknown fears of what might have been the cause. The greatest of these had blossomed into the fear that she might no longer even be with her father, but that it might be *she* who had married during his absence, not Florilyn. He also had to find out what days Gwyneth was working now, *if* she was still at the manor. No brief visit would suffice. He would visit the Barrie cottage tomorrow, when he hoped to learn all.

In the meantime, however, as he made his way out of the village, breathing in deeply of the coastal air, he took a brief detour along the promontory of Mochras Head. Notwithstanding his perplexity about the last time he had been here, he took time to walk to Gwyneth's special place. He sat down and gazed out over the azure sea as it prepared a few hours hence to receive the golden orb into itself in its nightly burial, that the earth and its inhabitants might have their daily season of rest. There was no fog on this day. He only prayed that an explanation presented itself about the events of that day two years before and the meaning of the bouquet he had seen on the street—some explanation that did not break his heart.

After ten or fifteen minutes of quiet reflection, as he allowed the peace of the "special place" to fill him again, Percy rose and continued on to Westbrooke Manor. He walked up the drive, keeping his eyes moving. He did not want to encounter Gwyneth like this, with a chance meeting as she was leaving the manor for home. But all was quiet, and he saw no one.

He walked toward the great house. There were the new stables, completed now though mostly unoccupied. His feet echoed softly over the flagged paving stones of the entryway. He paused at the front door. Even after an absence of two years, he felt no duty to ring the bell. This was home.

He turned the latch and went inside. The only voices he heard came from the kitchen in the distance, where the staff would be having their dinner. He walked through the entryway, along the corridor, and toward the dining room. At last he heard soft voices from the family. He paused, smiled to himself, then opened the door and walked into the room.

Four heads turned toward him at once. A stunned silence followed. In their shock at seeing him in their midst, aunt, uncle, and both cousins all seemed for the briefest of instants not to know him.

The silence did not last long. A great shriek sounded as Florilyn leaped from her chair, knocking it backward onto the floor behind her. "Percy!" she cried as she ran across the room to him and flung her arms about him.

SIXTY-NINE

Sonship

*L*ater that evening, when they had returned with the buggy after retrieving Percy's bags from town, Percy and Florilyn left the house as a warm dusk descended. Without conscious intent, their steps led them toward the garden east of the manor.

"So, it's law, is it?" said Florilyn. "When you were here last you were talking about engineering and the church as potential professions as well."

"You have a good memory!"

"I was paying attention." Florilyn smiled. "I also had the benefit of an occasional letter from your mother to mine. Otherwise I would know nothing about how you had spent the last two years. So I really must thank you for all those long, newsy letters."

Percy laughed. "I know, I know," he said. "I am sorry. I've been terrible."

"Yes, you have!"

"You have no idea how demanding school is."

"It takes every minute of your time?"

"Well, maybe not *every* minute. I admit that as a letter writer I am a failure."

"You write to your father, I hear."

394

"That's different."

"How so?"

"We don't talk about ourselves or what we are doing."

"What do you write each other about, then?"

"Ideas. . .theology."

"Sounds boring."

"Are you kidding? I love dialoguing back and forth with my father about the ideas of faith. What could be more exciting than that? But I apologize for not keeping in touch better. I thought about you all a lot, if that is any consolation."

"Well. . .maybe it makes up for it a little," said Florilyn playfully. "But *just* a little. A girl gets lonely, you know. She looks for letters in the post. Still. . .now that you're here, I *may* decide to forgive you. So what made you decide that you wanted to be a solicitor instead of a minister?"

"My father encouraged me in that direction."

"I would think he would have wanted you to follow him into the church."

"My father is too selfless for that."

"What do you mean?"

"He is trying to help me discover what is best for *me*, not what *he* might prefer. In the end, we both felt that my personality would be better suited for law."

"How did you come to that conclusion?"

Percy thought a moment. "It wasn't anything specific," he said. "We sought God's guidance, of course. But there were no telegrams from heaven. God doesn't reveal His will that way. My father says that the Lord speaks with a soft voice into our senses, with nudges into our hearts and brains, not shouts, with subtle pressures in one direction or another. He simply suggested we pray and see what we sensed, to see if we felt any of those gentle inward nudgings toward either ministry or law. By then we had pretty much omitted engineering."

"And did you. . .feel the nudging, I mean?"

"Gradually, yes. I can't say exactly how. Like my father says, it was subtle. I found myself thinking more about law and becoming enthusiastic about it. Then the offer of an internship came last summer from a solicitor's firm in Aberdeen. That was the confirmation of circumstance."

"What's that?"

"My father says that God makes His will in our lives known by the subtle inner nudges in response to our prayers, and He confirms that leading by circumstance. He says that the Lord uses circumstances to confirm His leading, even occasionally to change the direction of His leading. As long as we're not in a hurry and willing to wait, the two always line up at some point—the direction of the leading and the circumstances that make it possible to follow that leading. When the two line up, you can be confident that God might indeed be indicating a certain direction."

"*Might* be. That doesn't sound very definite."

"You never know 100 percent. There's a certain amount of guesswork involved in following the Lord's leading. My father says that our own desires can interfere and make us think God is leading when we are really just following what we want to do ourselves. It is also easy to *misinterpret* circumstances and think they're saying something they're not. That's why the most important thing in listening to God's voice is to set aside your own desires and ambitions. And then be willing to go *slow* in making decisions. That's another thing my father says, that God is never in a hurry."

"You make it sound like the decision of what you should pursue was your father's. Wasn't it ultimately your decision to make?"

"Sure. But I placed the decision before him and asked what he thought I should do. He is my father. My life is not entirely my own. It can never be."

"Your life is not your *own?*"

"I said not *entirely* my own. We are linked to those who came before. I believe we have a duty to them."

"You have a duty to do what your father wants you to do, even now that you are a grown man?"

"Not completely. Of course not. But to a degree, yes. The fact that he is paying for my education gives him the right to offer his input. And I genuinely want it. The generations of families is very important in God's economy. We have a duty to our ancestors, to live faithfully and to honor their names. It is not an idea that is much in vogue today when most perceive that they have no duty to anyone but themselves. But we *do* have duties that extend wider than that. In that lineage, my father is the one God placed immediately over me. That fact carries great weight. It carries the assumption that my father perceives it as his duty to help me find what God wants me to do. He does so not to please himself but to help me fulfill *my* place in God's plan."

"Do you think your father really thinks of all that every time you ask for his advice?"

"Absolutely. I know it for a fact. He seeks my best, not his own. He always seeks the best of others, not himself."

"He sounds like a remarkable man."

"He is. That's why I know I can place my uncertainties in his hands and that he will seek only my absolute best. That is the whole basis of the thing—my assurance that my father wants the very *best* for me. Even if he didn't, I would still consider it my duty to heed him, even to obey him if he made it a matter of obedience. But hey—you know all this. My mother says you have been reading MacDonald. My father is like David Elginbrod to me. I realize that not all fathers are as wise as mine. I can imagine it being very difficult to obey if you did not have the assurance that your father or mother was seeking your best. In a way, I suppose, I have it easy. I know that about my parents. It makes it easy to heed their advice, even to obey them on the rare occasions now when it might still come to that."

"Most people our age would laugh to hear you say such things," said Florilyn. "They would consider you loony. But you're right. It does sound like the sort of father-son relationship MacDonald talks about. I can hardly imagine what Courtenay would say!"

"I am sure that is true," smiled Percy. "But for the first time in my life I am at peace being the son of my father. I do not intend to lose out on what being a son can teach me. I am not anxious to be independent of him. And since I am still young, and since I spent some years in rebellion, my father is in a position to know what is best for me better than I am myself. That's what it means to trust his wisdom. It means trusting *him* to know my best even above my own desires, trusting him, in a sense, to speak for God in my life."

"You make it sound as though he makes all your decisions."

"Not at all. Every individual grows into an autonomy and independence as a man or woman in their own right. That is exactly what every parent ought to be working toward. My father wants that very thing for me. He doesn't tell me what to do. But I *want* his advice and counsel. He gives me his impressions, helps me focus on spiritual principles, points out factors I may not have considered. And he will sometimes urge me very strongly in one direction or another. But in the end, he always encourages me to make my own decisions. *Now*, at least that's what he does. Five years ago he *made* me come here. I had no choice then because I was incapable of wise choices. I was sixteen and rebellious. I had been in trouble with the police. It's different now. Part of that process is his trust of me, too."

"I think I begin to see. . .a little," said Florilyn thoughtfully.

"It's really a wonderful thing—the more I trust him, the more he trusts me. That's why our dialogue is based not on either of us trying to convince the other to any particular point of view but about mutually trying to figure out what is best. In that my father's vote, you might say, weighs very heavily, even though the ultimate decision rests with me. That probably sounds contradictory, but that is sort of how the mechanics of the thing work in practice."

"Will you ever consider yourself fully on your own, so that you *don't* think about what your father says?"

"I hope not. My father is a wise man. Why would I *ever* not want to glean as much of that wisdom as possible? As long as I live, he will always be ahead of me spiritually simply because he is older and has been listening to God's voice longer. And he still wants the wisdom of his father, even though, as you know, Grandpa has been in China for ten years. In the same way, I will always be spiritually ahead of *my* children, if I have any, in the same way. That's the way the generations are supposed to work. I will go to my grave, long after my father is dead, *still* doing my best to learn from his wisdom. I think that's the way God intended it to be with sons and fathers."

"I doubt that's the way Courtenay looks at it!" laughed Florilyn.

"Courtenay has not spent his life developing spiritual eyesight. It grieves me to say that for most of my life I didn't either. I have only been learning to see my father in this way for five years. That's why I am trying so hard to listen to him and learn from him now, even though I am no longer under his roof and technically, I suppose you might say, on my own. And as I said, my father still sees himself learning from his father, where *he* is the son. Of course, Grandpa recognizes him as a man of God in his own right, because that's what he prepared him to be. But my father looks up to him just as I look up to my father."

"It must be remarkable to be part of something like that," said Florilyn. "I knew that Grandfather and Grandmother Drummond had gone to China, but sad to say, Mother has learned not to talk about spiritual things around the rest of us. I feel bad about that now. I had no idea all that was at work between. . .well, all three of you, I guess."

"I admit that it is not very common. But as I said, I believe it is God's pattern."

They sat down on one of the garden's stone benches. Dusk was closing heavily around them. It was now after ten o'clock. The sounds of evening drifted toward them from the nearby trees. They sat for several minutes.

"What about. . .your future?" asked Florilyn, at length voicing the question that had been on her mind for two years. As she spoke, her voice betrayed a slight quiver.

"That's one of the things I hope to resolve while I am here," replied Percy.

As much hopefulness as Florilyn might have hoped to take from his answer, his expression revealed nothing. "What does your father think. . .about us?"

"He is pleased that we have become so close," replied Percy, again revealing nothing.

Once more it was quiet.

Percy drew in a deep breath. "It is getting late," he said. "Suddenly I am very tired. It's been a long day." Slowly he rose. "Shall we go in?" he asked.

"I think I will sit a little longer," replied Florilyn. "You've given me so much to think about. I have never heard anything like what you have described between you and your father. . .and even your grandfather's role in it. It sounds both wonderful and frightening. I've never considered that a father and son, or a daughter I suppose as well, could trust one another like that and be such. . . It sounds like your father is actually your best friend."

"He really is. That's exactly right. I know there would be many who would think me out of my mind to talk about my father this way. Others would think me a fool. I don't know, perhaps this is not a road everyone can walk. I don't even say everyone should. I don't know. I am still young. I am probably guilty of the common hubris of youth of thinking I know more than I really do. All I can say is that this is the way I have chosen to obey the command to honor my father and mother."

Florilyn smiled. "Well, I don't think you a fool. But I need time to absorb it all."

"All right. Well then, I'll leave you to your thoughts. How about a ride tomorrow afternoon? After we both sleep in!"

"I would like that," said Florilyn with a smile.

Percy turned to go.

"Oh, Percy," said Florilyn after him, "did you stop by to see anyone else in the village or on your way up here this evening?"

"I stopped in at the inn, then by the smithy, then I came straight here. Why?"

"Oh, nothing. It's just that there is something you need to know, something you ought to be prepared for. I've been trying to find a way to tell you all evening."

"What?"

Florilyn hesitated. "Come to think of it," she added with a smile, "there's no sense ruining your evening. I'll tell you in the morning. Though not too early!"

"I know. You like to sleep in. But now I will worry about what it might be. My night's ruined either way."

"I'm sorry," rejoined Florilyn. "I shouldn't have said anything. It will keep until tomorrow. If I know you, you won't worry about it for long. I'll tell you everything in the morning. Well, everything I know, which isn't much."

Assuming she had something to tell him about Rhawn Lorimer or one of the Burrenchobays, or possibly something to do with her brother and the university scandal Mistress Chattan had mentioned, Percy consented to wait. "Sure. . .okay. Good night, Florilyn."

"Good night, Percy. It's really nice to have you back."

SEVENTY

Old Wounds, New Beginnings

*E*xpecting to sleep till at least eight or nine, Percy was wide awake the next morning before seven. After a spirited visit with his aunt in the breakfast room, he decided to walk to the village. It was hours before Florilyn would make an appearance for the day after the late evening. With a ride planned for the afternoon, he wanted to wait no longer before visiting Grannie and Gwyneth.

Walking past the draper's shop on the afternoon of his arrival, Percy was reminded of the first time he had set eyes on Rhawn Lorimer. The momentary exchange that fateful day had seemed innocent enough. But even then, the flirtatious mischief had been evident in her eye.

He knew it well might stir up the old rumor, but he needed to see her. He had unfinished business with her, too, just as he did with Gwyneth—though of a much different nature. He had to look Rhawn in the eye and ask her *why*. If Florilyn's news concerned Rhawn, he might just as well find it out for himself.

While they ate breakfast, he asked his aunt about Rhawn.

"We have hardly seen her in the last two years," replied Katherine. "She and Florilyn never visit anymore."

"I would like to drop in on her this morning."

"Goodness, Percy. . .why?"

402

"It's just something I need to do. I am concerned about her, for one thing. I want to ask her why she did it."

"I wouldn't want to have anything to do with her. Aren't you afraid of stirring everything up again? People will talk."

"Who cares? And why would people talk? Are you saying . . . ? Is she not married? Did the father not come forward?"

"No to both," answered his aunt. "She is still living with her parents. She has a baby boy."

"No one ever owned up to it?"

Katherine shook her head.

"And Rhawn never divulged the truth?"

"No."

"Did she ever absolve me?" asked Percy.

"Yes, eventually she came clean and said she had lied about you."

Percy took in the information thoughtfully.

"*Must* you see her, Percy?" asked Katherine.

He thought about her question a moment. "I don't know if I *have* to, but I want to. Things need to be brought to resolution. It's something my dad's always talking about—reconciliation and healing. I *have* to see if there might be an opening with Rhawn. If not, at least I will have tried."

His aunt nodded then her lips broke into a smile. "That's your father, all right," she said. "Even as a teen he could not tolerate conflict. He was always trying to resolve differences between people. Why should I expect Edward's son to be any different? Like father, like son, I suppose."

"That's a great compliment coming from you, Aunt Katherine."

Percy left her and set out for Llanfryniog about eight thirty. He left Florilyn a brief note saying he would be back by noon. Whatever she had to tell him would have to wait for later in the day.

He walked straight to the village. He wanted to get that visit out of the way first. Then he would have plenty of time with Gwyneth afterward.

He made no attempt to hide his movements. He went directly to the magistrate's home. A woman whom he had never seen answered the door.

"Mrs. Lorimer?" said Percy.

"Yes," she answered, looking him over with a questioning eye.

"Is Rhawn here?" Percy asked. "I am a friend of hers."

"Do I know you?"

"No, ma'am. I've not been in Llanfryniog for two years."

Whatever suspicions Percy's statement might have aroused in Mrs. Lorimer's mind, she kept to herself. She disappeared into the house, leaving the door open and Percy standing outside.

A minute later Rhawn appeared.

"Hello, Rhawn," said Percy with a smile.

She stared back at him blankly, not believing her eyes. In the distance Percy heard the sounds of a child.

"Percy!" she said in a soft, almost questioning voice. Her eyes began to fill. The change that had come over her was remarkable. On her face was the look of a sad and broken young woman.

Percy stepped forward and embraced her.

She began to weep in earnest, though softly.

"Why have you come here, Percy?" she asked at length, stepping back and wiping her eyes. "Aren't you afraid of being seen. . .of what people will say?"

"No, I am not concerned."

"Are you. . .angry with me?" she asked, forcing a sad, almost frightened smile.

"No, not that either. I do have to say that I was surprised and disappointed."

"Have you come to rub salt in the wounds?"

"Rhawn! I would never do that."

"Why, then? Why would you want to see me?"

"I had to ask you *why*. . .why you did it. Why did you, Rhawn?"

She smiled again more sadly than before. "Can't you guess?"

"No, honestly I can't. What did I ever do to hurt you?"

"Nothing, Percy," she said, starting to cry again. "Nothing at all. That is the reason."

"I don't follow you."

"I knew the real father would never acknowledge his child. He had already turned his back on me. I knew he would never marry me. You were the nicest boy I had ever met. I suppose I hoped that maybe. . . But it was stupid and selfish of me. I was not in the habit back then of thinking of anyone but myself. I didn't think of the consequences to you. I am sorry for what I must have put you through. I just thought. . ."

She looked away and began to cry again. "I did it because I was selfish, Percy," she went on in a halting voice. "I kept trying to convince myself that you were smitten with me. All my life I had been able to make any boy I wanted fall all over me. You were the first boy who didn't. It made me crazy to conquer you. I told myself that you were playing hard to get, that you really loved me. But everyone knew how it was between you and Florilyn. I knew well enough that she was in love with you."

She was looking down as she spoke and did not see Percy's expression of surprise at her words.

"That made me angry, too," Rhawn went on, "that she might succeed where I had failed. I suppose I was trying to get back at you both, and at the same time I hoped that you might. . . I suppose I still hadn't given up on the idea that you might actually care for me in some way. I see now how foolish. . .that you never—" Rhawn glanced away, crying again.

She started a moment later when she felt two strong hands on her shoulders. She looked up. Percy was staring straight into her eyes with a more peaceful look of love and compassion than she had ever seen from anyone in her life.

"Rhawn," he said, smiling tenderly. "You were right. I did not love you in that way. I hope you do not mistake my visit today in thinking that has changed. I cannot love you as a man would. I cannot be a father to your child. But I want to be a friend to you. I would like us to make a new beginning, if you are willing. I think Florilyn is ready to be your friend again, as well."

"Oh, Percy. . .I don't know. Why would you treat me this way? After all I. . .I mean, why would you be so good to me?"

Percy smiled.

It was the old smile she remembered!

"Isn't that what friends are for?" he said.

Rhawn could hardly believe how kind and generous he was. "Would you. . .could you come in for a cup of tea?" she asked. "I would like you to meet my mother. . .and my son."

SEVENTY-ONE

Gone

*P*ercy left the Lorimer home thirty minutes later, full of many thoughts. Mostly he felt compassion for Rhawn. She was now reaping the fruit of the foolishness of her younger years. But all beginnings offer hope for new life. Perhaps this might be such a day for her.

He turned into the lane toward Grannie's. He hoped he might find Gwyneth there. After tea with Grannie, they could walk along the beach together.

It was great to be back, he thought. Just walking through the streets of Llanfryniog made him happy.

He couldn't wait to see Gwyneth again. He was nearly running by the time he reached Grannie's. He tried to calm himself, reminding himself how changed Gwyneth was last time. He had *almost* not recognized her that day he had first seen her working at the manor. In his eyes she would always be the nymph of the Snowdonian hills, the lake creature out of whose hands deer came to eat. Yet she was bound to be changed again. And still the question dogged him why she had not met him two years before.

He slowed. *Would she be taller?* he wondered with a smile. She would never be as tall as Florilyn. But she *might* grow to five feet, and then be not much more than a foot shorter than he.

She would be eighteen now. Would the same thing happen as before? Would he gaze upon the face beneath the head of white and wonder, *Is it really her?*

As he went, he also tried to prepare himself for the possibility that there could be a young man in her life…*if* she wasn't engaged or married already. He had *tried* to prepare himself for it. But he knew he wasn't *really* prepared for such news.

He reached Grannie's cottage. Strange, thought Percy, there was no smoke drifting out of the chimney. He went to the familiar door and knocked. There was no response from inside. A second knock, then a third produced the same result. He tried the latch. It was locked. Grannie *never* locked her door. Something felt wrong.

He thought a moment, then turned and quickly broke into a run in the direction of the cottage outside the village. He hoped the explanation was as simple as that Grannie was with them. With the premonition growing that something wasn't right, he ran across the moorland plateau. He ran straight to the door of the cottage and knocked.

It opened a minute later. A rough-looking man, unshaven for several days and with a scowl on his face, opened the door and stared at him. "What do you want, mate?" he growled.

"I came to see the Barries," said Percy, glancing into the house behind the man in perplexity.

"Ain't nobody by that name here."

"Codnor Barrie? He has a daughter by the name of Gwyneth?"

"Look, mate—this is my place. I ain't heard of no Barrie."

"How long have you lived here?"

"Seven months. Came from Australia to work in the mines. Now they ain't giving me the work they promised. Now beat it!" The door slammed in Percy's face.

He walked to the side of the house. Not a creature nor pen was to be seen behind it. In bewilderment Percy hurried back to the village. He went straight to Grannie's again. This time he knocked on the door of the house next to it. It opened, and he was met by Grannie's neighbor, a woman Percy had seen a few times in the past. "Good morning," he said.

"It's Mr. Drummond, isn't it?" she said.

"Yes, and I'm hoping you can tell me where Grannie is, and Gwyneth and her father. I just returned and found a stranger living in the cottage on the moor, and not a very friendly one. Grannie's door is locked up tight."

"I'm sorry to be the bearer of such tidings, Mr. Drummond," said the old woman, "but they're gone."

"*Gone. . .where?*"

"I don't know, Mr. Drummond."

"Why did they leave?"

"Nobody knows. It's a mystery. One day Mr. Barrie appeared with his cart at Grannie's and picked up a few things. I figured she was going up to live with them. She was ailing, Grannie was, and the lass had been coming down every day. But then I never saw her again. Next thing I knew folks were saying they'd disappeared—all three of them."

"*Disappeared!*" exclaimed Percy. "It makes no sense."

The woman shook her head, as if to say that she agreed with him but had no other answer to give.

"Grannie's place has been vacant ever since," she said. "But like you say, a fellow from the mines is living in Codnor's place, honest man, though he's a surly one."

"So I discovered. But how can it be that no one knows where they went? Did he have work elsewhere? Was he fired from the mine? There must be *some* explanation."

"That's why it's a mystery, Mr. Drummond."

Percy thanked the woman and left.

Not a young man prone to downcast moods, this was as shattering a blow as Percy had ever known in his life. He half stumbled out of town in the direction of the harbor in a stupor of desolation. A few fishermen were about, but he did not pause to speak with them. Unaware that Gwyneth had been sitting at that very spot waiting for him two years earlier, while he had been sitting on the promontory waiting for her, he passed the corner of the concrete quay and continued onto the beach.

He made his way slowly, memories flooding him as he went—his talks with Gwyneth, playing in the tide, the race with Florilyn—so many memories. He was in no playful mood today and plodded along heedless of his steps.

The tide was about halfway in, which made climbing over the rocks and boulders and tidepools at the end of the north beach more difficult. By the time he reached the south beach with the promontory rising high on his left, his boots and trousers were wet to the knees. He hardly noticed.

He glanced toward the cave, water almost to its mouth. He had no appetite to explore without Gwyneth. On he walked. He reached the base of the promontory path then slowly climbed up to the plateau of Mochras Head. Sighing dejectedly, he again sought Gwyneth's special place.

He sat down on the wet grass, just as he had on that misty morning two years before. It was clear today. He stared out across the blue sea, trying to imagine the Irish coastline, though he was never sure whether he *really* saw it.

"Oh. . .Gwyneth, Gwyneth," he whispered. "Where have you gone?"

Seventy-Two

The Viscount and His Factor

*P*ercy arrived back at Westbrooke Manor about ten thirty. He found Florilyn in the breakfast room. She had just read his note.

"Oh, Percy!" she said. "I had hoped to talk to you before you went into town. I can see from your face that you know."

He nodded, slumped into a chair, and buried his face in his hands.

"I am sorry, Percy," said Florilyn. "I know what Gwyneth meant to you. I wanted to find a way to tell you last night, but it just—I don't know...I couldn't find a way. She was my friend, too. I'm sorry."

Percy looked toward her and smiled sadly. "It's all right," he said. "As you said, you didn't want to ruin my evening. And it would have." He drew in a long breath and exhaled slowly. "I talked to Grannie's neighbor," he said. "The story she recounts is almost incomprehensible... that they left without a word to anyone."

"That is exactly how it was," rejoined Florilyn. "One day Gwyneth was working here and everything was fine. Two days later my father told me she would not be returning. I asked why. He said that she and her father had left Llanfryniog. I was stunned. She'd not said a word to me. There wasn't a hint of it ahead of time. Immediately I rode down to the cottage, but they were already gone. I never saw Gwyneth again. I am still completely bewildered."

"Your father must know *something*."

"He said his factor informed him that Barrie had given notice and told him he would not be renewing his rental of the cottage."

"Then I need to talk to Mr. Heygate. Someone *has* to know something."

"I tried," said Florilyn. "I finally gave up. I asked everyone in the village, every one of Grannie's neighbors. I rode up to the Muirs. Even they didn't know. Stevie and his mother were as surprised as I was. They didn't say good-bye to them either. I have done my best for eight months to find out something. Gwyneth and I had become very close. But they seem to have wanted no one to know where they had gone."

Percy listened in stunned disbelief. "Then maybe I need to hear it for myself," he said. Percy left Florilyn with her late breakfast and went upstairs.

He found Lord Snowdon in his study. Even more than on the previous evening, he noticed what Mistress Chattan had warned him of—that his uncle appeared to have aged more than a mere two years would account for. He was shocked at how gray he had become.

"Ah, Percy, my boy!" said his uncle. "Out for a ride so early on your first morning back with us, I see."

"No, sir," replied Percy. "I walked to town and then to visit my friends Codnor Barrie and his daughter."

"I, uh. . .am not familiar with the name," rejoined the viscount, who stood when Percy entered. In fact he knew the name better than that of any of his tenants, former or present.

"The girl worked here as a servant in the manor, Uncle Roderick. I don't see how you could not have known her."

"Well, er. . .of course, that is, you can hardly expect me to be on intimate terms with all my wife's maids," said his uncle as he sat down again. As he did, he winced visibly. "Blasted knee!" he muttered. "Don't ever get old, Percy, my boy. It plays havoc with your knees. I just hope I die before I get so decrepit I can't walk. But where were we? Ah, yes, some girl you mentioned that you say worked here. Perhaps. . .that is to say, perhaps I might recognize her face if I were to see her."

"Unfortunately, that is impossible."

"Why is that?"

"Because their cottage is now occupied by someone else," Percy answered. "The Barries have moved, up and gone without a trace. Florilyn tells me your factor was the one who spoke with Mr. Barrie. I would like to know what you know, Uncle Roderick. It is a matter of great personal urgency to me. Whatever it takes, I *have* to find them."

"What are these people to you, Percy, my boy. . .if you don't mind my asking?" said his uncle.

"They are close and dear friends. The girl, Gwyneth is her name, helped me more than anyone other than my own father, to see God's handiwork about me, as well as inside me. She is one of the most remarkable individuals I have ever met. She was also very close to Florilyn. I have to find her. . .for both our sakes."

"She, uh. . .sounds like an extraordinary young girl, you say. Yes, quite—and a peasant, the daughter of a miner, you say. Most extraordinary. How would, uh. . .such a one come to possess this vast knowledge about the church?"

"You mistake me, Uncle Roderick. It would not surprise me if the girl had never set foot inside a church in her life. What I said was that she had helped me to see God in His creation and within myself. Unless a man like my father is in the pulpit, judging by its success rate, church seems to me singularly ill equipped for the transmission of that revelation into human hearts."

"Ah, yes. . .I see. . .of course, of course. So then, er. . .Barrie is the name, you say. Hmm, yes, I seem to recall something about it. Yes, a very sudden departure it was, I believe."

"What exactly did your factor tell you?"

"Just that. . .if I recall, let me think. . .that the man told him he was leaving Llanfryniog and the slate mine."

"There was nothing else?"

"Not that I, uh. . .not that I recall."

Percy turned to go. "Do you know where I might find your factor?" he said.

"I could not say with certainty, though you might try his office. I believe he had business in Penrhyndeudraeth later. If I am not mistaken, he planned to spend the night there and take the train up to Llanfairpwllgwyngyllgogerychwyrndrobwllllantysiliogogogoch."

"To where?" exclaimed Percy.

His uncle chuckled. "It's a village in Anglesey," he said. "Translated it means, 'St. Mary's Church in the hollow of white hazel near the rushing whirlpool and Tysilio of the Red Cave's Church.' I thought I might get you with that one, Percy, my boy."

"What do people in a hurry call it?" asked Percy.

"Llanfair Pwllgwyngell, or just Llanfair. Tilman plans to visit his son's family on the peninsula for a day or two. Whether he has left yet I do not know."

"Then I had better try to catch him before he leaves."

Percy hastened downstairs and to the south wing. His knock at the factor's door was answered by a summons to enter.

"Ah, young Drummond!" said Tilman Heygate, rising to meet him and shaking his hand warmly.

"Hello, Mr. Heygate."

"I heard you were back. You're looking very well—healthy and with another inch or two to your credit."

"I've just come from the viscount," said Percy. "I hope you might be able to shed some light on the sudden disappearance of Codnor Barrie and his daughter."

"Barrie—he was the slate miner?" replied the factor, resuming his seat behind his desk.

"Yes, sir," said Percy, taking the chair opposite him.

"Rented a cottage from us out on the moor, about a mile east of the village, wasn't it?"

"That's right."

"Yes, I recall it now. I found it very strange," nodded Heygate thoughtfully.

"What exactly did Mr. Barrie say?" asked Percy.

"A note came here to the manor from him asking to see me," replied Heygate.

"Did you think that strange?"

"Not at all. I handle matters for all the viscount's tenants. They pay their rents to me. They bring their complaints to me."

"He didn't say what it was about?"

"Just that he wanted to see me. I knew he worked in the slates, so I rode down there the next evening. His daughter was with him and greeted me pleasantly. A nice girl, she struck me...worked at the manor as well, I believe."

"That's right." Percy nodded.

"The man said he needed to talk to me in private. The girl left the cottage. She kept a number of animals in pens and a fenced area behind the house. When we were alone, Barrie told me that a change had come to his situation. He and his daughter would be leaving Llanfryniog and quitting their tenancy. He said that they would be moving soon, adding that the viscount had been very kind to him. He asked me to thank him. Then he handed me three one pound notes for the rent that was due. He asked me to say nothing to anyone but the viscount. His daughter did not know of his plans yet, he said, nor another soul."

"Did you ask him why he was leaving?"

"I did. He merely said that an opportunity had arisen that would prove of great benefit to his daughter, that he hoped thereby perhaps even to secure for her an education beyond what was available here and give her opportunities she would never otherwise have. It was not an opportunity he could afford to pass up."

"Was it a more lucrative job somewhere?"

"I don't know, Percy," replied Heygate. "I had the idea that he might have come into money. Not wealth, mind you, but enough to make the move he was talking about and live comfortably. He said nothing specifically. It was simply the sense I had. He was vague. I asked when they were leaving. He said they would be gone the following day. I asked where they were going. He said he could not say. Again he adjured me to secrecy. But it was hardly necessary. I knew nothing anyway."

"And that was it?"

"I'm afraid so. We shook hands. I took the three pounds and returned to the manor and told the viscount what had transpired. He received the information without comment or overmuch curiosity. And that was it. A month later I rented the cottage to a man new to the mines. To my knowledge, no one has heard from the Barrie fellow or the girl since."

SEVENTY-THREE

Cousins Facing the Future

*F*or the rest of the day, Percy kept mostly to himself. Florilyn knew he needed time to adjust to the sudden shock of finding Gwyneth gone. They did not ride that afternoon.

There exist few better antidotes to the mental and emotional doldrums, however, than demanding physical exertion. After an afternoon watching him wander aimlessly about the manor, inspecting the stables he had helped build two years before, rekindling his friendships with Grey Tide and Red Rhud and several other horses, and chatting with Hollin Radnor and Stuart Wyckham, Florilyn determined that she would get her cousin away from the house the next morning.

Percy spent the evening with a George MacDonald title he had not seen, *Ranald Bannerman's Boyhood*. His aunt had handed it to him after dinner, telling him it had just come out that year, and that she had only recently finished it. However, he had a difficult time concentrating on the words on the page.

Florilyn appeared surprisingly early in the breakfast room the next morning. She was upbeat and cheerful, ready to do her best to bring life back to Percy's spirit. "It's a beautiful day, Percy," she said as they ate. "I am going for a ride. I hope you will join me."

"Sure," said Percy, though without his customary enthusiasm. "I guess I haven't been very good company. Sorry. . .but life goes on, as they say."

"That's the way I felt for weeks after Gwyneth disappeared," said Florilyn.

They agreed to meet at the stables at ten. Percy was already there when Florilyn arrived in her riding habit.

"Hollin has just been telling me about this beautiful black stallion," said Percy. He was standing at the stall of a jet-black powerful horse he had never seen before.

"A nasty brute," said Florilyn. "His name is Demon, and for good reason. He's a four-year-old. I'm surprised he hasn't snapped at you standing there. My father bought him hoping to race him. After getting him here, it became obvious why my father got him at the price he did. He's altogether unmanageable. What did Hollin tell you?"

"Exactly the same," replied Percy, "that he counseled your father against the purchase, but that Uncle Roderick had his heart set on a thoroughbred, and here was one to be had at a price he could afford."

"That about sums it up."

"Have you ridden him?" asked Percy.

Florilyn laughed, though the sound erupting from her mouth more resembled a snort. "I wouldn't be caught dead on that horse's back!"

"Does *anyone* ride him?"

"Courtenay can. Papa *thinks* he can. But it makes me nervous whenever he takes him out. We all pray he will come back alive! Mother has begged Papa to cut his losses and give the horse to Padrig Gwlwlwyd. My father is a good horseman. But he isn't as strong as he once was. He's not steady enough in the saddle for a dangerous horse like that. But he is a proud man. He doesn't want to admit that the horse is too much for him."

"Then I shall certainly keep my distance," said Percy. "Are Grey Tide and Red Rhud still the best choices for me?"

"That depends on what kind of mount you want."

"You know me—I'm a beginner, remember."

"Hardly!" rejoined Florilyn. "You can claim to be faster than me."

Even as she said the words, a flash of pain crossed Florilyn's face. "To answer your question, they are probably more reliable than ever. They are nine years old and not as fast as they once were but still the best two mounts in our stables. I think I will take out Crimson Sun."

"Who's that?"

"Red Rhud's foal. He's only a year and a half. We're still training him. But he is a gentle young stallion. I'll take him today, and he can get to know your voice and smell. Perhaps you can try him later."

"Sound's good. I'll stick with Grey Tide then."

Half an hour later, they left the grounds.

"Have you seen Harlech Castle?" asked Florilyn.

"No. North of here, isn't it?"

"Yes, about three or four miles. It's worth the ride."

They set out down the hill. Florilyn led along the main road, bypassing the village. They came in sight of what had for so long been the Barrie cottage, though neither mentioned it.

"How long will you be staying?" asked Florilyn as they clomped slowly along side by side. "Will you be here all summer?"

"You have no objection?" said Percy, a hint of fun returning to his tone.

"Goodness, no! I hope you do."

"Well that's good, because I still have a score to settle with you from five years ago."

"With me? What are you talking about?" Florilyn laughed.

"Our bet. . .on the race. . .that day on the beach. You *owe* me! The loser has to wait on the winner for a day."

"Hmm. . .I'd hoped you had forgotten that!" She smiled.

"I am simply biding my time, waiting for just the right moment to claim my winnings," rejoined Percy. "But to answer your question, I have no timetable. I have a good apprenticeship with a solicitor's firm in Aberdeen. Mr. Snyder, the man who's taken me under his wing, didn't want me to come south at all. I am supposed to be working for him right now. But I told him I had to take time to come to Wales again."

"He is expecting you back?"

Percy nodded. "But I gave no promises when that would be. There are things I wanted to settle before I return north."

"*Things?* About. . .what?"

"Just. . .things, you know. The future and all that. Sometimes you need to get away from your normal routine to put your life in perspective. I will graduate in a year. Then I plan to enter law school. There is much to consider."

"And after that?" probed Florilyn.

"I don't know—the practice of law, I suppose. I probably don't sound very enthusiastic. But I love law. It's fascinating to wrap your mind around all sides of a dilemma. But there are so many types of law. I haven't settled on an area of specialization yet. There are times I think nothing would be as rewarding as being a country solicitor in some small, out-of-the-way village where you would know everyone and be part of the community. You would have the chance to help people and be involved in their lives."

"Someplace like. . .Llanfryniog?" queried Florilyn.

"I suppose. Though I doubt the need for a solicitor's services is felt often enough in a village *this* small to make a poor lawyer much of a living." Percy chuckled. "But then I waver to the opposite extreme and think about the opportunities in a large city like Aberdeen or Edinburgh or Glasgow."

"I cannot imagine you as the big-city type." Florilyn smiled.

"I've been a city boy all my life except for my brief times here."

"Which is the real you?"

"Hmm. . .a good question. I'm not sure I know yet. Maybe that's one of those things I need to resolve. What about you?"

"What about me?"

"What are your plans?"

"You asked me that once before. I told you that women don't have plans. I am a country girl—I don't think there's any doubt about that. I once thought I would love the big city. London is exciting and vibrant and all that, but it's not for me. I could never live anywhere I couldn't ride for an hour without seeing another human being."

"I never took you for a loner."

Florilyn smiled. "I'm not sure that's the word I would use. I just like being out in the country, with nature all about me and with no sounds of bustle and activity."

They rode on in silence. In former years they would have been galloping and laughing and bantering and racing. On this day, however, their hearts were full of the thoughts that young men and young women often have who are not sure what the future holds. Theirs was an uncertain time in life. Adulthood beckoned, but the perplexities of youth remained. Those perplexities hung heavy on the hearts of the two cousins as they contemplated what lay ahead for them.

"I think a lot of you, Florilyn," said Percy at length. "I hope you know that."

"I think I do," replied Florilyn. "The feeling is mutual."

Again it was quiet. Both were thinking. Yet neither could divulge the full nature of their thoughts. The rest of the ride passed uneventfully.

Percy's mind was busier than he let on.

SEVENTY-FOUR

The Familiar Hills

*P*ercy's ride with Florilyn helped clarify his thoughts. It also added new complexities to his speculations.

There was much to think about, much to pray about. If ever he needed his father, that time was now. Unfortunately his father was three hundred miles away. Something also told him that the decision before him was one he needed to resolve on his own. If he was not sure enough to make up his own mind, then he was not sure *enough*. He had to be sure within *himself*.

He did not ride with Florilyn again for the rest of the week. He saw little of her. But he was watching. More and more, she filled his thoughts and prayers.

Roderick, Katherine, and Florilyn went to church on Sunday. Courtenay never accompanied them now. His aunt and uncle assumed Percy would go with them. But after comments he had heard in the village, Percy knew that sufficient speculation existed about his intentions toward his cousin without fueling it further by allowing half the town to see them together.

From his manner on their ride, Florilyn understood that it was time for her to wait. She accompanied her parents with a quiet, hopeful, patient heart.

Once they were on their way, Percy went to the stables, saddled Grey Tide, and set out northeastward into the Snowdonian hills. The moment he left the manor, he knew his destination.

Percy arrived at the overlook high above the translucent mountain lake an hour and a half later. At this place he had heard Gwyneth's wonderfully strange crooning voice beckoning to the animals that they could come to her without fear. He now knew the way down to the meadow as well. But he would never take that path again. The sights to which it led could be shared with only one person in the world.

Up here, however, this overlook was *his* private special place. Not even Gwyneth knew of that day he had watched her until the holiness of the moment had overwhelmed him.

This was another day like that one. Though Gwyneth would never know of it, his heart must again somehow connect with hers. He would give anything to know what she was thinking at this moment. The questions filling his mind were not merely about why she had left. She could not remain in Llanfryniog without her father and Grannie. Wherever they went, she would always go. They were her chief responsibility. He would never question that.

But why had there been no word to anyone? Not to Florilyn. . .no message left for him. Her leaving also left unanswered the nagging question why she had not met him on the promontory two years earlier. The unexpected turmoil of recent days left *too* much unanswered.

Why should he not be happy for Gwyneth? Whatever had taken place, wherever they had gone, Codnor Barrie would do nothing that was not for her best. He knew the man well enough to know that. According to Tilman Heygate, Gwyneth's future was the primary reason for the move. Perhaps they had inherited money from a distant relative.

Then why the mystery? Or had Codnor been offered a lucrative job elsewhere that would enable him to pay for further education for Gwyneth? Was it even possible that she had been betrothed to a man of means somewhere? Could *that* be the opportunity Barrie spoke of?

Whatever it was, how could he be sad for himself? Gwyneth was being given opportunities that Barrie could not have reason to expect from any other quarter. It was time for him to be *glad* for them, to rejoice for whatever future Gwyneth's father was now in a position to give her.

What, then, did this sudden change mean for him? Where did it leave his personal reasons for coming to Wales this summer? Had he become too anxious for God to reveal His will?

If Gwyneth was truly *gone*. . .forever. . .if he had no way to find her and would never see her again. . .what would she want him to do now? He could almost hear her voice as he recalled his previous visit: *"Miss Florilyn is expecting you to be her escort."*

At last the question that had been stirring and bubbling in the emotional confusion of his subconscious for days rose to the surface. The words were simple. But the implication was enormous: Would she want him to give his love to another? To one whom she herself loved as selflessly as he knew Gwyneth loved Florilyn?

Percy smiled. He knew the answer well enough. Gwyneth was so selfless, she would *never* think of herself. She would only think of him and those she loved. He knew beyond a doubt that he would have her blessing.

Could that perhaps be the reason she had not come to meet him at the promontory? Had she been trying to tell him two years ago that she knew Florilyn loved him and that ultimately he would have to choose between them? Had she been trying to make that choice easier for him even then?

And yet. . .he still had Florilyn's best to think of. Was it right. . .for *her*?

Percy had left Glasgow for Wales a week ago knowing that love beat in his heart. But was *love* the same as *affection*? And where did friendship between two young people fit into the kind of love that would last a lifetime? He had come here to find out the answers to such questions. But then immediately upon his arrival, so suddenly, circumstances had changed.

Pausing in his thoughts, Percy reflected on that word—*circumstances*. Was this an example of what his father so often said, that the Lord used circumstances to confirm His leading. . .occasionally even to *change* the direction of his leading?

"What are You trying to say to me, Lord?" Percy whispered aloud. "Are these *Your* circumstances speaking to me?"

Even his own soft voice seemed an intrusion upon the solemnity of the place where he sat.

Percy's thoughts filled with Florilyn. He knew that she loved him. Whether she was actually expecting a proposal he had no way of knowing. But if what Chandos said was universally known, she must have been *waiting* for one.

Could he love her as she deserved to be loved? Could he give her of his very best without a divided heart?

Then came a startling question: Were he and Florilyn being drawn together all along?

The question sent him into a new round of reflection. He had once told her he was proud of her. But it went far deeper than that. She had become a young woman of character. She had been a bratty girl during his first visit. She and Courtenay had been birds of a feather. But then who was *he* to be talking? He had been a bratty kid, too. He chuckled to himself at the thought.

It took a special kind of person, and genuine depth of character, to change. . .really *change*. Florilyn had done so. He admired her for it. He did not love her for that reason alone, but that depth of character certainly deepened his regard for her.

He had changed. Florilyn had changed. Perhaps *they* were now birds of a feather. . .a young man and young woman who had been on the same spiritual journey all along. Was it perhaps even a journey, because she had always been good, in some strange way, that it was *impossible* for Gwyneth fully to share?

Had he and Florilyn been meant for one another from the beginning? If God was indeed leading them together, could he trust Him, even trust Him for himself, that he *could* be the best for Florilyn? To accept God's leading also implied trusting Him enough to follow that leading.

Over the next few days, Percy continued to walk and ride alone. He visited many of his old haunts. He walked the hills praying and contemplating the future.

Over the coming days the sense—was it the divine nudging?— slowly grew on him that the answer to the big question was *yes*. He had come seeking resolution. Even more. . .a life companion. It seemed that God had now given him the answer he had been praying for.

After another week, he knew it was time to talk to Florilyn. This time about their future together.

SEVENTY-FIVE

Florilyn

By the sound of the knock, Florilyn knew who it was. She went to the door. There stood Percy. His look was unlike any expression she had seen on his countenance. He looked embarrassed, almost bashful.

"I need to talk to you, Florilyn," he said, glancing down at the floor. "I would *like* to talk to you, I should say. . .if you have time. . .or should I come back—"

"Goodness, no. Of course I have time, Percy."

He waited in the corridor.

She dashed into the room a moment then joined him and closed the door behind her.

They walked downstairs and left the house. It was silent for some time.

Percy led the way toward the garden. He was uncharacteristically agitated.

Florilyn waited.

"You have really changed, Florilyn," he said. "You are a different person than when I first came."

"You know why, don't you, Percy?" she asked softly.

"I suppose you grew up and began to see things differently. We all did. Remember what a jerk I was that first summer?"

"You were never a jerk, Percy."

"I made a pretty good impression of one! Maybe I should just say that I had a lot of growing up to do. So I changed, too. But so did you, and I am impressed and proud of you."

"You said that to me once before," rejoined Florilyn. "I wasn't quite sure what to think. I do now. . .at least I think so. It makes me happy to know you feel that way about me." Florilyn paused. "There's more to the changes in me than just being twenty now," she went on after a moment. "It's because of you, Percy. *You* helped me see things. You helped me grow up. You helped me see myself and helped me grow into someone better. Everything you told me about your father. . .that's how you have been to me. I learned to trust you in the same way that you trust your father."

"That is high praise," said Percy. His voice was soft and thoughtful. "That is a remarkable thing for one person to say to another."

"I mean every word."

"I know you do. That's what makes it remarkable. Thank you."

They walked on, descending more deeply into the depths of the garden. As they spoke softly together, Percy shared what was on his heart and the decision he had come to, which was to ask her to be his wife.

Florilyn's heart swelled. Slowly her eyes began to fill. "Do you really mean it, Percy?" she said.

He looked at her and smiled. "Of course I mean it."

"Oh, Percy," she said softly, her voice full of the tears that were flowing from her eyes, "you have made me the happiest girl in the world." She slipped her hand through his arm, and they continued to walk slowly through the garden.

"There is a question I have to ask, Percy," said Florilyn as they returned in the direction of the house some time later.

He waited.

"What about Gwyneth?"

Percy drew in a long sigh. "Nothing gets past you," he said with a smile.

"I know you loved her. At first I didn't realize it. But I grew to know it as I grew to love her, too."

"It's no secret," said Percy. "I loved you both. I love you for how you changed and for who you have become. I loved her with a sort of deep gratitude for helping me learn to see God. But I believe the circumstances as they developed were God's way of leading you and me together."

"Like what you told me your father talks about."

Percy nodded. Slowly a smile spread over his face. "Have I ever told you how I once wondered if Gwyneth was an angel?" he asked.

"No!" said Florilyn. "An *angel*?"

"I really did, at first. She was so different, so otherworldly. She would appear when you least expected it. And she helped me to change—like you said that I helped you."

Florilyn listened as Percy went on.

"Now I am wondering," he said. "I know it sounds crazy, but with her disappearing like this, maybe she really *was* an angel, sent in some strange way to lead us together. Then when her job was over, she left us."

"You don't *really* think so?"

"I don't know." Percy chuckled. "But it's a nice thought."

"She helped teach us *both* about God." Florilyn nodded. "That's what angels do, isn't it?"

"And about each other as well," agreed Percy. "I wonder if we would have come together without her. She will always be part of us."

"My only regret is that she cannot be at our wedding. I wish she could stand beside me. I will never forget her."

⚬☙⚬

Later that afternoon, a knock came on the viscount's door.

"Might I talk to you, Uncle Roderick?" said Percy when his uncle opened the door. "There is a personal matter I would like to discuss and an important question I need to ask you."

"Certainly, Percy, my boy! Come in and sit down. Was that you and

Florilyn I saw in the garden earlier?"

"Yes, sir. Actually that is what I would like to talk to you about." He closed the door behind him and took a seat with his uncle.

They remained in close conference for thirty minutes.

Feeling as if a great weight had been lifted from his shoulders, on the following morning Percy rode into Llanfryniog. He was in high spirits. At last he was ready to walk the streets and lanes and visit in the shops and walk to the harbor and beach. He was astonished to find people looking at him differently.

He was puzzled by the smiles until one woman stopped as he approached and extended her hand. "I hear congratulations are in order, Mr. Percy," she said. "May I offer my hand and wish you and Miss Florilyn all the best."

Percy shook her hand. "Does word really spread so fast?" He laughed. "All this only happened yesterday."

"The whole village knows, Mr. Percy," said the woman. "It doesn't take long for this kind of news to pass along. Good day to you, sir."

Percy watched her amble off, still amazed by the exchange. He didn't even know the woman's name, but she seemed to know everything about him.

SEVENTY-SIX

Joy Comes to the Manor

*T*hough some might have attributed his ebullient spirits to the relief of a father having a daughter off his hands, the viscount's joy went far deeper. He knew that Florilyn was engaged to a worthy young man whom he already loved as a son. His was a double portion of happiness.

Katherine's spirits and those of the entire staff of Westbrooke Manor were equally celebratory.

Stevie Muir had not been to work for two days. When he next appeared, therefore, he had heard nothing. Word of the engagement was the first news out of Hollin Radnor's mouth. Immediately Stevie went in search of Percy.

He encountered Florilyn on his way toward the house. "Miss Florilyn," he said excitedly, "I just heard the news about you and Percy. Congratulations!"

"Thank you, Stevie. I am very happy."

"You deserve it, Miss Florilyn."

She looked at him with a puzzled expression. "I don't. . . . How do you mean?" she said.

"Just that you are a young lady of quality and character," replied Stevie.

"What a nice thing to say!"

"I have been watching you for years. I have come to have great admiration for you. Not many girls in your position—from wealth and privilege, you know—not many grow to be the kind of young lady you have become. I know your parents are proud of you. You deserve a fine man like Percy. And he is lucky to have someone like you."

"Thank you, Stevie. No one has ever said something like that to me before except Percy."

"I mean it. I am happy for you both." Stevie continued in search of Percy.

Florilyn stared after him a moment with an odd expression. She had never paid much attention to Stevie Muir before. There was obviously more to him than met the eye.

"Percy, my boy," said the viscount as he and Percy walked down the main staircase together, "and at last I can legitimately call you that, eh!—how about father and prospective bridegroom going for a ride together? We need to talk about your future, yours and mine and my daughter's."

"I would like that, Uncle Roderick."

"That brings up another point of protocol to be decided. What will you call me after you are my son-in-law? Bit of a perplexity, what?"

"I'm sure we will be able to come to an amenable solution, *Uncle* Roderick!" laughed Percy.

They met Stevie in the entryway.

"Hello, Lord Snowdon," he said. "Percy, I was on my way to find you and offer my congratulations. I only heard this morning."

"Thank you, Stevie," smiled Percy as the two friends shook hands.

The three continued outside toward the stables.

"Stevie, my good man, Percy and I fancy a ride today. Saddle me the black demon. What is your fancy, Percy, my boy?"

"Red Rhud, I think," replied Percy. "But are you sure the stallion is wise, Uncle Roderick? Florilyn tells me he's dangerous."

"Bah! Women's talk. I can master any horse. I am in such high spirits I am ready to take on the world. You have made me a happy man, Percy, my boy."

Percy glanced toward Stevie with concern. Stevie's face registered the same anxiety. He was well acquainted with the dangerous temperament of the stallion.

But the viscount was insistent. Stevie therefore set about saddling him, while keeping a wary eye on the beast's eyes and ears.

SEVENTY-SEVEN

The River between the Ridges

*P*ercy and Lord Snowdon left the grounds eastward. Without intending it but with little choice, Percy's uncle led out at a reckless pace. The stallion had not been aired for days and was fierce with energy. It was all Percy could do to keep up.

This was his first ride this summer on Red Rhud's back. As he had noticed with Grey Tide, she had lost a step from previous visits. He was not able to draw alongside his uncle until they were a mile from the manor and the stallion's initial burst of fiery energy was somewhat dissipated.

"That is some spunky animal!" shouted Percy as he tried to catch up.

"A noble beast," rejoined his uncle over his shoulder. "As soon as I have the chance, I hope to race him in Manchester."

"Who will ride him?"

"I'll get someone. Maybe Courtenay. He can handle him."

"Are you sure racing a horse like that is a good idea?"

"Have you been talking to my wife and daughter?" laughed Westbrooke. "Horse racing is a man's business, Percy, my boy. You can't make money without risk. Perhaps we shall be partners."

As Percy at last drew even, the stallion Demon suddenly lurched sideways and snapped with great sharp teeth at Red Rhud's neck.

Percy swerved to the right with a startled cry, nearly toppling out of the saddle.

"Now I am sure that racing that animal is not a good idea."

"Nonsense, Percy, my boy!" rejoined the viscount. "Spirit, that's what's wanted in a champion thoroughbred. This Demon has it, and to spare. He is full of energy, that's all. He needs to be given the rein, the freedom to run. Let him go at top speed, and he is as easy to handle as any of my wife's mares."

With the words he dug in his heels and did just as he said, and again gave Demon the rein. Horse and rider shot off with a speed marvelous to behold had Percy not been terrified for his uncle's life.

Again he urged Red Rhud on as fast as he dared. But it was not enough to keep pace with his uncle. In spite of the lessons Gwyneth had given him, he was still not completely confident as a horseman. Within moments his uncle was out of sight.

Percy continued up the incline. As he crested the ridge, he gazed frantically for any sign of him. Halfway down the opposite slope far ahead, the black maniacal creature was tearing up great clods. His uncle appeared out of control, jostling about in the saddle.

In the distance, the stallion suddenly stopped abruptly and reared. As far away as he was, Percy heard great whinnying cries. They were not horse sounds of fright but of wrath. Percy galloped on.

His uncle had taken out his riding whip and was shouting and wielding it freely. In the contest of wills between man and enraged beast, however, the whip was not a wise instrument of mediation.

Suddenly Demon reared again and rose nearly erect. He was clearly trying to unseat his rider. His front hooves pawed violently at the air. The viscount only barely held to the saddle.

Demon crashed down on his forelegs, jumping and bucking wildly. Then without warning he broke into another furious gallop. Percy had still not reached them when the two receded again into the distance.

At the bottom of the valley between the two ridges flowed a small river, hardly worthy of the name but of more size than a mere stream.

It wound through a rocky channel of uneven terrain strewn with rocks of many sizes and some large boulders. It was a much different course than that of the stream through Gwyneth's special meadow. It was no place for a wild horse.

But there was no stopping Demon now. Some four hundred yards ahead, he reached the water and launched himself into the air.

Percy heard a great cry. A moment later he saw the black stallion flying up the hill on the opposite side of the river.

No rider was in the saddle.

He shouted to Red Rhud and hurried toward the scene. Gradually he slowed as the footing became treacherous. Reaching the stream, Percy reined in, jumped to the ground, and sloshed through the water.

He found his uncle lying motionless on the far side.

He ran to him and knelt down. A nasty gash was visible on the top of his head where he had crashed into a rock. Wet blood from it flowed into his hair. His hat was yards away. A huge welt rose from his skull.

"Ah, Percy, my boy," he said weakly, gasping for breath. "The brute threw me. You were right. . .a dangerous creature. I was a fool to think—"

"Just rest easy, Uncle Roderick," said Percy. "Don't try to talk. I saw the whole thing. The horse went wild."

"I can't. I'm cold, Percy, my boy."

Percy flung his riding jacket from him and laid it over his uncle's chest. The viscount's legs from the knees down lay wet in the streambed.

"I can't feel my legs, Percy, my boy. . .don't think I can ride. . .if that confounded horse. . .could ride back together. . .but I. . .don't think I have the strength. . .to climb up."

"Don't worry, Uncle Roderick," said Percy. "I'll ride back to the manor. We'll bring a cart. You just rest."

"Sorry to be a bother. . .Percy. . .my boy."

"Think nothing of it, Uncle Roderick."

Percy saw that he had begun to shiver. He yanked off his shirt and laid it under the jacket. He then splashed back through the water where Red Rhud waited patiently, mounted quickly, and galloped bare-chested in the direction of the manor.

There was no sign of Demon anywhere.

SEVENTY-EIGHT

The Ambulance Cart

*P*ercy galloped recklessly into the grounds shouting for Stevie and Hollin. By the time they had a small flatbed cart hitched to one of the sturdier horses and Percy had run inside for another shirt and jacket, the commotion had emptied the house with word that their master had had a serious fall.

"Where is he, Percy?" asked Florilyn as Percy mounted Red Rhud.

"Where the river runs through the valley, between the ridges on the path we took three days ago, you know, where the ford is so rocky."

"What where you doing there?"

"I'm not sure your uncle intended it. Demon was out of control."

"We'll be right behind you," said Katherine. She and Florilyn ran to the stables to saddle two more horses.

Seconds later Percy was flying eastward away from the manor. Stevie knew the place exactly from Percy's description. He and Hollin followed with the cart.

By the time Katherine and Florilyn arrived, Percy was seated beside the viscount. There was little he could do. His uncle was barely conscious.

The cart was only ten minutes behind, bumping down the rocks. They pulled it through the water then set about lifting the viscount onto it.

"Gently, gently!" exhorted Stevie. "Hollin, you and Percy lift by each shoulder. Lady Katherine and Lady Florilyn, you lift at his waist. I fear his right leg is broken. We must keep him flat."

Katherine's face had gone as pale as her husband's when she saw him lying broken among the rocks. "Will he. . . What do you think, Steven?" she asked.

"I cannot say, Lady Katherine," replied Stevie. "His head has been injured. We must get him to Dr. Rotherham with all the haste we dare."

The others stood by to follow Stevie's orders. None questioned his taking charge.

Katherine hesitated then knelt close to the viscount's face. It was ghostly white. "Oh, Roderick. . .Roderick," she said softly. "Be brave. . . be strong. We will get you home." She bent forward and kissed him.

His lips quivered and his eyelids fluttered. But he was unable to speak.

"Oh, dear Roderick—"

"Please, Lady Katherine," urged Stevie. "We must delay no longer." She stood.

"Place your hands under his waist, Lady Katherine," said Stevie, "just as Lady Florilyn is doing."

How much help she could provide in her condition was doubtful.

When he was in position beside the viscount's legs, Stevie nodded to the other two men. "All right, then," he said, "everyone lift. . .slowly, gently. . ."

He was not so heavy for five of them. But being dead weight and limp as a wet rag, he made an exceedingly awkward burden. A groan sounded from the viscount's mouth as they lifted him. They managed to get him high enough to lie on the blankets and pillows they had gathered to cushion the bed of the cart.

Even under the best of conditions, without a road, it would not be a comfortable ride. They had to bump their way over open fields, up and down the ridge, through woodland and across several streams. It took considerably longer than Stevie would have liked. But he chose to err on the side of caution and not add to the viscount's injuries.

Meanwhile, Katherine and Florilyn rode ahead. Florilyn galloped straight to town. Luckily she found Dr. Rotherham at home.

Katherine went on to the manor to prepare a sickroom on the ground floor. By the time the ambulance cart bearing her husband arrived, she had recovered from her initial shock and was again the strong matron of her home.

A bed was ready and a blazing fire roared in the hearth. Dry clothes were waiting. The entire staff was gathered at Katherine's side, anxious and ready to obey the slightest command. Florilyn and Dr. Rotherham had arrived only minutes before the cart clattered into the entryway.

Everyone ran outside. They looked on as Dr. Rotherham now took charge. With the men, he helped get the viscount, completely unconscious, inside and to bed. After giving what instructions were necessary, Dr. Rotherham left the manor to return to his surgery for the required supplies and tools to set the leg.

The bedside vigil began.

SEVENTY-NINE

At the Bedside

*I*n spite of his distant manner, the viscount was loved by his staff. His tenderness toward Katherine of late had had its effect on his overall demeanor.

The increase of smiles and kind words had spread among the rest of them as well. He grew appreciative of little things. He became free in expressing his gratitude, even plucked an occasional rose from the garden for Mrs. Drynwydd or Mrs. Llewellyn. This caused the two women to blush and babble a good deal but warmed their hearts more than the viscount ever knew. The accident, therefore, cast a cloud of gloom over the house.

Word quickly spread through Llanfryniog. The pall of hushed voices and tiptoed step extended throughout the whole village. On the following Sunday, prayers in all three churches were heavy of heart on the viscount's behalf.

All that day Kyvwlch Gwarthegydd's hammer was silent. The blacksmith would never have called the thoughts rising from his mind *prayers*. But God's heart is more open-minded than man's. He received the good man's compassion for the viscount and his family into His eternal bosom, nonetheless that the man denied His existence. God is the Father of Christians and atheists alike, though only the former get the full benefit of that Fatherhood by acknowledging their childness. But Gwarthegydd was *concerned*, and in his own way his unacknowledged Father in heaven received that concern on the viscount's behalf.

Dr. Rotherham set the leg but doubted, even if the patient recovered, whether it would ever be much use again. He was far more worried about the injury to the head and neck. The extremeties continued cold, the broken leg like a chunk of ice. He knew what dreadful danger that fact portended. There was little to be done but wait and see how rapidly and how far recovery spread through the viscount's body.

Courtenay, who had been away a few days, returned and was civil and courteous to all. He seemed genuinely shaken by the turn of events. He was horseman enough to know how dangerous a fall such as his father had taken could be. He was also perceptive enough to read on the doctor's face what he was not saying. Courtenay still knew nothing about how matters stood between Percy and his sister.

Eventually the murderer Demon wandered back to the manor. Hunger had somewhat quieted him, and Stevie was able to secure and return him to the stables. He immediately sought Katherine with his recommendation that the beast either be sold or put down. "You can never reform a bad-tempered horse," said Stevie. "If you are in agreement, with your permission, I would like to talk to Padrig Gwlwlwyd to see if he might have use for him. If he does, how much would you want for him, Lady Katherine?"

"If he wants him, Steven," she replied, "he may have him. I want nothing for him. I don't want a dangerous animal like that on my conscience. I would give him to Mr. Gwlwlwyd only on the condition that he never put the animal into the hands of one whom he might harm."

"A wise stipulation, Lady Katherine," Stevie nodded. "If Padrig does not think he can be reformed, I will put him down."

"Thank you, Steven."

Hearing of his mother's decision, Courtenay was furious. His anger stemmed not so much from the fact that the horse would be lost to him but that his mother had consulted Stevie Muir instead of him.

Hours went by and turned into days. Though the viscount did not regain consciousness, he was never alone. Someone sat at the bedside around the clock. Dr. Rotherham came every morning to see if there had been a change.

When the viscount awoke on the sixth day, Courtenay rode immediately for Llanfryniog and returned with the doctor. Great was the rejoicing of the entire community.

Though he kept his concerns to himself, Dr. Rotherham knew the joyous mood to be premature. Though the viscount appeared to have some of his strength back, circulation remained poor. The extremities were not warming as they should. The left leg was as numb to a poke of the needle as the right.

To Courtenay's great annoyance, as often as he was awake, his father seemed more to desire Percy near him than his own flesh and blood. In truth, the sickroom made Courtenay uncomfortable, and he was only too happy to yield his place. Nor did he feel any great filial affection toward his father. But the idea that Percy was so close to him rekindled his former antagonism toward his cousin.

At last Dr. Rotherham's professional ethics demanded that he tell someone what he feared. He shrank from making a full revelation to Lady Snowdon for fear of an emotional reaction that would ripple through the house and do no one any good. To tell the children and not the wife would hardly do. In the end, he realized he had no alternative but to speak to the viscount himself.

He went into the sick chamber, requested of Lady Florilyn that he be left alone for a few minutes with the patient, closed the door behind her, and then sat down in the chair beside the bed.

"Come to deliver the bad news in person, eh, doctor?" said the viscount, attempting with humor to mask his concern. He had seen the look on Rotherham's face the moment he entered.

"You are not so far wrong, Lord Snowdon," replied the doctor. "I would be remiss not to disclose the nature of your injuries to someone.

I hesitate to speak frankly with your wife. I am here to ask your will in the matter. Would you like your wife and son and daughter present?"

"Present for what?"

"For what I have to say."

"No, confound you," snapped the viscount, fear overpowering courtesy. "Just say it."

"You are certain you wouldn't like your family—"

"No, blast you—get on with it!"

The doctor sat patiently until the viscount calmed.

"Your leg is not recovering as I had hoped," said Rotherham after a few moments.

"Nonsense. I feel fine. Merely a little faintness."

"Your right leg is broken below the knee," Rotherham went on, ignoring the viscount's protestations. "The injury to both knee and leg are so severe it is unlikely you will walk normally again. Though I cannot be absolutely certain at this point, it may be that amputation will be necessary to save your life."

At the word, the viscount turned his face to the wall. The positive horror of the thought filled him with such dread that he was trembling like a child.

"I am yet more concerned about the injury to your head and neck, Lord Snowdon," Dr. Rotherham went on. "Your left leg, though to all appearances sound, does not respond to stimulation. I fear paralysis."

"Is there nothing you can do?"

"I fear not, my lord."

"Am I dying, then?"

"Absent a miracle from on high, sir, I fear. . ."

"Confounded doctors—can't give a man a straight answer," growled the viscount. "Blackguards, all of you! I'm dying—why can't you just say it? I'm man enough to take it. No one lives forever."

Again Dr. Rotherham waited. "What would you like me to do, my lord?" he asked at length.

"About what?" said the viscount testily.

"Your leg."

"Pooh—don't think I am going to give you leave to saw the thing off!" said the viscount, trembling again at the thought. "Where's the use if it's not going to save me? Let my head recover, and we'll talk about it then."

"By then it may be too late."

"Then it will be too late and the consequences will be mine!" cried the viscount.

"Would you like me to discuss the matter with your wife?" asked the doctor calmly.

"Good heavens, no! The poor woman would wither and go to pieces at the very idea." The viscount paused and grew serious. "There is one thing you can do for me, doctor," he said at length.

"Anything, my lord."

"Is there anyone you can trust, who can hold his tongue? If you could get a message to Porthmadog, a telegram or send someone to fetch my solicitor here—Murray is his name."

"I know the man. Yes, I could arrange it."

"Good. I would appreciate it. Thank you, doctor."

Dr. Rotherham left the room.

Florilyn returned. "Is everything all right, Daddy?" she said.

"Yes, yes, of course. Everything's fine."

She knew from his tone that he was lying. But she did not press it.

Her father closed his eyes and pretended to doze. Suddenly there was little time to put right what he had neglected for too many years. He had tried to make some amends a few months ago. Now suddenly the past returned upon him with renewed pangs of guilt.

But what could he do? How could it be managed? Whom could he trust?

He had tried to keep from hurting Katherine. Now he wondered if he had done the right thing. So long lethargic and drowsy, his conscience was coming awake. And it stung him.

Mr. Murray arrived the following afternoon. He presented himself and asked to see viscount Lord Snowdon.

Broakes vaguely recognized the man but asked whom should he say was calling.

"Lord Snowdon's solicitor, Hamilton Murray," the man replied.

It did not take long thereafter for word to circulate through the house, supplied with minor emendations by Broakes, that the viscount was closeted with his solicitor for the purpose of changing his will.

When the rumor reached Lady Katherine's ears not many minutes later, she put an immediate stop to it. "Don't be absurd, Mrs. Drynwydd," she said, walking into the kitchen and overhearing what had not been intended for her ears. "The disposition of the estate and Westbrooke Manor is decreed by the terms of the original grant of land centuries ago. The title goes with the manor to the eldest child. My husband could not change those terms if he wanted to. I can tell you of a certainty that he is not writing a new will."

Despite her strong words, Katherine left the kitchen shaken. She paused in the corridor, light-headed, and took two or three deep breaths to steady herself. She then hurried directly to the sick chamber. She found her husband and Mr. Murray alone.

"Ah, Katherine," said the viscount weakly, "you remember Mr. Murray?"

"Yes. . .of course."

"Hello again, Lady Snowdon," said the solicitor, extending his hand.

Katherine shook it but went straight to the bedside. "What is this all about, Roderick?" she asked.

"A mere formality, my dear," he answered. "It is only a precaution. I am having Mr. Murray draw up a document—just in case—naming you trustee of the estate until Courtenay is twenty-five. You remember the terms—he will not inherit until his twenty-fifth birthday. But should I. . .that is, in the unlikely event. . .that is, should something happen before that time. . .it is one of the ambiguities of the terms of the inheritance. I never bothered with it before now. But I want you protected. . .just in case."

"I see. Of course. That makes perfect sense. Well then," she said, turning to go, "I will. . .uh, leave the two of you—"

"No, please stay, Katherine," said the viscount. "This concerns you as well as me. I simply did not want to upset you. As long as you are here. . . please stay."

EIGHTY

Eternal Uncertainties

*T*emporarily at his ease for having legalized Katherine's trustee-ship over the estate, the viscount rested comfortably for the remainder of the day. He even seemed slightly improved.

The next morning, during Courtenay's brief daily visit to the sick chamber, his father motioned for him to sit down beside him. "So, Courtenay, lad," said the viscount, "you ought to, uh. . .know the state of affairs. They don't give me much hope, you see. . ."

Courtenay listened in silence. He was uncomfortable.

"It will soon be in your hands, you know," his father went on. "You know, I believe, how things stand. . .you will inherit when you are twenty-five. That time will be here before you know it. Only don't make the same mistakes I did, you know. . .foolishness of youth and all that. Keep a good head on your shoulders. . .take care of your mother and sister. . ."

Courtenay nodded and mumbled a few words of consent. But tenderness had never been a virtue that had existed between them. Neither father nor son knew how to call upon it when it was needed the most.

They spoke stiffly and haltingly for two or three minutes more. At length the viscount confessed himself fatigued and needing a rest, at which time Courtenay left him.

The interview with the solicitor Murray had at last awakened Katherine to the dire nature of her husband's condition. Though he tried to put an optimistic face on it for her sake, she knew that *he* considered the affidavit more than a precautionary measure. He thought he was dying and was certain that the trusteeship would be enforced. . .and soon.

Now the stark reality of the thing began to overwhelm her. Her father was a free thinker and had taught her and her brother Edward to trust more in God than in the doctrines of men. Nevertheless, Katherine could not prevent the natural anxiety of the pervasive judgmental mind-set so prevalent in the mildewed air of the church from filling her with a vague sense of dread.

Regular church attendance notwithstanding, Roderick had never been a spiritual man. She now began to fear for his soul. Despite her upbringing, despite her brother's influence, and despite the gentle whisperings of an eternally loving fatherhood from the pen of the prophet MacDonald, the terrible burden of the wrath of God began to fill her with horrifying images of flames and her poor Roderick in the midst of them.

When Reverend Ramsey came to call, in response to her expressed concern conveyed by the confidential note she had asked Percy to deliver, the viscount more than half suspected who had put him up to it. He grumbled a good deal about having to entertain a parson at a time like this. But he consented to the interview.

It was a formal, strained, almost businesslike affair. Though Fatherhood was the only side of God's nature capable of offering a hopeful glimpse of eternity, in truth Reverend Ramsey knew as little about the fatherhood of God as did Roderick Westbrooke. Ramsey exited the room after thirty minutes with the viscount's soul unchanged. He offered Katherine a few platitudes then left the manor with a sigh of relief. Consoling the dying and grieving was the part of his job he hated most.

Meanwhile, in the sick chamber, the clerical visit had at least served the purpose of turning Roderick Westbrooke's eyes inward, where all have to look eventually. The fact that the fellow Ramsey had had no more spiritual food to offer him at the deathbed than he did from the pulpit only made the viscount hunger the more for one who might possibly be able to tell him where he stood with God. Not that it would do him much good, he thought, but he would like to have some idea what to expect when he went to sleep for the last time and woke up somewhere *else*.

He had always looked down on the fellow, but he would give a thousand pounds right now for twenty minutes with Katherine's brother, Edward Drummond, or her father for that matter. There were two men who seemed to know something about God that had escaped the rest of the cloth. What did they teach ministers in their seminaries anyway? The fool Ramsey was useless.

Unfortunately, he did not have a thousand pounds. And Edward was hundreds of miles away!

I wonder how much the son has gleaned from the father, he thought to himself.

When Katherine again appeared after seeing Reverend Ramsey to the door, her husband asked her to send Percy to see him.

EIGHTY-ONE

High Questions

*A*h, Percy, my boy!" said the viscount when his nephew entered. "Come in, sit down, and offer some comfort to your uncle." His voice was weak and resigned, though surprisingly cheerful.

Percy had been in and out of the sickroom almost constantly since the accident. But he immediately sensed a change. He knew of neither the solicitor's visit nor the minister's. But he could tell something was different. He sat down beside the bedside.

"They tell me I am dying, Percy," said the viscount.

The bluntness of the statement stung Percy afresh. He was still a young man, not so well acquainted as his father with the cruel vicissitudes of life. "I am sorry, Uncle Roderick," he said.

"Ah, well, part of life they say, what?"

"I, uh. . . How long does the doctor think it will be?" asked Percy tentatively.

"Bah, who knows. You know what bunglers doctors are—can't save a man but won't give him a straight answer."

"And. . .there's nothing they can do?"

"The man wants to whack off my leg. Then he tells me my other is paralyzed, so what's the use? I'll never walk again with or without legs. Then he has the infernal cheek to tell me the problem is my

451

head. . .something about the spine, whatever that's got to do with it. Can't make up his mind. No wonder he's got no cure for what ails a man. Tell me, Percy, my boy, do you believe in heaven?"

The abruptness of the question took Percy off guard. "Uh, yes. . .yes, I do, Uncle Roderick," he said.

"I recall our first dinner together, when my daughter was baiting you. You were uncertain."

"I've grown stronger in my beliefs these last five years."

"Ah, well. . .good for you. Back then we were discussing the eternal destination of the old salt found on the beach. Now it's my turn, eh? So what do you think, now that you are five years older, Percy—will I go to heaven?"

"I don't know, Uncle Roderick. You really, uh. . .ought to be talking to my dad."

"Your father's not here."

"Isn't there someone. . .your minister in town that you would rather—"

"Bah, what he knows about God wouldn't fit through the eye of a needle, as the old saying goes. You've shown yourself a young man whom I respect, Percy, my boy. I want to know what *you* think. It wouldn't surprise me if you told me just what your father would anyway. So I ask you again, do *you* think I will go to heaven?"

"All right then, I would still say I don't know. I don't really know how you and God stand with one another."

"I've been a faithful churchman all my life. Does that count for anything?"

"No, I don't think it does."

"What does, then?"

"How you and God stand with one another. Whether you have made yourself His child."

"What do you mean by that? He's God the Father, isn't He? That includes everyone."

"Indeed. But have you made Him *your* Father?"

"You're talking in circles, Percy, my boy."

"I would never do that with you, Uncle Roderick."

"Then what in blazes do you mean?"

"That even though God is our Father, we must become His children. That is not something that happens in church."

"An incredible statement coming from a vicar's son."

"I learned it from my father. I *do* know that to be something he would say to you."

"What? Your father preaches that people don't have to go to church?"

"I didn't say that, Uncle Roderick. Of course my father wants people to go to church. But when they do, he tells them that it is not in church that they become God's children."

"Where is it then?"

"In their hearts."

"Ah, yes. . .well, there is that of course."

"It is a truth not widely preached. Again, those are my father's very words."

"So, Percy, my boy, do you think I will wake up in *hell*, then, when all this is over?"

"I could not say, Uncle Roderick. I would not presume to speak for God."

"Then I repeat. . .I merely ask your opinion."

"Then I would say the same thing I did before—that I am not personally aware how things stand between you and God."

"That's everything to you, then, is it—how a man stands with God?"

"Yes, that is everything."

"Even I don't know how I stand with Him. There are things in my past that hang heavy upon me, Percy, my boy. How am I to know what God thinks of it all?"

"I am certain of one thing—that He is a good Father," rejoined Percy, "and that He will forgive anything He is able to forgive. I know I am young, and I have little right to speak of such high truths. But there are things in my past that weigh upon my conscience, too."

"What regrets could a young fellow like you possibly have?" asked the viscount, not pausing to consider that the actions harrying his memory at present had been committed when he was younger than Percy.

"The regret of foolishness and youthful hubris, Uncle Roderick," replied Percy. "For years I did not recognize my father's wisdom. I treated him contemptibly. I will feel the pangs of that stupidity all my life."

"All young people are immature. Can't be too hard on yourself, Percy, my boy."

"The young may be immature. I'm sure I still am in many ways. But that is no excuse for willful blindness. Young people *choose* their rebellious attitudes just as I chose mine. They are not a mere part of youth that cannot be avoided. Therefore, I am responsible for my rebellious attitudes. But though my father has forgiven me, the most difficult part is forgiving myself. When I asked my father to forgive me, he said, 'You have always been forgiven. The forgiveness has existed within my heart all along.' That wonderful expression of love has been with me ever since. The forgiveness of my father's heart strengthens me to believe in God's forgiveness. I know God is saying the same to you at this moment. I truly believe those are God's words to you...right now."

"That would be a remarkable thing...if you are right."

"I believe it with all my heart. I believe that God is more forgiving toward us than most of us are toward ourselves. Then my father added these words, which maybe God says to us as well. He said, 'To complete the transaction, it was necessary for you to ask, that I might give it to you.'"

The viscount was silent for several long minutes. "What should I do, then," he said at length, "now that I am lying on my deathbed? What should I do now that it is nearly too late?"

"It is never too late."

"It is jolly well close to it if one is dying. So what is a man to do?"

"The same thing that God wants us to do every day of our lives.

Facing death changes nothing. It is no different for you at this moment than it is for me."

"What should I do, then?" repeated the viscount.

"Repent of your sins, and be His child."

The words seemed to jolt him, as if Percy had dashed him in the face with a cup of cold water. They bit deep into the long-repressed guilt that had been gnawing away at his conscience.

"*Child.* . .child, you say. Repent of my sins," he added softly. "If you only knew. . .not so easy as you think when there are others involved. I tried to find her, but she was gone, I tell you. Makes repentance dashed difficult, I dare say."

"Repentance is always possible."

"But what of the *child.* . .? It's too late for all that. So tell me, Percy," said his uncle, coming suddenly out of his mental wanderings, "what do you think of my daughter? She is my child, too, you know."

"I love her, Uncle Roderick."

"I am glad to hear it. I know you will take good care of her."

"I will."

"You will not let. . .that is to say, whatever happens. . .if she should. . . of course, her mother's money would still go to her, along with Courtenay, of course. . .but you would protect her? You would keep her from being hurt?"

"Of course. I will take care of her, Uncle Roderick. You may be assured of that."

The viscount paused. He thought for a long time. "There is another matter. . .of some delicacy, Percy, my boy," he resumed after a long silence. "I need to tell someone. You're right. It is not too late. Too late for *me*, I dare say, but perhaps not for you. You are a solicitor now, I understand."

"No, Uncle Roderick. I am merely studying toward that end."

"Perhaps it will be good enough. If I were to tell you something, would you be bound by confidentiality, a bit like the confessional, I dare say?"

"If you imposed it upon me, yes, I would honor your request."

"Well, it may be a little of the solicitor and priest together," said the viscount. "A confession and a legal document all rolled into one, eh? And here you are, a vicar's son and a future solicitor—I say you will do nicely, Percy, my boy. The perfect lawyer-priest. Go fetch paper and whatever else you need. I want you to take down a statement. Say nothing to anyone. Breathe not a word of it. Now go—get back here as soon as you can."

EIGHTY-TWO

Percy's Commission

*L*ess than five minutes had elapsed when Percy reentered the sick chamber. During that time, the viscount continued to relive much that had remained buried for decades. Percy's words had stung him with the necessity to set right what had remained unresolved from long before.

"Ah, good. . .back so soon?" he said. "You can use that writing desk over there. Is the door closed? You told no one what I asked you to do?"

"I hurried to my room and back without encountering a soul, Uncle Roderick."

"Then sit down. I will dictate. This will be a legal affidavit, will it not?"

"If you sign it, I would assume so," replied Percy. "But are you sure you wouldn't rather have your own solicitor—"

"I want you, Percy. I know I can trust you. This matter may have widespread consequences after I am gone. There is something I need you to do for me. Everything hinges on whether you are successful or not. . .someone I need you to find. But *if* you cannot find her, this need never come out. I am loath to hurt Katherine. But even if it comes late, one must do one's duty. That's part of repentance, is it not?"

"So I would assume, Uncle Roderick. But," Percy added, "if the estate is concerned, would you not rather speak to Courtenay? He is your heir, after all, and—"

"Bah—I could never trust *him* with this," said the viscount. "He would be consumed with self-interest. It is a terrible thing to have to say about one's own son, but in all candor, Percy, my boy, I don't trust the scoundrel. I half suspect him to be the father of the Lorimer girl's whelp, but he's not man enough to own up to it. No, I could not trust him to do the right thing."

Percy sat down across the room at a small table with paper, pen, and ink.

"You may disown me by the time I am through, Percy, my boy," said the viscount. "The story I have to tell is one I have never divulged to another soul. God forgive me, not even Katherine knows of it, though I kept it from her for her own sake. But I pray you will not take out your anger toward me on Florilyn."

"You need have no worry about that, Uncle Roderick. Nothing you could possibly say will change my affection for you."

"You are a good boy, Percy. After this, Florilyn may need you more than ever. So will Katherine. Be good to them, Percy."

"I will."

"You see, Percy, my boy. . ." his uncle began.

For the next thirty minutes, he told Percy of his early life, his travels, confessing alternate bouts of waywardness and repentance, of decisions made and decisions regretted. Soon he was rambling such that Percy could follow but portions of the disjointed narrative. He was not at all clear at every point who he was talking about.

"Promise me you will try to find her, Percy, my boy," he said several times.

"I will do all that is in my power."

"Tell her I'm sorry I didn't come back. . .didn't try harder. But she had disappeared, you see. . .had no idea. . .where she had gone. After a while. . .so long ago. . .couldn't go back. . .by then. . .your aunt, you see. I didn't want to hurt her."

After some time, the viscount was breathing heavily. He seemed spent. But he gathered himself once again, told Percy to start writing, and then began to dictate. He became lucid again. As the story unfolded, at last much of what he had said previously began to fit together.

The affidavit took an hour to compose. When it was completed, Percy took it to him to sign. It was with some difficulty that he was able to hold the pen to do so. By then he was exhausted.

"Keep it in a safe place, Percy, my boy," said the viscount. His voice was barely more than a whisper. "No one must see it unless your search is successful. Otherwise, Katherine need never know."

"I understand."

Within minutes his uncle was asleep, and Percy left him.

Eighty-Three

Farewell Prayer

*T*he visits with his solicitor, minister, and nephew had taxed what remained of the viscount's strength to its limit.

Having conducted with the former and latter what remained of the final business burdening his heart, almost from the moment Percy left him he began to fade. He had remained strong long enough to do what needed to be done. There was no more need for strength. He had put his affairs in order. His spirit now seemed to relax and give in to the inevitable.

The next days passed drearily. Dr. Rotherham came and went but had nothing to report. He knew the end was not far off. The efforts of the ministering staff of family and servants were now for the sole purpose of making the viscount comfortable. He said less and less, stopped eating, and eventually was able to drink only what was poured into his mouth a few drops at a time by spoon.

Late in the afternoon of the fifth day since they had been closeted together for purposes of the affidavit, an urgent knock came to Percy's door. He rose to answer it.

There stood Mrs. Drynwydd. "You're wanted, Mr. Percy," she said. "Quickly, sir. It's the viscount."

Percy ran along the corridor, flew down the staircase, resumed a walk, and tried to calm himself as he walked into the sickroom. There sat Katherine and Florilyn on either side of the bed. The viscount's two hands rested between each of theirs.

Percy approached. His uncle's skin seemed to have been stretched over the bones, his eyes sunken and dark, his flesh a ghastly gray. Seeing Percy approach, the viscount's eyes drifted toward him. His lips quivered as if trying to smile.

Katherine glanced toward Percy with a smile. "His breathing was labored," said Percy's aunt. "His eyes were closed. I was afraid. . .but he seems comfortable again."

Percy nodded and took the chair from the writing table, carried it to the bedside, then sat down beside her.

There was nothing to do but wait. The afternoon waned. The viscount dozed, woke, glanced about, tried to speak though could only mumble incoherently, and then dozed again.

That evening smells from the kitchen drifted in and revived him. He had not eaten in days, but the mere aroma of food was strengthening. Florilyn managed to get several spoonfuls of water into his mouth, moistening his tongue sufficiently that he was able to summon a few final fragments of halting speech.

"Percy. . .my boy," he said wearily, "and there's my Katy. . .and Flory. Where's Courtenay?"

"Steven has ridden to Sir Armond's for him," said Katherine. "He will be home soon. The rest of us are here, Roderick."

"Ah. . . ," sighed the viscount. He closed his eyes briefly then drew in a breath. "You're all. . .you've been so—good to me—I need to—I'm going. . .I've got to—got to make. . .an apology to—forgive me, Katy—I never meant—you were a good wife—better than I deserved—"

He sighed weakly. "I'm ready," he said after another minute. "I don't know—if God. . .that is. . .one never knows, but—if He will have me. . .I'm ready—see what He can make of me now. . .if He—" He did not have the strength to continue.

"Would you like me to pray, Uncle Roderick?" said Percy.

An imperceptible nod of the head was the viscount's only response.

The room fell silent. Percy thought a moment then drew in a breath. "Oh heavenly Father," he began, "we know so little of this strange thing we call death, which You invested with the power to give us life. Now, our Father, breathe more life into the soul of Your dying son to give him the courage and power to face the dawn of his new life. Heal our loved one at this time of his great need—heal him with the strength to die."

The faintest "Amen" came from the bed.

Katherine and Florilyn were weeping. What a mighty prayer had come spontaneously from the mouth of the vicar's son!

"You sent dear Roderick Westbrooke," Percy continued, "our husband and father and uncle—You sent him into the world as a tiny babe, just as You did Your own dear Son. Now help him out of it as Your child again and birth him into the new life that comes of being in Your presence. We dying men are Your children, and You take us back again into Yourself, into the eternal home of Your heart, to be with You and to be with Jesus, our elder brother, who conquered death on our behalf. Give Your dying child peace to yield himself into Your arms. Amen."

"Amen," the viscount whispered again.

"Be good to her. . .Percy. . .my boy. . . ."

"I will."

"And find—"

"Have no worries about anything," said Percy.

He clutched for Katherine's hand, which still held his. "Katy!" he murmured then glanced toward Florilyn with a smile. "Flory, my dear. I'm going— Percy, be good to— Katy—"

The sentence remained unfinished. The light went out of his eyes as his lids slowly closed. His head sank back into the pillow as a faint breath of air expired from his lungs.

He was dead.

Florilyn cried out and broke into heaving sobs as she turned faint. Katherine wept quietly. Percy saw Florilyn's eyes going back into her head. He jumped up and ran around the bed in time to catch her as she collapsed. He carried her limp in his arms toward the door.

As he walked from the room, he turned to see Katherine lay her head on her husband's chest. He hurried out with Florilyn, leaving his aunt to whisper in private her final good-byes to the man she had loved.

EIGHTY-FOUR

End or Beginning?

*E*dward and Mary Drummond had been receiving regular updates on their brother-in-law's condition. Plans were already in place to leave Glasgow for Wales the moment a telegram arrived announcing his passing. When it came, Katherine asked her brother to conduct the service. Percy's parents planned to stay as long as needed for Edward's sister's sake.

The whole village turned out for the funeral. Dignitaries from throughout Wales were present.

Llanfryniog's three ministers had the sadly unusual experience of being under the same roof at the same time, sharing the benches and stalls of the largest of their churches with parishioners from their three congregations. One could only conjecture whether they were too deeply entrenched in the learned doctrines of their denominations to receive Vicar Edward Drummond's triumphant assertion of the fatherhood of God as manna for their religiously trained intellects.

Percy's father took as text his favorite passage of Scripture save one, the parable of the prodigal son, emphasizing on the occasion of his brother-in-law's passing the father's implied words, "Welcome home, son!"

Time would tell whether the ministries of his three colleagues would change as a result of this new word spoken about the loving Father whom

Jesus called Abba. One thing was certain—such words had never been proclaimed prior to this day from any of Llanfryniog's pulpits.

Whether the clergymen would be or not, there was one seated among them who *would* forever be changed by what he heard. He had decided to attend the funeral at the last minute. He walked into the building he had so long despised with no little trepidation at what his fellow villagers were thinking to see him present. As he listened beside wife and great hulking son, Kyvwlch Gwarthegydd sat as one stunned. He walked out of the church fifty minutes later in a stupor. He had never heard the like before.

If God was like *this* man represented him, an actual Father. . .a good and loving *Father*. . .that changed everything!

Kyvwlch Gwarthegydd saw nothing in religion he liked or wanted. He never had. He hated the religious spirit with a passion. But one thing he knew as much about as he did the smithy's art was fatherhood. He was himself a father. He knew what love beat in his heart for Chandos. He would do *anything* for his son. He would give his very life for him.

If God was like *that*, then it meant the Creator was like *him*. . .just a Father! Could it be. . .was it possible that it was true after all?

What all the doctrines and sermons and persuasive arguments in the world would never achieve if the man lived to be two hundred had been accomplished in a few short minutes. The simple vision of the prodigal's open-hearted father, waiting to receive his son into his arms with a great smile on his face, had opened a window of lovely truth into the honest soul of the Welsh blacksmith.

Those who maintain that the threat of hell is the Christian's most effective tool for evangelism little understand the deepest rhythms of the human soul. Still less do they understand the heart of the Father of Jesus Christ.

The assembly walked quietly from the church to the surrounding cemetery where the viscount was laid to rest with the generations of Westbrookes who had gone before. One by one they greeted Katherine and Florilyn and Courtenay respectfully then slowly returned to their homes. The visitors who had come great distances returned in hired buggies to Dolgellau and Blaenau Ffestiniog, where most spent the night in the hotels and inns of North Wales before catching the train north or south on the following day. Among the last to leave the churchyard were Stevie and Adela Muir, both of whom hugged Katherine and Florilyn warmly.

The day after the funeral, Tilman Heygate sought Katherine in the parlor where she and Edward and Mary were seated together. "I am sorry to disturb you, Lady Katherine," he said. "But if I might have a minute of your time."

"Of course, Tilman," she said. "You can speak freely in front of my brother and sister-in-law."

"Yes, ma'am. Well, you see, it's like this. My son, he and his wife have been urging me to come up to the peninsula to be near them. The grandchildren are growing fast, you see. I've stayed on out of loyalty to your husband, but since there'll no doubt be changes coming, and I'm sorry for any inconvenience to yourself, Lady Katherine, but it's one of those things that can't be helped, you see. The long and the short of it is that I'm thinking that now is a good time." What the good man had not said was that he expected young Courtenay to be taking over general oversight of the manor, and he vowed that he would not spend a day in his employ.

"I understand, Tilman," said Katherine. "I will be sorry to lose you."

"Thank you, Lady Katherine. You and your husband have been very good to me."

"When is it you are thinking of making a change?"

"Maybe a month or two, Lady Katherine. As soon as you can find someone."

"I shall see what I can do."

"That doesn't sound good," said her brother when the factor had left them.

"I don't like to lose him," said Katherine. "He knows more about the estate than I do."

"Do you have anyone in mind?" asked Edward.

"Not that I can—" Suddenly Katherine stopped. A smile spread over her face. "What an intriguing idea!" she said, speaking almost to herself. "We have a young man here, a friend of Percy's actually, and about the same age. . . I know he is young, but he has shown that he can take charge in a crisis. He is bright, good with numbers, intelligent, dependable, decisive, completely trustworthy. He knows everyone for miles and is universally liked and respected. Now that I think about it, he strikes me as the perfect choice to help me run things around here until Courtenay is twenty-five."

"What is the lad's name?" asked Mary.

"Steven. . .Steven Muir. I know his mother quite well. She's begun reading MacDonald, too!"

"What better to recommend her son than that!" laughed Mary. "You will have the whole region reading the Scotsman before long."

"Is that when Courtenay inherits," asked Edward, "at twenty-five?"

Katherine nodded. "What it will be like after that, I can only imagine."

Later that day, Katherine went to Percy in private. "I have just been informed by Tilman Heygate," she told him, "that he will be leaving the manor and moving to be near his son's family. What would you think if I made Steven Muir my new factor?"

"I think it is a brilliant idea, Aunt Katherine," replied Percy enthusiastically. "But where do things stand with Courtenay?"

"The estate will not be his for another year and a half. He will no doubt be annoyed that I don't turn it over to him now, but I know him too well. As long as I am trustee, I must do what I consider best for the estate."

Eighty-Five

Knotted Strands

Two days after the funeral, from the window of her room, Florilyn saw Percy and his father walking away from the house in earnest conversation. She smiled to herself. She had no idea what they were saying. But at last she knew the nature of the discussion between them.

Watching the two for the last three days had been a revelation. She had never seen a father and son, or daughter and mother for that matter, talk so freely. . .like *friends*. They listened to each other, probed each other's thoughts, and mutually respected the other's ideas. They talked constantly. . .about *everything*!

She left her room and went downstairs to join her mother and aunt in the sitting room.

East of the house, Percy and his father continued slowly through the wood and up the gently rising slope east of the manor.

"There's something I need to ask you about, Dad," Percy said. "Before he died, Uncle Roderick made a request of me. It is extremely complicated and might require a good deal of time and travel, even expense. I'm not sure what I should do, how soon to begin, and where to place it in my considerations of school and the apprenticeship."

"What is it?" asked Percy's father.

"That's just it. I can't tell you. He asked that it remain confidential. Do you think the fact that he is dead changes that? I mean. . .is one still bound to a promise to a dead man?"

"An interesting question. It probably depends on the individual case. Are other people involved?"

Percy nodded.

"Could they be hurt if you divulged what you and Roderick talked about?"

"It's possible."

"Then it seems to me that you must honor your word as long as possible. It may in time become necessary to speak more openly. If it reaches a point where you absolutely have no idea what to do, we can rethink it. Perhaps you will need to tell me later. But for the immediate future, I think the safest policy is for you to keep your own counsel."

"I would give anything to tell you about it."

"The time may come when you will feel it right to do so. The Lord will show you what to do."

"Do you think I ought to begin immediately and take a leave of absence from school?"

"How urgent is the matter?"

"It didn't strike me as especially urgent. Actually, he never really said anything about *when*. Knowing he was dying, he simply wanted me to take care of it."

"Could it wait until you graduate?"

"I suppose. That would also give me time to consider how best to carry out Uncle Roderick's commission."

"And as well, if you are to be married, it seems in everyone's best interest for you to graduate first. That is another argument in favor of waiting."

"I see what you mean. Because of what's happened, though, I do think I ought to remain here for the summer. I wanted to ask your advice. . .what would you think of my writing to Mr. Snyder and telling him it will be impossible for me to apprentice with his firm this summer?"

"I think that is a wise decision," replied his father. "You are needed here. Florilyn and her mother are your primary responsibilities now. And I've heard Courtenay talking about taking a trip."

Father and son glanced up to see Florilyn, Mary, and Katherine approaching. They had come out of the house together.

"Hello, ladies!" said Edward, greeting them with a smile. "How are you managing, Katherine?" he said, walking toward her and embracing her affectionately.

His sister sighed and smiled sadly.

They all now turned and walked toward the garden.

"It will be hard for some time," said Katherine after a moment. "It was so sudden. But your message at the funeral helped more than you know. Sometimes I need to be reminded how good God really is. It is easy to forget. How do you do it, Edward—always put your finger on the exact point of truth needed?"

Her brother laughed.

Florilyn glanced toward him, struck suddenly at how very much like Percy's his laugh sounded.

"As I remember, you found that annoying when we were growing up!" Edward chuckled.

"Not anymore. Whenever I hear it now, it reminds me of Father."

"It is easy for us all to forget," said Edward after a moment. "I am trying to remember what our father taught us, too, Katherine. His vision of God is so much larger than mine. I am still learning. The natural human tendency is to doubt God rather than trust Him. I don't know why. I must constantly remind myself that God is on *our* side in this struggle we call life."

"That is just like what Father would say! At seventy-five, he is still hungry to know more about God."

"I hope you will be saying the same of me when I am seventy-five," rejoined Edward.

Florilyn walked between the men and slipped her hands into their two arms. "Percy speaks very highly of you, Uncle Edward," she said. "I have never seen a son honor a father as he does you. I feel that I know you almost as well as I know him."

"I am aware of it, Florilyn." The vicar smiled. "I am a man most fortunate to have such a son. *And* such a niece!"

"Now it looks as if you will be a father to me, as well as an uncle."

"It is an assignment I look forward to, my dear."

The five continued to walk about the grounds, speaking of many things. Not the least of which subjects that came up was the future of the two young people.

Percy shared with Katherine and Florilyn that he had decided not to return to Aberdeen for the summer apprenticeship, but to remain with them. . .with their permission, of course. Both were overjoyed and relieved beyond words. He then explained his conviction that he and his father felt it best that he return to complete his fourth year at the university so as to graduate before pursuing matrimonial plans.

Everyone agreed that it was a wise course of action. The other considerations that were on his mind, Percy kept to himself. Many questions remained.

Several days after the funeral, Rhawn Lorimer surprised everyone by appearing at Westbrooke Manor. Her son was with her, and a look of compassionate humility was on her face. She asked to see Florilyn and Katherine. She expressed her sympathies then added that she would like them to meet her son. Her tone was so gentle and her demeanor so changed, that they invited her to stay for tea—though it proved a somewhat rambunctious affair with a youngster about. From that day forward, she and Florilyn began a wonderful new friendship together.

Katherine consulted in private with Steven Muir, as she always called him. With quiet and humble gratitude, he accepted her offer. She added, however, that no announcement of it should be made until she made it herself. He must say nothing even to his mother.

After a few more days, Mary and Edward Drummond left on the

coach for Blaenau Ffestiniog where they caught the train that, after several connections, took them back to Scotland.

Two weeks later, declaring himself in need of a holiday, Courtenay Westbrooke left for the south of France, expecting at the end of his hiatus to find the weight of his father's responsibilities falling to his shoulders.

He did not return for three months. By then Percy had resumed his studies in Abereen. To Courtenay's great surprise and smoldering fury, Stevie Muir was confidently and capably in charge as Lady Katherine's factor at Westbrooke Manor.

No one quite knew why from the very day of the viscount's funeral the hammer and anvil of Kyvwlch Gwarthegydd's smithy were thereafter silent on Sundays. Nor did a soul ever know his dark secret—that when his wife and Chandos were occupied at church, he crept to his son's room to snatch peeks inside the Bible on the shelf, hoping to discover more about who God really was.

Percy's plans and what came of them will require another book.

Read the conclusion of The Green Hills of Snowdonia in
The Treasure of the Celtic Triangle.
Coming August 2012

Michael Phillips
and the Legacy of His Books

Native Californian Michael Phillips is one of the most versatile, prolific, and beloved Christian novelists of our time. To those unfamiliar with his work, the question, "What kind of books does Michael Phillips write?" has no easy answer.

He began his writing career in 1977 with nonfiction. Since that time he has authored more than twenty nonfiction books, most notably dealing with the nature and character of God and the fatherhood of God.

After turning to the writing of novels in the mid-1980s, Phillips has penned some sixty fiction titles of great variety. His works are read and loved by pastors, priests, and the laity, by prison inmates and college presidents, by men and women, young and old, elementary school children and graduate students alike. The enormous breadth of his faithful audience is testimony that his writings are universal in their appeal. He has likely written *something* to suit nearly every literary taste. Most of his series have been bestsellers in the Christian market. If you have not discovered his writings, you have years of enjoyment ahead of you!

Michael Phillips is also a coauthor. Nearly all his fourteen books in collaboration with friend Judith Pella have also been bestsellers.

Phillips's name is often linked to that of his spiritual and literary mentor, Victorian Scotsman George MacDonald. For those unfamiliar with the name, the books of George MacDonald were instrumental in leading C. S. Lewis out of atheism into Christianity. Lewis emphasized that George MacDonald was the most significant impetus in his own spiritual pilgrimage. MacDonald's writings can thus be seen as the spiritual soil out of which the faith of C. S. Lewis emerged. MacDonald's novels, fantasies, and fairy tales provided the imaginative foundation for Lewis's later writings, including the *Chronicles of Narnia*.

In spite of C. S. Lewis's frequent mention of his influence, Mac-Donald's name in the late twentieth century drifted into obscurity and his books became unavailable.

Fortunately, in the 1970s Michael Phillips, like C. S. Lewis before him, discovered the writings of MacDonald. A new generation of readers soon grew thankful for that discovery! For Phillips made it his life's work and passion to bring to public attention the literary and spiritual links between MacDonald and Lewis. To do so, Phillips set about preparing and releasing updated and edited editions of MacDonald's works. Phillips is most widely known as George MacDonald's redactor, publisher, and biographer, and the man whose vision and editorial expertise brought MacDonald back from obscurity when his name was nearly forgotten.

Phillips's efforts ignited the MacDonald renaissance of the 1980s and 1990s, an awakening that continues to this day. In addition to his redacted MacDonald titles, Phillips's publishing efforts in producing full-length facsimile editions spawned renewed interest in MacDonald's original work. Phillips is recognized, not only as the man responsible for the widespread renewal of MacDonald's influence, but as the world's foremost purveyor of MacDonald's message, with particular insight into MacDonald's heart and spiritual vision.

Michael Phillips and his wife, Judy, his lifelong partner in all aspects of his writing, bookselling, and publishing, divide their time between homes in California and Scotland, where they are working to heighten awareness of Scotland's own George MacDonald.

Both Phillipses love to hear from their readers. Though they receive mail from all over the world, they read and try to respond to every letter. You may learn more about Michael Phillips and his writings, as well as how to contact him and Judy and obtain their books, from the website: FatherOfTheInklings.com. You can also write to them at: P.O. Box 7003, Eureka, CA 95502.

Find an era and a Michael Phillips series that is to your taste! Most titles are available through local bookstores, from Christian Books, Amazon, or AbeBooks, or from FatherOfTheInklings.com. And these aren't all! For more titles by Michael Phillips, including his thought-provoking nonfiction writings on the nature of God, his Bible expositions, his acclaimed *Introductions to the Books of the Bible*, as well as available George MacDonald titles, go to FatherOfTheInklings.com.

19th-CENTURY SCOTLAND,
with Judith Pella
The Stonewycke Trilogy (1985–1986):
The Heather Hills of Stonewycke
Flight from Stonewycke
The Lady of Stonewycke
The Stonewycke Legacy (1987–1988):
A Stranger at Stonewycke
Shadows over Stonewycke
Treasure of Stonewycke
The Highland Collection (1987):
Jamie MacLeod, Highland Lass
Robbie Taggart, Highland Sailor

CALIFORNIA GOLD RUSH
The Journals of Corrie Belle Hollister (1990–1997):
My Father's World, with Judith Pella
Daughter of Grace, with Judith Pella
On the Trail of the Truth
A Place in the Sun
Sea to Shining Sea
Into the Long Dark Night
Land of the Brave and the Free
Grayfox
A Home for the Heart
The Braxtons of Miracle Springs
A New Beginning

19th-CENTURY RUSSIA,
with Judith Pella
The Russians (1991–1992):
The Crown and the Crucible
A House Divided
Travail and Triumph

WORLD WAR II & COLD WAR GERMANY
The Secret of the Rose (1993–1995):
The Eleventh Hour
A Rose Remembered
Escape to Freedom
Dawn of Liberty

WESTERN AMERICAN PRAIRIE
Mercy and Eagleflight (1996–1997):
Mercy and Eagleflight
A Dangerous Love

SPIRITUAL FANTASY (1998)
The Garden at the Edge of Beyond

CONTEMPORARY THRILLER
The Livingstone Chronicles (1997–2000):
Rift in Time
Hidden in Time

WORLD WAR I ENGLAND
The Secrets of Heathersleigh Hall (1998–2000):
Wild Grows the Heather in Devon
Wayward Winds
Heathersleigh Homecoming
A New Dawn over Devon

ANCIENT EPIC SCOTLAND
Caledonia (1999–2000):
Legend of the Celtic Stone
An Ancient Strife

CONTEMPORARY DRAMA
The Destiny Chronicles (2002):
Destiny Junction
King's Crossroads

AMERICAN CIVIL WAR
Shenandoah Sisters (2002–2004):
Angels Watching over Me
A Day to Pick Your Own Cotton
The Color of Your Skin Ain't the Color of Your Heart
Together Is All We Need
Carolina Cousins (2005–2007):
A Perilous Proposal
A Soldier's Lady
Never Too Late
Miss Katie's Rosewood
American Dreams (2005–2008):
Dream of Freedom
Dream of Life
Dream of Love

SCOTTISH DRAMA (2011)
Angel Harp
Heather Song

19th-CENTURY WALES
The Green Hills of Snowdonia (2012):
From Across the Ancient Waters
The Treasure of the Celtic Triangle

Discussion Questions

1. In chapter 7, in discussing the village of Llanfyniog, it was said that its religion "tended to see God as an Almighty magician and shaman, rather than as the loving Creator-Father of humankind." What did you think of this description of a Christianity which mingled remnants of paganism with the Christian Gospel? Have you encountered hints of the same thing in any of the churches you have been part of?

2. Nearly all of us have experienced family stresses not unlike what occurs in chapter 9 between Percy and his parents. Share a similar experience from your life—either as a parent or as a teen. How was it handled, and what was the end result? Many relational conflicts in families never do get satisfactorily resolved. What ongoing stresses are you attempting to come to terms with in your family?

3. Tell about an experience when you were aware of nature first "speaking" to you in new ways.

4. By chapter 25, nature has begun to get more deeply into Percy's soul than he ever anticipated. God speaks to every human heart by unique means. Nature is one of those ways. What are others? What have been your experiences in detecting God's voice and presence in new ways, whether through nature or other manifestations of His Being? What have been those "unique means" in your life?

5. What is your response to the spiritual inclinations of Kyvwlch Gwarthegydd and Hollin Radnor in chapter 28?

6. Respond to Vicar Edward Drummond's sermon on prodigality and reconciliation in chapters 29–33, both literarily and spiritually. Do you like this kind of thought-provoking spiritual content in a novel? Were you challenged to make right any relationships in your own life? Have

you wondered, with Edward and Mary, about the role of the prodigal's parents in the parable, what they were doing and thinking while their son was away? Have you been in such a position yourself?

7. What arrows of prayer were you challenged to send to God for your own loved ones after reading chapter 33?

8. Why is it, do you suppose, that young people in our day are not counseled, instructed, exhorted, and challenged to make their relationships with their parents right according to the pattern of chapter 50, and instead think it is enough to drift lazily back into speaking terms but little more? Why is today's church so lethargic about urging true repentance and homegoing? Why do today's counselors, even Christian counselors, invariably blame the parents for most problems, and do not confront young people with the scriptural imperative simply to humble themselves and repent?

9. Read between the lines of chapter 68 and interpret what you think is going on in Percy's thoughts.

10. As Percy describes the inner workings of his relationship with his father to Florilyn in chapter 69, what are your reactions? Many might read this and think *That is pretty idealistic. . .*or *That is the most ridiculous thing I have ever heard. . .*or *That sounds wonderful.* What do you think?

11. Has Percy made a sound decision (chapters 74–76)? He is facing an extremely difficult and delicate set of circumstances. When you were in similar situations, how did you arrive at clarity? Whom did you seek for counsel? If Percy had asked for your counsel in his predicament, what would have been your response?

12. What would you have said to Roderick Westbrooke in chapter 81 that Percy did not say?